Also by Henning Mankell in English translation

FACELESS KILLERS

THE FIFTH WOMAN

Henning Mankell

SIDETRACKED

Translated from the Swedish by
Steven T. Murray

THE HARVILL PRESS
LONDON

First published with the title *Villospår* by Ordfronts Förlag, Stockholm, 1995

First published in Great Britain by The Harvill Press in 2000

This paperback edition first published in 2001 by
The Harvill Press, 2 Aztec Row, Berners Road, London N1 0PW

www.harvill.com

3 5 7 9 8 6 4 2

© Henning Mankell, 1995
English translation © Steven T. Murray, 1999

Henning Mankell asserts the moral right to be identified as the author of this work

A CIP catalogue record for this book is available from the British Library

ISBN 1 86046 837 3

Designed and typeset in Minion at Libanus Press, Marlborough, Wiltshire

Printed and bound in Great Britain by Mackays of Chatham

To Jon

This is a novel. None of the characters in it are real people. However, not every similarity to real people is possible or even necessary to avoid. I am grateful to everyone who helped me with the work on this book.

Paderne,
July 1995

Shall I bend, in vain, shall I shake
the old, hard, immovable bars?
– they will not stretch, they will not break
for the bars are riveted and forged inside myself,
and the bars will not shatter until I shatter too

From "A Ghasel" by Gustaf Fröding

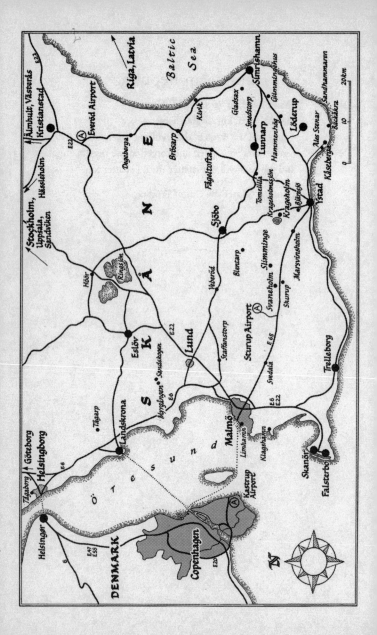

Dominican Republic

1978

PROLOGUE

Just before dawn, Pedro Santana woke. The kerosene lamp had started to smoke. When he opened his eyes he didn't know where he was. He had been roused from a dream in which he wandered through a peculiar, rocky landscape where the air was very thin, and he knew that all his memories were about to leave him. The smoking kerosene lamp had penetrated his consciousness like the distant smell of volcanic ash. But suddenly there was something else: a human sound, tormented, panting. And then the dream evaporated and he was forced to return to the dark room where he had now spent six days and six nights without sleeping more than a few minutes at a time.

The kerosene lamp had gone out. He lay completely still. The night was very warm. He smelt of sweat. It had been a long time since he had last managed to wash. He got up cautiously from the earthen floor and groped for the plastic jug of kerosene over by the door. It must have rained while he had slept. The floor was damp under his feet. Off in the distance he heard a rooster crow. Ramirez's rooster. It was always the first in the village to crow, before dawn. That rooster was like an impatient person. Like someone who lived in the city, someone who always seemed to have too much to do, but never did anything other than attend to his own haste. Life wasn't like that in the village: here everything moved as slowly as life itself. Why should people hurry when the plants that nourished them grew so slowly?

He found the jug of kerosene and pulled out the piece of cloth stuffed into the opening. The panting that filled the darkness grew more and more uneven. He found the lamp, pulled out the cork, and carefully poured in the kerosene. He struck a match, lifted the glass cover, and watched the wick start to burn.

Then he forced himself to turn around. He couldn't bear to see what was waiting for him. The woman lying in the bed next to the wall was going to die. He knew this now, even though for a long time he had tried to persuade himself that she would recover. His last attempt to flee had been in his dream. But a person could never escape death. Not his own, nor that of someone he loved.

He squatted down by the bed. The kerosene lamp threw restless shadows across the walls. He looked at her. She was still young. Even though her face was pale and sunken, she was beautiful. The last thing to leave my wife will be her beauty, he thought, as tears came to his eyes. He touched her forehead. The fever had risen again.

He glanced through the broken window patched with a piece of cardboard. Not dawn yet. If only it would come, he thought. Just let her have the strength to keep breathing until dawn. Then she won't leave me all alone in the night.

Suddenly her eyes flew open. He grasped her hand and tried to smile.

"Where is the child?" she asked in a voice so weak that he could hardly understand her.

"She's sleeping at my sister's house," he replied. "It's best that way."

She seemed reassured by his answer.

"How long have I been asleep?"

"For many hours."

"Have you been sitting here the whole time? You must rest. In a few days I won't need to lie here any longer."

"I've been sleeping," he replied. "Soon you're going to be well again."

He wondered whether she knew he was lying, whether she knew she would never get up again. Were both of them lying to each other in their despair? To make the inevitable easier?

"I'm so tired," she said.

"You must sleep so you'll get well," he answered, turning his head at the same time so she wouldn't see his face.

Soon the first light of dawn seeped in. She had slipped into unconsciousness again. He was so tired that he could no longer control his thoughts.

4

He had met Dolores when he was 21. He and his brother Juan walked the long road to Santiago de los Treinta Caballeros to see the carnival. Juan, who was older, had visited the city once before. But it was Pedro's first time. It took them three days to get there. Once in a while they got a ride for a few kilometres with an ox and cart. But they walked most of the way.

At last they reached their destination. It was a February day and the carnival was in full swing. Astonished, Pedro had stared at the garish costumes and the terrifying masks of devils and animals. The whole city was dancing to the beat of thousands of drums and guitars. Juan piloted him through the streets and alleys. At night they slept on benches in Parque Duarte. Pedro was afraid that Juan would disappear into the swirling crowds. He felt like a child frightened of losing his parents. But he didn't let on. He didn't want Juan to laugh at him.

On their last evening, Juan did suddenly vanish among the costumed, dancing people. They hadn't agreed on a place to meet if they were separated. Pedro searched for Juan all night. At daybreak he stopped by the fountain in the Plaza de Cultura.

A girl about his own age sat down beside him. She was the most beautiful girl he had ever seen. He watched as she took off her sandals and rubbed her sore feet. When she met his gaze, he lowered his eyes, embarrassed.

That was how he met Dolores. They sat by the fountain and started talking. Dolores had been looking for work as a housekeeper, going from house to house in the rich neighbourhood without success. She too was the child of a *campesino*, and her village was not far from Pedro's. They left the city together, plundered banana trees for food, and walked more and more slowly the closer they came to her village.

Two years later they were married, and moved into a little house in Pedro's village. Pedro worked on a sugar plantation while Dolores grew vegetables and sold them. They were poor, but they were happy.

Only one thing was not as it should be. After three years Dolores was not yet pregnant. They never talked about it, but Pedro sensed

Dolores's increasing anxiety. Without telling him, she had visited some *curiositas* on the Haitian border to seek help.

Eight years passed. And then one evening when Pedro was returning from the sugar plantation, Dolores met him on the road and told him she was pregnant. At the end of the eighth year of their marriage, she gave birth to a daughter. When Pedro saw his child for the first time, he could see at once that she had inherited her mother's beauty. That evening Pedro went to the village church and made an offering of some gold jewellery his mother had given him. Then he went home singing so loudly and fervently that the people he met thought he had drunk too much rum.

Dolores was asleep. She was breathing harder, and stirred restlessly.

"You can't die," whispered Pedro, no longer able to control his despair. "You can't die and leave me and our child."

Two hours later it was all over. For a brief moment her breathing grew completely calm. She opened her eyes and looked at him.

"You must baptise our daughter," she said. "You must baptise her and take care of her."

"You'll be well soon," he answered. "We'll baptise her together."

"I don't exist any more," she said and closed her eyes.

Then she was gone.

Two weeks later Pedro left the village, carrying his daughter in a basket on his back. His brother Juan followed him down the road.

"What are you doing?" he asked.

"What has to be done."

"Why must you go to the city to baptise your daughter? Why can't you have her baptised here in the village? That church has served us well. And our parents before us."

Pedro stopped and looked at his brother.

"For eight years we waited for a child. When our daughter finally came, Dolores died. She wasn't yet 30. She had to die. Because we are poor. Because of poverty's diseases. Now I will return to the big

6

cathedral on the plaza where we met. My daughter will be baptised in the biggest church there is in this country. That's the least I can do for Dolores."

He didn't wait for Juan's reply. Late that evening, when he reached the village Dolores had come from, he stopped at her mother's house. Again he explained where he was going. The old woman shook her head sadly.

"Your sorrow will drive you crazy," she said.

Early the next morning Pedro resumed his journey. As he walked he told his daughter everything he could remember about Dolores. When he had no more to say, he started again.

Pedro reached the city one afternoon as heavy rain clouds gathered on the horizon. He sat down to wait on the steps of the cathedral, Santiago Apóstol, and watched the black-clad priests passing by. They seemed either too young, or in too much of a hurry to be worthy of baptising his daughter. He waited many hours. At last an old priest came slowing towards the cathedral. Pedro stood up, took off his straw hat, and held out his daughter. The old priest listened patiently to his story. Then he nodded.

"I will baptise her," he said. "You have walked a long way for something you believe in. In our day that is rare. People seldom walk long distances for their faith. That's why the world looks the way it does."

Pedro followed the priest into the dim cathedral. He felt that Dolores was near him as they made their way to the font.

"What will the girl be named?" he asked.

"She will be named Dolores, after her mother. And María. Dolores María Santana."

After the baptism Pedro went out to the plaza and sat down where he had met Dolores ten years before. His daughter was asleep in the basket. He sat completely still, deep in thought.

I, Pedro Santana, am a simple man. I have inherited nothing but poverty and relentless misery. I have not even been allowed to keep

7

my wife. But I vow that our daughter will have a different life. I will do everything for her. I promise you, Dolores, that your daughter will live a long and happy and worthy life.

That evening Pedro left the city with his beloved daughter, Dolores María Santana. She was then eight months old.

Skåne

21–24 June 1994

CHAPTER 1

Before dawn he started his transformation.

He had planned everything meticulously so that nothing could go wrong. It would take him all day, and he didn't want to risk running out of time. He took up the first paintbrush and held it in front of him. From the cassette player on the floor he could hear the tape of drum music that he had recorded. He studied his face in the mirror. Then he drew the first black lines across his forehead. He noted that his hand was steady. So he wasn't nervous, at least. Even though this was the first time he had put on his war paint. Until this moment it had been merely an escape, his way of defending himself against the injustices he was continually subjected to. Now he went through the transformation in earnest. With each stroke that he painted on his face, he seemed to be leaving his old life behind. There was no turning back. This very evening the game would be over for good, he would go out into the war, and people were going to die.

The light in the room was very bright. He arranged the mirrors carefully, so that the glare didn't get in his eyes. When he had locked the door behind him, he had first checked that everything was where it was supposed to be: the well-cleaned brushes, the little porcelain cups of paint, the towels and water, next to the little lathe his weapons in rows on a black cloth – three axes, knives with blades of various lengths, and spray cans. This was the only decision still to be made. Before sundown he had to choose which to take with him. He couldn't take them all. But he knew that the choice would resolve itself once he had begun his transformation.

Before he sat down on the bench and started to paint his face, he tested the edges of his axes and knives. They were as sharp as could

11

be. He couldn't resist the temptation to press a little harder on one of the knives. His finger started to bleed. He wiped it and the knife with a towel. Then he sat down in front of the mirrors.

The first strokes on his forehead had to be black. It was as if he were slicing two deep cuts, opening his brain, and emptying the memories and thoughts that had haunted him all his life, tormenting him and humiliating him. Then the red and white stripes, the circles, the squares, and at last the snake-like designs on his cheeks. None of his white skin should be visible. Then the transformation would be complete. What was inside him would be gone. He would be born again in the guise of an animal, and he would never speak as a human being again. He would cut out his tongue if he had to.

Just after 6 p.m. he was done. By then he had chosen the largest of the three axes. He stuck the shaft into his thick leather belt. Two knives were already there in their sheaths. He looked around the room. Nothing was forgotten. He stuffed the spray cans in the inside pockets of his jacket.

He looked at his face in the mirror one last time, and shuddered. Carefully he pulled his motorcycle helmet over his head, switched off the light, and left the room barefoot, just as he had come in.

At 9.05 p.m. Gustaf Wetterstedt turned down the sound on his TV and phoned his mother. It was a nightly ritual. Ever since he had retired as minister of justice more than 25 years earlier, leaving behind all his political dealings, he had watched the news with repugnance. He couldn't come to terms with the fact that he was no longer involved. During his years as minister, a man in the absolute centre of the public eye, he appeared on TV at least once a week. Each appearance had been meticulously copied from film to video by a secretary and the tapes now covered a whole wall of shelves in his study. Once in a while he watched them again. It was a great source of satisfaction to see that never once in all those years as minister of justice had he lost his composure when confronted by an unexpected question from a malicious reporter. He would recall with unbounded contempt how many of his colleagues had been terrified of TV reporters, how they would stammer and get entangled in contradictions. That had never happened to him. He was a man who couldn't be trapped. The reporters had never beaten him. Nor had they discovered his secret.

He had turned on his TV at 9 p.m. to see the top stories. Now he turned down the sound. He pulled over the telephone and called his mother. She was now 94, but with a clear mind and full of energy. She lived alone in a big flat in Stockholm's innercity. Each time he lifted the receiver and dialled the number he prayed she wouldn't answer. He was more than 70, and he had begun to be afraid that she would outlive him. There was nothing he wanted more than for her to die. Then he'd be left alone. He wouldn't have to call her any more, and soon he'd forget what she even looked like.

The telephone rang at the other end. He watched the silent anchorman. At the fourth ring he began to hope that she was dead. Then she answered. He softened his voice as he spoke. He asked how she was feeling, how had her day been, but now he knew that she was still alive, he wanted to make the conversation as brief as possible.

Finally he hung up and sat with his hand resting on the receiver. She's never going to die, he thought. She'll never die unless I kill her. All he could hear was the roar of the sea, and then a lone moped going past the house. He walked over to the big balcony window facing the sea. The twilight was beautiful. The beach below his huge estate was deserted. Everyone is sitting in front of their TVs, he thought. There was a time when they sat there and watched me make mincemeat of the reporters, back when I was minister of justice. I should have been made foreign minister. But I never was.

He drew the heavy curtains, making sure that there were no gaps. Even though he tried to live as discreetly as possible in this house located just east of Ystad, occasional curiosity-seekers spied on him. Although it had been 25 years since he left office, he had not yet been entirely forgotten. He went out to the kitchen and poured himself a cup of coffee from a thermos he had bought during an official visit to Italy in the late 1960s. He vaguely recalled that he'd gone to discuss

13

efforts to prevent the spread of terrorism in Europe. All over his house there were reminders of the life he had lived. Sometimes he thought of throwing them away, but to make the effort seemed pointless.

He went back to the sofa with his coffee. He switched off the TV with the remote, and sat in the dark, thinking through the day's events. In the morning he'd had a visit from a journalist on one of the big monthly magazines. She was writing a series about famous people in retirement, but he couldn't really see why she had decided upon him. She had brought a photographer with her and they took pictures on the beach and inside the house. He had decided in advance that he would present the image of a kindly old man, reconciled with his past. He described his present life as very happy. He lived in seclusion so that he could meditate, he said, and he let slip with feigned embarrassment that he was thinking of writing his memoirs. The journalist, who was in her 40s, had been impressed and clearly respectful. Afterwards he escorted her and the photographer to their car and waved as they drove off.

He hadn't said a single thing that was true during the entire interview, he thought with satisfaction. This was one of the few things that still held any interest for him. To deceive without being discovered. To continue with the pretence. After all his years as a politician he realised all that was left was the lie. The truth disguised as a lie or the lie dressed up as the truth.

Slowly he drank the rest of his coffee. His sense of well-being grew. The evenings and nights were his best time. That was when his thoughts of all that he had lost sank beneath the surface, and he remembered only what no-one could rob him of. The most important thing. The utmost secret.

Sometimes he imagined himself as an image in a mirror that was both concave and convex at the same time. No-one had ever seen anything but the surface: the eminent jurist, the respected minister of justice, the kindly retiree strolling along the beach in Skåne. No-one would have guessed at his double-sided self. He had greeted kings and presidents, he had bowed with a smile, but in his head he was thinking, *if you only knew who I really am and what I think of you.* When he stood in front of the TV cameras he always held that thought – *if you only knew who I really am and what I think of you* – foremost in his mind. His secret. That he hated and despised the party he represented, the policies that he defended, and most of the people he met. His secret would stay hidden until he died. He had seen through the world, identified all its frailties, understood the meaninglessness of existence. But no-one knew about his insight, and that was the way it would stay.

He felt a growing pleasure at what was to come. Tomorrow evening his friends would arrive at the house just after 9 p.m., in the black Mercedes with tinted windows. They would drive straight into his garage and he would wait for them in the living-room with the curtains drawn, just as now. He could feel his expectation swell as he started to fantasise about what the girl they delivered to him this time would look like. He had told them there had been far too many blondes lately. Some of them had also been much too old, over 20. This time he wanted a younger one, preferably of mixed race. His friends would wait in the basement where he had installed a TV; he would take the girl with him to his bedroom. Before dawn they would be gone, and he would already be daydreaming about the girl they would bring the following week.

The thought of the next evening made him so excited that he got up from the sofa and went into his study. Before he turned on the light he drew the curtains. For a moment he thought he saw the shadow of someone down on the beach. He took off his glasses and squinted. Sometimes late-night strollers would stop on the edge of his property. On several occasions he had had to call the police in Ystad to complain of young people lighting bonfires on the beach and making noise.

He had a good relationship with the Ystad police. They came right away and moved anyone disturbing him. He never could have imagined the knowledge and contacts he had gained as minister of justice. Not only had he learned to understand the special mentality that prevails inside the police force, but he had methodically acquired friends in strategic places in the Swedish machinery of justice. As important were all the contacts he had made in the criminal world. There were intelligent criminals, individuals who worked alone as well as leaders of great crime syndicates, whom he had made his friends. Even though much had changed since he left office, he still enjoyed his old contacts. Especially the friends who saw to it that each week he had a visit from a girl of a suitable age.

He had imagined the shadow on the beach. He straightened the curtains and unlocked one of the cabinets in the desk he had inherited from his father, a distinguished professor of jurisprudence. He took out an expensive and beautifully decorated portfolio and opened it before him on the desk. Slowly, reverently, he leafed through his collection of pornographic pictures from the earliest days of photography. His oldest picture was a rarity, a daguerreotype from 1855 that he had acquired in Paris, of a naked woman embracing a dog. His collection was renowned in the discreet circle of men who shared his interest. His collection of pictures from the 1890s by Lecadre was surpassed only by the collection owned by an elderly steel magnate in the Ruhr. Slowly he turned the plastic-covered pages of the album. He lingered longest over the pages where the models were very young and one could see by their eyes that they were under the influence of drugs. He had often regretted that he himself had not begun to devote himself to photography earlier. Had he done so, he would today be in possession of an unrivalled collection.

When he had finished, he locked the album in the desk again. He had extracted a promise from his friends that upon his death they would offer the pictures to an antiquities dealer in Paris who specialised in the sale of such items. The money would be donated to a scholarship fund he had already established for young law students, which would be announced after his death. He switched off the desk lamp and remained sitting in the dark room. The sound of the surf was very faint. Once again he thought he heard a moped passing.

In spite of his age, he still found it difficult to imagine his own death. During trips to the United States, he had managed twice to be present anonymously at executions, the first by electric chair, the second in the gas chamber, which even then was rather rare. It had been a curiously pleasurable experience to watch people being killed. But his own death he could not contemplate. He left the study and poured a little glass of liqueur from the bar in the living-room. It was already approaching midnight. A short walk down to the sea was all that remained for him to do before he went to bed. He put on a jacket out in the hall, slipped his feet into a pair of worn clogs, and left the house.

Outside it was dead calm. His house was so isolated that he could not see the lights of any of his neighbours. The cars on the road to Kåseberga roared by in the distance. He followed the path that led through the garden and down to the locked gate to the beach. To his annoyance he discovered that the light on a pole next to the gate was out. The beach awaited him. He fished out his keys and unlocked the gate. He walked the short distance onto the sand and stopped at the water's edge. The sea was still. Far out on the horizon he saw the lights of a boat heading west. He unbuttoned his fly and peed into the water as he continued to fantasise about the visit he would have the next day.

Although he heard nothing, suddenly he knew that someone was standing behind him. He stiffened, seized with terror. Then he spun round.

The man standing there looked like an animal. Apart from a pair of shorts he was naked. The old man looked into his face with dread. He couldn't see if it was deformed or hidden behind a mask. In one hand the man held an axe. In his confusion the old man noticed that the hand around the shaft of the axe was very small, that the man was like a dwarf.

He screamed and started to run, back towards the garden gate.

He died the instant the edge of the axe severed his spine, just below the shoulder blades. And he knew no pain as the man, who was perhaps an animal, knelt down and slit an opening in his forehead and then with one violent wrench ripped most of the scalp from his skull.

It was a little after midnight. It was Tuesday, 21 June.

The motor of a moped started up somewhere nearby, and moments later died away.

Everything was once again very still.

CHAPTER 2

Around noon on 21 June, Kurt Wallander left the police station in Ystad. So that no-one would notice his going, he walked out through the garage entrance, got into his car, and drove down to the harbour. Since the day was warm he had left his sports jacket hanging over his chair at his desk. Anyone looking for him in the next few hours would assume he must be somewhere in the building. Wallander parked by the theatre, walked out on the inner pier and sat down on the bench next to the red hut belonging to the sea rescue service. He had brought along one of his notebooks, but realised that he hadn't brought a pen. Annoyed, he nearly tossed the notebook into the harbour. But this was impossible. His colleagues would never forgive him.

Despite his protests, they had appointed him to make a speech on their behalf at 3 p.m. that day for Björk, who was resigning his post as Ystad chief of police.

Wallander had never made a formal speech in his life. The closest he had come were the innumerable press conferences he had been obliged to hold during criminal investigations.

But how to thank a retiring chief of police? What did one actually thank him for? Did they have any reason to be thankful? Wallander would have preferred to voice his uneasiness and anxiety at the vast, apparently unthought-out reorganisations and cutbacks to which the force was increasingly subjected. He had left the station so he could think through what he was going to say in peace. He'd sat at his kitchen table until late the night before without getting anywhere. But now he had no choice. In less than three hours they would gather and present their farewell gift to Björk, who was to start work the next day in Malmö as head of the district board of immigration affairs.

Wallander got up from the bench and walked along the pier to the harbour café. The fishing boats rocked slowly in their moorings. He remembered idly that once, seven years ago, he had been involved in fishing a body out of this harbour. But he pushed away the memory. Right now, the speech he had to make for Björk was more important. One of the waitresses lent him a pen. He sat down at a table outside with a cup of coffee and forced himself to write a few sentences. By 1 p.m. he had put together half a page. He looked at it gloomily, knowing that it was the best that he could do. He motioned to the waitress, who came and refilled his cup.

"Summer seems to be taking its time," Wallander said to her.

"Maybe it won't get here at all," replied the waitress.

Apart from the difficulty of Björk's speech, Wallander was in a good mood. He would be going on holiday in a few weeks. He had a lot to be happy about. It had been a long, gruelling winter. He knew that he was in great need of a rest.

At 3 p.m. they gathered in the canteen of the station and Wallander made his speech to Björk. Svedberg gave him a fishing rod as a present, and Ann-Britt Höglund gave him flowers. Wallander managed to embellish his scanty speech on the spur of the moment by recounting a few of his escapades with Björk. There was great amusement as he recalled the time when they had both fallen into a pool of liquid manure after some scaffolding they were climbing collapsed. In his reply Björk wished his successor, a woman named Lisa Holgersson, good luck. She was from one of the bigger police districts in Småland and would take over at the end of the summer. For the time being Hansson would be the acting chief in Ystad. When the ceremony was over and Wallander had returned to his office, Martinsson knocked on his half-open door, and came in.

"That was a great speech," he said. "I didn't know you could do that sort of thing."

"I can't," said Wallander. "It was a lousy speech. You know it as well as I do."

Martinsson sat down cautiously in the broken visitor's chair.

"I wonder how it'll go with a woman chief," he said.

"Why wouldn't it go well?" replied Wallander. "You should be worrying instead about what's going to happen with all these cutbacks."

"That's exactly why I came to see you," said Martinsson. "There's a rumour going round that staff numbers are going to be cut back on Saturday and Sunday nights."

Wallander looked at Martinsson sceptically.

"That won't work," he said. "Who's going to deal with the people we've got in the cells?"

"Rumour has it that they're going to take tenders for that job from private security companies."

Wallander gave Martinsson a quizzical look.

"Security companies?"

"That's what I heard."

Wallander shook his head. Martinsson got up.

"I thought you ought to know about it," he said. "Do you have any idea what's going to happen within the force?"

"No," said Wallander. "Cross my heart."

Martinsson lingered in the office.

"Was there something else?"

Martinsson took a piece of paper out of his pocket.

"As you know, the World Cup has started. Sweden was 2–2 in the game against Cameroon. You bet 5–0 in favour of Cameroon. With this score, you came in last."

"How could I come in last? Either I bet right or wrong, didn't I?"

"We run statistics that show where we are in relation to everyone else."

"Good Lord! What's the point of that?"

"An officer was the only one who picked 2–2," said Martinsson, ignoring Wallander's question. "Now for the next match. Sweden against Russia."

Wallander was totally uninterested in football, although he had occasionally gone to watch Ystad's handball team, which had several times been ranked as one of the best in Sweden. But lately the entire country seemed to be obsessed by the World Cup. He couldn't turn on the TV or open a newspaper without being bombarded with speculation as to how the Swedish team would fare. He knew that he had no choice but to take part in the football pool. If he didn't, his colleagues would think he was arrogant. He took his wallet out of his back pocket.

"How much?"

"A hundred kronor. Same as last time."

He handed the note to Martinsson, who checked him off on his list.

"Don't I have to guess the score?"

"Sweden against Russia. What do you think?"

"4–4," said Wallander.

"It's pretty rare to have that many goals scored in football," Martinsson said, surprised. "That sounds more like ice hockey."

"All right, let's say 3–1 to Russia," said Wallander. "Will that do?"

Martinsson wrote it down.

"Maybe we can take the Brazil match while we're at it," Martinsson went on.

"3–0 to Brazil," said Wallander quickly.

"You don't have very high expectations for Sweden," said Martinsson.

"Not when it comes to football, anyway," replied Wallander, handing him another 100-krona note.

Martinsson left and Wallander began to mull over what he had been told, but then he dismissed the rumours with irritation. He would find out soon enough what was true and what wasn't. It was already 4.30 p.m. He pulled over a folder of material about an organised crime ring exporting stolen cars to the former Eastern-bloc countries. He had been working on the investigation for several months. So far the police had only succeeded in tracking down parts of the operation. He knew that this case would haunt him for many more months yet. During his leave, Svedberg would take over, but he suspected that very little would happen while he was gone.

There was a knock on the door, and Ann-Britt Höglund walked in. She had a black baseball cap on her head.

"How do I look?" she asked.

"Like a tourist," replied Wallander.

"This is what the new caps are going to look like," she said. "Just imagine the word POLICE above the peak. I've seen pictures of it."

"They'll never get one of those on my head," said Wallander. "I suppose that I should be glad I'm not in uniform any more."

"Someday we might discover that Björk was a really good chief," she said. "I think what you said in there was great."

"I know the speech wasn't any good," said Wallander, starting to feel annoyed. "But you are all responsible for having picked me."

Höglund stood up and looked out of the window. She had managed to live up to the reputation that preceded her when she came to Ystad the year before. At the police academy she had shown great aptitude for police work, and had developed even more since. She had filled part of the void left by Rydberg's death a few years ago. Rydberg was the detective who had taught Wallander most of what he knew, and sometimes Wallander felt that it was his task to guide Höglund in the same way.

"How's it going with the cars?" she asked.

"They keep on being stolen," said Wallander. "The organisation seems to have an incredible number of branches."

"Can we punch a hole in it?" she asked.

"We'll crack it," replied Wallander. "Sooner or later. There'll be a lull for a few months. Then it'll start up again."

"But it'll never end?"

"No, it'll never end. Because of Ystad's location. Just 200 kilometres from here, across the Baltic, there's an unlimited number of people who want what we've got. The only problem is they don't have the money to pay for it."

"I wonder how much stolen property is shipped with every ferry," she mused.

"You don't want to know," said Wallander.

Together they went and got some coffee. Höglund was supposed to go on holiday that week. Wallander knew that she was going to spend it in Ystad, since her husband, a machinery installer with the whole world as his market, was currently in Saudi Arabia.

"What are you going to do?" she asked when they started talking about their upcoming breaks.

"I'm going to Denmark, to Skagen," said Wallander.

"With the woman from Riga?" Höglund wondered with a smile.

Wallander was taken aback.

"How do you know about her?"

"Oh, everybody does," she said. "Didn't you realise? You might call it the result of an ongoing internal investigation."

Wallander had never told anyone about Baiba, whom he had met during a criminal investigation. She was the widow of a murdered Latvian policeman. She had been in Ystad over Christmas almost six months ago. During the Easter holiday Wallander had visited her in Riga. But he had never spoken about her or introduced her to any of his colleagues. Now he wondered why not. Even though their relationship was new, she had pulled him out of the melancholy that had marked his life since his divorce from Mona.

"All right," he said. "Yes, we'll be in Denmark together. Then I'm going to spend the rest of the summer with my father."

"And Linda?"

"She called a week ago and said she was taking a theatre class in Visby."

"I thought she was going to be a furniture upholsterer?"

"So did I. But now she's got it into her head that she's going to do some sort of stage performance with a girlfriend of hers."

"That sounds exciting, don't you think?"

Wallander nodded dubiously.

"I hope she comes here in July," he said. "I haven't seen her in a long time." They parted outside Wallander's door.

"Drop in and say hello this summer," she said. "With or without the woman from Riga. With or without your daughter."

"Her name is Baiba," said Wallander.

He promised he'd come by and visit.

After Ann-Britt left he worked on the file for a good hour. Twice he called the police in Göteborg, trying without success to reach a detective who was working on the same investigation. At 5.45 p.m. he decided to go out to eat. He pinched his stomach and noted that he was still losing weight. Baiba had complained that he was too fat. After that, he had no problem eating less. He had even squeezed into a tracksuit a few times and gone jogging, boring though he found it.

He put on his jacket. He would write to Baiba that evening. The telephone rang just as he was about to leave the office. For a moment he wondered whether to let it ring. But he went back to his desk and picked up the receiver.

It was Martinsson.

"Nice speech you made," said Martinsson. "Björk seemed genuinely moved."

"You said that already," said Wallander. "What is it? I'm on my way home."

"I just got a call that was a little odd," said Martinsson. "I thought I ought to check with you."

Wallander waited impatiently for him to go on.

"It was a farmer calling from out near Marsvinsholm. He claimed that there was a woman acting strangely in his rape field."

"Is that all?"

"Yes."

"A woman acting strangely out in a rape field? What was she doing?"

"If I understood him correctly, she wasn't doing anything. The peculiar thing was that she was out in the field."

Wallander thought for a moment before he replied.

"Send out a squad car. It sounds like something for them."

"The problem is that all the units seem to be busy right now. There were two car accidents almost simultaneously. One by the road into Svarte, the other outside the Hotel Continental."

"Serious?"

"No major injuries. But there seems to be quite a mess."

"They can drive out to Marsvinsholm when they have time, can't they?"

"That farmer seemed pretty upset. I can't quite explain it. If I didn't have to pick up my children, I'd go myself."

"All right, I can do it," said Wallander. "I'll meet you in the hall and get the name and directions."

A few minutes later Wallander drove off from the station. He turned left at the roundabout and took the road towards Malmö. On the seat next to him was a note Martinsson had written. The farmer's name was Salomonsson, and Wallander knew the road to take. When he got out onto the E65 he rolled down the window. The yellow rape fields stretched out on both sides of the road. He couldn't remember the last time he had felt as good as he did now. He stuck in a cassette of *The Marriage of Figaro* with Barbara Hendricks singing Susanna, and he thought about meeting Baiba in Copenhagen. When he reached the side road to Marsvinsholm he turned left, past the castle and the castle church, and turned left again. He glanced at Martinsson's directions and swung onto a narrow road that led across the fields. In the distance he caught a glimpse of the sea.

Salomonsson's house was an old, well-preserved Skåne farmhouse. Wallander got out of the car and looked around. Everywhere he looked were yellow rape fields. The man standing on the front steps was very old. He had a pair of binoculars in his hand. Wallander thought that he must have been imagining the whole thing. All too often, lonely old people out in the country let their imaginations run riot. He walked over to the steps and nodded.

"Kurt Wallander from the Ystad police," he said.

The man on the steps was unshaven and his feet were stuck into a pair of worn clogs.

"Edvin Salomonsson," said the man, stretching out a skinny hand.

"Tell me what happened," said Wallander.

The man pointed out at the rape field that lay to the right of the house. "I discovered her this morning," he began. "I get up early. She was already there at five. At first I thought it was a deer. Then I looked through the binoculars and saw that it was a woman."

"What was she doing?" asked Wallander.

"She was standing there."

"That's all?"

"She was standing and staring."

"Staring at what?"

"How should I know?"

Wallander sighed. Probably the old man *had* seen a deer. Then his imagination had taken over.

"Do you know who she is?" he asked.

"I've never seen her before," replied the man. "If I knew who she was, why would I call the police?"

"You saw her the first time early this morning," he went on, "but you didn't call the police until late this afternoon?"

"I wouldn't want to put you out for no reason," the man answered simply. "I assume the police have plenty to do."

"You saw her through your binoculars," said Wallander. "She was out in the field and you had never seen her before. What did you do?"

"I got dressed and went out to tell her to leave. She was trampling down the rape."

"Then what happened?"

"She ran."

"Ran?"

"She hid in the field. Crouched down so I couldn't see her. First I thought she was gone. Then I discovered her again through the binoculars. It happened over and over. Finally I got tired of it and called you."

"When did you see her last?"

"Just before I called."

"What was she doing then?"

"Standing there staring."

Wallander glanced out at the field. All he could see was the billowing rape.

"The officer you spoke with said that you seemed uneasy," said Wallander.

"Well, what's somebody doing standing in a rape field? There's got to be something odd about that."

Wallander decided he ought to end the conversation as rapidly as possible. It was clear to him now that the old man had imagined the whole thing. He would contact social services the next day.

"There's not really much I can do," said Wallander. "She's probably gone by now. And in that case, there's nothing to worry about."

"She's not gone at all," said Salomonsson. "I can see her right now."

Wallander spun around. He followed Salomonsson's pointing finger.

The woman was about 50 metres out in the rape field. Wallander could see that her hair was very dark. It stood out sharply against the yellow crop.

"I'll go and talk to her," said Wallander. "Wait here."

He took a pair of boots from his car, and put them on. Then he walked towards the field, feeling as though he were caught in something surreal. The woman was standing completely still, watching him. When he got closer he saw that not only did she have long black hair, but her skin was dark too. He stopped when he reached the edge of the crop. He raised one hand and tried to wave her over. She continued to stand motionless. Even though she was still quite far from him and the billowing rape hid her face every so often, he had the impression that she was rather beautiful. He shouted to her to come towards him. When she still didn't move he took a step into the field. At once she vanished. It happened so fast that she seemed like a frightened animal. He could feel himself getting angry. He went on walking out into the field, looking in every direction. When he caught sight of her again she had moved to the eastern corner of the field. So that she wouldn't get away, he started running. She moved swiftly, and Wallander was soon out of breath. When he got as close as 20 metres or so from her, they were out in the middle of the field. He shouted to her.

"Police!" he yelled. "Stop where you are!"

He started walking towards her. Then he pulled up short.

Everything happened very fast. She raised a plastic container over her head and started pouring a colourless liquid over her hair, her face, and her body. He thought fleetingly that she must have been carrying it the whole time. He could see that she was terrified. Her eyes were wide open and she was staring straight at him.

"Police!" he shouted again. "I just want to talk to you."

At the same moment a smell of petrol wafted towards him. Suddenly she had a flickering cigarette lighter in one hand, which she touched to her hair. Wallander cried out as she burst into flame. Paralysed, he watched her lurch around the field as the fire sizzled and blazed over her body. Wallander could hear himself screaming. But the woman on fire was silent. Afterwards he couldn't remember hearing her scream at all.

When he tried to run up to her the field exploded in flames. He was suddenly surrounded by smoke and fire. He held his hands in front of his face and ran, without knowing which direction he was heading. When he reached the edge of the field he tripped and tumbled into the ditch. He turned around and saw her one last time before she fell over and disappeared from his sight. She was holding her arms up as if appealing for mercy. The entire field was aflame.

Somewhere behind him he could hear Salomonsson wailing. Wallander got to his feet. His legs were shaking. Then he turned away and threw up.

CHAPTER 3

Afterwards Wallander would remember the burning girl in the rape field the way you remember, with the greatest reluctance, a distant nightmare sooner forgotten. If he appeared to maintain at least an outward sense of calm for the rest of that evening and far into the night, later he could recall nothing but trivial details. Martinsson, Hansson and especially Ann-Britt Höglund had been astonished by his calm. But they couldn't see through the shield he had set up to protect himself. Inside him there was devastation, like a house that had collapsed.

He got back to his flat just after 2 a.m. Only then, when he sat down on his sofa, still in his filthy clothes and muddy boots, did the shield crumble. He poured himself a glass of whisky. The doors of his balcony stood open and let in the balmy night, and he cried like a baby.

The girl had been a child. She reminded him of his own daughter Linda. During his years as a policeman he had learned to be prepared for whatever might await him when he arrived at a place where someone had met a violent or sudden death. He had seen people who had hanged themselves, stuck a shotgun in their mouth, or blown themselves to bits. Somehow he had learned to endure what he saw and push it aside. But he couldn't when there were children or young people involved. Then he was as vulnerable as when he was first a policeman. He knew that many of his colleagues reacted the same way. When children or young people died violently, for no reason, the defences erected out of habit collapsed. And that's how it would be for Wallander as long as he continued working as a policeman.

He had completed the initial phase of the investigation in an exemplary manner. With traces of vomit still clinging to his mouth he had run up to Salomonsson, who was watching his crop burn with astonishment, and asked where the telephone was. Since Salomonsson didn't seem to understand the question, maybe didn't even hear it, he dashed past him into the house. He was assailed by the acrid smell of the unwashed old man. In the hall he found the telephone. He dialled 90–000, and the operator said later that Wallander had sounded quite calm when he described what had happened and asked for a full team to be sent out.

The flames from the field were shining through the windows like floodlights lighting up the summer evening. He called Martinsson at home, talking first with his daughter and then his wife before Martinsson was called in from the back yard. As succinctly as possible he described what had happened and asked Martinsson to call Hansson and Höglund too. Then he went out to the kitchen and washed his face under the tap. When he came back outside, Salomonsson was still rooted to the same spot, as if mesmerised. A car arrived with some of his closest neighbours in it. But Wallander shouted to them to stay back, not allowing them to approach Salomonsson. In the distance he heard sirens from the fire engines, which almost always arrived first. Soon afterwards, two squad cars of uniformed officers and an ambulance arrived. Peter Edler was directing the firefighting, a man in whom Wallander had total confidence.

"What's going on?" he asked.

"I'll explain later," said Wallander. "But don't stamp around in the field. There's a body out there."

"The house isn't threatened," said Edler. "We'll work on containing the fire."

Edler turned to Salomonsson and asked how wide the tractor paths and the ditches between the fields were. One of the ambulance crew came over. Wallander had met him before but couldn't remember his name.

"Is anyone hurt?" he asked.

Wallander shook his head.

"One person dead," he replied. "She's lying out in the field."

"Then we'll need a hearse," said the ambulance driver. "What happened?"

Wallander didn't feel like answering. Instead he turned to Norén, who was the officer he knew best.

"There's a dead woman in the field," he said. "Until the fire is put out we can't do anything but block it off."

Norén nodded.

"Was it an accident?" he asked.

"More like a suicide," said Wallander.

A few minutes later, as Martinsson arrived, Norén handed him a paper cup of coffee. He stared at his hand and wondered why it wasn't shaking. Hansson and Ann-Britt Höglund arrived in Hansson's car, and he told his colleagues what had happened.

Again and again he used the same phrase: *She burned like a flare.*

"This is just terrible," said Höglund.

"It was worse than you can imagine," said Wallander. "Not to be able to do anything. I hope none of you ever has to experience anything like this."

Silently they watched the firefighters work. A large group of bystanders had gathered, but the police kept them back.

"What did she look like?" asked Martinsson. "Did you see her?"

Wallander nodded.

"Someone ought to talk to the old man," he said. "His name is Salomonsson."

Hansson took Salomonsson into his kitchen. Höglund went over and talked to Peter Edler. The fire had begun to die down. When she returned she told them it would be all over shortly.

"Rape burns fast," she said. "And the field is wet. It rained yesterday."

"She was young," said Wallander, "with black hair and dark skin. She was dressed in a yellow windcheater. I think she had jeans on. I don't know about her feet. And she was frightened."

"What of?" asked Martinsson.

Wallander thought a moment.

"She was frightened of me," he replied. "I'm not absolutely sure, but I think she was even more terrified when I called out that I was a policeman and told her to stop. But beyond that, I have no idea."

"She understood everything you said?"

"She understood the word 'police' at least. I'm certain of that."

All that remained of the fire was a thick pall of smoke.

"There was no-one else out there in the field?" asked Höglund. "You're sure she was alone?"

"No," said Wallander. "I'm not sure at all. But I didn't see anyone but her."

They stood in silence. *Who was she?* Wallander asked himself. *Where did she come from? Why did she set herself on fire? If she wanted to die, why did she choose to torture herself?*

Hansson came back from the house, where he had been talking with Salomonsson.

"We should do what they do in the States," he said. "We should have menthol to smear under our noses. Damn, the smell in there. Old men shouldn't be allowed to outlive their wives."

"Get one of the ambulance crew to ask him how he's feeling," said Wallander. "He must be suffering from shock."

Martinsson went to deliver the message. Peter Edler took off his helmet and stood next to Wallander.

"It's nearly out," he said. "But I'll leave a truck here tonight."

"When can we go out in the field?" asked Wallander.

"Within an hour. The smoke will hang around for a while yet. But the field has already started to cool off."

Wallander took Peter Edler aside.

"What am I going to see?" he asked. "She poured a five-litre container of petrol over herself. And the way everything exploded around her, she must have already poured more on the ground."

"It won't be pretty," Edler replied candidly. "There won't be a lot left."

Wallander said nothing. He turned to Hansson.

"No matter how we look at it, we know that it was suicide," said

Hansson. "We have the best witness we can get: a policeman."

"What did Salomonsson say?"

"That he'd never seen her before she appeared at 5 a.m. this morning. There's no reason to think he's not telling the truth."

"So we don't know who she is," said Wallander, "and we don't know what she was running from either."

Hansson looked at him in surprise.

"Why should she be running from something?" he asked.

"She was frightened," said Wallander. "She was hiding. And when a policeman arrived she set herself on fire."

"We don't know what she was thinking," said Hansson. "You may be imagining that she was frightened."

"No," said Wallander. "I've seen enough fear in my time to know what it looks like."

One of the ambulance crew came walking towards them.

"We're taking the old boy with us to the hospital," he said. "He looks in pretty bad shape."

Wallander nodded.

Soon the forensic team arrived. Wallander tried to point out where in the smoke the body might be located.

"Maybe you should go home," said Höglund. "You've seen enough this evening."

"No," said Wallander. "I'll stay."

Eventually the smoke had cleared, and Peter Edler said they could start their examination. Even though the summer evening was still light, Wallander had ordered floodlights to be brought in.

"There might be something out there apart from a body," said Wallander. "Watch your step, and everyone who doesn't have work to do out there should stay back."

He realised then that he really didn't want to do what had to be done. He would far rather have driven away and left the responsibility to the others. He walked out into the field alone. The others watched. He was afraid of what he would see, afraid that the knot he had in his stomach would burst.

He reached her. Her arms had stiffened in the upstretched motion he had seen her make before she died, surrounded by the raging flames. Her hair and face, along with her clothes, were burned off. All that was left was a blackened body that still radiated terror and desolation. Wallander turned around and walked back across the charred ground. For a moment he was afraid he was going to faint.

The forensic technicians started to work in the harsh glare of the floodlights, where moths swarmed. Hansson had opened Salomonsson's kitchen window to drive out the smell. They pulled out the chairs and sat around the kitchen table. At Höglund's suggestion they made coffee on Salomonsson's ancient stove.

"All he has is ground coffee," she said after searching through the drawers and cupboards. "Is that all right?"

"That's fine," said Wallander. "Just as long as it's strong."

Hanging on the wall beside the ancient cupboards with sliding doors was an old-fashioned clock. Wallander noticed that it had stopped. He had seen a clock like that once before, at Baiba's flat in Riga, and it too had had a pair of immobile hands. As though they were trying to ward off events that had not yet happened by stopping time, he thought. Baiba's husband was killed execution-style on a frozen night in Riga's harbour. A lone girl appears as if shipwrecked in a sea of rape and takes her life by inflicting the worst pain imaginable.

She had set herself on fire as though she were her own enemy, he thought. It wasn't him, the policeman with the waving arms, she had wanted to escape. It was herself.

He was jolted out of his reverie by the silence around the table. They were looking at him and waiting for him to take the initiative. Through the window he could see the technicians moving slowly about in the glare of the floodlights. A camera flash went off, then another.

"Did somebody call for the hearse?" asked Hansson.

For Wallander it was as if someone had struck him with a sledge-hammer. The simple, matter-of-fact question from Hansson brought him back to painful reality.

The images flickered inside his head. He imagined driving through the beautiful Swedish summertime, Barbara Hendricks's voice strong and clear. Then a girl skitters away like a frightened animal in the field of tall rape. The catastrophe strikes. Something happens that shouldn't. The hearse on its way to carry off the summer itself.

"Prytz knows what to do," said Martinsson, and Wallander recognised the ambulance driver whose name he'd forgotten earlier.

He knew he had to say something.

"What do we know?" he began tentatively, as if each word were offering resistance. "An elderly farmer, living alone, rises early and discovers a strange woman in his rape field. He tries calling to her, to get her to leave, since he doesn't want his crop destroyed. She hides and then reappears, again and again. He calls us late in the afternoon. I drive out here, since the regular officers are all busy. To be honest, I have trouble taking him seriously. I decide to leave and contact social services, since he seems so confused. But the woman suddenly pops up in the field again. So I try to reach her, but she moves away. She lifts a plastic container over her head, drenches herself in petrol, and sets fire to herself with a cigarette lighter. The rest you know. She was alone, she had a container of petrol, and she took her own life."

He broke off abruptly, as if he no longer knew what to say. A moment later he went on.

"We don't know who she is," he said. "We don't know why she killed herself. I can give a fairly good description of her. But that's all."

Ann-Britt Höglund got some cracked coffee cups out of a cupboard. Martinsson went out into the yard to have a pee. When he returned, Wallander continued his cautious summary.

"The most important thing is to find out who she was. We'll search through all missing persons. Since I think she was dark-skinned, we can start by putting a little extra focus on checking on refugees and the refugee camps. Then we'll have to wait for what the forensic technicians come up with."

"At any rate, we know there was no crime committed," said Hansson. "So our job is to determine who she was."

"She must have come from somewhere," said Höglund. "Did she walk here? Did she ride a bike? Did she drive? Where did she get the petrol?"

"And why here, of all places?" said Martinsson. "Why Salomonsson's place? This farm is way off the beaten track."

The questions hung in the air. Norén came into the kitchen and said that some reporters had arrived who wanted to know what happened. Wallander, who knew that he had to get moving, stood up.

"I'll talk to them," he said.

"Tell them the truth," said Hansson.

"What else?" Wallander replied in surprise.

He went out into the yard and recognised the two newspaper reporters. One was a young woman who worked for *Ystad Recorder*, the other an older man from *Labour News*.

"It looks like a film shoot," said the woman, pointing at the floodlights in the charred field.

"It's not," said Wallander.

He told them what had happened. A woman had died in a fire. There was no suspicion of criminal activity. Since they still didn't know who she was, he didn't want to say anything more at this time.

"Can we take some pictures?" asked the man from *Labour News*.

"You can take as many pictures as you like," replied Wallander. "But you'll have to take them from here. No-one is allowed to go into the field."

The reporters drove off in their cars. Wallander was about to return to the kitchen when he saw one of the technicians working out in the field waving to him. Wallander went over. It was Sven Nyberg, the surly but brilliant head of forensics. They stopped at the edge of the area covered by the floodlights. A slight breeze came wafting from the sea across the field. Wallander tried to avoid looking at the body, with its upstretched arms.

"I think we've found something," said Nyberg.

In his hand he had a little plastic bag. He handed it to Wallander, who moved under one of the floodlights. In the bag was a gold necklace with a tiny pendant.

"It has an inscription," said Nyberg. "The letters 'D.M.S.' and it's a picture of the Madonna."

"Why didn't it melt?" asked Wallander.

"A fire in a field doesn't generate enough heat to melt jewellery," Nyberg replied. He sounded tired.

"This is exactly what we needed," said Wallander.

"We'll be ready to take her away soon," said Nyberg, nodding towards the black hearse waiting at the edge of the field.

"How does it look?" Wallander asked cautiously.

Nyberg shrugged.

"The teeth should tell us something. The pathologists are excellent. They can find out how old she was. With DNA technology they can also tell you whether she was born in this country of Swedish parents or if she came from somewhere else."

"There's coffee in the kitchen," said Wallander.

"No thanks," said Nyberg. "I'll be done here pretty soon. In the morning we'll go over the entire field. Since there was no crime it can wait until then."

Wallander went back to the house. He laid the plastic bag containing the necklace on the kitchen table.

"Now we have something to go on," he said. "A pendant, a Madonna. Inscribed with the initials 'D.M.S.' I suggest you all go home now. I'll stay here a while longer."

"We'll meet at nine o'clock tomorrow morning," said Hansson, getting up.

"I wonder who she was," said Martinsson. "The Swedish summer-time is too beautiful and too brief for something like this to happen."

They parted in the yard. Höglund lingered behind.

"I'm thankful I didn't have to see it," she said. "I think I understand what you're going through."

"I'll see you tomorrow," he said.

When the cars had gone he sat down on the steps of the house. The floodlights shone as if over a bleak stage on which a play was being performed, with him the only spectator.

The wind had started to blow. They were still waiting for the warmth of summer. The night air was cold, and Wallander realised that he was freezing sitting there on the steps. How intensely he longed for the summer heat. He hoped it would come soon.

After a while he got up and went inside the house and washed the coffee cups.

CHAPTER 4

Wallander gave a start. Someone was trying to tear off one of his feet. When he opened his eyes he saw that his foot was caught in the broken bed frame. He turned over onto his side to free it. Then he lay still. The dawn light filtered through the crookedly drawn shade. He looked at the clock on the beside table. It was 4.30 a.m. He had hardly slept, and he was very tired. He found himself back out in the field again. He could see the girl much more clearly now. It wasn't me she was afraid of, he thought. She wasn't hiding from me or Salomonsson. There was someone else.

He got up and shuffled out to the kitchen. While he waited for the coffee to brew he went into his messy living-room and checked the answer machine. The red light was flashing. He pushed the replay button. First was his sister Kristina. "I need you to call me. Preferably in the next couple of days." It must be something to do with their father. Although he had married his care worker and no longer lived alone, he was still moody and unpredictable.

There was a scratchy, faint message from *Skåne Daily*, asking if he was interested in a subscription. He was just on his way back to the kitchen when he heard the next message. "It's Baiba. I'm going to Tallinn. I'll be back on Saturday."

He was seized with jealousy. Why was she going to Tallinn? She had said nothing about it the last time they spoke. He poured a cup of coffee, and called her number in Riga, but there was no answer. He dialled again. His unease was growing. She could hardly have left for Tallinn at 5 a.m. Why wasn't she home? Or if she was home, why didn't she answer?

He picked up his coffee cup, opened the balcony door facing

Mariagatan, and sat down. Once again he saw the girl running through the rape. For an instant she looked like Baiba. He forced himself to accept that his jealousy was unwarranted. They had agreed not to encumber their new relationship with promises of fidelity. He remembered how they had sat up on Christmas Eve and talked about what they wanted from one another. Most of all, Wallander wanted them to get married. But when Baiba spoke of her need for freedom, he had agreed with her. Rather than lose her, he would accept her terms.

The sky was clear blue and the air was already warm. He drank his coffee in slow sips and tried to keep from thinking of the girl. When he had finished he went into the bedroom and searched for a long time before finding a clean shirt. Next he gathered all the clothes strewn around the flat. He made a big pile in the middle of the living-room floor. He would have to go to the launderette today.

At 5.45 a.m. he left his flat and went down to the street. He got into his car and remembered that it was due for its M.O.T. by the end of June. He drove off down Regementsgatan and then out along Österleden. On the spur of the moment, he turned onto the road heading out of town and stopped at the new cemetery at Kronoholmsvägen. He left the car and strolled along the rows of gravestones. Now and then he would catch sight of a name he vaguely recognised. When he saw a year of birth the same as his own he averted his eyes. Some young men in blue overalls were unloading a mower from a trailer. When he reached the memorial grove, he sat on one of the benches. He hadn't been here since the windy autumn day four years ago when they had scattered Rydberg's ashes. Björk had been there, and Rydberg's distant and anonymous relatives. Wallander had often meant to come back. A gravestone with Rydberg's name on it would have been simpler, he thought. A focal point for my memories of him. In this grove, full of the spirits of the dead, I can find no trace of him.

He realised that he had difficulty remembering what Rydberg looked like. He's dying away inside me, he thought. Soon even my memories of him will be gone.

He stood up, suddenly distressed. He kept seeing the burning girl.

He drove straight to the station, went into his office, and closed the door, forcing himself to prepare a summary of the car theft investigation that he had to turn over to Svedberg. He moved folders onto the floor so that his desk would be completely clear.

He lifted up his desk blotter to see whether there were any items there that he'd forgotten about. He found a scratch-off lottery ticket he had bought several months before. He rubbed it with a ruler until the numbers appeared, and saw that he had won 25 kronor. From the hall he could hear Martinsson's voice, then Ann-Britt Höglund's. He leaned back in his chair, put his feet up on the desk, and closed his eyes. When he woke up he had a cramp in one of his calf muscles, but he'd slept for no more than ten minutes. The telephone rang. It was Per Åkeson from the prosecutors' office. They exchanged greetings, and some words about the weather. They had worked together for many years, and had slowly developed a rapport that had become like a friendship. They often disagreed about whether an arrest was justified or whether remanding an offender in custody was reasonable. But there was also a trust that went deep, although they almost never spent time together off duty.

"I read in the paper about the girl who burned to death in a field by Marsvinsholm," said Åkeson. "Is that something for me?"

"It was suicide," replied Wallander. "Other than a farmer named Salomonsson, I was the only witness."

"What in heaven's name were you doing there?"

"Salomonsson called. Normally a squad car would have dealt with it. But they were busy."

"The girl can't have been a pretty sight."

"It was worse than you could imagine. We have to find out who she was. The switchboard has already started taking calls from people worried about missing relatives."

"So you don't suspect foul play?"

Without understanding why, Wallander hesitated before answering.

"No," he said then. "I can't think of a more blatant way to take your own life."

"You don't sound entirely convinced."

"I had a bad night. It was as you say – a pretty horrible experience."

They fell silent. Wallander could tell that Åkeson had something else he wanted to talk about.

"There's another reason why I'm calling," he said finally. "But keep it between us."

"I usually know how to keep my mouth shut."

"Do you remember I told you a few years ago that I was thinking of doing something else? Before it's too late, before I get too old."

"I remember you talked about refugees and the UN. Was it the Sudan?"

"Uganda. And I've actually got an offer. Which I've decided to accept. In September I'm going to take a year's sabbatical."

"What does your wife think about this?"

"That's why I'm calling. For moral support. I haven't discussed it with her yet."

"Is she supposed to go with you?"

"No."

"Then I suspect she'll be a little surprised."

"Have you any idea how I should break it to her?"

"Unfortunately not. But I think you're doing the right thing. There has to be more to life than putting people in jail."

"I'll let you know how it goes."

They were just about to hang up when Wallander remembered that he had a question.

"Does this mean that Anette Brolin is coming back as your replacement?"

"She's changed sides; she's working as a criminal barrister in Stockholm now," said Åkeson. "Weren't you a little in love with her?"

"No," Wallander said. "I was just curious."

He hung up. He felt a pang of jealousy. He would have liked to travel to Uganda himself, to have a complete change. Nothing could undo the horror of seeing a young person set herself alight. He envied Per Åkeson, who wasn't going to let his desire to escape stop at mere dreams.

The joy he had felt yesterday was gone. He stood at the window and gazed out at the street. The grass by the old water tower was still green. Wallander thought about the year before, when he had been on sick leave for a long time after he had killed a man. Now he wondered whether he had ever really recovered from that depression. I ought to do something like Åkeson, he thought. There must be a Uganda for me somewhere. For Baiba and me.

He stood by the window for a long time, then went back to his desk and tried to reach his sister. Several times he got a busy signal. He spent the next half hour writing up a report of the events of the night before. Then he called the pathology department in Malmö but couldn't find a doctor who could tell him anything about the burned corpse.

Just before 9 a.m. he got a cup of coffee and went into one of the conference rooms. Höglund was on the phone, and Martinsson was leafing through a catalogue of garden equipment. Svedberg was in his usual spot, scratching the back of his neck with a pencil. One of the windows was open. Wallander stopped just inside the door with a strong feeling of déjà vu. Martinsson looked up from his catalogue and nodded, Svedberg muttered something unintelligible, while Höglund patiently explained something to one of her children. Hansson came into the room. He had a coffee cup in one hand and a plastic bag with the necklace that had been found in the field in the other.

"Don't you ever sleep?" asked Hansson.

Wallander felt himself bristle at the question.

"Why do you ask?"

"Have you taken a look in the mirror lately?"

"I didn't get home until early this morning. I sleep as much as I need to."

"It's those football matches," said Hansson. "They're on in the middle of the night."

"I don't watch them," said Wallander.

"I thought everyone stayed up to watch."

"I'm not that interested," Wallander admitted. "I know it's unusual, but as far as I know, the chief of the national police hasn't sent out any instruction that it's a dereliction of duty not to watch the games."

"This might be the last time we'll have a chance to see it," Hansson said sombrely.

"See what?"

"Sweden playing in the World Cup. I just hope our defence doesn't go pear-shaped."

"I see," Wallander said politely. Höglund was still talking on the phone.

"Ravelli," Hansson went on, referring to Sweden's goalkeeper.

Wallander waited for him to continue, but he didn't.

"What about him?"

"I'm worried about him."

"Why? Is he sick?"

"I think he's erratic. He didn't play well against Cameroon. Kicking the ball out at strange times, odd behaviour in the goal area."

"Policemen can also be erratic," said Wallander.

"You can't really compare them," said Hansson. "At least we don't have to make lightning-fast decisions about whether to rush out or stay back on the goal line."

"Hell, who knows?" said Wallander. "Maybe there's a similarity between the policeman who rushes to the scene of a crime and the goalie who rushes out on the field."

Hansson gave him a baffled look. The conversation died. They sat around the table and waited for Höglund to finish her call. Svedberg, who had a hard time accepting female police officers, drummed his pencil on the table in annoyance to let her know they were waiting for her. Soon Wallander would have to tell Svedberg to put a stop to these tiresome protests. Höglund was a good policewoman, in many ways much more talented than Svedberg.

A fly buzzed around his coffee cup. They waited.

Finally Höglund hung up and sat down at the table.

"A bike chain," she said. "Children have a hard time understanding that their mothers might have something more important to do than come straight home and fix it."

"Go ahead," said Wallander on impulse. "We can do this run-through without you."

She shook her head. "They'd come to expect it", she said.

Hansson put the necklace in its plastic bag on the table in front of him.

"A woman commits suicide," he said. "No crime has been committed. All we have to do is work out who she was."

Hansson was starting to act like Björk, thought Wallander, just managing not to burst out laughing. He caught Ann-Britt's eye. She seemed to be thinking the same thing.

"Calls have started coming in," said Martinsson. "I've put a man on it."

"I'll give him my description of her," said Wallander. "Otherwise we have to concentrate on people who've been reported missing. She might be one of them. If she's not on that list, someone is going to miss her soon."

"I'll take care of it," said Martinsson.

"The necklace," said Hansson, opening the plastic bag. "A Madonna and the letters D.M.S. I think it's solid gold."

"There's a database of abbreviations and acronyms," said Martinsson, who knew the most about computers. "We can put in the letters and see if we get anything."

Wallander reached for the necklace. It was still soot-marked.

"It's beautiful," he said. "But people in Sweden mostly wear a cross, don't they? Madonnas are more common in Catholic countries."

"It sounds as though you're talking about a refugee or immigrant," said Hansson.

"I'm talking about what the medallion represents," replied Wallander. "In any case, it has to be included in the description of the girl, and the person taking the calls has to know what it looks like."

"Shall we release a description?" Hansson asked.

Wallander shook his head.

"Not yet."

He was thinking about the night before. He knew he wouldn't give up until he knew what it was that had made the girl burn herself to death alone in the rape field. I'm living in a world where young people take their own lives because they can't stand it any more, he thought. I have to understand why, if I'm going to keep on being a policeman.

He gave a start. Hansson had spoken.

"Do we have anything more to discuss right now?" Hansson asked again.

"I'll take care of the pathologist in Malmö," Wallander said. "Has anyone been in touch with Sven Nyberg? If not, I'll drive over and talk to both of them."

The meeting was over. Wallander went to his office and got his jacket. He hesitated a moment, wondering whether he ought to make another attempt to get hold of his sister. Or Baiba in Riga. But he decided against doing either.

He drove first to Salomonsson's farm. Policemen were taking down the floodlights and rolling up the cables. The house was locked up, and he remembered that he must check and see how Salomonsson was doing. Maybe he had remembered something that would be of help.

He walked out into the field. The fire-blackened ground stood out sharply against the surrounding yellow crops. Nyberg was kneeling in the mud. In the distance he saw two other technicians who seemed to be searching along the edges of the burned area. Nyberg nodded curtly to Wallander. The sweat was running down his face.

"How's it going?" asked Wallander. "Have you found anything?"

"She must have had a lot of petrol with her," said Nyberg, getting up. "We found five half-melted containers. They were apparently empty when the fire broke out. If you draw a line through the spots where we found them, you can see that she had surrounded herself."

"What do you mean?" Wallander asked.

Nyberg threw out one arm in a sweeping gesture.

"I mean that she built a fortress around herself. She poured petrol

46

in a wide circle. It was a moat, and there was no way into her fortress. She was standing right in the middle, with the last container, which she had saved for herself. Maybe she was hysterical and depressed. Maybe she was mad or seriously ill. I don't know. But that's what she did. She knew full well what she was going to do."

"Can you tell me anything about how she got here?"

"I've sent for a dog unit," said Nyberg. "But they probably won't be able to pick up her trail. The smell of petrol has permeated the ground. The dogs will just be confused. We haven't found a bicycle. The tractor paths that lead down towards the E65 didn't have anything either. She could have landed in this field by parachute."

Nyberg took a roll of toilet paper out of one of his bags of equipment and wiped the sweat from his face.

"What do the doctors say?" he asked.

"Nothing yet," said Wallander. "I think they've got a difficult job ahead of them."

"Why would anyone do something like this?" Nyberg asked. "Could someone really have such strong reasons for dying that she'd end her life by torturing herself as much as she possibly could?"

"I've asked myself the same question," said Wallander.

Nyberg shook his head.

"What's happening?" he asked.

Wallander had no answer.

He went back to the car and called the station. Ebba answered. To avoid her concern, he pretended to be in a hurry.

"I'm going to see the farmer," he said. "I'll be in this afternoon."

He drove back to Ystad. In the cafeteria at the hospital he had some coffee and a sandwich. Then he looked for the ward where Salomonsson was. He stopped a nurse, introduced himself, and stated his business. She gave him a quizzical look.

"Edvin Salomonsson?"

"I don't remember whether his name was Edvin," Wallander said. "Did he come in last night after the fire outside Marsvinsholm?"

The nurse nodded.

"I'd like to speak with him," said Wallander. "If he's not too sick, that is."

"He's not sick," replied the nurse. "He's dead."

Wallander gave her an astonished look.

"Dead?"

"He died this morning in his sleep. Apparently it was a heart attack. It would probably be best if you spoke to one of the doctors."

"I just came by to see how he was doing," said Wallander. "Now I have my answer."

He left the hospital and walked out into the bright sunshine. He had no idea what to do next.

CHAPTER 5

Wallander drove home knowing that he must sleep if he were ever going to be able to think clearly again. No-one could be blamed for the old farmer's death. The person who might have been held responsible, the one who had set fire to his rape field, was already dead herself. It was the events themselves, the fact that any of this had happened, that made him feel sick at heart. He unplugged the phone and lay down on the sofa in the living-room with a flannel over his eyes. But sleep wouldn't come. After half an hour he gave up. He plugged in the telephone, lifted the receiver, and dialled Linda's number in Stockholm. On a sheet of paper by the phone he had a long list of numbers, each crossed out. Linda moved often, and her number was forever changing. He let it ring a long time. Then he dialled his sister's number. She answered almost at once. They didn't speak very often, and hardly ever about anything but their father. Sometimes Wallander thought that their contact would cease altogether when their father died.

They exchanged the usual pleasantries, without really being interested in the answers.

"You called," Wallander said.

"I'm worried about Dad," she said.

"Has something happened? Is he sick?"

"I don't know. When did you visit him last?"

Wallander tried to remember.

"About a week ago," he said, feeling guilty.

"Can you really not manage to see him more often?"

"I'm working almost round the clock. The department is hopelessly understaffed. I visit him as often as I can."

"I talked to Gertrud yesterday," she went on, without commenting on what Wallander had said. "I thought she gave an evasive answer when I asked how Dad was doing."

"Why would she?" said Wallander, surprised.

"I have no idea. That's why I'm calling."

"He was the same as always," Wallander said. "Cross that I was in a hurry and couldn't stay very long. But the whole time I was there he sat painting his picture and made out as though he didn't have time to talk to me. Gertrud was happy, as usual. I have to admit I don't understand how she puts up with him."

"Gertrud likes him," she said. "It's a question of love. Then you can put up with a lot."

Wallander wanted to end the conversation as quickly as possible. As she got older, his sister reminded him more and more of their mother. Wallander had never had a very happy relationship with his mother. When he was growing up it was as though the family had been divided into two camps – his sister and his mother against him and his father. Wallander had been very close to his father until his late teens, when he decided to become a policeman. Then a rift had developed. His father had never accepted Wallander's decision, but he couldn't explain to his son why he was so opposed to this career, or what he wanted him to do instead. After Wallander finished his training and started on the beat in Malmö, the rift had widened to a chasm. Some years later his mother was stricken with cancer. She was diagnosed at New Year and died in May. His sister Kristina left the house the same summer and moved to Stockholm, where she got a job in a company then known as L. M. Ericsson. She married, divorced, and married again. Wallander had met her first husband once, but he had no idea what her present husband even looked like. He knew that Linda had visited their home in Kärrtorp a few times, but he got the impression that the visits were never very successful. Wallander knew that the rift from their childhood and teenage years was still there, and that the day their father died it would widen for good.

"I'm going to see him tonight," said Wallander, thinking about the pile of dirty laundry on his floor.

"I'd appreciate it if you called me," she said.

Wallander promised he would. Then he called Riga. When the phone was picked up he thought it was Baiba at first. Then he realised that it was her housekeeper, who spoke nothing but Latvian. He hung up quickly. At the same moment his phone rang and he jumped.

He picked up the phone and heard Martinsson's voice.

"I hope I'm not bothering you," said Martinsson.

"I just stopped by to change my shirt," said Wallander, wondering why he always felt it necessary to excuse himself for being at home. "Has something happened?"

"A few calls have come in about missing persons," said Martinsson. "Ann-Britt is busy going through them."

"I was thinking more of what you had come up with on the computer."

"The mainframe has been down all morning," Martinsson replied glumly. "I called Stockholm a while ago. Somebody there thought it might be up and running again in an hour, but he wasn't sure."

"We're not chasing crooks," Wallander said. "We can wait."

"A doctor called from Malmö," Martinsson continued. "A woman. Her name was Malmström. I promised her you'd call."

"Why couldn't she talk to you?"

"She wanted to talk to *you*. I suppose it's because you were the last one to see the woman alive."

Wallander wrote down the number. "I was out there today," he said. "Nyberg was on his knees in the filth, sweating. He was waiting for a police dog."

"He's like a dog himself," said Martinsson, not disguising his dislike of Nyberg.

"He can be grumpy," Wallander protested. "But he knows his stuff."

He was about to hang up when he remembered Salomonsson.

"The farmer died," he said.

"Who?"

"The man whose kitchen we were drinking coffee in last night. He had a heart attack."

After he hung up, Wallander went to the kitchen and drank some water. For a long time he sat at the kitchen table doing nothing. Eventually he called Malmö. He had to wait while the doctor named Malmström was called to the phone. From her voice he could hear that she was very young. Wallander introduced himself and apologised for the delay in returning her call.

"Has any new information come to light that indicates that a crime was committed?" she asked.

"No."

"In that case we won't have to do an autopsy," she replied. "That will make it easier. She burned herself to death using petrol – leaded."

Wallander felt that he was about to be sick. He imagined her blackened body, as if it were lying right next to the woman he was speaking to.

"We don't know who she was," he said. "We need to know as much as possible about her in order to be able to give a clear description."

"It's always hard with a burned body," she said, without emotion. "All the skin is burned away. The dental examination isn't ready yet. But she had good teeth. No fillings. She was 163 centimetres tall. She had never broken a bone."

"I need her age," said Wallander. "That's almost the most important thing."

"That'll take a few more days. We can base it on her teeth."

"What would you guess?"

"I'd rather not."

"I saw her from 20 metres away," said Wallander. "I think she was about 17. Am I wrong?"

The female doctor thought a moment before she replied.

"I don't like to guess," she said at last. "But I think she was younger."

"What makes you think so?"

"I'll tell you when I know. But I wouldn't be surprised if it turned out she was only 15."

"Could a 15-year-old really kill herself in that way?" Wallander asked. "I have a hard time believing that."

"Last week I put together the pieces of a seven-year-old girl who blew herself up," replied the doctor. "She had planned it very carefully. She made certain that no-one else would be hurt. Since she could barely write, she left behind a drawing as her farewell letter. And recently I heard of a four-year-old who tried to poke his own eyes out because he was afraid of his father."

"That just isn't possible," said Wallander. "Not here in Sweden."

"It was here, all right," she said. "In Sweden. In the centre of the universe. In the middle of summer."

Wallander's eyes filled with tears.

"As we don't know who she was, we'll keep her here," the doctor said.

"I have a question," said Wallander. "Is it incredibly painful to burn to death?"

"People have known that through the ages," she replied. "That's why they used fire as one of the worst punishments or tortures that someone could be subjected to. They burned Joan of Arc, they burned witches. In every era people have been tortured by fire. The pain is beyond imagining. And, you don't lose consciousness as fast as you would hope. There's an instinct to run from the flames that's stronger than the desire to escape the pain. That's why your mind forces you not to pass out. Then you reach a limit. For a while the burned nerves become numbed. There are examples of people with 90 per cent of their body burned who for a brief time felt uninjured. But when the numbness wears off . . ."

She didn't finish her sentence.

"She burned like a flare," said Wallander.

"The best thing you can do is stop thinking about it," she said. "Death can actually be a liberator. No matter how reluctant we are to accept that."

When the conversation was over, Wallander got up, grabbed his jacket, and left the flat. The wind had started blowing outside. Cloud cover had moved in from the north. On the way to the station he pulled in to the M.O.T. garage and made an appointment. When he arrived at the garage, he stopped at the reception desk. Ebba had recently slipped and broken her hand. He asked how she was feeling.

"It reminds me that I'm getting old," she said.

"You'll never get old," said Wallander.

"That's a nice thing to say," she said. "But it's not true."

On the way to his office Wallander stopped to see Martinsson, who was sitting in front of his computer.

"They got it up and running 20 minutes ago," he said. "I'm just checking the description to see whether there are any missing persons who fit."

"Add that she was 163 centimetres tall," said Wallander. "And that she was between 15 and 17 years old."

Martinsson gave him a baffled look.

"Only 15? That can't be possible, can it?"

"I wish it weren't true," said Wallander. "But for now we have to consider it a possibility. How's it going with the initials?"

"I haven't got that far yet," said Martinsson. "But I was planning to stay late this evening."

"We're trying to make an identification," said Wallander. "We're not searching for a fugitive."

"There's no-one at home tonight anyway," said Martinsson. "I don't like going back to an empty house."

Wallander left Martinsson and looked in on Höglund's room, which was empty. He went back down the hall to the operations centre, where the emergency alerts and phone calls were received. Höglund was sitting at a table with a senior officer, going through a pile of papers.

"Any leads?" he asked.

"We've got a couple of tip-offs we have to look into more closely," she said. "One is a girl from Tomelilla Folk College who's been missing for two days."

54

"Our girl was 163 centimetres tall," said Wallander. "She had perfect teeth. She was between 15 and 17 years old."

"That young?" she asked in amazement.

"Yep," said Wallander. "That young."

"Then it's not the girl from Tomelilla, anyway," said Höglund, putting down the paper in her hand. "She's 23 and tall."

She searched through the stack of papers for a moment.

"Here's another one," she said. "A 16-year-old girl named Mari Lippmansson. She lives here in Ystad and works in a bakery. She's been missing from her job for three days. It was the baker who called. He was furious. Her parents evidently don't care about her at all."

"Take a look at her," Wallander said encouragingly. But he knew she wasn't the one.

He got a cup of coffee and went to his room. The folder on the car thefts was still lying on the floor. He'd better turn the case over to Svedberg now. He hoped no serious crimes would be committed before he started his holiday.

Later that afternoon they met in the conference room. Nyberg was back from the farm, where he had finished his search. It was a short meeting. Hansson had excused himself because he had to read an urgent memo from national headquarters.

"Let's be brief," said Wallander. "Tomorrow we'll go over all the cases that can't wait."

He turned to Nyberg, sitting at the end of the table.

"How'd it go with the dog?" he asked.

"He didn't find a thing," Nyberg replied. "If there was ever anything to give him a scent, it was covered up by the odour of petrol."

Wallander thought for a moment.

"You found five melted petrol containers," he said. "That means that she must have come to Salomonsson's field in some sort of vehicle. She couldn't have carried all that petrol by herself. Unless she walked there several times. There's one more possibility, of course. That she didn't come alone. But that doesn't seem reasonable, to say the least. Who would help a young girl commit suicide?"

"We could try to trace the petrol containers," said Nyberg dubiously. "But is it really necessary?"

"As long as we don't know who she was, we have to trace her by any leads we have," Wallander replied. "She must have come from somewhere, somehow."

"Did anyone look in Salomonsson's barn?" asked Höglund. "Maybe the petrol containers came from there."

Wallander nodded.

"Someone had better drive out there and check," he said.

Höglund volunteered.

"We'll have to wait for Martinsson's results," Wallander said, winding up the meeting. "And the pathologists' work in Malmö. They're going to give us an exact age tomorrow."

"And the gold medallion?" asked Svedberg.

"We'll wait until we have some idea of what the letters on it might mean," said Wallander.

He suddenly realised something he had completely overlooked earlier. Behind the dead girl there were other people. Who would mourn her. Who would forever see her running like a living flare in their heads, in a totally different way from him. The fire would stay with them like scars. It would gradually fade away from him like nightmare.

They went their separate ways. Svedberg went with Wallander to get the papers on the car thefts. Wallander gave him a brief run-down. When they were done, Svedberg didn't get up, and Wallander sensed that there was something he wanted to talk about.

"We ought to get together and talk," said Svedberg hesitantly. "About what's going on."

"You're thinking about the cuts? And security companies taking over the custody of suspects?"

Svedberg nodded glumly. "What use are new uniforms if we can't do our jobs?"

"I don't really think it'll help to talk about it," Wallander said warily. "We have a union that's paid to take care of these matters."

"We ought to protest, at least," said Svedberg. "We ought to talk to people on the street about what's going to happen."

"People have their own troubles," replied Wallander, and at the same time it occurred to him that Svedberg was quite right. The public was prepared to bend over backwards to save their police stations.

Svedberg stood up. "That's about it," he said.

"Set up a meeting," Wallander said. "I promise I'll come. But wait until summer's over."

"I'll think about it," said Svedberg and left the room with the files under his arm.

It was late afternoon. Through the window Wallander could see that it was about to rain. He decided to have a pizza before he drove out to see his father in Löderup. On the way out he stopped in on Martinsson.

"Don't stay there too long," he said.

"I haven't found anything yet," said Martinsson.

"See you tomorrow."

Wallander went out to his car, which was already spattered with raindrops. He was just about to drive away when Martinsson ran out waving his arms. We've got her, he thought, and felt a knot in his stomach. He rolled down the window.

"Did you find her?" he asked.

"No," said Martinsson.

Wallander realised something serious had happened. He got out of the car.

"What is it?" he asked.

"Someone phoned in," said Martinsson. "A body has been found on the beach out past Sandskogen."

Damn, thought Wallander. Not now. Not that.

"It sounds like a murder," Martinsson went on. "It was a man that called. He was unusually lucid, even though I think he was in shock."

"Get your jacket," said Wallander. "It's raining."

Martinsson didn't move.

"The man who called seemed to know who the victim was."

Wallander could tell by Martinsson's face that he ought to dread what would come next.

"He said it was Wetterstedt. The former minister of justice."

Wallander stared at Martinsson.

"What?"

"Gustaf Wetterstedt. The minister of justice. And he said it looked as if he'd been scalped."

It was Wednesday, 22 June.

CHAPTER 6

The rain was coming down harder by the time they got to the beach. On the way there they had spoken very little. Martinsson gave directions. They turned off onto a narrow road past the tennis courts. Wallander tried to picture what awaited them. What he wanted least of all had happened. If the man who called the station turned out to be right, his leave was in danger. Hansson would appeal to him to postpone it, and eventually he would have to give in. What he had been hoping for – that his desk would be cleared of pressing matters at the end of June – was not going to happen.

They saw the dunes ahead of them and stopped. A man came forward to meet them. To Wallander's surprise, he didn't seem older than 30. If it was Wetterstedt who had died, this man couldn't have been more than ten when the minister of justice had retired and vanished from public view. Wallander had been a young detective at the time. In the car he had tried to remember Wetterstedt's face. He wore his hair cropped short, and glasses without frames. Wallander vaguely recalled his voice: blaring, invariably self-confident, never willing to admit a mistake.

The young man introduced himself as Göran Lindgren. He was dressed in shorts and a thin sweater, and he seemed very agitated. They followed him down to the beach, deserted now that it had started to rain. Lindgren led them over to a big rowing boat turned upside down. On the far side there was a wide gap between the sand and the boat's gunwale.

"He's under there," said Lindgren in an unsteady voice.

Wallander and Martinsson looked at each other, still hoping the man had imagined it. They knelt down and peered in under the boat. In the dim light they could see a body lying there.

"We'll have to turn the boat over," said Martinsson in a low voice, as if afraid the dead man would hear him.

"No," said Wallander, "we're not turning anything over." He got up quickly and turned to Göran Lindgren.

"I assume you have a torch," he said. "Otherwise you couldn't have described the body in such detail."

The man nodded in surprise and pulled a torch out of a plastic bag near the boat. Wallander bent down again and shone the light inside.

"Holy shit," said Martinsson at his side.

The dead man's face was covered with blood. But they could see that the skin from the forehead up over his skull was torn off, and Lindgren had been right. It was Wetterstedt under the boat. They stood up. Wallander handed back the torch.

"How did you know it was Wetterstedt?" he asked.

"He lives here," said Lindgren, pointing up towards a villa to the left of the boat. "Besides, everyone knows him. You don't forget a politician who was on TV all the time."

Wallander nodded doubtfully.

"We'll need a full team out here," he said to Martinsson. "Go and call. I'll wait here."

Martinsson hurried off. It was raining harder now.

"When did you find him?" asked Wallander.

"I don't have a watch on me," said Lindgren. "But it couldn't have been more than half an hour ago."

"Where did you call from?"

Lindgren pointed to the plastic bag.

"I have a mobile phone."

Wallander regarded him with interest.

"He's lying under an overturned boat," he said. "He's invisible from outside. You must have bent down to be able to see him?"

"It's my boat," said Lindgren simply. "Or my father's, to be exact. I usually walk here on the beach when I finish work. Since it was starting to rain, I thought I'd put my things under the boat. When

I felt the bag bump into something I bent down. At first I thought it was a plank, but then I saw him."

"It's really none of my business," said Wallander, "but I wonder why you had a torch with you?"

"We have a summer cottage in the woods at Sandskogen," replied Lindgren. "Over by Myrgången. We're in the process of rewiring it, so it has no lights. My father and I are electricians."

Wallander nodded. "You'll have to wait here," he said. "We'll have to ask you these questions again in a while. Have you touched anything?"

Lindgren shook his head.

"Has anyone other than you seen him?"

"No."

"When did you or your father last turn over this boat?"

Lindgren thought for a moment.

"It was over a week ago," he said.

Wallander had no more questions. He stood there thinking for a moment and then left the boat and walked in a wide arc up towards the villa where Wetterstedt lived. He tried the gate. It was locked. He waved Lindgren over.

"Do you live nearby?" he asked.

"No," he said. "I live in Åkesholm. My car is parked on the road."

"But you knew that Wetterstedt lived in this house?"

"He used to walk along the beach here. Sometimes he stopped to watch while we were working on the boat, Dad and I. But he never spoke to us. He was rather arrogant."

"Was he married?"

"Dad said that he'd read in a magazine that he was divorced."

Wallander nodded.

"That's fine," he said. "Don't you have a raincoat in that bag?"

"It's up in the car."

"Go ahead and get it," Wallander said. "Did you call anyone besides the police and tell them about this?"

"I think I ought to call Dad. It's his boat, after all."

"Hold off for the time being," said Wallander. "Leave the phone here, and go and get your raincoat."

Lindgren did as he was told. Wallander went back to the boat. He stood looking at it and tried to imagine what had happened. He knew that the first impression of a crime scene was often crucial. During an investigation that was long and difficult, he would return to that first moment.

Some things he was already sure of. It was out of the question that Wetterstedt had been murdered underneath the boat. Someone had wanted to hide him. Since Wetterstedt's villa was so close, there was a good chance that he had died there. Besides, Wallander had a hunch that the killer couldn't have acted alone. The boat must have been lifted to get the body underneath. And it was the old-fashioned kind, clinker-built and heavy.

Wallander turned his mind to the torn-off scalp. What was it that Martinsson had said? Lindgren had told him on the phone that the man had been "scalped". Wallander tried to imagine what other reasons there might be for the wound to the head. They didn't know how Wetterstedt had died. It wasn't natural to think that someone would intentionally have torn off his hair. Wallander felt uneasy. The torn-off skin disturbed him.

Just then the police cars started to arrive. Martinsson had been smart enough to tell them not to turn on their sirens and lights. Wallander walked about ten metres away from the boat so that the others wouldn't trample the sand around it.

"There's a dead man underneath the boat," said Wallander when the police had gathered. "Apparently it's Gustaf Wetterstedt, who was once our top boss. Anyone as old as I am, at least, will remember the days when he was minister of justice. He was living here in retirement. And now he's dead. We have to assume that he was murdered. So we'll start by cordoning off the area."

"It's a good thing the game isn't on tonight," said Martinsson.

"No doubt the person who did this is a football fan too," said Wallander. He was getting annoyed at the constant references to the World Cup, but he hid his irritation from Martinsson.

"Nyberg is on his way," said Martinsson.

"We'll have to work on this all night," said Wallander. "We might as well get started."

Svedberg and Ann-Britt Höglund were in one of the first cars. Hansson showed up right after they did. Lindgren reappeared in a yellow raincoat. He explained again how he had found the dead man while Svedberg took notes. It was raining hard now, and they gathered under a tree at the top of one of the dunes. When Lindgren had finished, Wallander asked him to wait. Since he still didn't want to turn the boat over, the doctor had to dig out some sand to get far enough in under the boat to confirm that Wetterstedt was indeed dead.

"Apparently he was divorced," said Wallander. "But we'll have to get confirmation on that. Some of you will have to stay here. Ann-Britt and I will go up to his house."

"Keys," said Svedberg.

Martinsson went down to the boat, lay on his stomach, and reached in. After a minute or so he managed to find a key ring in Wetterstedt's jacket pocket. Covered in wet sand, Martinsson handed Wallander the keys.

"We've got to put up a canopy," Wallander said testily. "Where is Nyberg? Why the delay?"

"He's coming," said Svedberg. "Today is his sauna day."

Wallander and Höglund made their way up to Wetterstedt's villa.

"I remember him from the police academy," she said. "Somebody put up a photo of him on the wall and used it as a dartboard."

"He was never popular with the police," Wallander said. "It was during his administration that we noticed something new was coming, a change that snuck up on us. I remember it felt like someone had pulled a hood over our eyes. It was almost shameful to be a policeman then. People seemed to worry more about how the prisoners were doing than the fact that crime was steadily on the rise."

"There's a lot I can't recall," said Höglund. "But wasn't he mixed up in some sort of scandal?"

"There were a lot of rumours," said Wallander. "About one thing and another. But nothing was ever proven. A number of police officers in Stockholm were said to be quite upset."

"Maybe time caught up with him," she said.

Wallander looked at her in surprise. But he said nothing.

They had reached the gate.

"I've been here before, you know," she said suddenly. "He used to call the police and complain about young people sitting on the beach and singing on summer nights. One of those young people wrote a letter to the editor of *Ystad Recorder* to complain. Björk asked me to look into it."

"Look into what?"

"I'm not really sure," she answered. "But Björk was very sensitive to criticism."

"That was one of his best traits," said Wallander. "He always defended us and that isn't always the case."

They found the key and opened the gate. Wallander noticed that the light was burned out. The garden they stepped into was well tended. There were no fallen leaves on the lawn. There was a little fountain with two nude plaster children squirting water at each other from their mouths. A swing hung in the arbour. On a flagstone patio stood a marble-topped table and chairs.

"Well cared for and expensive," said Höglund. "What do you think a marble table like that costs?"

Wallander didn't answer, since he had no idea. They continued up towards the villa. He guessed that it had been built around the turn of the century. They followed the flagstone path around to the front of the house. Wallander rang the bell. He waited for over a minute before he rang again. Then he looked for the key and unlocked the door. They stepped into a lit hall. Wallander called out into the silence, but there was no-one there.

"Wetterstedt wasn't killed under the boat," said Wallander. "Of course he could have been attacked on the beach. But I think it happened here."

"Why's that?" she asked.

"I don't know," he said. "Just a hunch."

They went through the house slowly, from the basement to the attic, without touching anything but the light switches. It was a cursory examination. Yet for Wallander it was important. The man who now lay dead on the beach had lived in this house. They had to seek clues as to how his death had come about.

But they didn't find the slightest sign of disorder. Wallander looked in vain for the place where the crime might have taken place. At the front door he had looked for signs of a break-in. As they had stood in the hall listening to the silence, Wallander had told Höglund to take off her shoes. Now they padded soundlessly through the huge villa, which seemed to grow with each step they took. Wallander could feel his colleague looking as much at him as at the objects in the rooms they passed through. He remembered how he had done the same thing with Rydberg, when he was still a young, inexperienced detective. Instead of considering it flattering, it depressed him. The changing of the guard was under way already. She was the one on the way in, he was on the way out.

He remembered when they had first met, almost two years ago. She was a pale, plain young woman who had graduated from the police academy with top marks. But the first thing that she said to him was that he'd teach her everything that the academy couldn't about the unpredictability of the real world. But maybe it was the other way round, he thought, as he looked at a rather blurry lithograph. Imperceptibly, the transition had taken place.

They stopped by a window on the upper floor where they had a view of the beach. The floodlights were in place; Nyberg was gesticulating angrily as he supervised the arrangement of a plastic canopy over the rowing boat. The cordon was guarded by policemen in raincoats. Only a few people stood outside the cordon in the driving rain.

"I'm beginning to think I was wrong," Wallander said as he watched the canopy finally settle into place. "There are no signs that Wetterstedt was killed in here."

"The killer might have cleaned up," Höglund suggested.

"We'll find that out after Nyberg goes through the house with a fine-tooth comb," said Wallander. "But I'm sure it happened outside."

They went back downstairs in silence.

"There was no mail on the floor inside the front door," she said. "The property is walled off. There must be a letter box somewhere."

"We'll take that up later," said Wallander.

He walked into the living-room and stood in the middle. She watched from the doorway, as though expecting him to make an impromptu speech.

"I make a habit of asking myself what I'm missing," Wallander said. "But everything here seems in place. A man living alone in a house where everything is orderly, no bills are unpaid, and where loneliness lingers like old cigar smoke. The only thing that doesn't fit is that the man in question is now lying dead underneath a rowing boat down on the beach."

Then he corrected himself, "No, there's one other thing," he said. "The light by the garden gate isn't working."

"It may have just burned out," she said, surprised.

"Right," said Wallander, "but it still breaks the pattern."

There was a knock on the door. When Wallander opened it, Hansson was standing there, raindrops streaming down his face.

"Neither Nyberg nor the doctor are going to get anywhere unless we turn that boat over," he said.

"Turn it over," said Wallander. "I'll be right there."

Hansson disappeared into the rain.

"We have to start looking for his relatives," Wallander said. "He must have an address book somewhere."

"There's one thing that's odd," said Höglund. "This house is full of souvenirs from a long life with lots of travel and countless meetings with people. But there are no family photographs."

They were back in the living-room. Wallander looked around and saw that she was right. It bothered him that he hadn't thought of it himself.

"Maybe he didn't want to be reminded that he was old," Wallander said without conviction.

"A woman would never be able to live without pictures of her family," she said. "That's probably why I thought of it."

There was a telephone on a table next to the sofa.

"There's a phone in his study too," he said, pointing. "You look in there, and I'll start here."

Wallander squatted by the low telephone stand. Next to the phone was the remote control for the TV. Wetterstedt could talk on the phone and watch TV at the same time, he thought. Just like me. We live in a world where people can't bear not to be able to change channel and talk on the phone at the same time. He riffled through the phone books, but didn't find any private notes. Next he pulled out two drawers in a bureau behind the telephone stand. In one there was a stamp album, in the other some tubes of glue and a box of napkin rings.

As he was walking towards the study, the phone rang. He stopped. Höglund appeared at once in the doorway to the study. Wallander sat down carefully on the corner of the sofa and picked up the receiver.

"Hello," said a woman's voice. "Gustaf? Why haven't you called me?"

"Who's speaking, please?" asked Wallander.

The woman's voice suddenly turned formal. "This is Gustaf Wetterstedt's mother calling," she said. "With whom am I speaking?"

"My name is Kurt Wallander. I'm a police officer here in Ystad."

He could hear the woman breathing. He realised that she must be very old if she was Gustaf Wetterstedt's mother. He made a face at Höglund, who was standing looking at him.

"Has something happened?" asked the woman.

Wallander didn't know how to react. It went against all written and unwritten procedures to inform the next of kin of a sudden death over the telephone. But he had already told her his name, and that he was a police officer.

"Hello?" said the woman. "Are you still there?"

Wallander didn't answer. He stared helplessly at Höglund. Then he did something which he couldn't decide was justified. He hung up.

"Who was that?" she asked.

Wallander shook his head. He picked up the phone and called the headquarters of the Stockholm police.

CHAPTER 7

Later that evening, Gustaf Wetterstedt's telephone rang again. By that time Wallander had arranged for his colleagues in Stockholm to tell Wetterstedt's mother of his death. An inspector who introduced himself as Hans Vikander was calling from the Östermalm police. In a few days, 1 July, the old name would disappear and be replaced by "city police".

"She's been informed," Vikander said. "Because she was so old I took a clergyman along with me. I must say she took it calmly, even though she's 94."

"Maybe that's why," said Wallander.

"We're trying to track down Wetterstedt's two children," Vikander went on. "The older, a son, works at the UN in New York. The daughter lives in Uppsala. We hope to reach them this evening."

"What about his ex-wife?" asked Wallander.

"Which one?" Vikander asked. "He was married three times."

"All three of them," said Wallander. "We'll have to contact them ourselves later."

"I've got something that might interest you," Vikander went on. "When we spoke with the mother she said that her son called her every night, at precisely nine o'clock."

Wallander looked at his watch. It was just after 9 p.m. At once he understood the significance of what Vikander had said.

"He didn't call yesterday" Vikander continued. "She waited until 9.30 p.m. Then she tried to call him. No-one answered, although she claimed she let it ring at least 15 times."

"And the night before?"

"She couldn't remember too well. She's 94, after all. She said that her short-term memory was pretty bad."

"Did she say anything else?"

"It was a little hard to know what to ask."

"We'll have to talk to her again," Wallander said. "Since she's already met you, it would be good if you could take it on."

"I'm going on holiday the second week in July," said Vikander. "Until then, that's no problem."

Wallander hung up. Höglund came into the hall. She had been checking the letter box.

"Newspapers from today and yesterday," she said. "A phone bill. No personal letters. He can't have been under that boat for very long."

Wallander got up from the sofa.

"Go through the house one more time," he said. "See if you can find any sign that something is missing. I'll go down and take a look at him."

It was raining even harder now. As Wallander hurried through the garden he remembered that he was supposed to be visiting his father tonight. With a grimace he went back to the house.

"Do me a favour," he asked Höglund. "Call my father and tell him I'm tied up with an urgent investigation. If he asks who you are, tell him you're the new chief of police."

She nodded and smiled. Wallander gave her the number. Then he went out into the rain.

The cordoned area was a ghostly spectacle, lit up by the powerful floodlights. With a strong feeling of unease, Wallander walked in under the temporary canopy. Wetterstedt's body lay stretched out on a plastic sheet. The doctor was shining a torch down Wetterstedt's throat. He stopped when he realised that Wallander had arrived.

"How are you?" asked the doctor.

Wallander hadn't recognised him until that moment. It was the doctor who had treated him in hospital a few years earlier when he'd thought he was having a heart attack.

"Apart from this business, I'm doing fine," said Wallander. "I never had a recurrence."

"Did you take my advice?" asked the doctor.

"Of course not," Wallander muttered.

He looked at the dead man, who gave the same impression in death as he had on the TV screen. There was something obstinate and unsympathetic about his face, even when covered with dried blood. Wallander leaned forward and looked at the wound on his forehead, which extended up towards the top of his head, where the skin and hair had been ripped away.

"How did he die?" asked Wallander.

"From a powerful blow to the spine with an axe," the doctor replied. "It would have killed him instantly. The spine is severed just below the shoulder blades. He was probably dead before he hit the ground."

"Are you sure it happened outside?" Wallander asked.

"I think so. The blow to the spine must have come from someone standing behind him. It's most likely that the force of the blow made him fall forwards. He has grains of sand in his mouth and eyes. It probably happened right nearby."

"There must be traces of blood somewhere," said Wallander.

"The rain makes it difficult," said the doctor. "But with a little luck maybe you can scrape through the surface layer and find some blood that seeped deep enough that the rain hasn't washed it away."

Wallander pointed at Wetterstedt's butchered head.

"How do you explain this?" he asked.

The doctor shrugged.

"The incision in the forehead was made with a sharp knife," he said. "Or maybe a razor. The skin and hair seem to have been torn off. I can't tell yet if it was done before or after he received the blow to the spine. That will be a job for the pathologist in Malmö."

"Malmström will have a lot to do," said Wallander.

"Who?"

"Yesterday we sent in the remains of a girl who burned herself to death. And now we're sending over a man who's been scalped. The pathologist I talked to was named Malmström. A woman."

"There's more than one," said the doctor. "I don't know her."

Wallander squatted next to the corpse.

"Give me your interpretation," he said to the doctor. "What do you think happened?"

"Whoever struck him in the back knew what he was doing," said the doctor. "A sharpshooter couldn't have done better. But to scalp him! That's the work of a madman."

"Or an American Indian," said Wallander.

He got up and felt a twinge in his knees. The days when he could squat without pain were over.

"I'm finished here," said the doctor. "I've already told Malmö that we're bringing him in."

Wallander didn't reply. He had noticed that Wetterstedt's fly was open.

"Did you touch his clothes?" he asked.

"Just on the back, around the wound to his spine," said the doctor.

Wallander nodded. He could feel the nausea rising.

"Could I ask you one thing?" he said. "Could you check inside Wetterstedt's fly and see if he's still got what's supposed to be there?"

The doctor gave Wallander a questioning look.

"If someone cut off half his scalp, they might cut off other things too," Wallander explained.

The doctor nodded and pulled on a pair of latex gloves. Then he cautiously stuck his hand in and felt around.

"Everything that's supposed to be there seems to be there," he said when he pulled out his hand.

Wallander nodded.

Wetterstedt's corpse was taken away. Wallander turned to Nyberg, who was kneeling next to the boat, which had been turned right side up.

"How's it going?" asked Wallander.

"I don't know," said Nyberg. "With this rain, everything is washing away."

"We'll have to dig tomorrow," said Wallander and told him what the doctor said. Nyberg nodded.

"If there's any blood, we'll find it. Any special place you want us to start looking?"

"Around the boat," said Wallander. "Then in the area from the garden gate down to the water."

Nyberg pointed at a case with the lid open. There were plastic bags inside.

"All I found in his pockets was a box of matches," said Nyberg. "You've got his keys. The clothes are expensive. Except for the clogs."

"The house seems to be untouched," Wallander said. "But I'd appreciate it if you could take a look at it tonight."

"I can't be in two places at once," Nyberg grumbled. "If we're going to secure any evidence out here, we'll have to do it before it's all washed away by the rain."

Wallander was just about to return to Wetterstedt's house when he noticed that Lindgren was still there. He went over to him. He could see that the young man was freezing.

"You can go home now," Wallander said.

"Can I phone my father and tell him about it?"

"Go ahead."

"What happened?" Lindgren asked.

"It's too soon to say," Wallander replied.

There were still a handful of people outside the cordon, watching the police work. Some senior citizens, a younger man with a dog, a boy on a moped. Wallander thought about the days that lay ahead with dread. A former minister of justice who had been found scalped with his spine chopped in half was the sort of juicy titbit that would drive the media wild. The only positive thing that he could think of was that the girl who burned herself to death in Salomonsson's rape field would not end up on the front pages after all.

He had to have a pee. He went down to the water and unzipped his fly. Maybe it's that simple, he thought. Wetterstedt's fly was open because he was standing taking a pee when he was attacked.

He started to walk back up towards the house, then stopped. He was overlooking something. He went back to Nyberg.

"Do you know where Svedberg is?" he asked.

"I think he's trying to find some more plastic sheeting and a couple of big tarpaulins. We've got to cover up the sand."

"I'll talk to him when he gets back," said Wallander. "Where are Martinsson and Hansson?"

"I think Martinsson went to get something to eat," said Nyberg sourly. "Who the hell has time for food?"

"We can arrange to get you something," said Wallander. "Where's Hansson?"

"He was going to speak to the prosecutors' office. And I don't want anything."

Wallander walked back to the house. After he hung up his soaked jacket and pulled off his boots he realised he was hungry. He went to the kitchen and turned on the light. He remembered how they had sat in Salomonsson's kitchen drinking coffee. Now Salomonsson was dead. Compared with the old farmer's kitchen, this was another world. Shiny copper pots hung on the walls. An open grill with a smoke hood attached to an old oven chimney stood in the middle of the room. He opened the refrigerator and took out a piece of cheese and a beer. He found some crispbread in one of the cupboards, and sat down at the kitchen table and ate, his mind empty. By the time Svedberg came in the front door he had finished.

"Nyberg said you wanted to talk to me?"

"How'd it go with the tarpaulins?"

"We're still trying to cover up the sand as best we can. Martinsson called the weather office and asked how long the rain was going to last. It's supposed to keep raining all night. Then we'll have a few hours' break before the next storm arrives. That one's expected to be a real summer gale."

A puddle had formed on the kitchen floor around Svedberg's boots. But Wallander didn't feel like asking him to take them off. They were unlikely to find the clue to Wetterstedt's death in his kitchen.

Svedberg sat down and dried off his hair with a handkerchief.

"I vaguely remember that you once told me you were interested in the history of the American Indians," Wallander began. "Or am I wrong?"

Svedberg gave him a puzzled look.

"You're right," he said. "I've read a lot about American Indians. I never liked watching movies that didn't tell the truth about them. I corresponded with an expert named Uncas. He won a prize on a TV show once. I think that was before I was born. But he taught me a lot."

"I assume you're wondering why I ask," Wallander went on.

"Actually, no," said Svedberg. "Wetterstedt was scalped, after all."

Wallander looked at him intently.

"Was he?"

"If scalping is an art, then in this case it was done almost perfectly. A cut with a sharp knife across the forehead. Then some cuts up by the temples. To get a firm grip."

"He died from a blow to the spine," said Wallander. "Just below the shoulder blades."

Svedberg shrugged.

"Native American warriors struck at the head," he said. "It's hard to hit the spine. You have to hold the axe at an angle. It's particularly hard, of course, if the person you're trying to kill is in motion."

"What if he's standing still?"

"In any case, it's not very warrior-like," said Svedberg. "In fact, it's not like an American Indian to kill someone from behind. Or to kill anyone at all, for that matter."

Wallander rested his head in his hands.

"Why are you asking about this?" said Svedberg. "It's hardly likely that an American Indian murdered Wetterstedt."

"Who would take his scalp?" asked Wallander.

"A madman," said Svedberg. "Anyone who does something like this has to be nuts. We must catch him as fast as possible."

"I know," said Wallander.

Svedberg stood up and left. Wallander got a mop and cleaned the floor. Then he went in to see Höglund in the study.

"Your father didn't sound too happy," she said. "But I think the main thing that was bothering him was that you hadn't called earlier."

"He's right about that," said Wallander. "What have you found?"

"Surprisingly little," she said. "On the surface nothing seems to have been stolen. No cabinets are broken open. I think he must have had a housekeeper to keep this big place clean."

"Why do you say that?"

"Two reasons. First, you can see the difference in the way a man and a woman clean. Don't ask me how. That's just the way it is."

"And the second reason?"

"There's a note in his diary that says 'charwoman' and then a time. The note comes up twice a month."

"Did he really write 'charwoman'?"

"A fine old contemptuous word."

"When was she here last?"

"Last Thursday."

"That explains why everything seems so clean and tidy."

Wallander sank down into a chair in front of the desk.

"How did it look down there?" she asked.

"An axe blow severed the spine. He died instantly. The killer cut off his scalp."

"Earlier you said there had to be at least two of them."

"I know I did. But now all I'm certain about is that I don't like this one bit. Why would someone murder an old man who's been living in seclusion for 20 years? And why take his scalp?"

They sat for a while in silence. Wallander thought about the burning girl. About the man with his hair torn off. And about the pouring rain. He tried to push these thoughts away by remembering himself and Baiba in a hollow behind a dune at Skagen in Denmark. But the girl kept running through the field with her hair on fire. And Wetterstedt lay scalped on a stretcher on the way to Malmö.

He forced himself to concentrate, and looked at Höglund.

"Give me a run-down," he said. "What do you think? What happened here? Describe it for me. Don't hold anything back."

"He went out," she said. "A walk down to the beach. To meet

75

someone. Or just to get some exercise. But he was only going for a short walk."

"Why?"

"The clogs. Old and worn out. Uncomfortable. But good enough if you're just going to be out for a short time."

"And then?"

"It happened at night. What did the doctor say about the time?"

"He's not sure yet. Keep going. Why at night?"

"The risk of being seen is too great in the daytime. At this time of year, the beach is never deserted."

"What else?"

"There's no obvious motive. But I think you can tell that the killer had a plan."

"Why?"

"He took time to hide the body."

"Why did he do that?"

"To delay its discovery. So he'd have time to get away."

"But nobody saw him, right? And why a man?"

"A woman would never sever someone's spine. A desperate woman might hit her husband with an axe. But she wouldn't scalp him. It's a man."

"What do we know about the killer?"

"Nothing. Unless you know something I don't."

Wallander shook his head.

"You've outlined everything we know," he said. "I think it's time for us to leave the house to Nyberg and his people."

"There's going to be a big commotion about this," she said.

"I know," said Wallander. "It'll start tomorrow. You can be glad you've got your holiday coming up."

"Hansson has already asked me whether I'd postpone it," she said. "I said yes."

"You should go home now," Wallander said. "I think I'll tell the others that we'll meet early tomorrow morning to plan the investigation."

Wallander knew that they had to form a picture of who Wetterstedt was. They knew that every evening at the same time he called his mother. But what about all the routines that they didn't know about? He went back to the kitchen and searched for some paper in one of the drawers. Then he made a list of things to remember for tomorrow morning's meeting. A few minutes later Nyberg came in. He took off his wet raincoat.

"What do you want us to look for?" he asked.

"I want to be able to rule out that he was killed inside. I want you to go over the house in your usual way," Wallander answered.

Nyberg nodded and left the kitchen. Wallander heard him reprimanding one of his crew. He knew he ought to drive home and sleep for a few hours, but instead he decided to go through the house one more time. He started with the basement. An hour later he was on the top floor. He went into Wetterstedt's spacious bedroom and opened his wardrobe. Pulling the suits back, he searched the bottom. Downstairs he could hear Nyberg's voice raised in anger. He was just about to close the wardrobe doors when he caught sight of a small case in one corner. He bent down and took it out, sat down on the edge of the bed, and opened it. Inside was a camera. Wallander guessed that it wasn't particularly expensive. He could see that it was more or less the same type as the one Linda had bought last year. There was film in it, and seven pictures out of 36 were exposed. He put it back in the bag. Then he went downstairs to Nyberg.

"There's a camera in this bag," he said. "I want you to get the photos developed as quickly as possible."

It was almost midnight when he left Wetterstedt's villa. It was still pouring outside. He drove straight home.

When he got to his flat he sat down at the kitchen table, wondering what the photographs would be of. The rain pounded against his windows, and he was aware of a feeling of foreboding. He sensed that what had happened was only the beginning of something much worse.

CHAPTER 8

On Thursday morning, 23 June, there was no Midsummer Eve mood in the Ystad station. Wallander had been woken at 3 a.m. by a reporter from *Daily News* in Stockholm who had heard about Wetterstedt's death from the Östermalm police. Just when Wallander finally managed to get back to sleep, the *Express* called. Hansson had also been woken during the night. They gathered in the conference room just after 7 a.m., everyone looking haggard and tired. Nyberg was there, even though he had been going through Wetterstedt's house until 5 a.m. Before the meeting, Hansson took Wallander aside and told him that he would have to run the investigation.

"I think Björk knew this would happen," said Hansson. "That's why he retired."

"He didn't retire," said Wallander. "He was promoted. Besides, seeing into the future was definitely not one of his talents. He worried enough about what was happening around him from day to day."

But Wallander knew that the responsibility for organising the hunt for Wetterstedt's killer would fall to him. The big difficulty was the fact that they would be short of staff all summer. He was grateful that Ann-Britt Höglund had agreed to postpone her holiday. But what was going to happen to his? He had counted on being on his way to Skagen with Baiba in two weeks.

He sat down at the table and took stock of the exhausted faces around him. It was still raining, but it was easing off. In front of him on the table he had a pile of messages that he had picked up at the reception desk. He pushed them aside and tapped on the table with a pencil.

"We have to get started," he said. "The worst thing possible has happened. We've had a murder during the summer holiday. We'll have to organise ourselves as best we can. We also have the Midsummer holiday coming up that will keep the uniformed officers busy. We'll have to plan our investigation with this in mind."

No-one spoke. Wallander turned to Nyberg and asked how the forensic investigation was going.

"If only it would stop raining for a few hours," said Nyberg. "To find the murder site we'll have to dig through the surface layer of the sand. That's almost impossible to do until it's dry. Otherwise we'll just end up with lumps of wet sand."

"I called the meteorologist at Sturup Airport a while ago," said Martinsson. "He's predicting that the rain will stop here just after 8 a.m. But a new storm will come in this afternoon, and we'll get more rain. After that it'll clear up."

"If it's not one thing it's another," said Wallander. "Usually it's easier for us if the weather's bad on Midsummer Eve."

"For once it looks like the football game will be a help," said Nyberg. "I don't think people will drink as much. They'll be glued to their TVs."

"What'll happen if Sweden loses to Russia?" asked Wallander.

"They won't," Nyberg proclaimed. "We're going to win."

Wallander hadn't realised that Nyberg was a football fan.

"I hope you're right," he said.

"Anyway, we haven't found anything of interest around the boat," Nyberg continued. "We also went over the part of the beach between Wetterstedt's gate, the boat, and down to the water. We picked up a number of items. But nothing that is likely to be of interest to us. With one possible exception."

Nyberg put one of his plastic bags on the table.

"One of the officers found this. It's a mace spray. The kind that women carry in their handbags to defend themselves if they're attacked."

"Aren't those illegal in Sweden?" asked Höglund.

"Yes, they are," said Nyberg. "But there it was, in the sand just outside the cordon. We're going to check it for prints. Maybe it'll turn up something."

Nyberg put the plastic bag back in his case.

"Could one man turn that boat over by himself?" asked Wallander.

"Not unless he's incredibly strong," said Nyberg.

"That means there were two of them," Wallander replied.

"The murderer could have dug out the sand under the boat," said Nyberg hesitantly. "And then pushed it back in after he shoved Wetterstedt underneath."

"That's a possibility," said Wallander. "But does it sound plausible?"

No-one at the table answered.

"There's nothing to indicate that the murder was committed inside the house," Nyberg continued. "We found no traces of blood or other signs of a crime. No-one broke in. We can't say whether anything was stolen, but it doesn't appear so."

"Did you find anything else that seemed unusual?" asked Wallander.

"I think the entire house is unusual," said Nyberg. "Wetterstedt must have had a lot of money."

They thought about that for a moment. Wallander realised he should sum up.

"It is important to find out when Wetterstedt was murdered," he began. "The doctor who examined the body thought that it probably happened on the beach. He found grains of sand in the mouth and eyes. But we'll have to wait to see what the doctors have to say. Since we don't have any clues to go on or any obvious motive, we'll have to proceed on a broad front. We have to find out what kind of man Wetterstedt was. Who did he associate with? What routines did he have? We have to understand his character, find out what his life was like. And we can't ignore the fact that 20 years ago he was very famous. He was the minister of justice. He was very popular with some people, and he was hated by others. There were rumours of scandals that he was involved in. Could revenge be part of the picture? He was cut down with an axe and had his hair ripped off. He was scalped. Has anything like this happened before? Can we find any similarities with previous murders? Martinsson will have to get his computer going. And Wetterstedt had a housekeeper we'll have to find and talk to, today."

"What about his political party?" asked Höglund.

"I was just getting to that. Did he have any unresolved political disputes? Did he continue to see old party allies? We have to clear this up too. Is there anything in his background that might point to a conceivable motive?"

"Since the news broke, two people have already called in to confess to the murder," said Svedberg. "One of them called from a phone booth in Malmö. He was so drunk it was hard to understand what he said. We asked our colleagues in Malmö to question him. The other one who called was a prisoner at Österåker. His last leave was in February. So it's quite clear that Gustaf Wetterstedt still arouses strong feelings."

"Those of us who have been around for a while know that the police hold a grudge too," said Wallander. "During his tenure as minister of justice, a lot of things happened that none of us can forget. Of all the ministers of justice and national police chiefs, in my time anyway, Wetterstedt was the one who did the least for us."

They went over the various assignments and divided them up. Wallander himself was going to question Wetterstedt's housekeeper. They agreed to meet again at 4 p.m.

"A few more items," said Wallander. "We're going to be invaded by reporters. We're going to be seeing headlines like 'The Scalp Murderer'. So we might as well hold a news conference today. I would prefer not to have to run it."

"You must," said Svedberg. "You have to take charge. Even if you don't want to, you're the one who does it best."

"All right, but I don't want to do it alone," said Wallander. "I want Hansson with me. And Ann-Britt. Shall we say 1 p.m.?"

They were all about to leave when Wallander asked them to wait.

"We can't stop the investigation into the girl who burned herself to death," he said.

"You think there's a connection?" Hansson asked in astonishment.

"Of course not," said Wallander. "But we still have to try and find out who she was, even though we're busy working on Wetterstedt."

"We've no positive leads on our database search," said Martinsson. "Not even on the combination of letters. But I promise to keep working on it."

"Someone must miss her," said Wallander. "A young girl. I think this is very odd."

"It's summer," said Svedberg. "A lot of young people are on the road. It could take a couple of weeks before someone is missed."

"You're right," Wallander admitted. "We'll have to be patient."

The meeting was over. Wallander had run it at a brisk pace since they all had a lot of work ahead of them. When he got to his office he went rapidly through his messages. Nothing looked urgent. He took a notebook out of a drawer, wrote "Gustaf Wetterstedt" at the top of the page, and leaned back in his chair and closed his eyes. What does his death tell me? What kind of person would kill him with an axe and scalp him? Wallander leaned over his desk again. He wrote:

"Nothing indicates that Wetterstedt was murdered by a burglar, but of course that can't be excluded yet. It wasn't a murder of convenience either, unless it was committed by someone insane. The killer took the time to hide the body. So the revenge motive remains. Who would want to take revenge on Gustaf Wetterstedt, to see him dead?"

Wallander put down his pen and read through the page with dissatisfaction. It's too soon to draw conclusions, he thought. I have to know more. He got up and left the room. When he walked out of the station it had stopped raining. The meteorologist at Sturup was right. Wallander drove straight to Wetterstedt's villa.

The cordon on the beach was still there. Nyberg was already at work. Along with his crew he was busy removing the tarpaulins over a section of the beach. There were a lot of spectators standing at the edge the cordon this morning.

Wallander unlocked the front door with Wetterstedt's key and then went straight to the study. Methodically he continued the search that Höglund had begun the night before. It took him almost half an hour to find the name of the woman Wetterstedt had called the "charwoman". Her name was Sara Björklund. She lived on Styrbordsgången, which Wallander knew lay just past the big warehouses at the west end of town. He picked up the telephone on the desk and dialled the number. Eventually a harsh male voice answered.

"I'm looking for Sara Björklund," said Wallander.

"She's not home," said the man.

"Where can I get in touch with her?"

"Who's asking?" said the man evasively.

"Inspector Kurt Wallander from the Ystad police."

There was a long silence at the other end.

"Are you still there?" said Wallander, not bothering to conceal his impatience.

"Does this have something to do with Wetterstedt?" asked the man. "Sara Björklund is my wife."

"I have to speak with her."

"She's in Malmö. She won't be back till this afternoon."

"When can I get hold of her? What time? Try to be exact!"

"I'm sure she'll be home by 5 p.m."

"I'll come by your house then," said Wallander and hung up.

He left the house and went down to Nyberg on the beach.

"Find anything?" he asked.

Nyberg was standing with a bucket of sand in one hand.

"Nothing," he said. "But if he was killed here and fell into the sand, there has to be some blood. Maybe not from his back. But from his head. It must have spurted blood. There are some big veins in the scalp."

Wallander nodded.

"Where did you find the spray can?" he asked.

Nyberg pointed to a spot beyond the cordon.

"I doubt it has anything to do with this," said Wallander.

"Me neither," said Nyberg.

Wallander was just about to go back to his car when he remembered that he had one more question for Nyberg.

"The light by the gate to the garden is out," he said. "Can you take a look at it?"

"What do you want me to do?" Nyberg wondered. "Change the bulb?"

"I just want to know why it's not working," said Wallander. "That's all."

He drove back to the station. The sky was grey, but it wasn't raining.

"Reporters are calling constantly," said Ebba as he passed the reception desk.

"They're welcome to come to the press conference at one o'clock," said Wallander. "Where's Ann-Britt?"

"She left a while ago. She didn't say where she was going."

"What about Hansson?"

"I think he's in Per Åkeson's office. Should I find him for you?"

"We have to get ready for the press conference. Get someone to bring more chairs into the conference room. There are going to be lots of people."

Wallander went to his office and started to prepare what he was going to say to the press. After about half an hour Höglund knocked on the door.

"I was at Salomonsson's farm," she said. "I think I know where that girl got the petrol from."

"Salomonsson had petrol in his barn?"

She nodded.

"Well, that's something," said Wallander. "That means that she actually could have walked to the farm. She wouldn't have had to come by car or bicycle."

"Could Salomonsson have known her?" she asked.

Wallander thought for a moment before he answered.

"No, Salomonsson wasn't lying. He'd never seen her before."

"So the girl walks to the farm from somewhere. She goes into Salomonsson's barn and finds a number of containers of petrol.

She takes five of them with her out into the rape. Then she sets herself on fire."

"That's about it," said Wallander. "Even if we manage to find out who she was, we'll probably never know the whole story."

They got coffee and discussed what they were going to say at the press conference. It was mid-morning when Hansson joined them.

"I talked to Per Åkeson," he said. "He told me he would contact the chief public prosecutor."

Wallander looked up from his papers in surprise.

"Why?"

"Wetterstedt was an important person. Ten years ago the prime minister of this country was murdered. Now we have a minister of justice murdered. I assume that he wants to know whether the investigation should be handled in any special way."

"If he were still in office I could understand it," said Wallander. "But he was an old man who had left his public duties behind a long time ago."

"You'll have to talk to Åkeson yourself," said Hansson. "I'm just telling you what he said."

At 1 p.m. they took their seats on the little dais at one end of the conference room. They had agreed to keep the meeting with the press as brief as possible. The main thing was to head off too many wild, unfounded speculations. So they decided to be vague when it came to answering how Wetterstedt had actually been killed. They wouldn't say anything at all about his having been scalped.

The room was crowded with reporters. Just as Wallander had imagined, the national newspapers were regarding Wetterstedt's murder as a major event. Wallander counted cameras from three different TV stations when he looked in the crowd.

It went unusually well. They were as terse as possible with their answers, citing the requirements of the investigation for limiting candour and withholding detail. Eventually the press realised they weren't going to get anything more. When the newspaper reporters had gone, Wallander allowed himself to be interviewed by the local radio station while Höglund answered questions for one of the TV stations. He looked at her and was relieved that for once he didn't have to be the one on camera.

At the end of the press conference Åkeson had slipped in unnoticed to the back of the room. Now he stood waiting for Wallander.

"I heard you were going to call up the chief public prosecutor," said Wallander. "Did he give you any directives?"

"He wants to be kept informed," said Åkeson. "The same way you keep me informed."

"You'll get a daily summary," said Wallander. "And hear as soon as we make a breakthrough."

"Nothing conclusive yet?"

"No."

The investigative team had a quick meeting at 4 p.m. Wallander knew that this was the time for work, not reports. He went rapidly around the table before asking everyone to go back to their tasks. They agreed to meet again at 8 a.m. the next morning, provided nothing crucial happened before then.

Just before 5 p.m. Wallander left the station and drove to Styrbordsgången, where Sara Björklund lived. It was a part of town that Wallander almost never visited. He parked and went in through the gate. The door was opened before he reached the house. The woman standing there was younger than he had expected. He guessed her to be around 30. And to Wetterstedt she had been a "charwoman". He wondered fleetingly whether she knew what Wetterstedt had called her.

"Good afternoon," said Wallander. "I called earlier today. Are you Sara Björklund?"

"I recognised you," she said, nodding.

She invited him in. She had set out a tray of buns and coffee in a thermos in the living-room. Wallander could hear a man upstairs scolding some children for making a racket. Wallander sat down in an armchair and looked around. He half expected one of his father's paintings to be hanging on the wall. That's all that's missing, he thought. Here's the old fisherman, the gypsy woman, and the crying child. My father's landscape is all that's needed. With or without the grouse.

"Would you like coffee, sir?" she asked.

"No need to call me sir," said Wallander. "Yes, please."

"You had to be formal with Wetterstedt," she said suddenly. "You had to call him Mr Wetterstedt. He gave strict instructions about that when I started working there."

Wallander was thankful to start right away on the matter in hand. He took out a notebook and pen.

"So you know that Gustaf Wetterstedt has been murdered," he began.

"It's terrible," she said. "Who could have done it?"

"We're wondering the same thing," said Wallander.

"Was he really lying on the beach? Under that ugly boat? The one you could see from upstairs?"

"Yes, he was," said Wallander. "But let's begin at the beginning. You cleaned the house for Mr Wetterstedt?"

"Yes."

"How long have you been with him?"

"Almost three years. I wasn't working. This house costs money so I was forced to look for cleaning work. I found the job in the paper."

"How often did you go to his house?"

"Twice a month. Every other Thursday."

Wallander made a note.

"Always on Thursdays?"

"Always."

"Did you have your own keys?"

"No. He never would have given them to me."

"Why do you say that?"

"When I was in the house he watched every step I took. It was incredibly nerve-wracking. But he paid well."

"Did you ever come across anything odd?"

"Such as?"

"Was there ever anyone else there?"

"No, never."

"He didn't have people to dinner?"

"Not that I know of. There were never any dishes waiting for me when I came."

Wallander paused for a moment before continuing.

"How would you describe him as a person?"

Her reply was swift and firm.

"He was the type you'd call arrogant."

"What do you mean by that?"

"He patronised me. To him I was nothing more than a cleaning woman. Despite the fact that he once belonged to the party that supposedly represented our cause. The cleaning women's cause."

"Did you know that he referred to you as a charwoman in his diary?"

"That doesn't surprise me in the least."

"But you stayed on with him?"

"I told you, he paid well."

"Try to remember your last visit. You were there last week?"

"Everything was as usual. He was just the way he always was."

"Over the past three years, then, nothing out of the ordinary happened?"

She hesitated before she answered. He was immediately on the alert.

"There was one time last year," she began tentatively. "In November. I don't know why, but I forgot what day it was. I went there on a Friday morning instead of Thursday. As I arrived, a big black car drove out of the garage. The kind with windows you can't see through. Then I rang the bell at the front door as I always do. It took a long time before he came to open the door. When he saw me he was furious. He slammed the door. I thought I was going to get the sack. But when I came back the next time he said nothing about it, just pretended that nothing had happened."

Wallander waited for her to go on.

"Was that all?"

"Yes."

"A big black car leaving his house?"

"That's right."

Wallander knew that he wouldn't get any further. He finished his coffee and stood up.

"If you remember anything else that might be helpful to the enquiry, I'd appreciate it if you'd call me," he said as he left.

He drove back to Ystad.

A big black car had visited Wetterstedt's house. Who was in the car? A strong wind began to blow, and the rain started again.

CHAPTER 9

By the time Wallander returned to Wetterstedt's house, Nyberg and his crew had moved back inside. They had carted off tons of sand without finding what they were looking for. When it started raining again, Nyberg immediately decided to lay out the tarpaulins. They couldn't carry on until the weather improved. Wallander returned to the house feeling that what Sara Björklund had said about showing up on the wrong day and the big black car meant they had knocked a small hole in Wetterstedt's shell. She had seen something that no-one was supposed to see. Wallander couldn't interpret Wetterstedt's rage in any other way, or the fact that he didn't fire her and never spoke of it again. The anger and the silence were two sides of the same temperament.

Nyberg was in Wetterstedt's living-room drinking coffee from an old thermos that reminded Wallander of the 1950s. He was sitting on a newspaper to protect the chair.

"We haven't found the murder site yet," said Nyberg "And now there's no point in looking because of the rain."

"I hope the tarpaulins are securely fastened," Wallander said. "It's blowing harder all the time."

"They won't move," said Nyberg.

"I thought I'd finish going through his desk," said Wallander.

"Hansson called. He has spoken to Wetterstedt's children."

"It took him this long?" said Wallander. "I thought he'd done that a while ago."

"I don't know anything about it," said Nyberg. "I'm just telling you what he said."

Wallander went into the study and sat down at the desk. He adjusted the lamp so that it cast its light in as big a circle as possible.

Then he pulled out one of the drawers in the left-hand cabinet. In it lay a copy of this year's tax return. Wallander placed it on the desk. He could see that Wetterstedt had declared an income of almost 1,000,000 kronor, and that the income came primarily from Wetterstedt's private pension plan and share dividends. A summary from the securities register centre revealed that Wetterstedt held shares in traditional Swedish heavy industry; Ericsson, Asea Brown Boveri, Volvo, and Rottneros. Apart from this income, Wetterstedt had reported an honorarium from the foreign ministry and royalties from Tidens publishing company. Under the entry "Net Worth" he had declared 5,000,000 kronor. Wallander memorised this figure.

He put the tax return back. The next drawer contained something that looked like a photo album. Here are the family pictures Ann-Britt was missing, he thought. But he leafed through the pages with growing astonishment: old-fashioned pornographic pictures, some of them quite sophisticated. Wallander noted that some of the pages fell open more easily than others. Wetterstedt had a preference for young models. Martinsson walked in. Wallander nodded and pointed to the open album.

"Some people collect stamps," said Martinsson, "others evidently collect pictures like this."

Wallander closed the album and put it back in the desk drawer.

"A lawyer named Sjögren called from Malmö," said Martinsson. "He said he had Wetterstedt's will. There are rather large assets in the estate. I asked him whether there were any unexpected beneficiaries. But everything goes to the direct heirs. Wetterstedt had also set up a foundation to distribute scholarships to young law students. But he put the money into it long ago and paid tax on it."

"So, we know that Gustaf Wetterstedt was a wealthy man. But wasn't he born the son of a poor docker?"

"Svedberg is working on his background," said Martinsson. "I gather he's found an old party secretary with a good memory who had a lot to say about Wetterstedt. But I wanted to have a word about the girl who committed suicide."

"Did you find out who she was?"

"No. But through the computer I've found more than 2,000 possibilities for what the letter combination might mean. It was a pretty long print-out."

"We'll have to put it out on Interpol," said Wallander after a pause. "And what's the new one called? Europol?"

"That's right."

"Send out a query with her description. Tomorrow we'll take a photo of the medallion. Even if everything else is getting pushed aside in the wake of Wetterstedt's death, we have to try and get that picture in the papers."

"I had a jeweller look at it," said Martinsson. "He said it was solid gold."

"Surely somebody is missing her," said Wallander. "It's rare for someone to have no relatives at all."

Martinsson yawned and asked whether Wallander needed any help.

"Not tonight," he said, and Martinsson left the house. Wallander spent another hour going through the desk. Then he turned off the lamp and sat there in the dark. Who was Gustaf Wetterstedt? The picture he had of him was still unclear.

An idea came to him. He looked up a name in the telephone book. He dialled the number and got an answer almost at once. He explained who it was and asked whether he could come over. Then he hung up. He found Nyberg upstairs and told him he'd be back later that evening.

The wind and the rain lashed at him as he ran to his car. He drove into town, to a block of flats near Österport School. He rang the bell and the door was opened. When he reached the third floor Lars Magnusson was waiting for him in his stockinged feet. Beautiful piano music was playing.

"Long time no see," said Magnusson as they shook hands.

"You're right," said Wallander. "It must be more than five years."

Long ago Magnusson had been a journalist. After a number of years at the *Express* he had tired of city life and returned to his roots in

Ystad. He and Wallander met because their wives became friends. The two men discovered that they shared an interest in opera. It wasn't until many years later, after he and Mona had divorced, that Wallander found out Magnusson was an alcoholic. But when the truth finally did come out, it came out with a vengeance. By chance, Wallander had been at the station late one night when Magnusson was dragged in, so drunk that he couldn't stand up. He had been driving in that state, and lost control and gone straight through the plate-glass window of a bank. He'd ended up spending six months in jail.

When he returned to Ystad he didn't go back to his job. His wife had left their childless marriage. He continued drinking but managed not to step too far over the line. He gave up his career in journalism and made a living setting chess problems for a number of newspapers. The only reason he hadn't drunk himself to death was that every day he forced himself to hold off on that first drink until he had devised at least one chess problem. Now that he had a fax machine, he didn't even have to go to the post office.

Wallander walked into the simple flat. He could smell that Magnusson had been drinking. A bottle of vodka stood on the coffee table, but Wallander didn't see a glass.

Magnusson was a good many years older than Wallander. He had a mane of grey hair falling over his dirty collar. His face was red and swollen, but his eyes were curiously clear. No-one doubted Magnusson's intelligence. Rumour had it that he once had a collection of poems accepted by Bonniers, but had withdrawn it at the last minute and repaid the small advance.

"This is unexpected," said Magnusson. "Have a seat. What can I get you?"

"Nothing, thanks," said Wallander, moving a pile of newspapers and making himself comfortable on a sofa.

Magnusson casually took a swig from the bottle of vodka and sat down opposite Wallander. He had turned down the piano music.

"It's been a long time," said Wallander. "I'm trying to remember when it was."

"At the state off licence," Magnusson replied quickly. "Almost exactly five years ago. You were buying wine and I was buying everything else."

Wallander nodded. He remembered now.

"There's nothing wrong with your memory," he said.

"I haven't ruined *that* yet," said Magnusson. "I'm saving it for last."

"Have you ever considered quitting?"

"Every day. But I doubt you came here to talk me into going on the wagon."

"You've probably read that Gustaf Wetterstedt was murdered, haven't you?"

"I saw it on the TV."

"I seem to remember that you told me something about him once. About the scandals that were hushed up."

"And that was the biggest scandal of them all," Magnusson interrupted him.

"I'm trying to get a fix on what sort of man he was," Wallander went on. "I hoped you might be able to help me."

"The question is whether you want to hear the unsubstantiated rumours or whether you want to know the truth," said Magnusson. "I'm not sure I can tell them apart."

"Rumours don't usually get started without reason," said Wallander.

Magnusson pushed away the vodka bottle as though it was too close to him.

"I started as a 15-year-old trainee at one of the Stockholm newspapers," he said. "That was in the spring of 1955. There was an old night editor there named Ture Svanberg. He was almost as big a drunk as I am now. But he was meticulous at his work. And he was a genius at writing headlines that sold papers. He wouldn't stand for anything sloppily written. Once he flew into such a rage over a story that he tore up the copy and ate the pieces, chewed the paper and swallowed it. Then he said: 'This isn't coming out as anything but shit.' It was Svanberg who taught me to be a journalist. He used to say that there were two kinds of reporters. 'The first kind digs in the ground for the truth. He stands down in the hole shovelling out dirt. But up on top there's another man, shovelling the dirt back in. There's always a duel going on between these two. The fourth estate's eternal test of strength for dominance. Some journalists want to expose and reveal things, others run errands for those in power and help conceal what's really happening.'

"And that's how it really was. I learned fast, even though I was only 15. Men in power always ally themselves with symbolic cleaning companies and undertakers. There are plenty of journalists who won't hesitate to sell their souls to run errands for those men. To shovel the dirt back into the hole. Paste over the scandals. Pile on the semblance of truth, maintain the illusion of the squeaky-clean society."

With a grimace he reached for the bottle again and took a swig. Wallander saw that he'd put on weight around the middle.

"Wetterstedt," Magnusson said. "So what was it that actually happened?" He fished a crumpled packet of cigarettes out of his shirt pocket. He lit one and blew out a cloud of smoke.

"Whores and art," he said. "For years it was common knowledge that the good Gustaf had a girl delivered to the block of flats in Vasastan every week, where he kept a small hideaway his wife didn't know about. He had a right-hand man who took care of the whole thing. The rumour was that this man was hooked on morphine, supplied by Wetterstedt. He had a lot of doctor friends. The fact that he went to bed with whores wasn't something the papers bothered with. He was neither the first nor the last Swedish minister to do that. Sometimes I wonder whether we're talking about the rule or the exception. But one day it went too far. One of the hookers got her courage up and reported him to the police for assault."

"When was that?" Wallander interrupted.

"Mid-60s. Her complaint said he'd beaten her with a leather belt and cut the soles of her feet with a razor. It was probably the stuff with the razor and her feet that made the difference. Perversion was newsworthy. The only problem was that the police had lodged a complaint against the highest defender of Swedish law and order next to the king. So the whole thing was hushed up, and the police report disappeared."

"Disappeared?"

"It literally went up in smoke."

"But the girl who reported him? What happened to her?"

"Overnight she became the proprietor of a lucrative boutique in Västerås."

Wallander shook his head.

"How do you know all this?"

"I knew a journalist called Sten Lundberg. He dug around in the whole mess. But when the rumours started that he was about to snoop his way to the truth, he was frozen out, blacklisted."

"And he accepted it?"

"He had no choice. Unfortunately *he* had a weakness that couldn't be covered up. He gambled. Had huge debts. There was a rumour that those gambling debts suddenly went poof. The same way the hooker's assault report did. So everything was back to square one. And Wetterstedt went on sending his morphine addict out after girls."

"You said there was one more thing," Wallander said.

"There was a story that he was mixed up in some of those art thefts carried out during his term as minister of justice. Paintings that were never recovered, and which now hang on the walls of collectors who will never show them to the public. The police arrested a fence once, a middleman. Unintentionally, I'm afraid. The fence swore that Wetterstedt was involved. But it couldn't be proved. It was buried. There were more people filling up the hole than there were people standing down in it and tossing the dirt out."

"Not a pretty picture," said Wallander.

"Remember what I asked? Do you want the truth or the rumours? Because the rumour about Wetterstedt was that he was a talented politician, a loyal party member, an amiable human being. Educated and competent. That's how his obituaries will read. As long as none of the girls he whipped talk."

"Why did he leave office?" asked Wallander.

"I don't think he got along so well with some of the younger ministers. Especially the women. There was a big shift between the generations in those days. I think he realised that his time was over. Mine was too. I quit being a journalist. After he came to Ystad I never wasted a thought on him. Until now."

"Can you think of anyone who would want to kill him, so many years later?"

Magnusson shrugged.

"That's impossible to answer."

Wallander had just one question left.

"Have you ever heard of a murder in this country where the victim was scalped?"

Magnusson's eyes narrowed. He looked at Wallander with a sudden, alert interest.

"Was he scalped? They didn't say that on TV. They would have, if they knew about it."

"Just between the two of us," Wallander said, looking at Magnusson, who nodded.

"We didn't want to release it just yet," he went on. "We can always say we can't reveal it 'for investigative reasons'. The excuse the police have for presenting half-truths. But this time it's actually true."

"I believe you," said Magnusson. "Or I don't believe you. It doesn't really matter, since I'm no longer a journalist. But I can't recall a murderer who scalped people. That would have made a great headline. Ture Svanberg would have loved it. Can you avoid leaks?"

"I don't know," Wallander answered frankly. "I've had a number of bad experiences over the years."

"I won't sell the story," said Magnusson.

Then he accompanied Wallander to the door.

"How the hell can you stand being a policeman?" he asked.

"I don't know," said Wallander. "I'll let you know when I work it out."

Wallander drove back to Wetterstedt's house. The wind was gusting up to gale force. Some of Nyberg's men were taking fingerprints upstairs. Looking out of the balcony window, he saw Nyberg perched on a wobbly ladder leaning against the light pole by the garden gate. He was clinging to the pole, so the wind wouldn't blow the ladder over. Wallander went to help him, but saw Nyberg begin to climb down. They met in the hall.

"That could have waited," said Wallander. "You might have been blown off the ladder."

"If I fell off I might have hurt myself," Nyberg said sullenly. "And of course checking the light could have waited, but it might have been forgotten. Since you were the one who wondered about it, and I have a certain respect for your ability to do your job, I decided to look at the light. I can assure you that it was only because you were the one who asked me."

Wallander was surprised, but he tried not to show it.

"What did you find?" he asked instead.

"The bulb wasn't burnt out," said Nyberg. "It was unscrewed."

"Hold on a minute," Wallander said, and went into the living-room to call Sara Björklund. She answered.

"Excuse me for disturbing you so late at night," he began. "But I have an urgent question. Who changed the light bulbs in Wetterstedt's house?"

"He did that himself."

"Outside also?"

"I think so. He did all of his own gardening, and I think I was the only other person who set foot inside his house."

Except for whoever was in the black car, thought Wallander.

"There's a light by the garden gate," he said. "Was it usually turned on?"

"In the winter, when it was dark, he always kept it lit."

"That's all I wanted to know," said Wallander. "Thanks for your help."

"Can you manage to climb up the ladder one more time?" he asked Nyberg when he came back to the hall. "I'd like you to screw in a new bulb."

"The spare bulbs are in the room next to the garage," said Nyberg and started to pull on his boots.

They went back out into the storm. Wallander held the ladder while Nyberg climbed up and screwed in the bulb. It went on at once. Nyberg climbed back down the ladder. They walked out onto the beach.

"There's a big difference," said Wallander. "Now it's light all the way down to the water."

"Tell me what you're thinking," said Nyberg.

"I think the place where he was murdered is somewhere within this circle of light," said Wallander. "If we're lucky we can get fingerprints from the light fixture."

"So you think the murderer planned the whole thing? Unscrewed the bulb because it was too bright?"

"Yes," said Wallander, "that's pretty much what I'm thinking."

Nyberg went back into the garden with the ladder. Wallander stayed behind, the rain pelting against his face.

The cordons were still there. A police car was parked just above the dunes. Except for a man on a moped there were no onlookers left. Wallander turned around and went back inside the house.

CHAPTER 10

He stepped into the basement just after 7 a.m. The floor was cool under his bare feet. He stood still and listened. Then he closed the door behind him and locked it. He squatted to inspect the thin layer of flour he had dusted over the floor the last time he was here. No-one had intruded into his world. There were no footprints. Then he checked the traps. He had been lucky. He had a catch in all four cages. One of the cages held the biggest rat he had ever seen.

Once, towards the end of his life, Geronimo told the story of the Pawnee warrior he had vanquished in his youth. His name was Bear with Six Claws, since he had six fingers on his left hand. That had been his first enemy. Geronimo came close to dying that time, even though he was very young. He cut off his enemy's sixth finger and left it in the sun to dry. Then he carried it in a little leather pouch on his belt for many years.

He decided to try out one of his axes on the big rat. On the small ones he would test the effect of the can of mace.

But that would be much later. First he had to undergo the big transformation. He sat down before the mirrors, adjusted the light so that there was no glare, and then gazed at his face. He had made a small cut on his left cheek. The wound had already healed. It was the first step in his final transformation.

The blow had been perfect. It had been like chopping down a tree when he cut into the spine of the first monster. He had heard the jubilation of the spirit world from within him. He had flopped the monster over on his back and cut off his scalp, without hesitation. Now it lay where it belonged, buried in the earth, with one tuft of hair sticking up from the ground.

Soon another scalp would join it. He looked at his face and considered whether he ought to make the second cut next to the first one.

Or should the knife consecrate the other cheek? Really it made no difference. When he was finished, his face would be covered with cuts.

Carefully he began to prepare himself. From his backpack he pulled out his weapons, paints and brushes. Last of all he took out the red book in which the Revelations and the Mission were written. He set it down on the table between himself and the mirrors.

Last night he had buried the first scalp. There was a guard by the hospital grounds. But he knew where the fence had come down. The secure wing, where there were bars on the windows and doors, stood apart on the outskirts of the large grounds. When he had visited his sister he had established which window was hers. No light shone from it. A faint gleam from the hall light was all that escaped from the menacing building. He had buried the scalp and whispered to his sister that he had taken the first step. He would destroy the monsters, one by one. Then she would come out into the world again.

He pulled off his shirt. It was summer, but he shivered in the cool of the basement. He opened the red book and turned past what was written about the man named Wetterstedt, who had ceased to exist. On page 7 the second scalp was described. He read what his sister had written and decided that this time he would use the smallest axe.

He closed the book and looked at his face in the mirror. It was the same shape as his mother's, but he had his father's eyes. They were set deep, like two retracted cannon muzzles. Because of these eyes, he might have regretted that his father would have to be sacrificed too. But it was only a small doubt, one that he could easily conquer. Those eyes were his first childhood memory. They had stared at him, they had threatened him, and ever since then he could see his father only as a pair of enormous eyes with arms and legs and a bellowing voice.

He wiped his face with a towel. Then he dipped one of the wide brushes into the black paint and drew the first line across his brow, precisely where the knife had cut open the skin on Wetterstedt's forehead.

He had spent many hours outside the police cordon. It was exciting to see all these policemen expending their energy trying to find out what happened and who had killed the man lying under the boat. On several occasions he had felt a compulsion to call out that he was the one.

It was a weakness that he had still not completely mastered. What he was doing, the mission he had undertaken from his sister's book of revelations, was for her sake alone, not his. He must conquer this urge.

He drew the second line across his face. The transformation had barely begun, but he could feel his external identity starting to leave him.

He didn't know why he had been named Stefan. On one occasion, when his mother had been more or less sober, he had asked her. Why Stefan? Why that name and not something else? Her reply had been very vague. It's a fine name, she said. He remembered that. A fine name. A name that was popular. He would be spared from having a name that was different. He still remembered how upset he had been. He left her lying there on the sofa in their living-room, stormed from the house and rode his bike down to the sea. Walking along the beach, he chose himself a different name. He chose Hoover. After the head of the F.B.I. He had read a book about him. It was rumoured that Hoover had a drop of American Indian blood in his veins. He wondered whether there was some in his own blood. His grandfather had told him that many of their relatives had emigrated to America a long time ago. Maybe one of them had taken up with an American Indian. Even if the blood didn't run through his own veins, it might be in the family.

It wasn't until his sister had been locked up in the hospital that he decided to merge Geronimo and Hoover. He had remembered how his grandfather had shown him how to melt pewter and pour it into plaster moulds to make miniature soldiers. He had found the moulds and the pewter ladle when his grandfather died. He had changed the mould so that the molten pewter would make a figure that was both a policeman and an Indian. Late one evening when everyone was asleep and his father was in jail, so he wouldn't come storming into the flat, he locked himself in the kitchen and carried out the great ceremony. By melting Hoover and Geronimo together he created his own new identity. He was a feared policeman with the courage of an

American Indian warrior. He would be indestructible. Nothing would prevent him from seeking vengeance.

He continued drawing the curved black lines above his eyes. They made his eyes appear to sink even deeper into their sockets, where they lurked like beasts of prey. Two predators, watching. Methodically he rehearsed what awaited him. It was Midsummer Eve. It was rainy and windy, which would make the task more difficult, but it wouldn't stop him. He would have to dress warmly before the trip to Bjäresjö. He didn't know whether the party he was going to visit had been moved indoors because of the rain, but he would trust in his ability to wait. This was a virtue Hoover had always preached to his recruits. Just like Geronimo. There would always be a moment when the enemy's alertness flagged. That's when he had to strike, even if the party was moved indoors. Sooner or later the man he sought would have to leave the house. Then it would be time.

He had been there the day before. He had left his moped among some trees and made his way to the top of a hill where he could watch undisturbed. Arne Carlman's house was isolated, just like Wetterstedt's. There were no close neighbours. An avenue of trimmed willows led up to the old whitewashed Scanian farmhouse.

Preparations for the Midsummer festivities had already begun. He'd seen people unloading folding tables and stackable chairs from a van. In one corner of the garden they were putting up a serving tent.

Carlman was there too. Through his binoculars he could see the man he would visit the next day, directing the work. He was wearing a tracksuit and a beret.

He thought of his sister with this man, and nausea overwhelmed him. He hadn't needed to see any more after that, he'd known what his plan would be.

When he had finished painting his forehead and the shadows around his eyes, he drew two heavy white lines down each side of his nose. He could already feel Geronimo's heart pounding in his chest. He bent down and started the player on the basement floor. The drums were very loud. The spirits started talking inside him.

He didn't finish until late afternoon. He selected the weapons he would take with him. Then he released the four rats into a large box. In vain they tried to scramble up the sides. He aimed the axe he wanted to try at the biggest. It was so fast that the rat didn't even have time to squeak. The blow split it in two. The other rats scratched at the sides. He went to his leather jacket, and reached into the inside pocket for the spray can. But it was gone. He searched the other pockets. It wasn't there. For a moment he stood frozen. Had someone been here after all? That was impossible.

To collect his thoughts, he sat down in front of the mirrors again. The spray can must have fallen out of his jacket pocket. Slowly and methodically he went over the days since he had visited Gustaf Wetterstedt. He realised he must have dropped the can when he was watching the police from outside the cordon. He had taken off his jacket at one point so he could put on a sweater. That's how it had happened. He decided that it presented no danger. Anyone could have dropped a spray can. Even if his fingerprints were on it, the police didn't have them on file. Not even F.B.I. chief Hoover would have been able to trace that spray can.

He got up from his place in front of the mirrors and returned to the rats in the box. When they caught sight of him they began rushing back and forth. With three blows of his axe he killed them all. Then he tipped the bleeding bodies into a plastic bag, tied it carefully, and put it inside another. He wiped off the edge of the axe and then felt it with his fingertips.

By just after 6 p.m. he was ready. He had stuffed the weapons and the bag of rats into his backpack. He put on socks and running shoes with the pattern on the soles filed off. He turned off the light and left the basement. Before he went out on the street he pulled his helmet over his head.

Just past the turn off to Sturup he drove into a car park and stuffed the plastic bag containing the rats into a rubbish bin. Then he continued on towards Bjäresjö. The wind had died down. There had been a sudden change in the weather. The evening would be warm.

Midsummer Eve was one of art dealer Arne Carlman's biggest occasions of the year. For more than 15 years he had invited his friends to a party at the Scanian farm where he lived during the summer. In a certain circle of artists and gallery owners it was important to be invited to Carlman's party. He had a strong influence on everyone who bought and sold art in Sweden. He could create fame and fortune for any artist he decided to promote, and he could topple any who didn't follow his advice or do as he required. More than 30 years earlier he had travelled all over the country in an old car, peddling art. Those were lean years but they had taught him what kind of pictures he could sell to whom. He had learned the business, and divested himself of the notion that art was something above the control of market forces. He had saved enough to open a combined frame shop and gallery on Österlånggatan in Stockholm. With a ruthless mixture of flattery, alcohol and crisp banknotes he bought paintings from young artists and then built up their reputations. He bribed, threatened and lied his way to the top. Within ten years he owned 30 galleries all over Sweden, and had started selling art by mail order. By the mid-70s he was a wealthy man. He bought the farm in Skåne and began holding his summer parties a few years later. They had become famous for their extravagance. Each guest could expect a present that cost no less than 5,000 kronor. This year he had commissioned a limited edition fountain pen from an Italian designer.

When Arne Carlman woke up beside his wife early on Midsummer Eve morning, he went to the window and gazed over a landscape weighed down by rain and wind. He quickly quelled a wave of irritation and disappointment. He had learned to accept that he had no power over the weather. Five years before he had had a special collection of rainwear designed for his guests. Those who wanted to be in the garden could be, and those who preferred to be inside could be in the old barn, converted into a huge open space.

When the guests began arriving around 8 p.m, what had promised to be a wet, nasty Midsummer Eve had become a beautiful summer evening. Carlman appeared in a dinner jacket, one of his sons following him holding an umbrella. As always, he had invited 100 people, of whom half were first-time guests. Just after 10 p.m. he clinked a knife on his glass, and gave his traditional summer speech. He did so in the knowledge that many of his guests hated or despised him. But at the age of 66, he had stopped worrying about what people thought. His empire could speak for itself. Two of his sons were prepared to take over the business when he could no longer run it, although he wasn't ready to retire. This is what he said in his speech, which was devoted entirely to himself. They couldn't count him out yet. They could look forward to many more Midsummer parties – at which the weather, he hoped, would be better than this year. His words were met with half-hearted applause. Then an orchestra started playing in the barn. Most of the guests made their way inside. Carlman led off the dancing with his wife.

"What did you think of my little speech?" he asked her.

"You've never been more spiteful," she replied.

"Let them hate me," he said. "What do I care? What do *we* care? I still have a lot to do."

Just before midnight, Carlman strolled to an arbour at the edge of the huge garden with a young woman artist from Göteborg. One of his talent scouts had advised him to invite her to his summer party. He had seen a number of transparencies of her paintings and recognised at once that she had something. It was a new type of idyllic painting. Cold suburbs, stone deserts, lonely people, surrounded by Elysian fields of flowers. He already knew that he was going to promote the woman as the leading exponent of a new school of painting, which could be called New Illusionism. She was very young, he thought, as they walked towards the arbour. But she was neither beautiful nor mysterious. Carlman had learned that just as important as the painting was the image presented by the artist. He wondered what he was going to do with this skinny, pale young woman.

It was a magnificent evening. The dance was still in full swing. But many of the guests had started gathering around the TV sets. Sweden's football match against Russia would be starting shortly. He wanted to finish his conversation with her so that he could watch it too.

Carlman had a contract in his pocket. It would provide her with a large cash sum in exchange for his acquiring the exclusive right to sell her work for three years. On the surface it seemed a very advantageous contract. But the fine print, difficult to read in the pale light of the summer night, granted him certain rights to future paintings. He wiped off two chairs with a handkerchief and invited her to sit. It took him less than half an hour to persuade her to agree to the arrangement. Then he handed her one of the designer pens and she signed the contract.

She left the arbour and went back to the barn. Later she would claim with absolute certainty that it had been three minutes to midnight. For some reason she had looked at the time as she walked along the gravel path up towards the house. With equal conviction she told the police that Arne Carlman had given no impression that he was uneasy. Nor that he was waiting for anyone. He had said that he was going to sit there for a few minutes and enjoy the fresh air after the rain. She hadn't looked back. But she was certain that there was no-one else in that part of the garden.

Hoover had been hiding on top of the hill all evening. The damp ground made him cold. Now and then he got up to shake some life into his limbs. Just after 11 p.m. he had seen through his binoculars that the moment was approaching. There were fewer and fewer people in the garden. He took out his weapons and stuck them in his belt. He also took off his shoes and socks and put them in his backpack. Then, bent almost double, he slipped down the hill and ran along a tractor path in the cover of a rape field. When he reached the edge of the property, he sank onto the wet ground. Through the hedge he had a view of the garden.

It was not long before his wait was over. Carlman was walking straight towards him, accompanied by a young woman. They sat down in the arbour. Hoover couldn't hear what they were talking about. After about half an hour the woman got up, but Carlman remained seated. The garden was deserted. The music in the barn had stopped; instead he could hear the blare of TV sets. Hoover got up, drew his axe, and squeezed through the hedge right behind the arbour. Swiftly, he checked again that no-one was in the garden. Then all doubt vanished, and his sister's revelations exhorted him to carry out his task. He rushed into the arbour and buried the axe in Arne Carlman's face. The powerful blow split the skull all the way to the upper jaw. He was still sitting on the bench, with the two halves of his head pointing in opposite directions. Hoover pulled out his knife and cut off the hair on the part of Carlman's head that was closest. Then he left as quickly as he had come. He climbed up the hill, picked up his backpack, and ran down the other side to the little gravel road where he had left his moped leaning against one of the road workers' huts.

Two hours later he buried the scalp next to the other one, beneath his sister's window.

There wasn't a cloud in the sky, and the wind had died completely. Midsummer Day would be both fair and warm. Summer had arrived. More quickly than anyone could have imagined.

Skåne

25–28 June 1994

CHAPTER 11

The emergency call came in to the Ystad station just after 2 a.m.

Thomas Brolin had just scored for Sweden in the match against Russia. He rammed in a penalty kick. A cheer rose in the Swedish summer night. It had been an unusually calm Midsummer Eve. The officer who received the call did so standing, since he had leapt to his feet shouting. But he realised at once that the call was serious. The woman shrieking in his ear seemed sober. Her hysteria was real. The officer sent for Hansson, who had felt his temporary appointment as police chief to be such a responsibility that he hadn't risked leaving the station on Midsummer Eve. He'd been busy weighing how his limited resources could best be employed on each case. At 11 p.m. fights had broken out at two different parties. One was caused by jealousy. In the other the Swedish goalkeeper, Ravelli, was the cause of the tumult. In a report later drafted by Svedberg, he stated that it was Ravelli's action in the game against Cameroon, when Cameroon scored their second goal, that triggered a violent argument that left three people in hospital.

Hansson went out to the operations centre and spoke with the officer who had taken the call.

"Did she really say that a man had his head split in half?"

The officer nodded. Hansson pondered this.

"We'll have to ask Svedberg to drive out there," he said.

"But isn't he busy with that domestic violence case in Svarte?"

"Right, I forgot," said Hansson. "Call Wallander."

For the first time in over a week Wallander had managed to get to sleep before midnight. In a moment of weakness he considered joining the rest of the country watching the match against Russia. But he fell asleep while he was waiting for the players to take the field. When the telephone rang, he didn't know where he was for a moment. He fumbled on the table next to the bed.

"Did I wake you up?" asked Hansson.

"Yes," replied Wallander. "What is it?"

Wallander was surprised at himself. He usually claimed that he was awake when someone called, no matter what time it was.

Hansson told him about the call. Later Wallander would brood over why he hadn't immediately made the connection between what had happened in Bjäresjö and Wetterstedt's murder. Was it because he didn't want to believe that they had a serial killer on their hands? Or was he simply incapable of imagining that a murder like Wetterstedt's could be anything but an isolated event? The only thing he did now was to ask Hansson to dispatch a squad car to the scene ahead of him.

Just before 3 a.m. he pulled up outside the farm in Bjäresjö. On the car radio he heard Martin Dahlin score his second goal against Russia. He realised that Sweden was going to win and that he had lost another 100 kronor.

He saw Norén running over to him, and knew at once that it was serious. But it wasn't until he went into the garden and passed a number of people who were either hysterical or dumbstruck that he grasped the full extent of the horror. The man who had been sitting on the bench in the arbour had actually had his head split in half. On the left half of his head, someone had also sliced off a large piece of skin and hair.

Wallander stood there completely motionless for more than a minute. Norén said something, but it didn't register. He stared at the dead man and knew without doubt that it was the same killer who had axed Wetterstedt to death. Then for a brief moment he felt an indescribable sorrow.

Later, talking to Baiba, he tried to explain the unexpected and very un-policeman-like feeling that had struck him. It was as though a dam inside him had burst, and he knew that there were no longer invisible lines dividing Sweden. The violence of the large cities had reached his own police district once and for all. The world had shrunk and expanded at the same time.

Then sorrow gave way to horror. He turned to Norén, who was very pale.

"It looks like the same offender," said Norén.

Wallander nodded.

"Who's the victim?" he asked.

"His name is Arne Carlman. He's the one who owns this farm. There was a Midsummer party going on."

"No-one must leave yet. Find out if anyone saw anything."

Wallander took out his phone, punched in the number of the station, and asked for Hansson.

"It looks bad," he said when Hansson came on.

"How bad?"

"I'm having a hard time thinking of anything worse. There's no doubt it's the same person who killed Wetterstedt. This one was scalped too."

Wallander could hear Hansson's breathing.

"You'll have to mobilise everything we've got," Wallander went on "And I want Åkeson to come out here."

Wallander hung up before Hansson could ask questions. What will I do now? he thought. Who am I looking for? A psychopath? An offender who acts in a precise and calculated way?

Deep inside he knew the answer. There must be a connection between Gustaf Wetterstedt and Arne Carlman. That was the first thing he had to discover.

After 20 minutes the emergency vehicles started arriving. When Wallander caught sight of Nyberg, he ushered him straight to the arbour.

"Not a pretty sight," was Nyberg's first comment.

"This has got to be the same man," said Wallander. "He has struck again."

"It doesn't look as though we'll have trouble identifying the scene of the crime this time," said Nyberg, pointing at the blood sprayed over the hedge and the table. He summoned his crew and set to work.

Norén had assembled all the guests in the barn. The garden was strangely deserted. He came over to Wallander and pointed up towards the farmhouse.

"He's got a wife and three children in there. They're in shock."

"Maybe we ought to call a doctor."

"She called one herself."

"I'll talk to them," said Wallander. "When Martinsson and Ann-Britt and the others get here, tell them to talk to anyone who might have seen something. The rest can go home. But write down every name. And don't forget to ask for identification. Were there any witnesses?"

"Nobody has come forward."

"Have you got a time frame?"

Norén took a notebook out of his pocket.

"At 11.30 Carlman was seen alive. At 2 a.m. he was found dead. So the murder took place sometime in between."

"It must be possible to shorten the time span," said Wallander. "Try and find out who was the last one to see him alive. And of course who found him."

Wallander went inside. The old Scanian farmhouse had been lovingly restored. Wallander stepped into a large room that served as living-room, kitchen, and dining area. Oil paintings covered the walls. In one corner of the room, the dead man's family sat on a sofa upholstered in black leather. A woman in her 50s stood up and came over to him.

"Mrs Carlman?"

"Yes."

She had been crying. Wallander looked for signs that she might break down. But she seemed surprisingly calm.

"I'm sorry," said Wallander.

"It's just terrible."

Wallander noted something a little rehearsed in her answer.

"Do you have any idea who might have done such a thing?"

"No."

The answer came too quickly. She had been prepared for that

question. That means there are plenty of people who might have considered killing him, he told himself.

"May I ask what was your husband's job?"

"He was an art dealer."

Wallander stiffened. She misconstrued his intense gaze and repeated her answer.

"I heard you," said Wallander. "Excuse me for a moment."

Wallander went back outside. He thought about what the woman inside had said, connecting it with what Lars Magnusson had told him about the rumours about Wetterstedt. Stories of stolen art. And now an art dealer was dead, murdered by the hand that took Wetterstedt's life. He was about to go back inside when Ann-Britt Höglund came around the corner of the house. She was paler than usual and very tense. Wallander remembered his early years as a detective, when he took every violent crime to heart. From the start, Rydberg had taught him that a policeman could never permit himself to identify with a victim of violence. That lesson had taken Wallander a long time to learn.

"Another one?" she asked.

"Same offender," said Wallander. "Or offenders."

"This one scalped too?"

"Yes."

He saw her flinch involuntarily.

"I think I've found something that ties these two men together," Wallander went on, and explained. In the meantime Svedberg and Martinsson arrived. Wallander quickly repeated what he had told Höglund.

"You'll have to interview the guests," said Wallander. "If I understood Norén correctly, there are at least a hundred. And they all have to show some identification before they leave."

Wallander went back into the house. He pulled up a chair and sat down near the sofa where the family was gathered. Besides Carlman's widow there were two boys in their 20s and a girl a couple of years older. All of them seemed oddly calm.

"I promise that I'll only ask questions that we absolutely must have answers to tonight," he said. "The rest can wait."

Silence. None of them said a word.

"Do you know who the murderer is?" Wallander asked. "Was it one of the guests?"

"Who else could it be?" replied one of the sons. He had short-cropped blond hair. Wallander had an uneasy feeling that he could see a resemblance to the mutilated face he had just examined out in the arbour.

"Is there anyone in particular that comes to mind?" Wallander continued.

The boy shook his head.

"It doesn't seem very likely that someone would have chosen to come here when a big party was going on," said Mrs Carlman.

Someone cold-blooded enough wouldn't have hesitated, thought Wallander. Or someone crazy enough. Someone who doesn't care whether he gets caught or not.

"Your husband was an art dealer," Wallander went on. "Can you describe for me what that involves?"

"My husband has 30 galleries around the country," she said. "He also has galleries in the other Nordic countries. He sells paintings by mail order. He rents paintings to companies. He's responsible for a large number of art auctions each year. And much more."

"Did he have any enemies?"

"A successful man is always disliked by those who have the same ambitions but lack the talent."

"Did your husband ever say he felt threatened?"

"No."

Wallander looked at the children sitting on the sofa. They shook their heads almost simultaneously.

"When did you see him last?" he continued.

"I danced with him at around 10.30 p.m.," she said. "Then I saw him a few more times. It might have been around 11 p.m. when I saw him last."

None of the children had seen him any later than that. Wallander knew that all the other questions could wait. He put his notebook back in his pocket and stood up. He wanted to offer some words of sympathy, but couldn't think what to say, so he just nodded and left the house.

Sweden had won the football game 3–1. Ravelli had been brilliant; Cameroon was forgotten, and Martin Dahlin's headed goal was a work of genius. Wallander picked up fragments of conversations going on around him, and pieced them together. Höglund and two other police officers had guessed the right score. Wallander sensed that he had solidified his position as the biggest loser. He couldn't decide whether this annoyed or pleased him.

They worked hard and efficiently. Wallander set up his temporary headquarters in a storeroom attached to the barn. Just after 4 a.m. Höglund came in with a young woman who spoke a distinct Göteborg dialect.

"She was the last one to see him alive," said Höglund. "She was with Carlman in the arbour just before midnight."

Wallander asked her to sit down. She told him her name was Madelaine Rhedin and she was an artist.

"What were you doing in the arbour?" asked Wallander.

"Arne wanted me to sign a contract."

"What sort of contract?"

"To sell my paintings."

"And you signed it?"

"Yes."

"Then what happened?"

"Nothing."

"Nothing?"

"I got up and left. I looked at my watch. It was 11.57 p.m."

"Why did you look at your watch?"

"I usually do when something important happens."

"The contract was important?"

"I was supposed to get 200,000 kronor on Monday. For a poor artist that's a big deal."

"Was there anyone nearby when you were sitting in the arbour?"

"Not that I saw."

"And when you left?"

"The garden was deserted."

"What did Carlman do when you left?"

"He stayed there."

"How do you know? Did you turn around?"

"He told me he was going to enjoy the fresh air. I didn't hear him get up."

"Did he seem uneasy?"

"No, he was cheerful."

"Think it over," Wallander said. "Maybe tomorrow you'll remember something else. Anything might be important. I want you to keep in touch."

When she left the room, Åkeson came in from the other direction. He was totally white. He sat down heavily on the chair Madelaine Rhedin had just vacated.

"That's the most disgusting thing I've ever seen," he said.

"You didn't have to look at him," said Wallander. "That's not why I wanted you to come."

"I don't know how you stand it," said Åkeson.

"Me neither," said Wallander.

Suddenly Åkeson was all business.

"Is it the same man who killed Wetterstedt?" he asked.

"Without a doubt."

"In other words, he may strike again?"

Wallander nodded. Åkeson grimaced.

"If there was ever a time to give priority to an investigation, this is it," he said. "I assume you need more personnel, don't you? I can pull some strings if necessary."

"Not yet," said Wallander. "A large number of policemen might aid the capture if we knew the killer's name and what he looked like. But we're not that far yet."

He told him what Magnusson had said, and that Arne Carlman was an art dealer.

"There's a connection," he concluded "And that will make the work easier."

Åkeson was doubtful.

"I hope you won't put all your eggs in one basket too early," he said.

"I'm not closing any doors," said Wallander. "But I have to explore every avenue I find."

Åkeson stayed for another hour before he drove back to Ystad. By 5 a.m. reporters had begun to show up at the farm. Furious, Wallander called the station and demanded that Hansson deal with them. He knew already that they wouldn't be able to conceal the fact that Carlman had been scalped. Hansson held an improvised and exceedingly chaotic press conference on the road outside the farm. Meanwhile Martinsson, Svedberg and Höglund herded out the guests, who all had to undergo a short interrogation. Wallander interviewed the sculptor who had discovered Carlman's body. He was extremely drunk.

"Why did you go out to the garden?" asked Wallander.

"To throw up."

"And did you?"

"Yes."

"Where did you throw up?"

"Behind one of the apple trees."

"Then what happened?"

"I thought I'd sit in the arbour to clear my head."

"And then?"

"I found him."

Wallander had been forced to stop there, because the sculptor started feeling sick again. He got up and went down to the arbour. The sky was clear, and the sun was already high. Midsummer Day would be warm and beautiful. When he reached the arbour he saw to his relief that Nyberg had covered Carlman's head with an opaque plastic sheet. Nyberg was on his knees next to the hedge that separated the garden from the adjacent rape field.

"How's it going?" asked Wallander encouragingly.

"There's a slight trace of blood on the hedge here," he said. "It couldn't have sprayed this far from the arbour."

"What does that mean?" asked Wallander.

"It's your job to answer that," replied Nyberg.

He pointed at the hedge.

"Right here it's quite sparse," he said. "It would have been possible for someone with a slight build to slip in and out of the garden this way. We'll have to see what we find on the other side. But I suggest you get a dog out here. A.S.A.P."

Wallander nodded.

The officer, named Eskilsson, arrived with his German shepherd shortly afterwards, as the last of the guests were leaving the garden. Wallander nodded to him. The dog was old and had been in service for a long time. His name was Shot.

The dog picked up a scent in the arbour at once and started towards the hedge. He wanted to push through the hedge exactly at the spot where Nyberg had found the blood. Eskilsson and Wallander found another spot where the hedge was thin and emerged onto the path that ran between Carlman's property and the field. The dog found the scent again, following it alongside the field towards a dirt road that led away from the farm. At Wallander's suggestion Eskilsson released the dog. Wallander felt a surge of excitement. The dog sniffed along the dirt road and came to the end of the field. Here he seemed to lose his bearings for a moment. Then he found the scent and kept following it towards a hill, where the trail seemed to end. Eskilsson searched in various directions, but the dog couldn't find the scent again.

Wallander looked around. A single tree bent over by the wind stood on top of the hill. An old bicycle frame lay half-buried in the ground. Wallander stood next to the tree and looked at the farm in the distance. The view of the garden was excellent. With binoculars it would have been possible to see who was outside the house at any given time.

He shuddered at the thought that someone else, someone unknown to him, had stood on the same spot earlier that night. He went back to the garden. Hansson and Svedberg were sitting on the steps of the farmhouse. Their faces were grey with fatigue.

"Where's Ann-Britt?" asked Wallander.

"She's getting rid of the last guest," said Svedberg.

"Martinsson? What's he doing?"

"He's on the phone."

Wallander sat down next to the others on the steps. The sun was already starting to feel hot.

"We've got to keep at it a little longer," he said. "When Ann-Britt is done, we'll go back to Ystad. We have to summarise what we know and decide what to do next."

No-one spoke. Höglund emerged from the barn. She crouched in front of the others.

"To think that so many people can see so little," she said wearily. "It's beyond me."

Eskilsson passed by with his dog. They heard Nyberg's grumpy voice near the arbour.

Martinsson came striding around the corner of the house. He had a telephone in his hand.

"This may be irrelevant right now," he said. "But we've received a message from Interpol. They have a positive identification of the girl who burned herself to death."

Wallander looked at him quizzically.

"The girl in Salomonsson's field?"

"Yes."

Wallander got up.

"Who is she?"

"I don't know. But there's a message waiting for you at the station."

They left Bjäresjö at once and headed back to Ystad.

CHAPTER 12

Dolores María Santana.

It was 5.45 a.m. on Midsummer morning. Martinsson read out the message from Interpol identifying the girl.

"Where's she from?" asked Höglund.

"The message is from the Dominican Republic," replied Martinsson. "It came via Madrid."

Puzzled, he looked around the room.

Höglund knew the answer.

"The Dominican Republic is one half of the island where Haiti is," she said. "In the West Indies. Isn't it called Hispaniola?"

"How the hell did she wind up here, in a rape field?" asked Wallander. "Who is she? What else did Interpol say?"

"I haven't had time to go through the message in detail," said Martinsson. "But it seems that her father has been looking for her, and she was reported missing in late November last year. The report was originally filed in a city called Santiago."

"Isn't that in Chile?" Wallander interrupted, surprised.

"This city is called Santiago de los Treinta Caballeros," said Martinsson. "Don't we have an atlas somewhere?"

"I'll get one," said Svedberg and left the room.

A few minutes later he returned, shaking his head.

"It must have been Björk's," he said. "I couldn't find it."

"Call our bookseller and wake him up," said Wallander. "I want an atlas here now."

"Are you aware that it's not even six in the morning and it's Midsummer Day?" Svedberg asked.

"It can't be helped. Call him. And send a car over to get it."

Wallander took a 100-krona note out of his wallet and gave it to Svedberg. A few minutes later Svedberg had roused the bookseller and the car was on its way.

They got coffee and went into the conference room. Hansson told them that they wouldn't be disturbed by anyone except Nyberg. Wallander took a look around the table. He met the gazes of the group of weary faces and wondered how he looked himself.

"We'll have to come back to the girl later," he began. "Right now we need to concentrate on what happened last night. And we might as well assume from the start that the same person who killed Gustaf Wetterstedt has struck again. The *modus operandi* is the same, even though Carlman was struck in the head and Wetterstedt had his spine severed. But both of them were scalped."

"I've never seen anything like it," said Svedberg. "The man who did this must be a complete animal."

Wallander held up his hand.

"Hold on a minute," he said. "There's something else we know too. Arne Carlman was an art dealer. And now I'm going to tell you something I learnt yesterday."

Wallander told them about his conversation with Lars Magnusson, and the rumours about Wetterstedt.

"So we have a conceivable link," he concluded. "Art: stolen art and fenced art. And somewhere, when we find the point that connects the two men, we'll find the offender."

No-one spoke. Everyone seemed to be considering what Wallander had said.

"We know where to concentrate our investigation," Wallander continued. "Finding the connection between Wetterstedt and Carlman. But we have another problem."

He looked around the table and could see that they understood.

"The killer could strike again," said Wallander. "We don't know why he killed either man. So we don't know whether he's after other people too. And we don't know who they might be. The only thing we can hope for is that the people threatened are aware of it."

"Another thing we don't know," said Martinsson. "Is the man insane? We don't know whether the motive is revenge or something else. We can't even be sure that he hasn't simply invented a motive. No-one can predict the workings of an insane mind."

"You're right, of course," replied Wallander. "We're dealing with many unknowns."

"Maybe this is just the beginning," Hansson said grimly. "Do you think we've got a serial killer on our hands?"

"It could be that bad," said Wallander firmly. "That's why I also think we should get some help from outside, from the criminal psychiatric division in Stockholm. Since this man's *modus operandi* is so remarkable, perhaps they can do a psychiatric profile of him."

"Has this offender killed before?" asked Svedberg. "Or is this the first time?"

"I don't know," said Wallander. "But he's cautious. I get a feeling that he plans what he does very carefully. When he strikes he does it without hesitation. There could be at least two reasons for this. First, he doesn't want to get caught. Second, he doesn't want to be interrupted before he finishes what he set out to do."

A shudder of revulsion passed through the group.

"This is where we have to start," he said. "Where is the connection between Wetterstedt and Carlman? Where do their paths cross? That's what we have to clarify. And we have to do it as quickly as possible."

"We should also realise that we won't be working in peace," said Hansson. "Reporters will be swarming around us. They know that Carlman was scalped. They have the story they've been longing for. For some strange reason Swedes love to read about crime when they're on holiday."

"That might not be such a bad thing," said Wallander. "At least it might send a warning to anyone who might be on the hit list."

"We ought to stress that we want clues from the public," said Höglund. "If we assume that you're right, that the murderer has a list he's working through, and that other people could realise that they're on it, then there may be a chance that some of them have an idea of who the killer is."

"You're right," said Wallander, turning to Hansson. "Call a press conference as soon as possible. We'll tell the press everything we know. That we're looking for a single killer. And that we need all the clues we can get."

Svedberg got up and opened a window. Martinsson yawned loudly.

"I know we're all tired," said Wallander. "But we have to carry on. Try to grab some sleep when you get a chance."

There was a knock on the door. An officer handed over an atlas. They set it on the table and found the Dominican Republic and the city of Santiago.

"We'll have to deal with this girl later," said Wallander. "We can't worry about it now."

"I'll send a reply," said Martinsson. "And ask for more information about her disappearance."

"How did she end up here?" muttered Wallander.

"The message from Interpol gives her age as 17," said Martinsson. "And her height as about 160 centimetres."

"Send them a description of the medallion," said Wallander. "If the father can identify it, the case is closed."

They left the conference room. Martinsson went home to talk to his family and cancel their holiday. Svedberg went down to the basement and took a shower. Hansson vanished down the hall to organise the press conference. Wallander followed Höglund into her office.

"Do you think we'll catch him?" she asked gravely.

"I don't know," said Wallander. "We have a lead that seems solid. This isn't an offender who simply kills anyone who gets in his way. He's after something. The scalps are his trophies."

She sat down in her chair as Wallander leaned against the door-frame.

"Why do people take trophies?" she asked.

"So they can brag about them."

"To themselves or to others?"

"Both."

Suddenly he realised why she had asked about the trophies.

"You think that he took these scalps so he could show them to somebody?"

"It can't be ruled out," she said.

"No," said Wallander, "it can't be ruled out. Nothing can."

He was just about to leave the room, but turned around.

"Will you call Stockholm?" he asked.

"It's Midsummer Day," she said. "I don't think they'll be on duty."

"You'll have to call someone at home," said Wallander. "Since we don't know whether he's going to strike again, we've got no time to lose."

Wallander went to his own office and sat down heavily in the visitor's chair. One of its legs creaked precariously. He leaned his head back and closed his eyes. Soon he was asleep.

He woke up with a start when someone entered the room. He glanced at his watch and saw that he'd been asleep for almost an hour. He still had a headache, but he wasn't quite so tired.

It was Nyberg. His eyes were bloodshot and his hair was standing on end.

"I didn't mean to wake you," he said apologetically.

"I was just dozing," said Wallander. "Have you got any news?"

Nyberg shook his head.

"All I can come up with is that the person who killed Carlman must have had his clothes drenched with blood. Subject to the forensic examination, I think we can assume that the blow came from directly overhead. That would mean that the person holding the axe was standing quite close."

"Are you sure it was an axe?"

"No," said Nyberg. "It could have been a heavy sabre. Or something else. But Carlman's head was split like a log."

Wallander felt sick.

"All right, then," he said. "So the killer got his clothes covered with blood. Someone might have seen him. And that clears all of the guests."

"We looked along the hedge," said Nyberg. "We searched all the way along the rape field and up towards that hill. The farmer who owns the fields around Carlman's farmhouse came and asked whether he could harvest the rape. I said that he could."

"A wise decision," said Wallander. "Isn't it late already?"

"I think so," said Nyberg. "It's Midsummer, after all."

"What about the hill?" asked Wallander.

"The grass was trampled down. At one spot it looked as if someone had been sitting there. We took samples of the grass and the soil."

"Anything else?"

"I don't think that old bicycle is of any interest to us," said Nyberg.

"The police dog lost the scent. Why?"

"You'll have to ask the officer about that," said Nyberg. "But it could be that another smell is so strong that the dog loses the scent he was originally following. There are plenty of reasons why trails suddenly stop."

"Go home and get some sleep," said Wallander. "You look exhausted."

"I am," said Nyberg.

After Nyberg left, Wallander went into the canteen and fixed himself a sandwich. A girl from the front desk came and gave him a pile of messages. He leafed through them and saw that reporters were calling. He knew he ought to go home and change his clothes, but instead he decided to do something entirely different. He knocked on the door of Hansson's office and told him he was driving out to Carlman's farm.

"I said we'd talk to the press at one o'clock," said Hansson.

"I'll be back by then," replied Wallander. "But unless something crucial happens, I don't want anyone to look for me. I need to think."

"And everybody needs to get some sleep," said Hansson. "I never imagined we'd wind up in such a nightmare."

"It always happens when you least expect it," said Wallander.

He drove out towards Bjäresjö in the beautiful summer morning, the windows rolled down. He ought to visit his father today. And call Linda too. Tomorrow Baiba would be back in Riga after her trip to Tallinn. In less than two weeks his holiday should be starting.

He parked the car by the cordon surrounding Carlman's farm. Small groups of people had gathered on the road. Wallander nodded to the officer guarding the cordon. Then he walked around the garden and followed the dirt road up towards the hill. He stood at the spot where the dog had lost the scent and looked around.

He had chosen the hill with care. From here he could see everything going on in the garden. He also must have been able to hear the music coming from inside the barn. Late in the evening the crowd in the garden thinned out. The guests had all said that everyone went indoors. At about 11.30 p.m. Carlman came walking towards the arbour with Madelaine Rhedin. Then what did you do?

Wallander didn't try to answer the question. Instead he turned around and looked down the other side of the hill. At the bottom there were tractor tracks. He followed the grassy slope until he reached the road. In one direction the tractor tracks led into a wood, and in the other down towards a road to the motorway to Malmö and Ystad. Wallander followed the tracks towards the woods. He walked under a clump of tall beech trees. The sunshine shimmered through the foliage. He could smell the earth. The tractor tracks stopped at a site where some newly felled trees were stacked.

Wallander searched in vain for a path. He tried to picture the roads. Anyone wanting to reach the motorway from the woods would have to pass two houses and several fields. The motorway was about two kilometres away. He retraced his steps and continued in the opposite direction. After almost a kilometre he came to the place where the road reached the E65.

By the side of the road was a road workers' hut, which was locked. He stood there and looked around. Then he went around to the back, finding a folded tarpaulin and a couple of iron pipes. Something was lying on the ground. He bent down and saw that it was a piece torn from a brown paper bag. It had some dark spots on it. Carefully he placed the piece of paper back on the ground. He looked underneath the hut, which was raised on four concrete blocks, and saw the rest of the paper bag. He reached in and pulled it out. There were no spots on the bag itself. He stood motionless, thinking. Then he put down the bag and called the station. He got hold of Martinsson, who had just got back.

"I need Eskilsson and his dog," said Wallander.

"Where are you? Did something happen?"

"I'm out by Carlman's farm," replied Wallander. "I just want to make sure of one thing."

After a short while Eskilsson arrived with his dog. Wallander explained what he wanted.

"Go over to the hill where the dog lost the scent," he said. "Then come back here."

Eskilsson left. After about ten minutes he returned. Wallander saw that the dog had stopped searching. But just as he reached the hut he reacted. Eskilsson gave Wallander a questioning look.

"Let him go," said Wallander.

The dog went straight for the piece of paper and halted. But when Eskilsson tried to get him to continue his search he quickly gave up. The scent had disappeared again.

"Is it blood?" asked Eskilsson, pointing at the piece of torn paper.

"I think so," said Wallander "At any rate, we've found something associated with the man who was up on the hill."

Eskilsson left with his dog. Wallander was just about to call Nyberg when he found that he had a plastic bag in one pocket. Carefully he deposited the piece of paper in it.

It couldn't have taken you more than a few minutes to get here from Carlman's farm. Presumably there was a bicycle here. You changed clothes since you had blood all over them. But you also wiped an object. Maybe a knife or an axe. Then you took off, either towards Malmö or Ystad. You probably crossed the motorway and chose one of the many small roads that criss-cross this area. I can follow you this far right now. But no further.

Wallander walked back to Carlman's farm. He asked the officer guarding the cordon whether the family was still there.

"I haven't seen anybody," he said. "But no-one has left the house."

Wallander nodded and walked to his car. There was a crowd of onlookers standing outside the cordon. Wallander glanced at them hastily and wondered what kind of people would give up a summer morning for the opportunity to smell blood.

He didn't realise until he drove off that he had seen something important. He slowed down and tried to remember what it was.

It had something to do with the people who were standing outside the cordon. What was it he had thought? Something about people sacrificing a summer morning?

He braked and made a U-turn in the middle of the road. When he got back to Carlman's house the onlookers were still there outside the cordon. Wallander looked around without finding any explanation for his reaction. He asked the officer whether anyone had just left.

"Maybe. People come and go all the time."

"Nobody special that you recall?"

The officer thought for a moment. "No."

Wallander went back to his car.

It was 9.10 a.m. on the morning of Midsummer Day.

CHAPTER 13

When Wallander got back to the station, the girl in reception told him he had a visitor waiting in his office. Wallander lost his temper and shouted at the girl, a summer intern, that no-one, no matter who it was, was to be allowed into his office. He stormed down the hall and threw open the door, coming face to face with his father, sitting in the visitor's chair.

"The way you tear open doors," said his father. "Somebody might think you were in a rage."

"All they told me was that someone was waiting in my office," said Wallander, astonished. "Not that it was you."

Wallander's father had never visited him at work. When he was a young officer, his father had even refused to let him into the house in uniform. But now here he was, wearing his best suit.

"I'm surprised," said Wallander. "Who drove you here?"

"My wife has both a driver's licence and a car," replied his father. "She went to see one of her relatives while I came here. Did you see the game last night?"

"No. I was working."

"It was great. I remember the way it was back in '58, when the World Cup was held in Sweden."

"But you were never interested in football, were you?"

"I've always liked football."

Wallander stared at him in surprise.

"I didn't know that."

"There's a lot of things you don't know. In 1958 Sweden had a defender named Sven Axbom. He was having big problems with one of Brazil's wingers, as I recall. Have you forgotten about that?"

"How old was I in 1958? I was a baby."

"You never were much for playing football. Maybe that's why you became a policeman."

"I bet that Russia would win," said Wallander.

"That's not hard to believe," said his father. "I bet 2–0 myself. Gertrud, on the other hand, was cautious. She thought it would be 1–1."

"Would you like some coffee?" asked Wallander.

"Yes, please."

In the hall Wallander ran into Hansson.

"Will you see to it that I'm not disturbed for the next half hour?" he said.

Hansson gave him a worried look.

"I absolutely must speak with you."

Hansson's formal manner irritated Wallander.

"In half an hour," he repeated. "Then we'll talk as much as you like."

He went back to his room and closed the door. His father took the plastic cup in both hands. Wallander sat down behind the desk.

"I never thought I'd see you in the station," he said.

"I wouldn't have come if I didn't have to," his father replied.

Wallander set his plastic cup on the desk. He should have known straight away that it must be something very important for his father to visit him here.

"What's happened?" Wallander asked.

"Nothing, except that I'm sick," replied his father simply.

Wallander felt a knot in his stomach.

"What do you mean?" he asked.

"I'm starting to lose my mind," his father went on calmly. "It's a disease with a name I can't remember. It's like getting senile. But it can make you angry at everything. And it can progress very fast."

Wallander knew what his father meant. Svedberg's mother was stricken with it. But he couldn't remember the name either.

"How do you know?" he asked. "Have you been to the doctor? Why didn't you say something before now?"

"I've even been to a specialist, in Lund," said his father. "Gertrud drove me there."

Wallander didn't know what to say.

"Actually, I came here to ask you something," his father said, looking at him.

The telephone rang. Wallander put the receiver on the desk.

"I've got time to wait," said his father.

"I told them I didn't want to be disturbed. So tell me what it is you want."

"I've always dreamed of going to Italy," his father said. "Before it's too late, I'd like to take a trip there. And I thought you might come with me. Gertrud doesn't have any interest in Italy. I don't think she wants to go. I'll pay for the whole thing. I've got the money."

Wallander looked at his father. He seemed small and shrunken sitting there in the chair. At that moment he suddenly looked his age. Almost 80.

"Of course, let's go to Italy," said Wallander. "When did you have in mind?"

"It's probably best that we don't wait too long. Apparently it's not too hot in September. But will you have time then?"

"I can take a week off any time. Or did you want longer than that?"

"A week would be fine."

His father leaned forward, put down the coffee cup, and stood up.

"Well, I won't bother you any longer," he said. "I'll wait for Gertrud outside."

"You can wait here," said Wallander.

His father waved his cane at him.

"You've got a lot to do," he said. "I'll wait outside."

Wallander accompanied him out to reception, where his father sat down on a sofa.

"I don't want you to wait with me," said his father. "Gertrud will be here soon."

Wallander nodded.

"We'll go to Italy together," he said. "And I'll come out and see you as soon as I can."

"The trip might be fun," said his father. "You never know."

Wallander left him and went over to the girl at the front desk.

"I'm sorry," he said. "It was quite right of you to let my father wait in my office."

He went back to his room, tears welling in his eyes. Even though his relationship with his father was strained, coloured by guilt, he felt a great sorrow. He stood by the window and looked out at the beautiful summer weather.

There was a time when we were so close that nothing could come between us, he thought. That was back when the silk knights, as we called them, used to come in their shiny American cars that we called land yachts and buy your paintings. Even then you talked about going to Italy. Another time, only a few years ago, you actually set off. I found you, dressed in pyjamas, with a suitcase in your hand in the middle of a field. And now we have to make that trip. I won't allow anything to stop us.

Wallander returned to his desk and called his sister in Stockholm. The answer machine informed him that she wouldn't be back until that evening.

It took him a long while to push aside his father's visit and collect his thoughts. He couldn't seem to accept that what his father had told him was true.

After talking to Hansson he made an extensive review of the investigation. Just before 11 a.m. he called Per Åkeson at home and gave him an update. Then he drove over to Mariagatan, took a shower, and changed his clothes. By midday he was back at the station. On the way to his room he stopped to see Ann-Britt Höglund. He told her about the paper he'd found behind the road workers' hut.

"Did you get hold of the psychologists in Stockholm?" he asked.

"I found a man named Roland Möller," she said. "He was at his summer house outside Vaxholm. But Hansson must make a formal request as acting chief."

"Did you talk to him?"

"He's done it."

"Good," said Wallander. "Now, something else. Do criminals return to the scene of the crime?"

"It's both a myth and a truth."

"In what sense is it a myth?"

"In that it's supposed to be something that always happens."

"And what's the reality?"

"That it actually does happen once in a while. The most classic example in our own legal history is probably from here in Skåne. The policeman who committed a series of murders in the early 1950s and was later on the team investigating what happened."

"That's not a good example," Wallander objected. "He was forced to return. I'm talking about the ones who return of their own accord. Why?"

"To taunt the police. To gloat. Or to find out how much the police actually know."

Wallander nodded thoughtfully.

"Why are you asking me this?"

"I had a peculiar experience," said Wallander. "I got a feeling that I saw someone out by Carlman's farm that I'd also seen outside the cordon near Wetterstedt's villa."

"Why couldn't it be the same person?" she asked, surprised.

"No reason. But there was something odd about this person. I just can't put my finger on what it was."

"I don't think I can help you."

"I know," said Wallander. "But in the future I want someone to photograph everyone standing outside the cordon, as discreetly as possible."

"In the future?"

Wallander knew that he had said too much. He tapped on the desk three times with his index finger.

"Naturally I hope nothing else will happen," he said. "But if it does."

Wallander accompanied Höglund back to her office. Then he continued out of the station. His father was gone. He drove to a restaurant on the edge of town and ate a hamburger. On a thermometer he saw that it was 26°C.

The press conference on Midsummer Day at the Ystad station was memorable because Wallander lost his temper and left the room before it was over. Afterwards he refused to apologise. Most of his colleagues thought he did the right thing. But the next day Wallander got a phone call from the director of the national police board, telling him that it was highly unsuitable for the police to make abusive comments to journalists. The relationship was strained enough as it was, and no additional aggravation could be tolerated.

Towards the end of the press conference, a journalist from an evening paper had stood up and started to question Wallander about the fact that the offender had taken the scalps of his victims. Wallander tried hard to avoid going into the gory details. He had replied that some of the hair of both Wetterstedt and Carlman had been torn off. But the reporter persisted, demanding details even when Wallander said that he couldn't give more information because of the forensic investigation. By then Wallander had developed a splitting headache. When the reporter accused him of hiding behind the requirements of the investigation, and said that it seemed like pure hypocrisy to withhold details when the police had called the press conference, Wallander had had enough. He banged his fist on the table and stood up.

"I will not let police policy be dictated by a journalist who doesn't know when to stop!" he shouted.

The flashbulbs went off in an explosion as he left the room. Afterwards, when he had calmed down, he asked Hansson to excuse his behaviour.

"I hardly think that it will change the way the headlines will read tomorrow morning," Hansson replied.

"I had to draw the line somewhere," said Wallander.

"I'm on your side, of course," said Hansson. "But I suspect there are others who won't be."

"They can suspend me," said Wallander. "They can fire me. But they can't ever make me apologise to that reporter."

"That apology will probably be discreetly given by the national police board to the editor-in-chief of the newspaper," said Hansson. "And we won't ever hear about it."

At 4 p.m. the investigative group shut themselves behind closed doors. Hansson had given strict instructions that they were not to be disturbed. At Wallander's request a squad car had gone to pick up Åkeson.

He knew that the decisions they made this afternoon would be crucial. They would be forced to go in so many directions at once. All options had to be explored. But at the same time Wallander knew that they had to concentrate on the main lead.

Wallander borrowed a couple of aspirin from Höglund and thought again about what Lars Magnusson had said, about the connection between Wetterstedt and Carlman. Was there something else he'd missed? He searched his weary mind without coming up with anything. They would concentrate their investigation on art sales and art thefts. They would have to dig deep into the rumours, some almost 30 years old, surrounding Wetterstedt, and they would have to move fast. Wallander knew they wouldn't get help along the way. Lars Magnusson had talked about the collaborators who cleaned up the mess left by those wielding power. Wallander would have to find a way of throwing light on these activities, but it would be very difficult.

The investigative meeting was one of the longest Wallander had ever attended. They sat for almost nine hours before Hansson blew the final whistle. By then everyone was exhausted. Höglund's bottle of aspirin was empty. Plastic coffee cups covered the table. Cartons of half-eaten pizza were piled in a corner of the room.

But this meeting was also one of the best Wallander had ever experienced. Concentration hadn't flagged, everyone contributed their opinions, and logical plans for the investigation had developed as a result.

Svedberg went over the telephone conversations he had had with

Wetterstedt's two children and his third ex-wife, but no-one could see a possible motive. Hansson had also managed to talk with the 80-year-old who had been party secretary during Wetterstedt's term as minister of justice. He had confirmed that Wetterstedt had often been the subject of rumours within the party. But no-one had been able to ignore his unflagging loyalty.

Martinsson reported on his interview with Carlman's widow. She was still very calm, leading Martinsson to think she must be on sedatives. Neither she nor any of the children was able to suggest a motive for the murder. Wallander outlined his talk with Sara Björklund, Wetterstedt's "charwoman". He also told them that the light bulb on the pole by the gate had been unscrewed. And finally, he told them about the bloody piece of paper he had found behind the road workers' hut.

None of his colleagues knew that his father was constantly on his mind. After the meeting he asked Höglund whether she had noticed how distracted he had been. She told him she hadn't noticed this, that he had seemed more dogged and focused than ever.

At 9 p.m. they took a break. Martinsson and Höglund called home, and Wallander finally got hold of his sister. She had wept when he told her about their father's visit and his illness. Wallander tried to console her as best he could, but he fought back tears himself. At last they agreed that she should talk to Gertrud the next day and that she would visit as soon as possible. She asked whether she really believed that their father would be able to manage a trip to Italy. Wallander answered honestly – he didn't know. But he reminded her that their father had dreamed of going to Italy since they were children.

During the break Wallander also tried to call Linda. After 15 rings he gave up. Annoyed, he decided he would have to give her the money to buy an answer machine.

When they returned to the meeting room Wallander started by discussing the connection between the two victims. That was what they had to seek, without ruling out other possibilities.

"Carlman's widow was sure that her husband had never had

anything to do with Wetterstedt," said Martinsson. "Her children said the same thing. They searched through all his address books without finding Wetterstedt's name."

"Carlman wasn't in Wetterstedt's address book either," said Höglund.

"So the link is invisible," said Wallander. "Or, more precisely, elusive. Somewhere we must be able to find it. If we do, we may also catch sight of the killer. Or at least a motive. We have to dig deep and fast."

"Before he strikes again," said Hansson. "There is no knowing whether that will happen."

"We also don't know who to warn," said Wallander. "The only thing we know about the killer or killers, is that they plan the murders."

"Do we know that?" Åkeson interjected. "It seems to me you're jumping to that conclusion prematurely."

"Well there's no indication that we're dealing with someone who kills on impulse, who has a spontaneous desire to rip the hair off his victims," replied Wallander, feeling his temper rise.

"It's the conclusion that I'm having trouble with," said Åkeson. "That's not the same thing as discrediting the evidence."

The mood in the room grew oppressive. No-one could miss the tension between the two men. Normally, Wallander wouldn't hesitate to argue with Åkeson in public. But this evening he chose to back down, mainly because he was exhausted and knew he would have to keep the meeting going for hours yet.

"I agree," was all he said. "We'll scrub that conclusion and settle for saying that the murders appear planned."

"A psychologist from Stockholm is coming down tomorrow," said Hansson. "I'm going to pick him up at Sturup Airport. Let's hope he can help us."

Wallander nodded. Then he threw out a question that he hadn't really prepared. But now seemed a suitable time.

"The murderer," he said. "For the sake of argument let's think of him for the time being as a man who acts alone. What do you see? What do you think?"

"Strong," said Nyberg. "The axe blows were delivered with tremendous force."

"I'm afraid he's collecting trophies," said Martinsson. "Only an insane person would do something like that."

"Or someone who intends to throw us off the track with the scalps," said Wallander.

"I have no idea," said Höglund. "But it must be someone who's profoundly disturbed."

In the end the character of the killer was left. Wallander summed up in one last run-through, in which they planned the investigative work to be done and divided up the tasks. At around midnight Åkeson left, saying that he would help out by arranging for reinforcements for the investigative team whenever they thought it necessary. Although they were all exhausted, Wallander went over the work one more time.

"None of us is going to get a lot of sleep for the next few days," he said in closing. "And I realise that this will throw many of your holiday plans into chaos. But we have to muster all our forces. We have no option."

"We'll need reinforcements," said Hansson.

"Let's decide about that on Monday," said Wallander. "Let's wait until then."

They decided to meet again the following afternoon. Before then Wallander and Hansson would present the case to the psychologist from Stockholm.

Then they broke up and went their separate ways. Wallander stood by his car and looked up at the pale night sky. He tried to think about his father. But something else kept intruding. Fear that the killer would strike again.

CHAPTER 14

Early on Sunday morning, 26 June, the doorbell rang at Wallander's flat on Mariagatan in central Ystad. He was wrenched out of a deep sleep and at first thought the telephone was ringing. When the doorbell rang again he got up quickly, found his dressing gown lying halfway under the bed, and went to the door. It was Linda with a friend Wallander hadn't met. He hardly recognised Linda either, since she had cropped her long blonde hair and dyed it red. But he was relieved and happy to see her.

He let them in and said hello to Linda's friend, who introduced herself as Kajsa. Wallander was full of questions. How did they come to be ringing his doorbell so early on a Sunday morning? Were there really train connections this early? Linda explained that they had arrived the night before, but they had stayed at the house of a girl she had gone to school with, whose parents were away. They would be staying there for the whole week. They came over so early because after reading the papers in the past few days, Linda knew it would be hard to get hold of her father.

Wallander made a breakfast of leftovers he dug out of his refrigerator. While they ate they told him they'd be spending the week rehearsing a play they had written. Then they were going to the island of Gotland to take part in a theatre seminar. Wallander listened, trying to disguise how disappointed he was that Linda had abandoned her dream to become a furniture upholsterer, settle down in Ystad, and open her own shop. He also yearned to talk to her about her grandfather. He knew how close she was to him.

"There's so much going on. I'd like to talk with you in peace and quiet, just you and me," he said, when Kajsa was out of the room.

"That's the best thing about you," she said. "You're always so glad to see me." She wrote down her phone number and promised to come over when he called.

"I saw the papers," she said. "Is it really as bad as they make out?"

"It's worse," Wallander said. "I've got so much to do that I don't know how I'm going to cope. It was pure luck that you caught me at home."

They sat and talked until Hansson called and said he was at Sturup Airport with the psychologist. They agreed to meet at the station at 9 a.m.

"I have to go now," he told Linda.

"We do, too," she said.

"Does this play you're putting on have a name?" Wallander wondered when they got out to the street.

"It's not a play," replied Linda. "It's a revue."

"I see," said Wallander, trying to remember what the difference was. "And does it have a name?"

"Not yet," said Kajsa.

"Can I see it?" Wallander asked tentatively.

"When it's ready," said Linda. "Not before."

Wallander asked whether he could drive them somewhere.

"I'm going to show her the town," said Linda.

"Where are you from?" he asked Kajsa.

"Sandviken, up north," she said. "I've never been to Skåne before."

"Then we're even," said Wallander. "I've never been to Sandviken."

He watched them disappear around the corner. The fine weather was holding. It would be even warmer today. He felt cheerful because of his daughter's unexpected visit, even though he couldn't adjust to the drastic way she had been experimenting with her looks the past few years. But when she'd stood in the doorway, he'd seen for the first time what many people had told him before. Linda looked like him. He had discovered his own face in hers.

He arrived at the station, feeling renewed vigour after Linda's unexpected visit. He strode down the hall, thinking that he clumped along like an overweight elephant, and threw off his jacket when he entered his room. He grabbed the telephone before he even sat down and asked the receptionist to get hold of Nyberg. Just as he'd fallen asleep the night before, an idea had come to him that he wanted to explore. It took five minutes before the girl at the front desk managed to locate Nyberg.

"It's Wallander," he said. "Do you remember telling me about a can of some sort of spray that you found outside the cordon on the beach?"

"Of course I remember," snapped Nyberg.

Wallander ignored the fact that Nyberg was obviously in a bad mood.

"I thought we ought to check it for fingerprints," he said. "And compare them to whatever you can find on that piece of paper I found near Carlman's house."

"Will do," said Nyberg. "But we would have done it anyway, even if you hadn't asked us to."

"I know," said Wallander. "But you know how it is."

"No, I don't," said Nyberg. "You'll have the results as soon as I've got something."

Wallander slammed down the receiver, full of energy. He stood by the window and looked out at the old water tower while he went through what he wanted to get done that day. He knew from experience that something almost always came along to spoil the plan. If he managed to get half the things done he'd be pleased.

At 9 a.m. he left his office, got some coffee, and went into one of the small meeting rooms, where Hansson was waiting with the psychologist from Stockholm. The man introduced himself as Mats Ekholm. He was around 60, with a firm handshake. Wallander had an immediately favourable impression of him. Like many police officers, Wallander had always felt sceptical about what psychologists could contribute in a criminal investigation. But from conversations with Ann-Britt Höglund he had begun to realise that this was wrong. He decided to give Ekholm a chance to show them what he could do.

The investigation files were set out on the table.

"I've read through them as best I could," said Ekholm. "I suggest that we start by talking about what isn't in the files."

"It's all there," said Hansson, surprised. "If there's one thing the police are forced to learn, it's how to write reports."

"I suppose you want to know what *we* think," interrupted Wallander. "Isn't that right?"

Ekholm nodded.

"There's a fundamental rule that says that the police are always searching for something specific," he answered. "If they don't know what an offender looks like they include an approximation. Quite often the phantom image turns out to have similarities with the offender who is finally apprehended."

Wallander recognised his own reactions in Ekholm's description. He always created an image of a criminal that he carried with him during an investigation.

"Two murders have been committed," Ekholm continued. "The *modus operandi* is the same, even though there are some interesting differences. Wetterstedt was killed from behind. The murderer struck him in the back, not in the head. He chose the more difficult alternative. Or could it be that he wanted to avoid smashing Wetterstedt's head? We don't know. After the blow he cut off his scalp and took the time to hide the body. If we look at Carlman's death, we can easily identify the similarities and differences. Carlman was also struck down with an axe. He too had a piece of his scalp torn off. But he was killed from directly in front. He must have seen his attacker. The offender chose a time when there were many people nearby, so the risk of discovery was high. He made no attempt to hide the body, realising that it would be virtually impossible. The first question we have to ask is: which are more important? The similarities or the differences?"

"He's a murderer," said Wallander. "He selected two people. He made plans. He must have visited the beach outside Wetterstedt's house several times. He even took the time to unscrew a bulb to obscure the area between the garden gate and the sea."

"Do we know whether Wetterstedt was in the habit of taking an evening walk on the beach?" Ekholm interjected.

"No," said Wallander. "But of course we ought to find out."

"Keep going," said Ekholm.

"On the surface the pattern looks completely different when it comes to Carlman," said Wallander. "Surrounded by people at a Midsummer party. But maybe the killer didn't see it that way. Maybe he thought he could make use of the fact that no-one sees anything at all at a party. Nothing is as difficult as obtaining a detailed impression of events from a large group of people."

"To answer that question we have to examine what alternatives he may have had," said Ekholm. "Carlman was a businessman who moved around a lot. Always surrounded by people. Maybe the party was the right choice after all."

"The similarity or the difference," said Wallander. "Which one is crucial?"

Ekholm threw out his hands.

"It's too early to say, of course. What we can be sure of is that he plans his crimes carefully and that he's extremely cold-blooded."

"He takes scalps," said Wallander. "He collects trophies. What does that mean?"

"He's exercising power," said Ekholm. "The trophies are the proof of his actions. For him it's no more peculiar than a hunter putting up a pair of horns on his wall."

"But the decision to scalp," Wallander went on. "Where does that come from?"

"It's not that strange," said Ekholm. "I don't want to seem cynical. But what part of a human being is more suitable to be taken as a trophy? A human body rots. A piece of skin with hair on it is easy to preserve."

"I guess I still can't stop thinking of American Indians," said Wallander.

"Naturally it can't be excluded that your killer has a fixation on an American Indian warrior," said Ekholm. "People who find themselves

145

in a psychic borderland often choose to hide behind another person's identity. Or transform themselves into a mythological figure."

"Borderland?" said Wallander. "What does that involve?"

"Your killer has already committed two murders. We can't rule out that he intends to commit more, since we don't know his motive. This indicates he has probably passed a psychological boundary, that he has freed himself from our normal inhibitions. A person can commit murder or manslaughter without premeditation. A killer who repeats his actions is following completely different psychological laws. He finds himself in a twilight zone where all the boundaries that exist for him are of his own making. On the surface he can live a completely normal life. He can go to a job every morning. He can have a family and devote his evenings to playing golf or tending his garden. He can sit on his sofa with his children around him and watch the news reports on the murders he himself has committed. He can deplore the crimes, and wonder why such people are on the loose. He has two different identities that he controls utterly. He pulls his own strings. He is both marionette and puppet master."

Wallander thought about what Ekholm had said.

"Who is he?" he finally asked. "What does he look like? How old is he? I can't hunt someone who looks entirely normal on the surface. I must search for a specific person."

"I can't answer that yet," said Ekholm. "I need time to get into the material before I can create a profile of the killer."

"I hope you're not considering today a day of rest," said Wallander wearily. "We'll need that profile as soon as possible."

"I'll try to get something together by tomorrow," said Ekholm. "But you and your colleagues have to realise that the difficulties and the margins of error are daunting."

"I realise that," said Wallander. "We still need all the help you can give us."

When the meeting was over Wallander drove down to the harbour and walked out onto the pier, where he had sat a few days earlier trying to write his speech for Björk. He sat and watched a fishing boat on its way out to sea. He unbuttoned his shirt and closed his eyes, facing the sun. Somewhere close by he heard children laughing. He tried to empty his mind and enjoy the heat. But after a few minutes he stood up and left.

Your killer has already committed two murders. We can't rule out that he intends to commit more, since we don't know his motive.

Ekholm's words might have been his own. He would not relax until they had caught Wetterstedt and Carlman's killer. Wallander knew his strength was his determination. And sometimes he had moments of insight. But his weakness was also clear. He couldn't keep his job from becoming a personal matter. Your killer, Ekholm had said. There was no better description of his weakness. The man who killed Wetterstedt and Carlman was actually his own responsibility. Whether he liked it or not.

He went back to his car, deciding to follow the plan he had made that morning. He drove out to Wetterstedt's villa. The cordons on the beach were gone. Lindgren and an older man, who he assumed was Lindgren's father, were busy sanding the boat. He didn't feel like saying hello.

He still had Wetterstedt's keys, and he unlocked the front door. The silence was deafening. He sat down in one of the leather chairs in the living-room. He could just hear sounds from the beach. He looked around the room. What did it tell him? Had the killer ever been inside the house? He was having a hard time gathering his thoughts. He got up and went over to the big window facing the garden, the beach and the sea. Wetterstedt had stood here many times. He could see that the parquet floor was worn at this spot. He looked out of the window. Someone had shut off the water to the fountain in the garden. He let his gaze wander as he went over the thoughts he'd had earlier.

On the hill outside Carlman's house my killer stood and observed the party. He may have been there many times. From there he could see without being seen. Where is the hill from which you would have the same view of Wetterstedt? From what point could you see him without being seen?

He walked around the house, stopping at each window. From the kitchen he looked for a long time at a pair of trees growing just outside Wetterstedt's property. But they were young birches that wouldn't have held a person's weight.

Not until he came to the study and looked out of the window did he realise that he had found the answer. From the projecting garage roof it was possible to see straight into the room. He left the house and went around the garage. A younger, fit man could jump up, grab hold of the eaves and pull himself up. Wallander went and got a ladder he had seen on the other side of the house. He leaned it against the garage roof and climbed up. The roof was the old-fashioned tar-paper type. Since he wasn't sure how much weight it would hold, he crawled on all fours over to a spot where he could look straight into Wetterstedt's study. He searched until he found the point farthest away from the window that still had a good view inside. On his hands and knees he inspected the tar-paper. Almost at once he discovered some cuts in it criss-crossing each other. He ran his fingertips across the tar-paper. Someone had slashed it with a knife. He looked around. It was impossible to be seen either from the beach or from the road above Wetterstedt's house.

Wallander climbed down and put the ladder back. Carefully he inspected the ground next to the garage, but all he found were some tattered pages from a magazine that had blown onto the property. He went back into the house. The silence was oppressive. He went upstairs. Through the window in Wetterstedt's bedroom he could see Lindgren and his father turning their boat right side up. He could see that it took two people to turn it over.

And yet he now knew that the killer had been alone, both here and when he killed Carlman. Though there were few clues, his intuition told him that it had been one person sitting on Wetterstedt's roof and on the hill above Carlman's.

I'm dealing with a lone killer, he thought. A lone man who leaves his borderland and hacks people to death so he can then take their scalps as trophies.

He left Wetterstedt's house, emerging into the sunshine again with relief. He drove over to a café and ate lunch at the counter. A young woman at a table nearby nodded to him and said hello. He replied, unable to remember who she was. Not until he left did he recall that she was Britta-Lena Bodén, the bank teller whose excellent memory had been so important during an investigation.

By midday he was back at the station. Ann-Britt Höglund met him in the foyer.

"I saw you from my window," she said.

Wallander knew at once that something had happened. He waited, tense, for her to continue.

"There is a point of contact," she said. "In the late 1960s Carlman did some time in prison. At Långholmen. Wetterstedt was minister of justice at the time."

"That isn't enough," said Wallander.

"I'm not finished. Carlman wrote a letter to Wetterstedt. And when he got out of prison they met."

Wallander stood motionless.

"How do you know this?"

"Come to my office and I'll tell you."

Wallander knew what this meant. If there was a connection, they had broken through the hard, outermost shell of the investigation.

CHAPTER 15

It had started with a telephone call.

Ann-Britt Höglund had been on her way down the hall to talk to Martinsson when she was paged. She returned to her office and took the call. It was a man who spoke so softly that at first she thought he was sick or injured. But she understood that he wanted to talk to Wallander. No-one else would do, least of all a woman. She explained that Wallander had gone out and no-one could say when he was coming back. But the man was extremely persistent, although she didn't understand how a man who spoke so softly could seem so strong-willed. She considered transferring the call to Martinsson and having him pretend to be Wallander. But something told her that he might know Wallander's voice.

He said that he had important information. She asked him whether it had to do with Wetterstedt's death. Maybe, he replied. Then she asked whether it was about Carlman. Maybe, he said once again. She knew that somehow she had to keep him talking. He had refused to give his name or phone number.

He finally resolved the impasse. He had been silent for so long that Höglund thought he had hung up, but then he asked for the station fax number. Give the fax to Wallander, the man had said. Not to anyone else.

An hour later the fax had arrived. She handed it to Wallander. To his astonishment he saw that it was sent from Skoglund's Hardware in Stockholm.

"I looked up the number and called them," she said. "I also thought it was strange that a hardware shop would be open on Sunday. From a message on their answer machine I got hold of the owner via his mobile phone. He had no idea either how someone could have sent a fax from his office. He was on his way to play golf but promised to look into the matter. Half an hour later he called and reported that someone had broken into his office."

"How strange," said Wallander.

He read the fax. It was hand-written and hard to read. He must get reading glasses soon. He couldn't pretend any longer he was just tired or stressed. The fax seemed to have been written in great haste. Wallander read it silently. Then he read it aloud to make sure he hadn't misunderstood anything.

"'Arne Carlman was in Långholmen during the spring of 1969 for fraud and fencing stolen goods. At that time Gustaf Wetterstedt was minister of justice. Carlman wrote letters to him. He bragged about it. When he got out he met with Wetterstedt. What did they talk about? What did they do? We don't know. But things went well for Carlman. He never went to prison again. And now they're dead. Both of them.' Have I read this correctly?"

"I came up with the same thing," she said.

"No signature," said Wallander. "And what is he really getting at? Who is he? How does he know this stuff? Is any of it true?"

"I don't know," she said. "But I had a feeling that this man knew what he was talking about. Anyway, it's not hard to check whether Carlman was really at Långholmen in the spring of 1969. We know that Wetterstedt was minister of justice then."

"Wasn't Långholmen closed by then?" Wallander asked.

"That was a few years later, in 1975, I think. I can check on exactly when."

Wallander waved it off.

"Why did he only want to talk to me?" he asked. "Did he give any explanation?"

"I got a feeling he'd heard about you."

"So he wasn't claiming that he knew me?"

"No."

Wallander thought for a moment.

"Let's hope what he wrote is true," he said. "Then we've established the connection."

"It shouldn't be too hard to verify," said Höglund. "Even if it is Sunday."

"I'll go out and talk to Carlman's widow right now. She must know whether her husband was ever in prison," said Wallander.

"Do you want me to come along?"

"No."

Half an hour later Wallander parked his car outside the cordon in Bjäresjö. A bored-looking officer sat in a squad car reading the paper. He straightened up when he saw Wallander approaching.

"Is Nyberg still working here?" asked Wallander in surprise. "Isn't the forensic investigation finished?"

"I haven't seen any technicians around," said the officer.

"Call Ystad and ask them why the cordons haven't been removed," said Wallander. "Is the family home?"

"The widow is probably there," said the officer. "And the daughter. But the sons left in a car a few hours ago."

Wallander entered the grounds of the farm. The bench and the table in the arbour were gone. In the beautiful summer weather the events of the last few days seemed unbelievable. He knocked on the door. Carlman's widow opened it almost at once.

"I'm sorry to bother you," said Wallander. "But I have a few questions that I need answered as soon as possible."

She was very pale. As he stepped inside he smelled a faint whiff of alcohol. Somewhere inside, Carlman's daughter shouted, asking who was at the door. Wallander tried to remember the name of the woman leading the way. Had he ever heard it? Yes – it was Anita. He'd heard Svedberg use it during the long investigative meeting. He sat down on the sofa facing her. She lit a cigarette. She was wearing a flimsy summer dress. Wallander felt vaguely disapproving. Even if she didn't love her husband, he had been murdered. Didn't people believe in showing respect for the dead any more? Couldn't she have chosen more sombre attire? He had such conservative views sometimes that he surprised himself. Sorrow and respect didn't follow a colour scheme.

"Would the inspector like something to drink?" she asked.

"No thank you," said Wallander. "I'll be as brief as I can."

She shot a glance past his face. He turned around. Her daughter, Erika, had entered the room silently and was sitting in the background. She was smoking and seemed nervous.

"Do you mind if I listen?" she asked in a belligerent voice.

"Not at all," he said. "You're welcome to join us."

"I'm fine here," she said.

Her mother shook her head almost imperceptibly. She seemed resigned about her daughter's behaviour.

"Actually I came here because it's Sunday," Wallander began. "Which means that it's difficult to get information from archives. And since we need to have an answer as soon as possible, I came to you."

"You don't have to excuse yourself," said the woman. "What is it you want to know?"

"Was your husband in prison in the spring of 1969?"

Her reply was swift and resolute.

"He was in Långholmen between the 9th of February and the 19th of June. I drove him there and I picked him up. He was convicted of fraud and fencing stolen goods."

Her frankness made Wallander lose his train of thought. But what had he expected? That she would deny it?

"Was this the first time he was sentenced to a prison term?"

"The first and the last."

"Can you tell me any more about the convictions?"

"He denied having either received stolen paintings or forged any cheques. Other people did it in his name."

"So you think he was innocent?"

"It's not a matter of what I think. He was innocent."

Wallander decided to change tack.

"It has come to light that your husband knew Gustaf Wetterstedt, despite the fact that both you and your children claimed earlier that this was not the case."

"If he knew Gustaf Wetterstedt then I would have known about it."

"Could he have had contact with him without your knowledge?"

She thought for a moment before she replied.

"I would find that very difficult to believe," she said.

Wallander knew at once that she was lying. But he couldn't see why. Since he had no more questions he stood up.

"Perhaps you can find your own way out," said the woman on the sofa. She seemed very tired suddenly.

Wallander walked to the door. As he approached the daughter, who had been watching him intently, she stood up and blocked his way, holding her cigarette in her left hand.

Out of nowhere came a slap that struck Wallander hard on his left cheek. He was so surprised that he took a step back, tripped, and fell to the floor.

"Why did you let it happen?" she shrieked.

Then she started pummelling Wallander, who managed to fend her off as he tried to get up. Mrs Carlman came to his rescue. She did the same thing as the girl had just done to Wallander. She slapped her daughter hard in the face. When the girl calmed down, her mother led her over to the sofa. Then she returned to Wallander, who was standing there with his burning cheek, torn between rage and astonishment.

"Erika's been so depressed about what happened," said Anita Carlman. "She's lost control. The inspector must forgive her."

"Maybe she should see a doctor," said Wallander, noticing that his voice was shaking.

"She already has."

Wallander nodded and went out of the door. He tried to remember the last time he had been struck. It was more than ten years ago. He was interrogating a man suspected of burglary. Suddenly the man had jumped up from the table and slugged him in the mouth. That time Wallander struck back. His rage was so fierce that he broke the man's nose. Afterwards the man tried to sue Wallander for police brutality, but he was found innocent. The man later sent a complaint to the ombudsman about Wallander, but that too was dropped with no measures taken.

He had never been hit by a woman before. When his wife Mona had lost control, she had thrown things at him. But she had never tried to slap him. He often wondered what would have happened if she had. Would he have hit back? He knew there was a good chance he would.

He stood in the garden touching his stinging cheek. All the energy he had felt that morning had evaporated. He was so tired that he couldn't even manage to hold on to the feeling the girls' visit had given him.

He walked back to his car. The officer was slowly rolling up the yellow tape.

He put *The Marriage of Figaro* in the cassette deck. He turned up the volume so high that it thundered inside the car. His cheek stung. In the rear-view mirror he could see that it was red. When he got to Ystad he turned into the big car park by the furniture shop. Everything was closed, the car park deserted. He opened the car door and let the music flow. Barbara Hendricks made him forget about Wetterstedt and Carlman for a moment. But the girl in flames still ran through his mind. The field seemed endless. She kept running and running. And burning and burning.

He turned down the music and started pacing back and forth in the car park. As always when he was thinking, he walked along staring at the ground. And so Wallander didn't notice the photographer who saw him by chance, and took a picture of him through a telephoto lens as he paced around the empty car park. A few weeks later, when an astonished Wallander saw the picture, he'd even forgotten that he'd stopped there to try and clear his head.

The team met very briefly that afternoon. Mats Ekholm joined them and ran through what he had discussed earlier with Hansson and Wallander. Höglund told the team about the fax, and Wallander reported that Anita Carlman had confirmed the information it contained. He didn't mention being slapped. When Hansson asked tentatively whether he'd consider talking to the reporters camped out around the station who seemed to know when a meeting had taken place, he refused.

"We have to teach these reporters that we're working on a legal matter," Wallander said, and could hear how affected he sounded. "Ann-Britt can take care of them. I'm not interested."

"Is there anything I shouldn't say?" she asked.

"Don't say we have a suspect," said Wallander. "Because we don't."

After the meeting Wallander exchanged a few words with Martinsson.

"Has anything more been discovered about the girl?" he asked.

"Not yet," said Martinsson.

"Let me know as soon as something happens."

Wallander went to his room. The telephone rang immediately, making him jump. Every time it rang he expected to be told of another murder. But it was his sister. She told him that she had talked to Gertrud. There was no doubt that their father had Alzheimer's disease. Wallander could hear how upset she was.

"He's almost 80," he consoled her. "Sooner or later something had to happen."

"But even so," she said.

Wallander knew what she meant. He could have used the same words himself. All too often life was reduced to those powerless words of protest, *but even so*.

"He won't be able to handle a trip to Italy," she said.

"If he wants to, then he will," said Wallander. "Besides, I promised him."

"Maybe I should come with you."

"No. It's our trip."

He hung up, wondering whether she was offended that he didn't invite her to join them. But he put aside those thoughts and decided that he really had to go and visit his father. He located the scrap of paper on which he had written Linda's phone number and called her. He was surprised when Kajsa answered at once, expecting them to be outside on such a beautiful day. When Linda came on he asked whether she'd leave her rehearsal and drive out with him to see her grandfather.

"Can Kajsa come too?" she asked.

"Normally I'd say yes," replied Wallander. "But today I'd prefer it if it was just you and me. There's something I need to talk to you about."

He picked her up in Österport Square. On the way to Löderup he told her about his father's visit to the station, and that he was ill.

"No-one knows how fast it will progress," said Wallander. "But he will be leaving us. Sort of like a ship sailing farther and farther out towards the horizon. We'll still be able to see him clearly, but for him we'll seem more and more like shapes in the fog. Our faces, our words, our common memories, everything will become indistinct and finally disappear altogether. He might be cruel without realising he's doing it. He could turn into a totally different person."

Wallander could tell that she was upset.

"Can't anything be done?" she asked after sitting for a long time in silence.

"Only Gertrud can answer that," he said. "But I don't think there is a cure."

He also told her about the trip that he and his father wanted to take to Italy.

"It'll be just him and me," said Wallander. "Maybe we can work out all the problems we've had."

Gertrud met them on the steps when they pulled into the courtyard. Linda ran to see her grandfather, who was painting out in the studio he had made in the old barn. Wallander sat down in the kitchen and talked to Gertrud. It was just as he thought. There was nothing to be done but try to live a normal life and wait.

"Will he be able to travel to Italy?" asked Wallander.

"That's all he talks about," she said. "And if he should die while he's there, it wouldn't be the worst thing."

She told him that his father had taken the news of his illness calmly.

This surprised Wallander, who had known his father to fret about the slightest ailment.

"I think he's come to terms with old age," said Gertrud. "He probably thinks that by and large he would live the same life again if he had the chance."

"But in that life he would have stopped me from becoming a policeman," said Wallander.

"It's terrible, what I read in the papers," she said. "All the horrible things you have to deal with."

"Someone has to do it," said Wallander. "That's just the way it is."

They stayed and ate dinner in the garden. Wallander could see that his father was in an unusually good mood. He assumed that Linda was the reason. It was already 11 p.m. by the time they left.

"Adults can be so childlike," Linda said suddenly. "Sometimes because they're showing off, trying to act young. But Grandpa can seem childlike in a way that seems totally unaffected."

"Your grandpa is a very special person," said Wallander.

"Do you know you're starting to look like him?" she asked. "You two are becoming more alike every year."

"I know," said Wallander. "But I don't know if I like it."

He dropped her off where he'd picked her up. They decided that she would call in a few days. He watched her disappear past Österport School and realised to his astonishment that he hadn't thought about the investigation once the whole evening. He immediately felt guilty, then pushed the feeling away. He knew that he couldn't do any more than he had already done today.

He drove to the station. None of the detectives were in. There weren't any messages important enough to answer that evening. He drove home, parked his car, and went up to his flat.

Wallander stayed up for a long time that night. He had the windows open to the warm summer air. On his stereo he played some music by Puccini. He poured himself the last of the whisky. He felt some of the happiness he had felt the afternoon he was driving out to Salomonsson's farm, before the catastrophe had struck. Now he was in the middle of an investigation that was marked by two things. First, they had very little to help them identify the killer. Second, it was quite possible that he was busy carrying out his third murder at that very moment. Still, Wallander tried to put the case out of his mind. And for a short time the burning girl disappeared from his thoughts too. He had to admit that he couldn't single-handedly solve every violent crime that happened in Ystad. He could only do his best. That's all anyone could do.

He lay down on the sofa and dozed off to the music and the summer night with the whisky glass within reach.

But something drew him back to the surface again. It was something that Linda had said in the car. Some words that suddenly took on a whole new meaning. He sat up on the sofa, frowning. What was it she had said? *Adults can be so childlike.* There was something there that he couldn't grasp. *Adults can be so childlike.*

Then he realised what it was. And he couldn't understand how he could have been so sloppy. He put on his shoes, found a torch in one of the kitchen drawers, and left the flat. He drove out along Österleden, turned right, and stopped outside Wetterstedt's house, which lay in darkness. He opened the gate to the front yard. He gave a start when a cat vanished like a shadow among the bushes. He shone the torch along the base of the garage, and didn't have to search long before he found what he was looking for. He took the torn-out pages of the magazine between his thumb and forefinger and shone the light on them. They were from an issue of *The Phantom*. He searched in his pockets for a plastic bag and put the pages inside.

Then he drove home. He was still annoyed that he had been so sloppy.

Adults can be so childlike.

A grown man could very well have sat on the garage roof reading an issue of *The Phantom*.

CHAPTER 16

When Wallander awoke just before 5 a.m., on Monday 27 June, a cloud bank had drifted in from the west and reached Ystad, but there was still no rain. Wallander lay in bed and tried in vain to go back to sleep. At 6 a.m. he got up, showered and made coffee. The fatigue was like a dull pain. Ten or 15 years ago he'd almost never felt tired in the morning, no matter how little sleep he'd got, he thought with regret. But those days were gone forever.

Just before 7 a.m. he walked into the station. Ebba had already arrived, and she smiled at him as she handed him some phone messages.

"I thought you were on holiday," said Wallander in surprise.

"Hansson asked me to stay a few extra days," said Ebba. "Now that there's so much happening."

"How's your hand?"

"Like I said. It's no fun getting old. Everything just starts to fall apart."

Wallander couldn't recall ever having heard Ebba make such a dramatic statement. He wondered whether to tell her about his father and his illness, but decided against it. He got some coffee and sat down at his desk. After looking through the phone messages and stacking them on top of the pile from the night before, he called Riga, feeling a pang of guilt at making a personal call. He was still old-fashioned enough not to want to burden his employer. He remembered how a few years ago Hansson had been consumed by a passion for betting on the horses. He had spent half his working day calling racetracks all over the country for tips. Everyone had known about it, but no-one had complained. Wallander had been surprised that only he had thought someone should talk to Hansson. But then one day all the form guides and half-completed betting slips vanished from Hansson's desk. Through the grapevine Wallander heard that Hansson had decided to stop before he wound up in debt.

Baiba picked up the phone after the third ring. Wallander was nervous. Each time he called he was afraid that she'd tell him they shouldn't see each other again. He was as unsure of her feelings as he was sure of his own. But she sounded happy, and her happiness was infectious. Her decision to go to Tallinn had been made quite hastily, she explained. One of her friends was going and asked Baiba to go with her. She had no classes at the university that week, and the translation job she was working on didn't have a pressing deadline. She told him about the trip and then asked how he was. Wallander decided not to mention that their trip to Skagen might be jeopardised. He said that everything was fine. They agreed that he would call her that evening. Afterwards, Wallander sat worrying about how she'd react if he had to postpone their holiday.

Worry was a bad habit, which seemed to grow worse the older he got. He worried about everything. He worried when Baiba went to Tallinn, he worried that he was going to get sick, he worried that he might oversleep or that his car might break down. He wrapped himself in clouds of anxiety. With a grimace he wondered whether Mats Ekholm might be able to do a psychological profile of him and suggest how he could free himself from all the problems he created.

Svedberg knocked on his half-open door and walked in. He hadn't been careful in the sun the day before. The top of his head was completely sunburnt, as were his forehead and nose.

"I'll never learn," Svedberg complained. "It hurts like hell."

Wallander thought about the burning sensation he'd felt after being slapped the day before. But he didn't mention it.

"I spent yesterday talking to the people who live near Wetterstedt," Svedberg said. "He went for walks quite often. He was always polite and said hello to the people he met. But he didn't socialise with anyone in the neighbourhood."

"Did he also make a habit of taking walks at night?"

Svedberg checked his notes. "He used to go down to the beach."

"So this was a routine?"

"As far as I can tell, yes."

Wallander nodded. "Just as I thought," he said.

"Something else came up that might be of interest," Svedberg continued. "A retired civil servant named Lantz told me that a reporter had rung his doorbell on Monday 20 June, and asked for directions to Wetterstedt's house. Lantz understood that the reporter and a photographer were going there to do a story. That means someone was at his house on the last day of his life."

"And that there are photographs," said Wallander. "Which newspaper was it?"

"Lantz didn't know."

"You'll have to get someone to make some calls," said Wallander. "This could be important."

Svedberg nodded and left the room.

"And you ought to put some cream on that sunburn," Wallander called after him. "It doesn't look good."

Wallander called Nyberg. A few minutes later he came in.

"I don't think your man came on a bicycle," said Nyberg. "We found some tracks behind the hut from a moped or a motorcycle. And every worker on the road team drives a car."

An image flashed through Wallander's mind, but he couldn't hold on to it. He wrote down what Nyberg had said.

"What do you expect me to do with this?" asked Nyberg, holding up the bag with the pages from *The Phantom*.

"Check for fingerprints," said Wallander. "Which may match other prints."

"I thought only children read *The Phantom*," said Nyberg.

"No," replied Wallander. "There you're wrong."

When Nyberg had gone, Wallander hesitated. Rydberg had taught him that a policeman must always tackle what was most important at a given moment. But what was now? No one thing could yet be assumed to be more important than another. Wallander knew that what mattered now was to trust his patience.

He went out into the hall, knocked on the door of the office that had been assigned to Ekholm and opened the door. Ekholm was sitting with his feet on the desk, reading through some papers. He nodded towards the visitor's chair and tossed the papers on the desk.

"How's it going?" asked Wallander.

"Not so good," said Ekholm evenly. "It's hard to pin down this person. It's a shame we don't have a little more material to go on."

"He needs to have committed more murders?"

"To put it bluntly, that would make the case easier," said Ekholm. "In many investigations into serial murders conducted by the F.B.I., a breakthrough comes only after the third or fourth crime. Then it's possible to sift out the things that are particular to each killing, and start to see an overall pattern. And a pattern is what we're looking for, one that enables us to see the mind behind the crimes."

"What can you say about adults who read comic books?" asked Wallander.

Ekholm raised his eyebrows.

"Does this have something to do with the case?"

"Maybe."

Wallander told him about his discovery. Ekholm listened intently.

"Emotional immaturity or abnormality is almost always present in individuals who commit serial murders," said Ekholm. "They don't value other human beings. That's why they don't comprehend the suffering they cause."

"But all adults who read *The Phantom* aren't murderers," said Wallander.

"Just as there have been examples of serial killers who were experts on Dostoevsky," replied Ekholm. "You have to take a piece of the puzzle and see whether it fits anywhere."

Wallander was starting to get impatient. He didn't have time to get into a theoretical discussion with Ekholm.

"Now that you've read through our material," he said, "what sort of conclusions have you made?"

"Just one, actually," said Ekholm. "That he will strike again."

Wallander waited for something more, an explanation, but it didn't come.

"Why?"

"Something about the total picture tells me so. And I can't say why except that it's based on experience. From other cases with trophy hunters."

"What kind of image do you see?" asked Wallander. "Tell me what you're thinking right now. Anything at all. And I promise I won't hold you to it later."

"An adult," replied Ekholm. "Considering the age of the victims and his possible connection to them, I'd say he's at least 30, but maybe older. The possible identification with a myth, perhaps of an American Indian, makes me think that he's in very good physical condition. He's both cautious and cunning. Which means that he's the calculating type. I think he lives a regular, orderly life. He hides his inner life beneath a surface of normality."

"And he's going to strike again?"

Ekholm threw out his hands.

"Let's hope I'm wrong. But you asked me to tell you what I think."

"Wetterstedt and Carlman died three days apart," said Wallander. "If he keeps to that pattern, he'll kill someone today."

"That's not inevitable," said Ekholm. "Since he's cunning, the time factor won't be crucial. He strikes when he's sure of success. Something might happen today. But it could also take several weeks. Or years."

Wallander had no more questions. He asked Ekholm to attend the team meeting an hour later. He went back to his room feeling increasingly anxious. The man they were looking for, of whom they knew nothing, would strike again.

He took out the notebook in which he had written Nyberg's words, and tried to recapture the fleeting image that had passed through his mind. He was sure that this was important, and that it had something to do with the road workers' hut. But he couldn't pin it down. He got up and went to the conference room. He missed Rydberg more than ever now.

Wallander sat in his usual seat at one end of the table. He looked around. Everyone was there. He sensed that the group hoped they were going to make a breakthrough. Wallander knew they'd be disappointed. But none of them would show it. The detectives gathered in this room were professionals.

"Let's start with a review of what's happened in the scalping case in the past 24 hours," he began.

He hadn't planned to say *the scalping case*. But from that moment on the investigation wasn't called anything else.

Wallander usually waited until last to give his report, since he was expected to sum up and provide further directions. It was natural for Höglund to speak first. She passed around the fax that had come from Skoglund's Hardware. What Anita Carlman had confirmed had also been checked in the national prison register. Höglund had just begun the most difficult task – to find evidence or even copies of the letters that Carlman was said to have written to Wetterstedt.

"It all happened so long ago," she concluded. "Although archives are generally well organised in this country, it takes a long time to find documents from more than 25 years ago. We're dealing with a time before computers were in use."

"We must keep looking, though," said Wallander. "The connection between Wetterstedt and Carlman is crucial."

"The man who rang," said Svedberg, rubbing his burnt nose. "Why wouldn't he say who he was? Who would break into a shop just to send a fax?"

"I've thought about that," said Höglund. "There could be a lot of reasons why he wants to protect his identity, perhaps because he's scared. And he obviously wanted to point us in a particular direction."

The room fell silent. Wallander could see that Höglund was on the right track. He nodded to her to continue.

"Naturally we're guessing. But if he feels threatened by the man who killed Wetterstedt and Carlman, he would be extremely eager for us to capture him. Without revealing his own identity."

"In that case he should have told us more," said Martinsson.

"Maybe he couldn't," Höglund objected. "If I'm right, that he contacted us because he's frightened, then he probably told us everything he knows."

Wallander lifted his hand.

"Let's take this even further," he said. "The man gave us information relating to Carlman. Not Wetterstedt. That's crucial. He claims that Carlman wrote to Wetterstedt and that they met after Carlman was released from prison. Who would know this?"

"Another inmate," said Höglund.

"That was exactly my thought," said Wallander. "But your theory is that he's contacting us out of fear. Would that fit if he was only Carlman's fellow prisoner?"

"There's more to it," said Höglund. "He knows that Carlman and Wetterstedt met after Carlman got out. So contact continued outside of prison."

"He could have witnessed something," said Hansson, who had been silent until now. "For some reason this has led to two murders 25 years later."

Wallander turned to Ekholm, who was sitting by himself at the end of the table.

"25 years is a long time," he said.

"The desire for revenge can go on indefinitely," said Ekholm. "There are no prescribed time limits. It's one of the oldest truths in criminology that an avenger can wait forever. If these are revenge killings, that is."

"What else could they be?" asked Wallander. "We can rule out crimes against property, probably with Wetterstedt, and with complete certainty in Carlman's case."

"A motive can have many components," said Ekholm. "A serial killer may choose his victims for reasons that seem inexplicable. Take the scalps, for instance: we might ask whether he's after a special kind of hair. Wetterstedt and Carlman had the same full head of grey hair. We can't exclude anything. But as a layman, I agree that right now the point of contact ought to be the most important thing to focus on."

"Is it possible that we're thinking along the wrong lines altogether?" asked Martinsson suddenly. "Maybe for the killer there's a *symbolic* link between Wetterstedt and Carlman. While we search for facts, maybe he sees a connection that's invisible to us. Something that's completely inconceivable to our rational minds."

Wallander knew that Martinsson had the ability to turn an investigation around on its axis and get it back on the right track.

"You're thinking of something," he said. "Keep going."

Martinsson shrugged his shoulders and seemed about to change his mind.

"Wetterstedt and Carlman were wealthy men," he said. "They both belonged to a certain social class. They were representatives of political and economic power."

"Are you suggesting a political motive?" Wallander asked, surprised.

"I'm not suggesting anything," said Martinsson. "I'm listening to you and trying to see the case clearly myself. I'm as afraid as everyone else in this room that he's going to strike again."

Wallander looked around the table. Pale, serious faces. Except for Svedberg with his sunburn. Only now did he see that they were all as frightened as he was. He wasn't the only one who dreaded the next ring of the telephone.

The meeting broke up before 10 a.m., but Wallander asked Martinsson to stay behind.

"What is happening with the girl?" he asked. "Dolores María Santana?"

"I'm still waiting to hear from Interpol."

"Give them a nudge," said Wallander.

Martinsson gave him a puzzled look.

"Do we really have time for her now?"

"No. But we can't just let it drop either."

Martinsson promised to send off another request. Wallander went in his office and called Lars Magnusson. He answered after a long time. Wallander could hear that he was drunk.

"I need to continue our conversation," he said.

"I don't conduct conversations at this time of day," said Magnusson.

"Make some coffee," said Wallander. "And put away the bottles. I'm coming over in half an hour." He hung up on Magnusson's protests.

Someone had placed two preliminary autopsy reports on his desk. Wallander had gradually learned to decipher the language used by pathologists and forensic doctors. Many years ago he had taken a course in Uppsala arranged by the national police board. Wallander remembered how unpleasant it was to visit an autopsy room.

There was nothing unexpected in the reports. He put them aside and looked out the window, trying to visualise the killer. What did he look like? What was he doing right now? But Wallander saw nothing but darkness before him. Depressed, he got up and left.

CHAPTER 17

When Wallander left Lars Magnusson's flat after more than two hours of trying to conduct a coherent conversation, all he wanted to do was go home and take a bath. He hadn't noticed the filth on his first visit, but this time it was obvious. The front door was ajar when Wallander arrived. Magnusson was lying on the sofa while a saucepan of coffee boiled over in the kitchen. He'd greeted Wallander by telling him to go to hell.

"Don't come around here, just get out and forget there's anyone called Lars Magnusson," he'd shouted.

But Wallander stood his ground. The coffee on the stove indicated that Magnusson had thought he might talk to someone in the daytime after all. Wallander searched in vain for clean cups. In the sink were plates on which the food and grease seemed have fossilised. Eventually he found two cups, which he washed and carried into the living-room.

Magnusson wore only a pair of dirty shorts. He was unshaven and clutched a bottle of dessert wine like a crucifix. Wallander was horrified at his dissipation. What he found most disgusting was that Lars Magnusson was losing his teeth. Wallander grew annoyed and then angry that the man on the sofa wasn't listening to him. He yanked the bottle away from him and demanded answers to his questions. He had no idea what authority he was acting on. But Magnusson did as he was told. He even hauled himself up to a sitting position. Wallander wanted to get more of a sense of the time when Wetterstedt was minister of justice, of the rumours and scandal. But Magnusson seemed to have forgotten everything. He couldn't even remember what he'd said on Wallander's last visit. Finally, Wallander gave him back the bottle and once he had taken a few more slugs, feeble memories begin to surface.

Wallander left the flat with one lead. In an unexpected moment of clarity, Magnusson remembered that there was a policeman on the Stockholm vice squad who had developed a particular interest in Wetterstedt. Rumour had it that this man, who Magnusson remembered was Hugo Sandin, had created a dossier on Wetterstedt. As far as Magnusson knew, nothing had ever come of it. He'd heard that Sandin had moved south when he retired and now lived with his son, who had a pottery workshop outside Hässleholm.

"If he's still alive," Magnusson said, smiling his toothless smile, as though he hoped that Hugo Sandin had died before him.

Wallander drove back to the station, feeling determined to locate Sandin. In reception he ran into Svedberg, whose burnt face was still troubling him.

"Wetterstedt was interviewed by a journalist from *MagaZenith*," said Svedberg.

Wallander had never heard of the magazine.

"Retirees get it," Svedberg told him. "The journalist's name was Anna-Lisa Blomgren, and she did take a photographer with her. Now that Wetterstedt is dead they aren't going to publish the article."

"Talk to her," said Wallander. "And ask for the pictures."

Wallander went to his office. He called the switchboard and asked them to find Nyberg, who called back 15 minutes later.

"Do you remember the camera from Wetterstedt's house?" Wallander asked.

"Of course I remember," said Nyberg grumpily.

"Has the film been developed yet? There were seven pictures exposed."

"Didn't you get them?" Nyberg asked, surprised.

"No."

"They should have been sent over to you last Saturday."

"I never got them."

"Are you sure?"

"Maybe they're lying around somewhere."

"I'll have to look into this," said Nyberg. "I'll get back to you."

Somebody would bear the brunt of Nyberg's wrath, and Wallander was glad that it wouldn't be him.

He found the number of the Hässleholm police and after some difficulty managed to get hold of Hugo Sandin's phone number. When Wallander asked about Sandin, he was told that he was about 85 years old but that his mind was still sharp.

"He usually stops by to visit a couple of times a year," said the officer Wallander spoke to, who introduced himself as Mörk.

Wallander wrote down the number and thanked him. Then he called Malmö and asked for the doctor who had done the autopsy on Wetterstedt.

"There's nothing in the report about the time of death," Wallander said to him. "That's very important for us."

The doctor asked him to wait a moment while he got his file. After a moment he returned and apologised.

"It was left out of the report. Sometimes my dictaphone acts up. But Wetterstedt died less than 24 hours before he was found. We're still waiting for some results from the laboratory that will enable us to narrow the time span further."

"I'll wait for those results," said Wallander and thanked him.

He went in to see Svedberg, who was at his computer.

"Did you talk to that journalist?"

"I'm just typing up a report."

"Did you get the time of their visit?"

Svedberg looked through his notes.

"They got to Wetterstedt's house at 10 a.m. and stayed until 1 p.m."

"After that, nobody else saw him alive?"

Svedberg thought for a moment. "Not that I know of."

"So, we know that much," said Wallander and left the room.

He was just about to call Hugo Sandin, when Martinsson came in.

"Have you got a minute?" he asked.

"Always," said Wallander. "What's up?"

Martinsson waved a letter.

"This came in the mail today," he said. "It's from someone who says he gave a girl a ride from Helsingborg to Tomelilla on Monday, 20 June. He's seen the description of the girl in the papers, and thinks it might have been her."

Martinsson handed the envelope to Wallander, who took out the letter and read it.

"No signature," he said.

"But the letterhead is interesting."

Wallander nodded. "Smedstorp Parish," he said. "Official church stationery."

"We'll have to look into it," said Martinsson.

"We certainly will," said Wallander. "If you take care of Interpol and the other things you're busy with, I'll look after this."

"I still don't see how we have time," said Martinsson.

"We'll make time," said Wallander.

After Martinsson left, Wallander realised that he'd been subtly criticised for not leaving the suicide case for the moment. Martinsson might be right, he thought. There was no space for anything but Wetterstedt and Carlman. But then he decided the criticism was unjustified. They must make time to handle every case.

As if to prove that he was right, Wallander left the station and drove out of town towards Tomelilla and Smedstorp. The drive gave him time to think about the murders. The summer landscape seemed a surreal backdrop to his thoughts. Two men are axed to death and scalped, he thought. A young girl walks into a rape field and sets herself on fire. And all around me it's summertime. Skåne couldn't be more beautiful than this. There's a paradise hidden in every corner of this countryside. To find it, all you have to do is keep your eyes open. But you might also glimpse hearses on the roads.

The parish offices were in Smedstorp. After he passed Lunnarp he turned left. He knew that the office kept irregular hours, but there were cars parked outside the whitewashed building. A man was mowing the lawn. Wallander tried the door. It was locked. He rang the bell, noting from the brass plate that the office wouldn't be open until Wednesday. He waited. Then he rang again and knocked on the door.

The lawnmower hummed in the background. Wallander was just about to leave when a window on the floor above opened. A woman stuck out her head.

"We're open on Wednesdays and Fridays," she shouted.

"I know," Wallander replied. "But this is urgent. I'm from the Ystad police."

Her head disappeared. Then the door opened. A blonde woman dressed in black stood before him, heavily made up and wearing high heels. What surprised Wallander was the white clerical collar set against all that black. He introduced himself.

"Gunnel Nilsson," she replied. "I'm the vicar of this parish."

Wallander followed her inside. If I were walking into a nightclub I could better understand it, he thought. The clergy don't look the way I'd imagine these days.

She opened the door to an office and asked him to have a seat. Gunnel Nilsson was a very attractive woman, although Wallander couldn't decide whether the fact that she was a vicar made her seem more so.

He saw a letter lying on her desk. He recognised the parish letterhead.

"The police received a letter on your letterhead. That's why I'm here."

He told her about the girl. The vicar seemed upset. When he asked her why, she explained that she had been sick for a few days and hadn't read the papers. Wallander showed her the letter.

"Do you have any idea who wrote it? Or who has access to your letterhead?"

She shook her head.

"Only women work here."

"It's not clear whether a man or a woman wrote the letter," Wallander pointed out.

"I don't know who it could be," she said.

"Does anyone in the office live in Helsingborg? Or drive there often?"

She shook her head again. Wallander could see that she was trying to be helpful.

"How many people work here?" he asked.

"There are four of us. And there's Andersson, who takes care of the garden. We also have a full-time watchman, Sture Rosell. But he mainly stays out at our churches. Any of them could have taken some letterhead from here, of course. Plus anyone who visited the vicar's office on business."

"You don't recognise the handwriting?"

"No."

"It's not illegal to pick up hitchhikers," said Wallander. "So why would someone write an anonymous letter? Because they wanted to hide the fact that they'd had been in Helsingborg? It's puzzling."

"I could ask whether anyone here was in Helsingborg that day," she said. "And try to match the handwriting."

"I'd appreciate your help," said Wallander, standing up. "You can reach me at the Ystad police station."

He wrote his phone number down for her. She followed him out.

"I've never met a female vicar before," he said.

"Many people are still surprised," she replied.

"In Ystad we have our first woman chief of police," he said. "Everything changes."

"For the better, I hope," she said and smiled.

Wallander looked at her, deciding she was quite beautiful. He didn't see a ring on her finger. He couldn't help thinking forbidden thoughts. She really was terribly attractive.

The man cutting the grass was now sitting on a bench smoking. Without really knowing why, Wallander sat down on the bench and started talking to him. He was about 60, and dressed in a blue work shirt, dirty corduroy trousers and a pair of ancient tennis shoes. Wallander noted that he was smoking unfiltered Chesterfields, the brand that his father had smoked when he was a child.

"She doesn't open the door when the office is closed," the man said thoughtfully. "This is the first time it's ever happened."

"The vicar is quite good-looking," said Wallander.

"She's nice too," said the man. "And she gives a good sermon. I don't know whether we've ever had such a good vicar. But many people would still rather have a man."

"They would?" said Wallander absentmindedly.

"Quite a few people would never think of having a woman. People in Skåne are conservative. For the most part."

The conversation died. It was as if both men had run out of steam. Wallander listened to the birds. He could smell the freshly mown grass. He remembered that he should contact Hans Vikander at the Östermalm police, and find out how the interview with Gustaf Wetterstedt's mother had gone. He had a lot to do. He certainly didn't have time to sit on a bench outside the parish offices in Smedstorp.

"Were you here to get a change of address certificate?" the man asked suddenly.

"I had a few questions to ask," he said, getting up.

The man squinted at him.

"I recognise you," he said. "Are you from Tomelilla?"

"No," said Wallander. "I'm originally from Malmö. But I've lived in Ystad for many years."

He was about to say goodbye when he noticed the white T-shirt showing under the man's unbuttoned work shirt. It advertised the ferry line between Helsingborg and Helsingør, in Denmark. He knew it could be a coincidence, but decided that it wasn't. He sat back down on the bench. The man stubbed out his cigarette in the grass, about to get up.

"Just a moment," said Wallander. "There's something I'd like to ask you about."

The man heard the change in Wallander's voice. He gave him a wary look.

"I'm a police officer," said Wallander. "I didn't come here to talk to the vicar. I came to talk to you. Why didn't you sign the letter you sent? About the girl you gave a lift from Helsingborg?"

It was a reckless move, he knew, in defiance of everything he had been taught. It was a punch below the belt – the police didn't have the right to lie to extract information, especially when no crime had been committed.

But it worked. The man jumped, caught off guard. Wallander could see him wondering how he could know about the letter.

"It's not against the law to write anonymous letters," he said. "Or to pick up hitchhikers. I just want to know why you did. And what time you picked her up and where you took her. The exact time. And whether she said anything during the journey."

"Now I recognise you," muttered the man. "You're the policeman who shot a man in the fog a few years ago. On the shooting range outside Ystad."

"You're right," said Wallander. "That was me. My name is Kurt Wallander."

"She was standing at the slip road of the southbound motorway," said the man suddenly. "It was 7 p.m. I had driven over to Helsingborg to buy a pair of shoes. My cousin has a shoe shop there. He gives me a discount. I don't usually pick up hitchhikers. But she looked so forlorn."

"What happened?"

"Nothing happened. What do you mean?"

"When you stopped the car. What language did she speak?"

"I have no idea what language it was, but it certainly wasn't Swedish. And I don't speak English. I said I was going to Tomelilla. She nodded. She nodded to everything I said."

"Did she have any luggage?"

"Not a thing."

"Not even a handbag?"

"Nothing."

"And then you drove off?"

"She sat in the back seat. She didn't speak. I thought there was something odd about the whole thing. I was sorry I'd picked her up."

"Why's that?"

"Maybe she wasn't going to Tomelilla at all. Who the hell goes to Tomelilla?"

"So she didn't say a word?"

"Not a word."

"What did she do?"

"Do?"

"Did she sleep? Look out the window? What?"

The man tried to remember.

"There was one thing I worried about afterwards. Every time a car passed us she crouched down. As if she didn't want to be seen."

"So she was frightened?"

"Definitely."

"What happened next?"

"I stopped at the roundabout on the outskirts of Tomelilla and let her out. To tell you the truth, I don't think she had any idea where she was."

"So she wasn't going to Tomelilla?"

"I think she just wanted to get out of Helsingborg. I drove off. But when I was almost home I thought, I can't just leave her there. So I drove back. But she was gone."

"How long did it take you to go back?"

"Not more than ten minutes."

Wallander thought for a moment.

"When you picked her up outside Helsingborg, she was standing at the slip road. Is it possible she'd had a lift to Helsingborg? Or was she coming from there?"

The man thought for a while.

"From Helsingborg," he said. "If she'd had a lift down from the north, she wouldn't have been standing where she was."

"And you never saw her again? You didn't look for her?"

"Why would I?"

"What time was this?"

"I let her off at 8 p.m. I remember the news came on the car radio just as she got out of the car."

Wallander thought about what he had heard. He knew he'd been lucky.

"Why did you write to the police?" he asked. "Why anonymously?"

"I read about the girl who'd burned herself to death," he said. "And I had a feeling that it might have been her. But I decided not to identify myself. I'm a married man. The fact that I picked up a female hitchhiker might have been misinterpreted."

Wallander could see that he was telling the truth.

"This conversation is off the record," he said. "But I will still have to ask you for your name and telephone number."

"My name is Sven Andersson," said the man. "I hope there won't be any trouble."

"Not if you've told me the truth," Wallander replied.

He wrote down the number.

"One more thing," he said. "Can you remember whether she was wearing a necklace?"

Andersson thought. Then he shook his head. Wallander got up and shook his hand.

"You've been a great help," he said.

"Was it her?" Andersson asked.

"Possibly," said Wallander. "The question we must answer is what she was doing in Helsingborg."

He left Andersson and walked to his car. Just as he opened the door his phone rang. His first thought was that the killer had struck again.

CHAPTER 18

Wallander answered the phone and spoke to Nyberg, who told him that the developed photos were on his desk. He felt great relief that it wasn't news of a third killing. As he drove away from Smedstorp, he realised he should learn to control his anxiety. There was no knowing whether the man had more victims on his list, but Wallander couldn't shake a sense of foreboding. They must continue the investigation as though nothing else was going to happen. Otherwise they'd waste their energy with fruitless worry. On the way back to Ystad, Wallander decided he would drive up to Hässleholm later that day to talk to Hugo Sandin.

He went straight to his office and wrote up a report of his conversation with Andersson. He tried to get hold of Martinsson, but all Ebba could tell him was that he had left the station without saying where he was going. Wallander tried to reach him on his mobile phone, but it was turned off. He was annoyed that Martinsson was often impossible to contact. At the next meeting, he would state that everyone must be contactable at all times. Then he remembered the photos. He had put his notebook on top of the envelope without noticing it. He turned on his desk lamp and looked at them one by one. Although he didn't really know what he had expected, he was disappointed. The photos showed nothing more than the view from Wetterstedt's house. They were taken from upstairs. He could see Lindgren's overturned boat and the sea, which was calm. There were no people in the pictures. The beach was deserted. Two of the pictures were blurry. He wondered why Wetterstedt had taken them – if, indeed, he had. He found a magnifying glass in a desk drawer, but still couldn't see anything of interest. He put them back in the envelope, deciding he'd ask someone else on the team to have a look, just to confirm he hadn't missed anything.

He was just about to call Hässleholm when a secretary knocked on the door with a fax from Hans Vikander in Stockholm. It was a report, five single-spaced pages, of the conversation he had had with Wetterstedt's mother. He read through it quickly. It was a precise report, but completely lacking in imagination. Every question was routine. An interview related to a criminal investigation should balance general enquiries with surprise questions. But perhaps he was being unfair to Hans Vikander. What was the chance that a woman in her 90s would say something unexpected about her son, whom she hardly ever saw and only exchanged brief phone calls with?

As he got some coffee, he thought idly about the female vicar in Smedstorp. Back in his room, he called the number in Hässleholm. A young man answered. Wallander introduced himself. It took several minutes for Hugo Sandin to come to the phone. He had a clear, resolute voice. Sandin told Wallander that he would meet him that same day. Wallander grabbed his notebook and wrote down the directions.

On the way to Hässleholm he stopped to eat. It was late afternoon when he turned off at the sign for the pottery shop and drove to the renovated mill. An old man was in the garden pulling up dandelions. When Wallander got out of the car the man came towards him, wiping his hands. Wallander couldn't believe that this vigorous man was over 80, that Sandin and his own father were almost the same age.

"I don't get many visitors," said Sandin. "All my friends are gone. I have one colleague from the old homicide squad who's still alive. But now he's in a home outside Stockholm and can't remember anything that happened after 1960. Old age really is shitty."

Sandin sounded just like Ebba. His own father almost never complained about his age. In an old coach house that had been converted into a showroom for the pottery there was a table with a thermos and cups set out. Out of courtesy, Wallander spent a few minutes admiring the ceramics on display. Sandin sat down at the table and served coffee.

"You're the first policeman I've met who's interested in ceramics," he said.

Wallander sat down. "Actually, I'm not," he admitted.

"Policemen usually like to fish," said Sandin. "In lonely, isolated mountain lakes. Or deep in the forests of Småland."

"I didn't know that," said Wallander. "I never go fishing."

Sandin looked at him intently.

"What do you do when you're not working?"

"I have a pretty hard time relaxing."

Sandin nodded in approval.

"Being a policeman is a calling," he said. "Just like being a doctor. We're always on duty. Whether we're in uniform or not."

Wallander said nothing, even though he disagreed. Once he might have believed that a policeman's job was his calling. But not any more. At least he didn't think so.

"So," Sandin prompted. "I read in the papers about what's going on in Ystad. Tell me what they left out."

Wallander recounted the circumstances surrounding the two murders. Now and then Sandin would interrupt with a question, always pertinent.

"So he may kill again," he said when Wallander had finished.

"We can't ignore that possibility."

Sandin shoved his chair back from the table and stretched out his legs.

"And you want me to tell you about Gustaf Wetterstedt," he said. "I'll be happy to. May I first ask you how you found out that a long time ago, I took a special interest in him?"

"A journalist in Ystad told me. Lars Magnusson. Unfortunately, quite an alcoholic."

"I don't recognise the name."

"Well, he's the one who knew about you."

Sandin sat silently, stroking his lips with one finger. Wallander sensed that he was looking for the right place to begin.

"The truth about Wetterstedt is straightforward," said Sandin. "He was a crook. He may have appeared to be a competent minister of justice. But he was totally unsuitable for the role."

181

"Why?"

"His activities were governed by attention to his career rather than the good of the country. That's the worst testimonial you can give a government minister."

"And yet he was in line to be leader of the party?"

Sandin shook his head vigorously.

"That's not true," he said. "That was media speculation. Within the party it was obvious that he could never be their leader. It's hard to see why he was even a member."

"But he was minister of justice for years. He couldn't have been totally unsuitable."

"You're too young to remember. But there was a change sometime in the 1950s. It was barely perceptible, but it happened. Sweden was sailing along on unbelievably fair winds. It seemed as though unlimited funds were available to obliterate poverty. At the same a change occurred in political life. Politicians were turning into professionals. Career politicians. Before, idealism had been a dominant part of political life. Now this idealism began to be diluted. People like Wetterstedt began their ascent. Youth associations became the hatcheries for the politicians of the future."

"Let's talk about the scandals," said Wallander, afraid that Sandin would get lost in political reminiscences.

"He used prostitutes," said Sandin. "He wasn't the only one, of course. But he had certain predilections that he subjected the girls to."

"I heard that one girl filed a complaint," said Wallander.

"Her name was Karin Bengtsson," said Sandin. "She came from an unhappy background in Eksjö. She ran away to Stockholm and came to our notice for the first time in 1954. A few years later she wound up with the group from which Wetterstedt picked his girls. In January 1957 she filed a complaint against him. He had slashed her feet with a razor blade. I met her myself at the time. She could hardly walk. Wetterstedt knew he'd gone too far. The complaint was dropped, and Bengtsson was paid off. She received money to invest in a clothing boutique in Västerås. In 1959, money magically appeared in her bank account, enough to buy a house. In 1960, she started holidaying in Mallorca every year."

"Who came up with the money?"

"Even then there were slush funds. The Swedish royal family had established a precedent by paying off women who had been intimate with the old king."

"Is Karin Bengtsson still alive?"

"She died in 1984. She never married. I didn't see her after she moved to Västerås. But she called once in a while, right until the last year of her life. She was usually drunk."

"Why did she call?"

"As soon as I heard that there was a prostitute who wanted to file a complaint against Wetterstedt, I got in touch with her. I wanted to help her. Her life had been destroyed. Her self-esteem wasn't very high."

"Why did you get involved?"

"I was pretty radical in those days. Too many policemen accepted the corruption. I didn't. No more than I do now."

"What happened later, when Karin Bengtsson was out of the picture?"

"Wetterstedt carried on as before. He slashed lots of girls. But none of them filed a complaint. Two of them did disappear."

"What do you mean?"

Sandin looked at Wallander in surprise.

"I mean they were never heard from again. We searched for them, tried to trace them. But they were gone."

"What do you think happened?"

"They were killed, of course. Dissolved in lime, dumped in the sea. How do I know?"

Wallander couldn't believe what he was hearing.

"Can this be true?" he said doubtfully. "It sounds incredible."

"What is the saying? Amazing but true?"

"You think Wetterstedt committed murder?"

Sandin shook his head.

"I'm not saying that. Actually I'm convinced he didn't. I don't know exactly what happened, probably never will. But we can still draw conclusions, even if there's no real evidence."

"I'm having a hard time accepting this is true," said Wallander.

"It's absolutely true," said Sandin firmly. "Wetterstedt had no conscience. But nothing could be proved."

"There were many rumours about him."

"And they were all justified. Wetterstedt used his position and his power to satisfy his perverted sexual desires. But he was also mixed up in secret deals that made him rich."

"Art deals?"

"Art thefts, more likely. In my free time I tried to track down all the connections. I dreamed that one day I'd be able to slam such an airtight report down on the prosecutor's desk that Wetterstedt would not only be forced to resign, but would end up with a long prison sentence. Unfortunately I never got that far."

"You must have a great deal of material from those days, don't you?"

"I burnt it all a few years ago. In my son's kiln. At least ten kilos of paper."

Wallander swore under his breath. He hadn't dreamed that Sandin would get rid of the material he had gathered so laboriously.

"I still have a good memory," said Sandin. "I could probably remember everything I burned."

"Arne Carlman," said Wallander "Who was he?"

"A man who raised peddling art to a higher level," replied Sandin.

"In the spring of 1969 he was in Långholmen prison," said Wallander. "We got an anonymous tip-off that he had contacted Wetterstedt. And that they met after Carlman got out of jail."

"Carlman popped up now and then in reports. I think he wound up in Långholmen for something as simple as passing a bad cheque."

"Did you find links between him and Wetterstedt?"

"There was evidence that they had met as early as the late 1950s. Apparently they had a mutual interest in betting on the horses. Their names came up in connection with a raid on Täby racetrack around 1962. Wetterstedt's name was removed, since it wasn't considered wise to tell the public that the minister of justice had been frequenting a racetrack."

"What kind of dealings did they have?"

"Nothing we could pin down. They circled like planets in separate orbits which happened to cross now and then."

"I need to find that connection," said Wallander. "I'm convinced we have to find it to identify their killer."

"You can usually find what you're looking for if you look hard enough," said Sandin.

Wallander's mobile phone rang. He felt an icy fear. But he was wrong again. It was Hansson.

"I just wanted to know whether you'll be back today. Otherwise I'll set up a meeting for tomorrow."

"Has anything happened?"

"Nothing crucial. Everyone's up to their eyes in their own assignments."

"Tomorrow morning at 8 a.m.," said Wallander. "Not tonight."

"Svedberg went to the hospital to get his sunburn looked at," said Hansson.

"This happens every year," said Wallander. He hung up.

"You're in the papers a lot," said Sandin. "You seem to have gone your own way occasionally."

"Most of what they say isn't true," said Wallander.

"I often ask myself what it's like to be a policeman nowadays," said Sandin.

"So do I," said Wallander.

They got up and walked to Wallander's car. It was a beautiful evening.

"Can you think of anyone who might have wanted to kill Wetterstedt?" asked Wallander.

"There are probably quite a few," said Sandin.

Wallander stopped short.

"Maybe we're thinking about this the wrong way," he said. "Maybe we should separate the investigations. Not look for a common denominator, but for two separate solutions. And find the connection that way."

"The murders were committed by the same man," said Sandin, "so the investigations have to be interlinked. Otherwise you might end up on the wrong track."

Wallander nodded.

"Call me again sometime," said Sandin. "I have all the time in the world. Growing old means loneliness. A long wait for the inevitable."

"Did you ever regret joining the police?" asked Wallander.

"Never," said Sandin. "Why would I?"

"Just wondering," said Wallander. "Thanks for taking the time to talk to me."

"You'll catch him," said Sandin encouragingly. "Even if it takes a while."

Wallander nodded and got into the car. As he drove off he could see Sandin in the rear-view mirror, pulling dandelions from the lawn.

It was 7.45 p.m. by the time Wallander got back to Ystad. He parked the car outside his building and was just about to walk through the main door when he remembered that he hadn't any food in the house. And that he had forgotten to have the car inspected again. He swore out loud.

He walked into town and ate dinner at the Chinese restaurant on the square. He was the only customer. After dinner he strolled down to the harbour and walked out on the pier. As he watched the boats rocking in their moorings he thought about the two conversations he had had that day.

Dolores María Santana had stood at the motorway slip road from Helsingborg one evening, looking for a ride. She didn't speak Swedish and she was frightened. All they knew about her was that she was born in the Dominican Republic.

He stared at an old, well-kept wooden boat as he formulated his questions. Why and how did she come to Sweden? What was she running from? Why had she burned herself to death?

He walked farther out along the pier.

There was a party going on board a yacht. Someone raised a glass and said "*Skål*" to Wallander. He nodded back and raised an invisible glass.

At the end of the pier he sat down on a bollard and went over his conversation with Sandin. Everything was one big tangle. He couldn't see any openings, anything that might lead to a breakthrough.

At the same time he still felt a sense of dread. He couldn't get away from the possibility that it might happen again. He tossed a fistful of gravel into the water and got up. The party on the yacht was in full swing. He walked back through town. The heap of dirty clothes still lay in the middle of his floor. He wrote himself a note and put it on the kitchen table. *M.O.T., damn it!* Then he switched on the TV and lay down on the sofa.

A little later he phoned Baiba. Her voice was clear and close by.

"You sound tired," she said. "Have you got a lot to do?"

"It's not so bad," he lied. "But I miss you."

He heard her laugh.

"We'll see each other soon," she said.

"What were you really doing in Tallinn?"

She laughed again.

"Meeting another man. What did you think?"

"Just that."

"You need some sleep," she said. "I can hear that all the way from Riga. I hear Sweden's doing well in the World Cup."

"Are you interested in sports?" asked Wallander, surprised.

"Sometimes. Especially when Latvia is playing."

"People here are completely nuts about it."

"But not you?"

"I promise to improve. When Sweden plays Brazil I'll try to stay up and watch."

He heard her laugh again. He wanted to say something more, but he couldn't think of anything. After he hung up he went back to the TV. For a while he tried to watch a movie. Then he turned it off and went to bed. Before he fell asleep he thought about his father. This autumn they would take a trip to Italy.

CHAPTER 19

The fluorescent hands of the clock twisted like snakes and showed 7.10 p.m. on Tuesday 28 June. A few hours later Sweden would play Brazil. This was part of his plan. Everybody would be focused on their TV sets. No-one would think about what was happening outside in the summer night.

The basement floor was cool under his bare feet. He had been sitting in front of his mirrors since early morning. He had completed his great transformation several hours earlier, changing the pattern on his right cheek. He had painted the circular decoration with blue-black paint. Until now he had used blood-red paint. His face was even more frightening.

He put down the last brush and thought about the task awaiting him. It would be the greatest sacrifice for his sister yet, even though he had been forced to alter his plans. For a brief moment the evil forces surrounding him had got the upper hand. He had spent an entire night in the shadows below his sister's window planning his strategy. He'd sat between the two scalps and waited for the power from the earth to enter him. With his torch he had read from the holy book she had given him, and he realised that nothing prevented him from changing the order that he had prepared.

The last victim was to have been their evil father. But since the man who was supposed to meet his fate this evening had left the country suddenly, the sequence would have to be changed.

He had listened to Geronimo's heart beating in his chest. The beats were like signals from the past. His heart drummed a message: the most important thing was not to waver from his sacred task. The earth under his feet was already crying out for the third retribution.

He would wait until the third man returned from abroad. Their father would have to take his place.

As he'd sat in front of the mirrors, undergoing the great transformation, he'd looked forward to meeting his father with special anticipation. This mission required careful preparation. He'd begun by readying his tools. It had taken him more than two hours to attach a blade to the toy axe he had been given by his father as a birthday present. He was seven at the time. Even then he knew that one day he would use it against the man who had given it to him. Now the moment had finally arrived. He had reinforced the badly decorated plastic shaft with special tape used by ice hockey players.

You don't know what it's called. It's not for chopping wood. It's a tomahawk.

He felt violent contempt when he remembered how his father had given the toy to him so long ago. It was a plastic replica manufactured in an Asian country. Now, with a proper blade, he had transformed it into a real axe.

He waited until 8.30, going over the plan once more. He checked his hands, noting that they weren't shaking. Everything was under control. The arrangements he had made over the past two days would ensure that things would go well.

He packed up his weapons, a glass bottle wrapped in a handkerchief, and a rope in his backpack. Then he pulled on his helmet, turned out the light, and left the room. When he came out onto the street he looked up at the sky. It was cloudy. It could rain. He started up the moped he had stolen the day before and rode to the centre of Malmö. At the train station he entered a phone booth. He had selected one in advance that was out of the way. On one side of the window he had pasted up a fake poster for a concert at a youth club. There was no-one around. He pulled off his helmet and stood with his face pressed against the poster. Then he stuck in his phone card and dialled the number. With his left hand he held a rag over his mouth. It was just before 9 p.m. He waited as the phone rang. He was totally calm. His father answered. Hoover could hear his irritation.

That meant he had started drinking and didn't want to be disturbed.

He spoke into the rag, holding the receiver away from his mouth.

"This is Peter," he said. "I've got something that should interest you."

"What is it?" His father was still annoyed. But he believed it was Peter calling.

"Stamps. Worth almost half a million."

His father hesitated.

"Are you sure?"

"At least half a million. Maybe more."

"Speak up a little, will you?"

"We must have a bad connection."

"Where are they coming from?"

"A house in Limhamn."

His father sounded less irritable. His interest was caught. Hoover had chosen stamps because his father had once taken his own collection – which Hoover had worked on for a long time – and sold it.

"Can't it wait until tomorrow? The match against Brazil is starting soon."

"I'm leaving for Denmark tomorrow. Either you take them tonight, or someone else will."

Hoover knew his father would never let such a large sum of money fetch up in someone else's pocket. He waited, still completely calm.

"All right, I'll come," his father said. "Where are you?"

"At the boat club in Limhamn. The car park."

"Why aren't you in Malmö?"

"I told you it was a house in Limhamn, didn't I?"

"I'll be there," said his father.

Hoover hung up and put on his helmet.

He left the telephone card sitting in the phone. He had plenty of time to ride out to Limhamn. His father always got undressed before he started drinking. And he never did anything in a hurry. His laziness was as vast as his greed. He started up the moped and rode through the city until he came out on the road that led to Limhamn. There were only a few cars in the car park outside the boat club. He ditched the moped behind some bushes and threw away the keys. He pulled off his helmet and took out the axe. He put the helmet into his backpack carefully so he wouldn't damage the glass bottle.

Then he waited. His father usually parked his van in one corner of the car park when he was delivering stolen property. Hoover guessed that he would do so now. His father was a creature of habit. And he was already drunk, his judgement muddled and reactions dulled.

After 20 minutes Hoover heard the van. The headlights swept across the trees before his father turned into the car park. Just as Hoover had expected, he stopped in the corner. Hoover ran barefoot across the car park until he reached the van. When he heard his father open the driver's door, he moved quickly around to the other side. His father looked out towards the car park with his back to him. Hoover raised the axe and struck him on the back of the head with the blunt end. This was the most critical moment. He didn't want to hit him so hard that he'd die, but hard enough that his father, who was big and very strong, would be knocked out.

His father fell without a sound to the pavement. Hoover waited a moment with the axe raised, but he lay still. He reached for the car keys and unlocked the side doors of the van, dragging him over to it. It took Hoover several minutes to get the whole body inside. He got his backpack, climbed into the van, and shut the doors. He turned on the overhead light. His father was still unconscious. With the rope he tied his hands behind his back, and then his legs to a post supporting one of the seats. Next he taped his mouth shut and turned off the light. He climbed into the driver's seat and started the engine. His father had taught him to drive a few years earlier. He pulled out of the car park and headed towards the ring road that skirted Malmö. Since his face was painted he didn't want to drive where the streetlights could shine through the van's windows. He drove out onto the E65 and continued east. It was just before 10 p.m. The game was about to begin.

He had found the place by accident. He had been on his way back to Malmö after observing the police at work on the beach outside Ystad, the beach where he had carried out the first sacred task given to him by his sister. He was driving along the coast when he discovered the dock, which was almost impossible to see from the road. He realised at once that he had found the right place.

An hour later he reached the place and turned off the road with his headlights off. His father was still unconscious but was moaning softly. He hurried to loosen the rope tied to the seat and pulled him out of the van. The man groaned as Hoover dragged his body down to the dock. He turned him over on his back and tied his arms and legs to its iron rings. His father looked like an animal skin stretched out to dry. He was dressed in a wrinkled suit, his shirt unbuttoned down to his belly. Hoover pulled off his shoes and socks. Then he got the backpack from the van. There was a light breeze. A few cars drove past up on the road, but their headlights missed the dock.

When he returned, his father was conscious. His eyes were wide. He jerked his head back and forth, thrashing his arms and legs. Hoover couldn't resist stopping in the shadows to watch him. He no longer saw a human being before him. His father had undergone the transformation he had planned for him. He was an animal.

Hoover came out of the shadows and went out on the dock. His father stared at him. Hoover realised he didn't recognise him. He thought about the fear he had felt when his father stared at him. Now the tables were turned. Terror had changed its shape. He leaned down close to his father's face, so that he could see through the paint and realise it was his own son. This would be the last thing he would see. This would be the image he would carry with him when he died.

Hoover had unscrewed the cap on the glass bottle and was holding it behind his back. Quickly he poured a few drops of hydrochloric acid into his father's left eye. Somewhere underneath the tape the man started screaming. He struggled with all his might. Hoover pulled open his other eyelid and poured acid into that eye. Then he stood up and threw the bottle into the sea. Before him was a beast thrashing back and forth in its death throes. Hoover looked down at his own hands again. His fingers were quivering a little. That was all. The beast lying on the dock in front of him was twitching spasmodically.

Hoover took his knife out of his backpack and cut off the skin from the top of the animal's head. He raised the scalp to the night sky. Then he took his axe and smashed it straight through the beast's forehead with such force that the blade stuck in the wood underneath.

It was over. Soon his sister would be brought back to life.

Just before 1 a.m. he drove into Ystad. The town was deserted. For a long time he had wondered whether he was doing the right thing. But Geronimo's beating heart had convinced him. He had seen the police fumbling on the beach, he had watched them move as if in a fog outside the farm he had visited. Geronimo had exhorted him to defy them.

He turned in at the railway station. He had already picked the spot. Work was under way to replace some old sewerage pipes. There was a tarpaulin covering the excavation. He turned off the headlights and rolled down the window. From a distance he could hear some men yelling drunkenly. He got out of the van and drew back part of the tarpaulin. Then he listened again. Silence. Quickly he opened the doors of the van, dragged his father's body out, and shoved him into the hole. He replaced the tarpaulin, started the engine and drove off. It was just before 2 a.m. when he parked the van in the outdoor car park at Sturup Airport. He checked carefully to see if he had forgotten anything. There was a lot of blood in the van. He had blood on his feet. He thought about all the confusion he was going to cause, how the police would fumble even more.

Suddenly he stopped and stood motionless.

The man who had left the country might not return. He'd need a replacement. He thought about the policemen he had seen on the beach by the overturned boat. He thought about the ones he had seen outside the farmhouse where the Midsummer party was held. One of them. One of them would be sacrificed so that his sister could come back to life. He would choose one. He would find out their names and then toss stones onto a grid, just as Geronimo had done, and he would kill the one that chance selected for him.

He pulled the helmet down over his head. Then he went over to his moped, which he had ridden there the day before and left parked under a lamppost, taking a bus back to Malmö. He started up the engine and rode off. It was already light when he buried his father's scalp underneath his sister's window.

Carefully he unlocked the door to the flat in Rosengård. He stood still and listened. Then he peeked into the room where his brother lay sleeping. Everything was quiet. His mother's bed was empty. She was lying on the sofa in the living-room, sleeping with her mouth open. Next to her on the table stood a half-empty wine bottle. He covered her gently with a blanket. Then he locked himself in the bathroom and wiped the paint from his face.

It was almost 6 a.m. before he undressed and went to bed. He could hear a man coughing outside on the street. His mind was completely blank. He fell asleep at once.

Skåne

29 June–4 July 1994

CHAPTER 20

The man who lifted the tarpaulin screamed. Then he fled.

One of the ticket agents was standing outside the railway station smoking a cigarette. It was just before 7 a.m. on the morning of 29 June, and it was going to be a hot day. The agent was wrenched from his thoughts, which were focused less on selling tickets than on the trip he was about to take to Greece. He turned when he heard the scream. He saw the man drop the tarpaulin and run off towards the ferry terminal. The ticket agent flicked away his cigarette butt and walked over to the pit. He stared down at a bloody head for a moment, then dropped the tarpaulin as if it had burned him. He ran into the station, tripping over a couple of suitcases left in the middle of the floor, and grabbed one of the phones inside the stationmaster's office.

The call arrived at the Ystad station on the 90–000 line just after 7 a.m. Svedberg, who was in unusually early that morning, was summoned to take the call. When he heard the agent talking about a bloody head he froze. His hand shook as he wrote down a single word, *station*, and hung up. He dialled the wrong number twice before managing to get hold of Wallander.

"I think it's happened again," said Svedberg.

For a few brief seconds Wallander didn't understand what Svedberg meant, even though every time the phone rang he feared that very thing. But now he experienced a moment of shock, or perhaps a desperate attempt at denial.

He knew he would never forget this moment. Fleetingly he thought that it was like having a premonition of his own death, a moment when denial and escape were impossible. *I think it's happened again.* He felt as if he were a wind-up toy. Svedberg's stammered words were like hands twisting the key attached to his back. He was wrenched out of his sleep and his bed, out of dreams he couldn't remember but which might have been pleasant. He got dressed in a desperate frenzy, buttons popping off, and his shoelaces flopped untied as he raced down the stairs and outside.

When he came screeching to a stop in his car, which still needed its M.O.T., Svedberg was already there. Directed by Norén, some officers were busy rolling out the striped crime-scene tape. Svedberg was awkwardly patting the weeping ticket agent on the shoulder, while some men in blue overalls stared into the pit, now transformed into a nightmare. Wallander left his door open and ran over to Svedberg. Why he ran he didn't really know. Maybe his internal police mechanism had started to speed up. Or maybe he was so afraid of what he was going to see that he simply didn't dare approach it slowly.

Svedberg was white in the face. He nodded towards the pit. Wallander walked slowly over and took several deep breaths before looking into the hole.

It was worse than he could have imagined. He was looking straight into a dead man's brain. Ann-Britt Höglund arrived next to Wallander. She flinched and turned away. Her reaction made him start to think clearly.

"No doubt about it," he said to Höglund, turning back to the pit. "It's him again."

She was very pale. Wallander was afraid she was going to faint. He put his arm around her shoulders.

"Are you OK?" he asked.

She nodded.

Martinsson arrived with Hansson. Wallander saw them both give a start when they looked in the hole. He was overcome with rage. The man who had done this had to be stopped.

"It must be the same killer," said Hansson in an unsteady voice. "Isn't it ever going to end? I can't take responsibility for this any more. Did Björk know about this before he left? I'm going to ask for reinforcements from the National Criminal Bureau."

"Do that," said Wallander. "But first let's get him out of there and see whether we can solve this ourselves."

Hansson stared in disbelief at Wallander, who realised that Hansson thought they were going to have to lift the dead man out themselves.

A large crowd had gathered outside the cordon. Wallander remembered what he had sensed in connection with Carlman's murder. He took Norén aside and asked him to borrow a camera from Nyberg and take pictures, as discreetly as possible, of the people standing outside the cordon. Meanwhile the emergency van from the fire department had arrived on the scene. Nyberg was directing his crew around the pit. Wallander went over to him, trying to avoid looking at the corpse.

"Once again," said Nyberg. He wasn't being cynical. Their eyes met.

"We've got to catch him," said Wallander.

"As soon as possible, I hope," said Nyberg. He lay down on his stomach so he could study the dead man's face. When he straightened up again he called to Wallander, who was just heading off to talk to Svedberg. He came back.

"Did you see his eyes?" asked Nyberg.

Wallander shook his head.

"What about them?"

Nyberg grimaced.

"Apparently the murderer wasn't content with taking a scalp this time," said Nyberg. "It looks like he poked his eyes out too."

"What do you mean?"

"The man in the pit doesn't have any eyes," said Nyberg. "There are two holes where they used to be."

It took them two hours to get the body out. Wallander talked to the workman who had lifted the tarpaulin and the ticket agent who had stood by the steps of the station dreaming of Greece. He noted the times that they had seen the body. He asked Nyberg to search the dead man's pockets to see if they could establish his identity, but they were empty.

"Nothing at all?" asked Wallander in surprise.

"Not a thing," said Nyberg. "But something may have fallen out. We'll look around down there."

They hauled him up in a sling. Wallander forced himself to look at his face. Nyberg was right. The man had no eyes. The torn-off hair made it seem that it was a dead animal, not a human being lying on the plastic sheet at his feet.

Wallander sat down on the steps of the station. He studied his notes. He called Martinsson, who was talking to a doctor.

"We know he hasn't been here long," he said. "I talked to the workmen replacing the sewerage pipes. They put the tarpaulin down at 4 p.m. yesterday. So the body was put there between then and 7 a.m. this morning."

"There are a lot of people around here in the evenings," said Martinsson. "People taking a walk, traffic to and from the station and the ferry terminal. It must have happened during the night."

"How long has he been dead?" asked Wallander. "That's what I want to know. And who he is."

Nyberg hadn't found a wallet. They had nothing to help establish the man's identity. Höglund came over and sat down next to them.

"Hansson's talking about requesting reinforcements from the National Criminal Bureau," she said.

"I know," said Wallander. "But he won't do anything until I tell him to. What did the doctor say?"

She looked at her notes.

"About 45 years old," she said. "Strong, well-built."

"That makes him the youngest one so far," said Wallander.

"Strange place to hide the body," said Martinsson. "Did he think that work would stop during the summer holiday?"

"Maybe he just wanted to get rid of it," said Höglund.

"Then why did he pick this pit?" asked Martinsson. "It must have been a lot of trouble to get him into it. And there was the risk that someone might see him."

"Maybe he wanted the body to be found," Wallander said thoughtfully. "We can't rule out that possibility."

They looked at him in astonishment, waiting for him to explain, but he remained silent.

The body was taken away to Malmö. They left for the police station. Norén had been taking pictures of the large crowd milling around outside the cordoned-off area.

Mats Ekholm had shown up earlier that morning, and stared at the corpse for a long time. Wallander had gone over to him.

"You got your wish," he said. "Another victim."

"I didn't wish for this," replied Ekholm, shaking his head.

Now Wallander regretted his remark. He would have to explain to Ekholm what he'd meant.

Just after 10 a.m. they closed the door to the conference room, Hansson again giving instructions that calls weren't to be put through. But they had barely started the meeting when the phone rang. Hansson snatched the receiver and barked into it, red with anger. But he sank slowly back in his chair. Wallander knew at once that someone very important was on the line. Hansson adopted Björk's obsequiousness. He made some brief comments, answered questions, but mostly listened. When the call was over he placed the receiver back as if it were a fragile antique.

"Let me guess – the national police board," said Wallander. "Or the chief public prosecutor. Or a TV reporter."

"The commissioner of the national police," replied Hansson. "He expressed as much dissatisfaction as encouragement."

"Sounds like a strange combination," Höglund said drily.

"He's welcome to come down here and help," said Svedberg.

"What does he know about police work?" Martinsson spluttered. "Absolutely nothing."

Wallander tapped his pen on the table. Everyone was upset and uncertain of what to do next, and he knew they had very little time before they would be subjected to a barrage of criticism. They would never be totally immune from outside pressure. They could only counteract it by focusing their attention inward on the shifting centre of the search. He tried to collect his thoughts, knowing that they didn't have a thing to go on.

"What do we know?" Wallander began, looking around the table. He felt like a vicar who had lost his faith. But he had to say something to spur them on again as a unit.

"The man wound up in that pit sometime last night. Let's assume that it took place in the early hours. We can assume that he wasn't murdered there. There would have been a lot of blood at the place where he was killed. Nyberg hadn't found a thing by the time we left, so he must have been transported there in a vehicle. Maybe the people working at the hot dog stand next to the railway crossing noticed something. It appears that he was killed by a powerful blow from the front that went all the way through his skull."

Martinsson turned completely white. He got up and left the room without a word. Wallander decided to carry on without him.

"He was scalped like the others. And he had his eyes put out. The doctor wasn't sure how, but there were some spots near the eyes that might indicate a corrosive agent. Maybe our specialist has some opinion on what this indicates."

Wallander turned to Ekholm.

"Not yet," said Ekholm. "It's too soon."

"We don't need a comprehensive analysis," said Wallander firmly. "At this stage we have to think out loud. Maybe we'll uncover the truth. We don't believe in miracles. But we don't have much else to go on."

"I think the fact that the eyes were put out means something," said Ekholm. "We can assume that the same man is involved. This victim was younger than the other two. And he suffered the loss of his sight, presumably while he was still alive. It must have been excruciating. The murderer took scalps from the first two he killed, and this time too. But he also blinded his victim. Why? What kind of revenge was he exacting this time?"

"The man must be a psychopath," said Hansson suddenly. "A serial killer of the kind I thought existed only in the United States. But here? In Ystad? In Skåne?"

"There's still something controlled about him," said Ekholm. "He knows what he wants. He kills and scalps. He pokes out or dissolves the eyes. There's nothing to indicate unbridled rage. Psychopath, yes. But one in control of his actions."

"Are there instances of something like this having happened before?" asked Höglund.

"Not that I can recall," replied Ekholm. "At least not here in Sweden. In America studies have been done on the role that eyes have played in psychopathic killings. I'll read about it today."

Wallander had been half-listening to the conversation. A thought that he couldn't quite yet grasp had popped into his head. It was something about eyes. Something somebody had said about eyes. What was it? He turned his attention to the meeting. But the thought lingered like an uneasy ache.

"Anything else?" he asked Ekholm.

"Not at the moment."

Martinsson came back into the room. He was still very pale.

"I've got an idea," said Wallander. "After hearing Mats I'm convinced that the murder took place elsewhere. The man must have screamed. Someone would have seen or heard something if it happened outside the railway station. We'll have to confirm this. But for the time being let's say I'm right. Why then did he pick that pit to hide the body? I talked to one of the workmen. Persson was his name, Erik Persson. He said that the pit had been excavated on Monday afternoon. Less than two days ago. The killer could have stumbled on it by chance, of course. But that doesn't fit with the fact that he seems to plan everything he does carefully. The killer must have been outside the railway station at some time after Monday afternoon. He must have looked into the pit to see if it was deep enough. We'll need to interview all the workmen. Did they notice anybody hanging around? And did the staff at the railway station notice anything?"

Everyone around the table was listening intently, making him feel that his ideas weren't completely off track.

"I also think the question of whether it was meant as a hiding place is crucial," he went on. "He must have known that the body would be found the next morning. So why did he choose the pit? So it would be discovered? Or is there another explanation?"

Everyone in the room waited for him to continue.

"Is he taunting us?" said Wallander. "Does he want to help us? Or is he trying to fool us? Does he want to trick me into thinking exactly the way I'm thinking now? What would the alternative be?"

No-one answered him.

"The timing is also important," said Wallander. "This murder was very recent. That might assist us."

"For that we need help," said Hansson. Clearly he'd been waiting for an opportunity to bring up the question of reinforcements.

"Not yet," said Wallander. "Let's decide later on today. Or maybe tomorrow. As far as I know, no-one in this room is going on holiday soon. Let's keep it to this group for a few more days. Then we can seek reinforcements if necessary."

"What about the connection?" said Wallander in conclusion. "Now there's one more person to fit into the puzzle we're trying to piece together."

He looked around the table once more.

"We have to realise that he could strike again," he said. "In fact, we should assume that he will."

The meeting was over. They all knew what they had to do. Wallander remained sitting at the table while the others filed out of the door. He was trying to recapture that thought. He was sure that it was something someone had said in relation to the investigation. Somebody had mentioned eyes. He thought back to the day he'd first heard that Wetterstedt had been found murdered. He searched his memory, but found nothing. Irritated, he tossed his pen aside and went out to the canteen for a cup of coffee. When he got back to his office he set the coffee cup on his desk and was about to shut the door when he saw Svedberg coming down the hall. Svedberg was walking fast. He only did that when something important had happened. Wallander instantly got a knot in his stomach. Not another one, he thought. We just can't cope.

"I think we've found the scene of the crime," said Svedberg.

"Where?"

"Our colleagues at Sturup found a delivery van soaked in blood in the airport car park."

A van. That would fit.

A few minutes later they left the station. Wallander couldn't remember ever in his life feeling that he had so little time. When they reached the edge of town he told Svedberg to turn on the police lights. In the fields beside the road a farmer was harvesting his rape.

CHAPTER 21

They arrived at Sturup Airport. The air felt stagnant in the oppressive heat of the late morning. In a very short period of time they determined that the murder had very likely taken place in the van. They also thought they knew who the dead man was.

The van was a late-1960s Ford, with sliding side doors, and painted black sloppily, the original grey showing through in patches. The body was dented in many places. Parked in an isolated spot, it resembled an old prizefighter who had just been counted out, hanging on the ropes in his corner.

Wallander knew some of the officers at Sturup. He also knew that he wasn't particularly popular after an incident that had occurred the year before. The side doors of the Ford were standing open. Some forensic technicians were already inspecting it. An officer named Waldemarsson came to meet them. Even though they had driven like madmen from Ystad, Wallander tried to appear totally nonchalant.

"It's not a pretty sight," said Waldemarsson as they shook hands.

Wallander and Svedberg went over to the Ford and looked in. Waldemarsson shone a torch inside. The floor of the van was covered with blood.

"We heard on the morning news that he had struck again," said Waldemarsson. "I called and talked to a woman detective whose name I can't remember."

"Ann-Britt Höglund," said Svedberg.

"Whatever her name is, she said you were looking for a crime scene," Waldemarsson went on. "And a vehicle."

Wallander nodded.

"When did you find the van?" he asked.

"We check the car park every day. We've had a number of car thefts here. But you know all about that."

Wallander nodded again. During the investigation into the export of stolen cars to Poland he had been in contact with the airport police several times.

"The van wasn't here yesterday afternoon," said Waldemarsson. "It couldn't have been here more than 18 hours."

"Who's the owner?" asked Wallander.

Waldemarsson took a notebook out of his pocket.

"Björn Fredman," he said. "He lives in Malmö. We called his number but didn't get an answer."

"Could he be the one we found in the pit?"

"We know something about Fredman," said Waldemarsson. "Malmö has given us information. He was known as a fence, and has done time on several occasions."

"A fence," said Wallander, feeling a flash of excitement. "For works of art?"

"They didn't say. You'll have to talk with our colleagues."

"Who should I ask for?" he demanded, taking his mobile phone out of his pocket.

"An Inspector Sten Forsfält."

Wallander got hold of Forsfält. He explained who he was. For a few seconds the conversation was drowned out by the noise of a plane. Wallander thought of the trip to Italy he planned to take with his father.

"First of all, we have to identify the man," said Wallander when the plane had climbed away in the direction of Stockholm.

"What did he look like?" asked Forsfält. "I met Fredman several times."

Wallander gave as accurate a description as he could.

"It might be him," said Forsfält. "He was big, at any rate."

Wallander thought for a moment.

"Can you drive to the hospital?" he asked. "We need a positive identification as quickly as possible."

"Sure, I can do that," said Forsfält.

"Prepare yourself, because it's a hideous sight," said Wallander. "He had his eyes poked out. Or burnt away."

Forsfält didn't reply.

"We're coming to Malmö," said Wallander. "We need some help getting into his flat. Did he have any family?"

"He was divorced," said Forsfält. "Last time he was in, it was for battery."

"I thought it was for fencing stolen property."

"That too. Fredman kept busy. But not doing anything legal. He was consistent on that score."

Wallander said goodbye and called Hansson to give him a brief run-down.

"Good," said Hansson. "Let me know as soon as you have more information. By the way, do you know who called?"

"The national commissioner again?"

"Almost. Lisa Holgersson. Björk's successor. She wished us luck. Said she just wanted to check on the situation."

"It's great that people are wishing us luck," said Wallander, who couldn't understand why Hansson was telling him about the call in such an ironic tone.

Wallander borrowed Waldemarsson's torch and shone it inside the van. He saw a footprint in the blood. He leaned forward.

"That's not a shoe print. It's a left foot."

"A bare foot?" said Svedberg. "So he wades around barefoot in the blood of the people he kills?"

"We don't know that it's a he," said Wallander dubiously.

They said goodbye to Waldemarsson and his colleagues. Wallander waited in the car while Svedberg ran to the airport café and bought some sandwiches.

"The prices are outrageous," he complained when he returned. Wallander didn't bother answering.

"Just drive," was all he said.

It was past midday when they stopped outside the police station in

Malmö. As he stepped out of the car Wallander saw Björk heading towards him. Björk stopped and stared, as if he had caught Wallander doing something he shouldn't.

"You, here?" he said.

"We need you back," said Wallander in an attempt at a joke. Then he explained what had happened.

"It's appalling what's going on," said Björk, and Wallander could hear that his anxious tone was genuine. It hadn't occurred to him before that Björk might miss the people he worked with for so many years in Ystad.

"Nothing is quite the same," said Wallander.

"How's Hansson doing?"

"I don't think he's enjoying his role."

"He can call if he needs any help."

"I'll tell him."

Björk left and they went into the station. Forsfält still wasn't back from the hospital. They drank coffee in the canteen while they waited.

"I wonder what it would be like to work here," said Svedberg, looking around at all the policemen eating lunch.

"One day we may all wind up here," said Wallander. "If they close down the district. One police station per county."

"That would never work."

"No, but it could happen. The national police board and those bureaucrats have one thing in common. They always try to do the impossible."

Forsfält appeared. They stood up, shook hands, and followed him to his office. Wallander had a favourable impression of him. He reminded him of Rydberg. Forsfält was at least 60, with a friendly face. He had a slight limp. Wallander sat down and looked at some pictures of laughing children tacked up on the wall. He guessed that they were Forsfält's grandchildren.

"Björn Fredman," said Forsfält. "It's him, all right. He looked appalling. Who would do such a thing?"

"If we only knew," said Wallander. "Who was Fredman?"

"A man of about 45 who never had an honest job in his life," Forsfält began. "I don't have all of the details. But I've asked the computer people for his records. He was a fence and he did time for battery. Quite violent attacks, as I recall."

"Was he involved in fencing stolen art?"

"Not that I can remember."

"That's a pity," said Wallander. "That would have linked him to Wetterstedt and Carlman."

"I have a hard time imagining that Fredman and Wetterstedt could have had much use for each other," said Forsfält.

"Why not?"

"Let me put it bluntly," said Forsfält. "Björn Fredman was what used to be called a rough customer. He drank a lot and got into fights. His education was nearly nonexistent, although he could read, write, and do arithmetic tolerably well. His interests could hardly be called sophisticated. And he was a brutal man. I interrogated him myself a number of times. His vocabulary consisted almost exclusively of swear words."

Wallander listened. When Forsfält stopped he looked at Svedberg.

"We're back to square one again," Wallander said slowly. "If there's no connection between Fredman and the other two."

"There could be things I don't know about," said Forsfält.

"I'm just thinking out loud," said Wallander.

"What about his family?" said Svedberg. "Do they live here in Malmö?"

"He's been divorced for a number of years," said Forsfält. "I'm sure of that."

He picked up the phone and made a call. After a few minutes a secretary came in with a file on Fredman and handed it to Forsfält. He took a quick look and then put it down on the table.

"He got divorced in 1991. His wife stayed in their flat with the children. It's in Rosengård. There are three children. The youngest was just a baby when they split up. Fredman moved back to a flat on Stenbrottsgatan that he'd kept for many years. He used it mostly as an office and storeroom. I don't think his wife knew about it. That's where he also took his other women."

"We'll start with his flat," said Wallander. "The family can wait. You'll see that they're notified of his death?"

Forsfält nodded. Svedberg had gone out to the hall to call Ystad. Wallander stood by the window, trying to decide what was most important. There seemed to be no link between the first two victims and Fredman. For the first time he had a premonition that they were following a false lead. Was there a completely different explanation for the murders? He decided he would go over all the investigative material that evening with an open mind. Svedberg came back and stood next to him.

"Hansson was relieved," he said.

Wallander nodded. But he didn't say a word.

"According to Martinsson an important message came from Interpol about the girl," Svedberg went on.

Wallander hadn't been paying attention. He had to ask Svedberg to repeat himself. The girl seemed to be part of something that had happened a long time ago. And yet he knew that sooner or later he'd have to take up her case again. They stood in silence.

"I don't like it in Malmö," said Svedberg suddenly. "I only feel happy when I'm home in Ystad."

Svedberg hated to leave the town of his birth. At the station it had become a running joke. Wallander wondered when he himself ever really felt happy. But then he remembered the last time. When Linda appeared at his door so early on Sunday morning.

Forsfält came to get them. They took the lift down to the car park and then drove out towards an industrial area north of the city. The wind had started to blow. The sky was still cloudless. Wallander sat next to Forsfält in the front seat.

"Did you know Rydberg?" he asked.

"Did I know Rydberg?" he replied slowly. "I certainly did. Quite well. He used to come to Malmö sometimes."

Wallander was surprised at his answer. He'd always thought that

211

Rydberg had discarded everything to do with the job, including his friends.

"He was the one who taught me everything I know," said Wallander.

"It was tragic that he left us so soon," said Forsfält. "He should have lived longer. He'd always dreamed of going to Iceland."

"Iceland?"

Forsfält nodded.

"That was his big dream. To go to Iceland. But it didn't happen." Wallander was struck by the realisation that Rydberg had kept something from him. He wouldn't have guessed that Rydberg dreamt of a pilgrimage to Iceland. He hadn't imagined that Rydberg had any dreams at all, or indeed any secrets.

Forsfält pulled up outside a three-storey block of flats. He pointed to a row of windows on the ground floor with the curtains drawn. The building was old and poorly maintained. The glass on the main door was boarded up with a piece of wood. Wallander had a feeling that he was walking into a building that should no longer exist. Isn't this building's existence in defiance of the constitution? he thought sarcastically. There was a stench of urine in the stairwell.

Forsfält unlocked the door. Wallander wondered where he'd got the keys. They walked into the hall and turned on the light. Some junk mail lay on the floor. Wallander let Forsfält lead the way. They walked through the flat. It consisted of three rooms and a tiny, cramped kitchen that looked out on a warehouse. Apart from the bed, which appeared new, the flat seemed neglected. The furniture was strewn haphazardly around the rooms. Some dusty, cheap porcelain figures stood on a 1950s-style bookshelf in the living-room. In one corner was a stack of magazines and some dumbbells. To his great surprise Wallander noticed a CD of Turkish folk music on the sofa. The curtains were drawn.

Forsfält went around turning on all the lights. Wallander followed him, while Svedberg took a seat on a chair in the kitchen and called Hansson. Wallander pushed open the door to the pantry with his foot. Inside were several unopened boxes of Grant's whisky. They had been shipped from the Scottish distillery to a wine merchant in Belgium. He wondered how they had ended up in Fredman's flat.

Forsfält came into the kitchen with a couple of photographs of the owner. Wallander nodded. There was no doubt that it was him they'd found. He went back to the living-room and tried to decide what he really hoped to discover. Fredman's flat was the exact opposite of Wetterstedt's and Carlman's houses. This is what Sweden is like, he thought. The differences between people are just as great now as they were when some lived in manor houses and others in hovels.

He noticed a desk piled with magazines about antiques. They must be related to Fredman's activities as a fence. There was only one drawer in the desk. Inside was a stack of receipts, broken pens, a cigarette case, and a framed photograph. It was of Fredman and his family. He was smiling broadly at the camera. Next to him sat his wife, holding a newborn baby in her arms. Behind the mother stood a girl in her early teens. She was staring into the camera, a look of terror in her eyes. Next to her, directly behind the mother, stood a boy a few years younger. His face was pinched, as if he was resisting something. Wallander took the photo over to the window and pulled back the curtain. He stared at it for a long time. An unhappy family? A family that hadn't yet encountered unhappiness? A newborn child who had no idea what awaited him? There was something in the picture that disturbed him, but he couldn't put his finger on it. He took it into the bedroom, where Forsfält was looking under the bed.

"You said that he did time for battery," said Wallander.

Forsfält got up and looked at the photo.

"He beat his wife senseless," he said. "He beat her up when she was pregnant. He beat her when the child was a baby. But strangely enough, he never went to prison for it. Once he broke a cab driver's nose. He beat a former partner half to death when he suspected him of cheating."

They continued searching the flat. Svedberg had finished talking to Hansson. He shook his head when Wallander asked him if anything had happened. It took them two hours to search the place. Wallander's flat was idyllic compared to Fredman's. They found nothing but a travel bag with antique candlesticks in it. Wallander understood why Fredman's language was peppered with swear words. The flat was just as empty and inarticulate as his vocabulary.

Finally they left the flat. The wind had picked up. Forsfält called the station and got word that Fredman's family had been informed of his death.

"I'd like to talk to them," said Wallander when they got into the car. "But it's probably better to wait until tomorrow."

He knew he wasn't being honest. He hated disturbing a family whose relative had suffered a violent death. Above all, he couldn't bear talking to children who had just lost a parent. Waiting until the next day would make no difference to them. But it gave Wallander breathing space.

They said goodbye outside the station. Forsfält would get hold of Hansson to clear up formalities between the two police districts. He made an appointment to meet with Wallander the next morning.

Wallander and Svedberg drove back towards Ystad. Wallander's mind was swarming with ideas. They remained silent.

CHAPTER 22

Copenhagen's skyline was just visible across the Sound in the hazy sunlight.

Wallander wondered whether he'd get to meet Baiba there or whether the killer they sought – about whom they seemed to know less, if that were possible – would force him to postpone his holiday.

He stood waiting outside the hovercraft terminal in Malmö. It was the morning of the last day of June. Wallander had decided the night before to take Höglund rather than Svedberg when he returned to Malmö to talk to Fredman's family. She'd asked whether they could leave early enough for her to do an errand on the way. Svedberg hadn't complained in the least at being left behind. His relief at not having to leave Ystad two days in a row was unmistakable. While Höglund took care of her errand in the terminal – Wallander hadn't asked what it was – he'd walked along the pier. A hydrofoil, the *Runner*, he thought it said, was on its way out of the harbour. It was hot. He took off his jacket and slung it over his shoulder, yawning.

After they'd returned from Malmö the night before, he'd called a meeting with the investigative team, since they were all still there. He and Hansson had also held an impromptu press conference. Ekholm had attended the meeting. He was still working on a psychological profile of the killer. But they had agreed that Wallander should inform the press that they were looking for someone who wasn't considered dangerous to the public, but who was certainly extremely dangerous to his victims.

There had been differing opinions on whether it would be wise to take this action. But Wallander had insisted that they couldn't ignore the possibility that someone might come forward out of sheer self-preservation. The press were delighted with this information, but Wallander felt uncomfortable, knowing that they were giving the public the best possible news, since the nation was about to close down for the summer holiday. Afterwards, when both the meeting and the press conference were over, he was exhausted.

He still hadn't gone over the telex from Interpol with Martinsson. The girl had vanished from Santiago de los Treinta Caballeros in December. Her father, Pedro Santana, a farm worker, had reported her disappearance to the police on 14 January. Dolores María, who was then 16 years old, but who had turned 17 on 18 February – a fact that made Wallander particularly depressed – had been in Santiago looking for work as a housekeeper. Before then she had lived with her father in a little village 70 kilometres outside the city. She had been staying with a distant relative when she had disappeared. Judging by the scanty report, the Dominican police had not taken much interest in her case, though her father had hounded them to keep looking for her, managing to get a journalist involved, but eventually the police decided that she had probably left the country.

The trail ended there. Interpol's comments were brief. Dolores María Santana hadn't been seen in any of the countries belonging to the international police network. Until now.

"She disappears in a city called Santiago," said Wallander. "About six months later she pops up in farmer Salomonsson's rape field, where she burns herself to death. What does that mean?"

Martinsson shook his head dejectedly. Wallander was so tired he could hardly think, but he roused himself. Martinsson's apathy made him furious.

"We know that she didn't vanish from the face of the earth," he said with determination. "We know that she had been in Helsingborg and got a lift from a man from Smedstorp. She seemed to be fleeing something. And we know she's dead. We should send a message back to Interpol telling them all this. And I want you to make a special request that the girl's father be properly informed of her death. When this other nightmare is over, we'll have to find out what terrified her in Helsingborg. I suggest you make contact with our colleagues there tomorrow. They might have some idea what happened."

After this muted outburst, Wallander drove home. He stopped and ordered a hamburger. Newspaper placards were posted everywhere, proclaiming the latest news on the World Cup. He had a powerful urge to rip them down and scream that enough was enough. But instead he waited patiently in line, paid, picked up his hamburger, and went back to his car.

When he got home he sat down at the kitchen table, tore open the bag and ate. He drank a glass of water with the hamburger. Then he made some strong coffee and cleared the table, forcing himself to go over all the investigative material again. The feeling that they had been sidetracked was still with him. Wallander hadn't laid the clues they were following. But he *was* the one who was leading the investigative group, and determining the course that they took. He tried to see where they should have paid more attention, whether the link between Wetterstedt and Carlman was already clearly visible, but unnoticed.

He went over all the evidence that they had gathered, sometimes solid, sometimes not. Next to him he had a notebook in which he listed all the unanswered questions. It troubled him that the results from many of the forensic tests still weren't available. Although it was past midnight, he was sorely tempted to call up Nyberg and ask him whether the laboratory in Linköping had closed for the summer. But he refrained. He sat bent over his papers until his back hurt and the letters began blurring on the page.

He didn't give up until after 2 a.m., when he'd concluded that they couldn't do anything but continue on the path that they had chosen. There must be a connection between the murdered men. Perhaps the fact that Björn Fredman didn't seem to fit with the others might point to the solution.

The pile of dirty laundry was still on the floor, reminding him of the chaos inside his own head. Once again he had forgotten to get an appointment for his car. Would they have to request reinforcements from the National Criminal Bureau? He decided to talk to Hansson about it first thing, after a few hours' sleep.

But by the time he got up at 6 a.m., he'd changed his mind. He wanted to wait one more day. Instead he called Nyberg and complained about the laboratory. He had expected Nyberg to be angry, but to Wallander's great surprise he had agreed that it was taking an unusually long time and promised to follow the matter up. They'd discussed Nyberg's examination of the pit where they'd found Fredman. Traces of blood indicated that the killer had parked his car right next to it. Nyberg had also managed to get out to Sturup Airport and look at Fredman's van. There was no doubt that it had been used to transport the body. But Nyberg didn't think that the murder could have taken place in it.

"Fredman was big and strong," he said. "I can't see how he could have been killed inside the van. I think the murder happened somewhere else."

"So we must find out who drove the van," said Wallander, "and where the murder occurred."

Wallander had arrived at the station just after 7 a.m. He'd called Ekholm at his hotel and found him in the breakfast room.

"I want you to concentrate on the eyes," he said. "I don't know why. But I'm convinced they're important. Maybe crucial. Why would he do that to Fredman and not to the others? That's what I want to know."

"The whole thing has to be viewed in its entirety," said Ekholm. "A psychopath almost always creates rituals, which he then follows as if they were written in a sacred book. The eyes have to fit into that framework."

"Whatever," Wallander said curtly. "But I want to know why only Fredman had his eyes put out. Framework or no framework."

"It was probably acid," said Ekholm.

Wallander had forgotten to ask Nyberg about that.

"Can we assume that's the case?" he asked.

"It seems so. Someone poured acid in Fredman's eyes."

Wallander grimaced.

"We'll talk this afternoon," he said and hung up.

Soon afterwards he had left Ystad with Höglund. It was a relief to get out of the station. Reporters were calling all the time. And now the public had started calling too. The hunt for the killer had become a national concern. Wallander knew that this was inevitable, and also useful. But it was an enormous task to record and check on all the information that was flooding in.

Höglund emerged from the terminal and caught up with him on the pier.

"I wonder what kind of summer it'll be this year," he said.

"My grandmother in Älmhult predicts the weather," said Höglund. "She says it's going to be long, hot and dry."

"Is she usually right?"

"Almost always."

"I think it'll be the opposite. Rainy and cold and crappy."

"Can you predict the weather too?"

"No."

They walked back to the car. Wallander wondered what she'd been doing in the terminal. But he didn't ask.

They pulled up in front of the Malmö police station at 9.30 a.m. Forsfält was waiting on the footpath. He got into the back seat and gave Wallander directions, talking to Höglund about the weather at the same time. When they stopped outside the block of flats in Rosengård he told them what had happened the day before.

"The ex-wife took the news of Fredman's death calmly. One of my colleagues smelt alcohol on her breath. The place was a mess. The younger boy is only four. He probably won't comprehend that his father, whom he almost never saw, is dead. But the older son understood. The daughter wasn't home."

"What's her name?" asked Wallander.

"The daughter?"

"The wife. The ex-wife."

"Anette Fredman."

"Does she have a job?"

"Not that I know of."

"How does she make a living?"

"No idea. But I doubt that Fredman was very generous to his family."

They got out of the car and went inside, taking the lift up to the fifth floor. Someone had smashed a bottle on the floor of the lift. Wallander glanced at Höglund and shook his head. Forsfält rang the doorbell. After a while the door opened. The woman standing before them was very thin and pale, and dressed all in black. She looked with terror at the two unfamiliar faces. As they hung up their coats in the hall, Wallander saw someone peer quickly through the doorway to the flat and then disappear. He guessed it was the older son or the daughter.

Forsfält introduced them, speaking gently and calmly. There was nothing hurried in his demeanour. Wallander could see he might be able to learn from Forsfält as he once had from Rydberg.

They went into the living-room. It looked as though she had cleaned up. The living-room had a sofa and chairs that looked almost unused. There was a stereo, a video, and a Bang & Olufsen TV, a Danish brand Wallander had had his eye on but couldn't afford. She had set out cups and saucers. Wallander listened. There was a four-year-old boy in the family. Children that age weren't quiet. They sat down.

"Let me say how sorry I am for the inconvenience," he said, trying to be as friendly as Forsfält.

"Thank you," she replied in a low, fragile voice, that sounded as if it might break at any moment.

"Unfortunately I have to ask you some questions," continued Wallander. "I wish they could wait."

She nodded but said nothing. At that moment the door into the living-room opened. A well-built boy of about 14 entered. He had an open, friendly face, but his eyes were wary.

"This is my son," she said. "His name is Stefan."

The boy was very polite, Wallander noticed. He came and shook hands with each of them. Then he sat down next to his mother on the sofa.

"I'd like him to hear this too," she said.

"That's fine," said Wallander. "I'm sorry about what happened to your father."

"We didn't see each other very much," replied the boy. "But thank you."

Wallander was impressed. He seemed mature for his age, perhaps because he'd had to fill the void left by his father.

"You have another son, don't you?" Wallander went on.

"He's with a friend of mine, playing with her son," said Anette Fredman. "I thought it would be better. His name is Jens."

Wallander nodded to Höglund, who was taking notes.

"And a daughter too?"

"Her name is Louise."

"But she's not here?"

"She's away for a few days, resting."

It was the boy who'd answered. He took over from his mother, as if he wanted to spare her a heavy burden. His answer had been calm and polite. But something wasn't quite right. It had come a little too quickly. Or was it that the boy had hesitated before replying? Wallander was immediately on the alert.

"I understand that this must be trying for her," he continued cautiously.

"She's very sensitive," replied her brother.

Something doesn't add up here, Wallander thought again. He knew he shouldn't press this now. It would be better to come back to the girl later. He glanced at Höglund, but she didn't seem to have noticed.

"I won't have to repeat the questions you've already answered," said Wallander, pouring himself a cup of coffee, to show that everything was normal. The boy had his eyes fixed on him. There was a wariness in his eyes that reminded Wallander of a bird, as though he'd been forced to take on responsibility too soon. The thought depressed him.

Nothing troubled Wallander more than seeing children and young people damaged.

"I know that you hadn't seen Mr Fredman in several weeks," he went on. "Was that true of Louise too?"

This time it was the mother who answered.

"The last time he was home, Louise was out," she said. "It's been several months since she saw him."

Wallander approached the most difficult questions gingerly. He knew that he would provoke painful memories, but he tried to move as gently as he could.

"He was murdered," he said. "Do either of you have any idea who might have done it?"

Anette Fredman looked at him with a surprised expression on her face. Her reply was shrill, her previous reticence gone.

"You ought to be asking who wouldn't have killed him. I don't know how many times I wished I'd had the strength to do it myself."

Her son put his arm around her.

"I don't think that's what the detective meant," he said soothingly. She quickly pulled herself together after her outburst.

"I don't know," she said. "And I don't want to know. But I don't feel guilty for being relieved that he won't be walking through this door again."

She stood up abruptly and left the room. Wallander could tell that Höglund couldn't decide whether she should follow. But she remained seated as the boy began to speak.

"Mummy is extremely upset," he said.

"We understand that," said Wallander with sympathy. "But you seem to be calm. Maybe you have some thoughts. I know this must be unpleasant for you."

"I don't think it could be anybody except one of Dad's friends. My Dad was a thief," he added. "He also used to beat people up. I'm not sure, but I think he was what people call an enforcer. He collected debts, he threatened people."

"How do you know that?"

"I don't know."

"Are you thinking about somebody in particular?"

"No."

Wallander let him think.

"No," he repeated. "I don't know."

Anette Fredman returned.

"Can either of you recall whether he had any contact with a man named Gustaf Wetterstedt? He was the minister of justice for a time. Or an art dealer named Arne Carlman?"

After looking at each other for confirmation, they both shook their heads. The interview limped along. Wallander tried to help them remember details. Now and then Forsfält interjected. Finally Wallander could see that they weren't going to get any further. He decided not to ask about the daughter again. Instead he nodded to Höglund and Forsfält that he was finished. But as they said goodbye out in the hall he told them he would have to call on them again, probably quite soon. He gave them his phone numbers at the station and at home.

Out on the street he saw Anette Fredman standing in the window looking down at them.

"The daughter," said Wallander. "Louise Fredman. What do we know about her?"

"She wasn't here yesterday either," said Forsfält. "She may have left home, of course. She's 17."

Wallander stood for a moment in thought.

"I want to talk to her," he said.

The others didn't react. He knew that he was the only one who had noticed the rapid change when he asked about her. He thought about the boy, Stefan, with his wary eyes. He felt sorry for him.

"That'll be all for now," said Wallander when they parted outside the Malmö police station. "But let's keep in touch."

They shook hands with Forsfält and said goodbye.

They drove back towards Ystad, through the countryside of Skåne during the most beautiful time of the year. Höglund leaned back in her seat and closed her eyes. Wallander could hear her humming.

He wished he could share her ability to switch off from the investigation, which made him so anxious. Rydberg had said many times that a police officer was never completely free. For once, Wallander wished that Rydberg was wrong.

Just after they passed the exit to Skurup he noticed that Höglund had fallen asleep. He drove as smoothly as he could, not wanting to wake her. She didn't open her eyes until he had to stop at the roundabout on the outskirts of Ystad. At that moment the phone rang. He nodded to her to answer it. He couldn't tell who it was, but he saw at once that something serious had happened. She listened in silence. They were almost at the station when she hung up.

"That was Svedberg," she said. "Carlman's daughter is on a respirator at the hospital. She tried to commit suicide."

Wallander was silent until he had parked and switched off the engine. Then he turned to her. He knew she hadn't told him everything yet.

"What else?"

"She's probably not going to live."

Wallander stared out of the window. He thought about how she had slapped him. He got out of the car without a word.

CHAPTER 23

It was hot. Wallander was sweating as he walked down the hill from the station towards the hospital.

He hadn't even gone to the front desk to see whether he had any messages. He had stood motionless by the car, as if he'd lost his bearings, and then slowly, almost drawling, he told Höglund that she would have to report on their interview while he went to the hospital where Carlman's daughter lay dying. He hadn't waited for an answer, but simply turned and left. It was then, on the hill, that he realised that the summer might indeed be long, hot and dry.

He didn't notice when Svedberg drove past and waved. As always when he was preoccupied, he walked looking down at the footpath. He was trying to follow a train of thought. The starting point was quite simple. In less than ten days, a girl had burned herself to death, another had tried to commit suicide after her father was murdered, and a third, whose father had also been murdered, had perhaps disappeared or was being hidden. They were of different ages; Carlman's daughter was the oldest, but all of them were young. Two of the girls had been affected by the same killer, while the third had killed herself. On the face of it, the third had no connection to the other two. But Wallander felt as if he had once again assumed personal responsibility for all three on behalf of his own generation, and especially as the bad father he felt he had been himself. Wallander had a tendency to self-criticise, growing gloomy, filled with melancholy. Often this led to a string of sleepless nights. But since he was now forced to carry on working in spite of everything, as a policeman in a tiny corner of the world, and as the head of a team, he did his best to shake off his unease and clear his head by taking a walk.

What kind of a world was he living in? A world in which young people burned themselves to death or tried to kill themselves by some other means. They were living in what could be called the Age of Failure. Something the Swedish people had believed in and built had turned out to be less solid than expected. All they had done was raise a monument to a forgotten ideal. Now society seemed to collapse around him, as if the political system was about to tip over, and no-one knew which architects were waiting to put a new one in place, or what that system would be. It was terrifying, even in the beautiful summertime. Young people took their own lives. People lived to forget, not remember. Houses were hiding places rather than cosy homes. And the police stood by helpless, waiting for the time when their jails would be guarded by men in other uniforms, men from private security companies.

This was enough, thought Wallander, wiping the sweat from his brow. He couldn't take any more. A mental picture of the boy with the wary eyes sitting next to his mother became muddled with an image of Linda.

He reached the hospital. Svedberg was standing on the steps waiting for him. Wallander staggered, as if about to fall, suddenly dizzy. Svedberg took a step towards him, reaching out his hand. But Wallander waved him away and continued up the hospital steps. To protect himself from the sun, Svedberg was wearing a ridiculous cap that was much too big for him. Wallander muttered something unintelligible, and dragged him into the cafeteria to the right of the entrance. Pale people in wheelchairs, some connected to intravenous drips sat with friends and relatives, who probably wanted nothing more than to be out in the sunshine, and forget hospitals, death and misery. Wallander bought coffee and a sandwich, while Svedberg settled for a glass of water.

"Carlman's widow phoned," said Svedberg. "She was hysterical."

"What did the girl do?" asked Wallander.

"She took pills. She was discovered quite by chance, in a deep coma. Her heart stopped just as they got to the hospital. She's in very bad shape. You won't be able to talk to her."

Wallander nodded. This walk to the hospital had been more for his own state of mind than for any investigative reason.

"What did her mother say?" he asked. "Was there a letter? Any explanation?"

"No. Apparently it was quite unexpected."

Wallander recalled how the girl had slapped him.

"She seemed unbalanced when I met her," he said. "She really didn't leave a note?"

"If she did, the mother didn't mention it."

Wallander thought for a moment.

"Do me a favour," he said. "Drive there and find out if there was a note or not. If there *is* something, you'll have to check it carefully."

They left the cafeteria. Wallander went back to the station with Svedberg. He might as well get hold of a doctor by phone to hear how the girl was.

"I put a few reports on your desk," said Svedberg. "I did a phone interview with the reporter and photographer who visited Wetterstedt the day he died."

"Anything new?"

"Only a confirmation of what we already know. That Wetterstedt was his usual self. There didn't seem to be anything threatening him. Nothing he was aware of, anyway."

"So I don't need to read the report?"

Svedberg shrugged.

"It's always better to have four eyes look at something than two."

"I'm not so sure about that," said Wallander distractedly.

"Ekholm is busy putting the finishing touches to his psychological profile," said Svedberg.

Wallander muttered something in reply. Svedberg dropped him off outside the station and drove on to talk to Carlman's widow. Wallander picked up his messages at the front desk. A new girl was there again. He asked about Ebba and was told that she was at the hospital having the cast taken off her wrist. I could have stopped in and said hello to her, thought Wallander. Since I was over there anyway. If it was possible to say hello to someone who was just having a cast removed.

He went to his office and opened the window wide. Without sitting down he riffled through the reports Svedberg had mentioned. Then he remembered that he had also asked to see the photographs taken by the magazine. Where were they? Unable to control his impatience, he found Svedberg's mobile number and called him.

"The photos," he asked. "Where are they?"

"Aren't they on your desk?" Svedberg replied, surprised.

"There's nothing here."

"Then they're in my office. I must have forgotten them. They were in today's post."

They were in a brown envelope on Svedberg's tidy desk. Wallander spread them out and sat in Svedberg's chair. Wetterstedt posing in his home, in the garden, and on the beach. In one of the pictures the overturned rowing boat could be seen in the background. Wetterstedt was smiling at the camera. The grey hair which would soon be torn from his head was ruffled by the wind. The photos showed a man who seemed at peace with his old age. Nothing in the pictures hinted at what was to happen. Wetterstedt had less than 15 hours left to live when the pictures were taken. The photos lying before him showed how he'd looked on the last day of his life. Wallander studied the pictures for a few minutes more before stuffing them back in the envelope. He started towards his office but changed his mind and stopped outside Höglund's door, which was always open.

She was bent over some papers.

"Am I interrupting you?" he asked.

"Not at all."

He went in and sat down. They exchanged a few words about Carlman's daughter.

"Svedberg is out at the farmhouse hunting for a suicide note," said Wallander. "If there is one."

"She must have been very close to her father," said Höglund.

Wallander didn't reply. He changed the subject.

"Did you notice anything strange when we were visiting the Fredman family?"

"Strange?"

"A chill that settled over the room?"

He immediately regretted his description. Höglund wrinkled her brow as if he had said something out of line.

"I mean that they seemed evasive when I asked questions about Louise," he explained.

"No, I didn't," she replied. "But I did notice that you acted differently."

He told her of the feeling he'd had. She thought before she answered.

"You might be right," she said. "Now that you mention it, they did seem to be on their guard. That chill you were talking about."

"The question is whether they both were, or only one of them," said Wallander.

"Was that the case?"

"I'm not sure. It's just a feeling I had."

"Didn't the boy start answering the questions you were actually asking his mother?"

Wallander nodded.

"That's it," he said. "And I wonder why."

"Still, you have to ask yourself whether it's really important," she said.

"Of course," he admitted. "Sometimes I have a tendency to get hung up on unimportant details. But I still want to have a talk with that girl."

This time she was the one who changed the subject.

"It frightens me to think about what Anette Fredman said. That she felt relief that her husband would never walk through their door again. I can't imagine what it means to live like that."

"He was abusing her," said Wallander. "Maybe he beat the children too. But none of them filed a complaint."

"The boy seemed quite normal," she said. "And well brought up, too."

"Children learn to survive," said Wallander, reflecting for a moment on his own childhood and Linda's. He stood up.

"I'm going to try and get hold of Louise Fredman. Tomorrow if I can. I've got a hunch that she hasn't gone away at all."

He got a cup of coffee and headed towards his room. He almost collided with Norén and remembered the photos he had asked to have taken of the crowd standing outside the cordon watching the police work.

"I gave the film to Nyberg," said Norén. "But I don't think I'm much of a photographer."

"Who the hell is?" said Wallander, in a kindly tone. He went into his room and closed the door. He sat staring at his telephone, collecting his thoughts before he called the M.O.T. garage and asked for a new appointment for his car. The slot they offered him was during the time he had intended to spend at Skagen with Baiba. When he angrily informed them of the atrocities he was trying to solve, a time that had been reserved inexplicably became free. He wondered who that slot had been assigned to. After he hung up he decided to do his laundry that evening.

The phone rang. It was Nyberg.

"You were right," he said. "The fingerprints on that piece of paper you found behind the road workers' hut match the ones we found on the pages from the comic book. So there's no doubt that the same person is involved. In a couple of hours we'll also know whether we can tie him to the van at Sturup. We're also going to try and get some prints from Fredman's face."

"Is that possible?"

"To pour acid into Fredman's eyes the killer must have used one hand to hold his eyelids open," said Nyberg. "It's unpleasant, but if we're lucky we'll find prints on the lids themselves."

"It's a good thing people can't hear the way we talk to each other," said Wallander. "How about that bulb? The light at Wetterstedt's garden gate."

"I was just getting to that," said Nyberg. "You were right about that too. We found fingerprints."

Wallander sat up straight in his chair. His bad mood was gone. He could feel his excitement rising. The investigation was showing signs of breaking wide open.

"Have we got the prints in the archives?" he asked.

"I'm afraid not," said Nyberg. "But I've asked central records to double check."

"Let's assume for a moment that we don't. That means we're dealing with someone without a record."

"Could be," Nyberg replied.

"Run the prints through Interpol too," said Wallander. "And Europol. Ask for highest priority. Tell them it concerns a serial killer."

Wallander hung up and asked the girl at the switchboard to find Ekholm. In a few minutes she called back and said he'd gone out for lunch.

"Where?" asked Wallander.

"I think he said the Continental."

"Get hold of him there," said Wallander. "Tell him to get over here right away."

A while later Ekholm knocked on the door. Wallander was talking to Per Åkeson. He pointed to a chair. Wallander was busy trying to convince a sceptical Åkeson that the investigation wouldn't be aided by a larger team, at least in the short term. Åkeson finally gave in, and they postponed the decision for a few more days.

Wallander leaned back in his chair and clasped his hands behind his head. He told Ekholm about the fingerprints.

"The prints we're going to find on Björn Fredman's body will be the same ones too," he said. "We know for certain that we're dealing with the same killer. The only question is: who is he?"

"I've been thinking about the eyes," said Ekholm. "All available information tells us that aside from the genitals, the eyes are the part of the body most often subjected to a final revenge."

"What does that mean?"

"That killers seldom begin by putting out someone's eyes. They save that for last."

Wallander nodded for him to continue.

"We can approach it from two directions," said Ekholm. "We might ask why Fredman was the one to have his eyes put out. We could also turn the whole thing around and ask why the eyes of the other two men weren't violated."

"What's your conclusion?"

"I don't have one," Ekholm said. "When we're talking about someone's psyche, especially that of a disturbed or sick person, we're getting into territory in which there are no absolute answers."

Ekholm looked as if he was waiting for a comment. But Wallander just shook his head.

"I see a pattern," Ekholm went on. "The person who did this selected his victims in advance. He has some kind of relationship with these men. It's not necessary for him to have known the first two personally. It might be a symbolic relationship. But I'm fairly certain that the mutilation of Fredman's eyes reveals that the killer knew his victim. And knew him well."

Wallander leaned forward and gave Ekholm a penetrating look.

"How well?" he asked.

"They might have been friends. Colleagues. Rivals."

"And something happened?"

"Something happened, yes. In reality or in the killer's imagination."

Wallander tried to see the implications of Ekholm's words. At the same time he asked himself whether he accepted his theory.

"So we ought to concentrate on Björn Fredman," he said after he had thought carefully.

"That's one possibility."

Wallander was irritated by Ekholm's tendency to avoid taking a decisive view. It bothered him, even though he knew that it was right to keep their options open.

"Let's say you were in my place," said Wallander. "I promise not to quote you. Or blame you if you're wrong. But what would you do?"

"I would concentrate on retracing Fredman's life," he said. "But I'd keep my eyes open."

Wallander nodded. He understood.

"What *kind* of person are we looking for?" he asked.

Ekholm batted at a bee that had flown in through the window.

"The basic conclusions you can draw yourself," he said. "That it's a man. That he's strong. That he's practical, meticulous and not squeamish."

"And his prints aren't in the criminal records," Wallander added. "He's a first-timer."

"This reinforces my belief that he leads a quite normal life," said Ekholm. "The psychotic side to his nature, the mental collapse, is well hidden. He could sit down at the dinner table with the scalps in his pocket and eat his meal with a healthy appetite."

"In other words, there are two ways we can set about catching him," Wallander said. "Either in the act, or by gathering a body of evidence that spells out his name in big neon letters."

"That's right. It's not an easy task that we have ahead of us."

Just as Ekholm was about to leave, Wallander asked one more question.

"Will he strike again?"

"It might be over," said Ekholm. "Björn Fredman as the grand finale."

"Is that what you think?"

"No. He'll strike again. What we've seen so far is the beginning of a long series of murders."

When Wallander was alone he shooed the bee out of the window with his jacket. He sat quite still with his eyes closed, thinking through everything Ekholm had said. At 4 p.m. he went to get some more coffee. Then he went to the conference room, where the rest of the team were waiting for him.

He began by asking Ekholm to repeat his theory. When Ekholm had finished the room was quiet for a long time. Wallander waited out the silence, knowing that each of them was trying to grasp the significance of what they had just heard. They're each absorbing this information, he thought. Then we'll work on determining the collective opinion of the team.

They agreed with Ekholm. They would make Björn Fredman's life the prime focus. Having settled the next steps in the investigation, they ended the meeting at around 6 p.m. Martinsson was the only one who left the station, to go and collect his children. The rest of them went back to work.

Wallander stood by his window looking out at the summer evening. The thought that they were still on the wrong track gnawed at him. *What was he missing?* He turned and looked around the room, as if an invisible visitor had come in.

So that's how things are, he thought. I'm chasing a ghost when I ought to be searching for a living human being. He sat there pondering the case until midnight. Only when he left the station did he remember the dirty laundry still heaped on the floor.

CHAPTER 24

Next morning at dawn Wallander went downstairs to the laundry room, still half asleep, and discovered to his dismay that someone had got there first. The washing machine was in use, and he had to sign up for a slot that afternoon. He kept trying to recapture the dream he'd had during the night. It had been erotic, frenzied, and passionate, and Wallander had watched himself from a distance, participating in a drama he never would have come close to in his waking life. But the woman in his dream wasn't Baiba. Not until he was on his way back upstairs did he realise that the woman reminded him of the female vicar he had met at Smedstorp. At first it surprised him, and then he felt a little ashamed. Later, when he got back to his flat, it dissolved into what it actually was, something beyond his control.

He sat at the kitchen table and drank coffee, the heat already coming through the half-open window. Maybe Ann-Britt's grandmother was right: they were in for a truly beautiful summer. He thought of his father. Often, especially in the morning, his thoughts would wander back in time, to the era of the "silk knights", when he woke each morning knowing he was a child loved by his father. Now, more than 40 years later, he found it hard to remember what his father had been like as a young man. His paintings were just the same even then: he had painted that landscape with or without the grouse with total determination not to change a thing from one painting to the next. His father had only painted one single picture in his whole life. He never tried to improve on it. The result had been perfect from the first attempt.

He drank the last of his coffee and tried to imagine a world without his father. He wondered what he would do when his constant feelings of guilt were gone. The trip to Italy would probably be their last chance to understand each other, maybe even to reconcile. He didn't want his good memories to end at the time when he had helped his father to cart out the paintings and place them in a huge American car, and then stood by his side, both of them waving to the silk knight driving off in a cloud of dust, on his way to sell them for three or four times what he had just paid for them.

At 6.30 a.m. he became a policeman again, sweeping the memories aside. As he dressed he tried to decide how he'd go about all the tasks he had set himself that day. At 7 a.m. he walked through the door of the station, exchanging a few words with Norén, who arrived at the same time. Norén was actually supposed to be on holiday, but he had postponed it, just as many of the others had.

"No doubt it'll start raining as soon as we catch the killer," he said. "What does a weather god care about a simple policeman when there's a serial killer on the loose?"

Wallander muttered something in reply, but he did not discount the possibility that there might be some grim truth in Norén's words.

He went in to see Hansson, who seemed now to spend all his time at the station, weighed down by anxiety. His face was as grey as concrete. He was shaving with an ancient electric razor. His shirt was wrinkled and his eyes bloodshot.

"You've got to try and get a few hours' sleep once in a while," said Wallander. "Your responsibility isn't any greater than anyone else's."

Hansson turned off the shaver and gloomily observed the result in a pocket mirror.

"I took a sleeping pill yesterday," he said. "But I still didn't get any sleep. All I got was a headache."

Wallander looked at Hansson in silence. He felt sorry for him. Being chief had never been one of Hansson's dreams.

"I'm going back to Malmö," he said. "I want to talk to the members of Fredman's family again. Especially the ones who weren't there yesterday."

Hansson gave him a quizzical look.

"Are you going to interrogate a four-year-old boy? That's not legally permitted."

"I was thinking of the daughter," said Wallander. "She's 17. And I don't intend to 'interrogate' anyone."

Hansson nodded and got up slowly. He pointed to a book lying open on the desk.

"I got this from Ekholm," he said. "Behavioural science based on a number of case studies of serial killers. It's unbelievable the things people will do if they're sufficiently deranged."

"Is there anything about scalping?" asked Wallander.

"That's one of the milder forms of trophy collecting. If you only knew the things that have been found in people's homes, it would make you sick."

"I feel sick enough already," said Wallander. "I'll leave the rest to my imagination."

"Ordinary human beings," said Hansson in dismay. "Completely normal on the surface. Underneath, mentally ill beasts of prey. A man in France, the foreman of a coal depot, used to cut open the stomachs of his victims and stick his head inside to try and suffocate himself. That's one example."

"That'll do," said Wallander, trying to discourage him.

"Ekholm wanted me to give you the book when I've read it," said Hansson.

"I bet he did," said Wallander. "But I really don't have the time. Or the inclination."

Wallander made himself a sandwich in the canteen and took it with him. As he ate it in the car, he wondered whether he should call Linda. But he decided not to. It was still too early.

He arrived in Malmö at around 8.30 a.m. The summer calm had already started to descend on the countryside. The traffic on the roads that intersected the motorway into Malmö was lighter than usual. He headed towards Rosengård and pulled up outside the block of flats he had visited the day before. He turned off the engine, wondering why he had come back so soon. They had decided to investigate Björn Fredman's life. Besides, it was necessary that he meet the absent daughter. The little boy was less important.

He found a dirty petrol receipt in the glove compartment and took out a pen. To his great irritation he saw that it had leaked ink around the breast pocket where he kept it. The spot was half the size of his hand. On the white shirt it looked as if he'd been shot through the heart. The shirt was almost new. Baiba had bought it for him at Christmas after she'd been through his wardrobe and cleaned out the old, worn-out clothes.

His immediate impulse was to return to Ystad and go back to bed. He didn't know how many shirts he'd had to throw away because he forgot to cap the pen properly before he put it in his pocket. Perhaps he should go and buy a new shirt. But he'd have to wait at least an hour until the shops opened, so he decided against it. He tossed the leaking pen out the window and then looked for another one in the messy glove compartment. He wrote down some key words on the back of the receipt. *BF's friends. Then and now. Unexpected events.* He crumpled up the note and was just about to stuff it in his breast pocket when he stopped himself. He got out of the car and took off his jacket. The ink from his shirt pocket hadn't reached the jacket lining. He went into the building and pushed open the lift door. The broken glass was still there. He got out on the fifth floor and rang the doorbell. There was no sound from inside the flat. Maybe they were still asleep. He waited more than a minute. Then he rang again. The door opened. It was the boy, Stefan. He seemed surprised to see Wallander. He smiled, but his eyes were wary.

"I hope I haven't come too early," said Wallander. "I should have called first, of course. But I was in Malmö anyway. I thought I'd pop in."

It was a flimsy lie, but it was the best he could come up with. The boy let him into the hall. He was dressed in a cut-off T-shirt and a pair of jeans. He was barefoot.

"I'm here by myself," he said. "My mother went out with my little brother. They were going to Copenhagen."

"It's a great day for a trip to Copenhagen," said Wallander warmly.

"Yes, she likes going there a lot. To get away from it all."

His words echoed disconsolately in the hall. Wallander thought the boy had sounded strangely unmoved last time when he mentioned the death of his father. They went into the living-room. Wallander laid his jacket on a chair and pointed at the ink spot.

"This happens all the time," he said.

"It never happens to me," said the boy, smiling. "I can make some coffee if you want."

"No thanks."

They sat down at opposite ends of the table. A blanket and pillow on the sofa indicated that someone had slept there. Wallander glimpsed the neck of an empty wine bottle under a chair. The boy noticed at once that he had seen it. His attention didn't flag for an instant. Wallander hastily asked himself whether he had the right to question a minor about his father's death without a relative present. But he didn't want to pass up this opportunity. And the boy was incredibly mature for 14. Wallander felt as though he was talking to someone his own age. Even Linda, who was several years older, seemed childish in comparison.

"What are you going to do this summer?" asked Wallander. "We've got fine weather."

The boy smiled. "I've got plenty to do," he replied.

Wallander waited for more, but he didn't continue.

"What class are you going to be in this autumn?"

"Eighth."

"Is school going well?"

"Yes."

"What's your favourite subject?"

"None of them. But maths is the easiest. We've started a club to study numerology."

"I'm not sure I know what that is."

"The Holy Trinity. The seven lean years. Trying to predict your future by combining the numbers in your life."

"That sounds interesting."

"It is."

Wallander could feel himself becoming fascinated by the boy sitting across from him. His strong body contrasted sharply with his childish face, but there was obviously nothing wrong with his mind.

Wallander took the crumpled gas receipt out of his jacket. His house keys dropped out of the pocket. He put them back and sat down again.

"I have a few questions," he said. "But this is not an interrogation, by any means. If you want to wait until your mother comes home, just say so."

"That's not necessary. I'll answer if I can."

"Your sister," said Wallander. "When is she coming back?"

"I don't know."

The boy looked at him. The question didn't seem to bother him. He had answered without hesitation. Wallander began to wonder if he had been mistaken the day before.

"I assume that you're in contact with her? That you know where she is?"

"She just took off. It's not the first time. She'll come home when she feels like it."

"I hope you understand that I think that sounds a little unusual."

"Not for us."

Wallander was convinced that the boy knew where his sister was. But he wouldn't be able to force an answer out of him. Nor could he disregard the possibility that the girl was so upset that she really had run away.

"Isn't it true that she's in Copenhagen?" he asked cautiously. "And that your mother went there today to see her?"

"She went over to buy some shoes."

Wallander nodded. "Well, let's talk about something else," he went on. "You've had time to think now. Do you have any idea who might have killed your father?"

"No."

"Do you agree with your mother, that a lot of people might have wanted to?"

"Yes."

"Why's that?"

For the first time it seemed as though the boy's polite exterior was about to crack. He replied with unexpected vehemence.

"My father was an evil man," he said. "He lost the right to live a long time ago."

Wallander was shaken. How could a young person be so full of hatred?

"That's not something you ought to say," he replied. "That a person has lost his right to live. No matter what he did."

The boy was unmoved.

"What did he do that was so bad?" Wallander asked. "Lots of people are thieves. Lots of them sell stolen goods. They don't have to be monsters because of that."

"He scared us."

"How'd he do that?"

"We were all afraid of him."

"Even you?"

"Yes. But not for the past year."

"Why not?"

"The fear went away."

"And your mother?"

"She was scared."

"Your brother?"

"He'd run and hide when he thought Dad was coming home."

"Your sister?"

"She was more afraid than any of us."

Wallander heard an almost imperceptible shift in the boy's voice. There had been an instant of hesitation, he was sure of it.

"Why?" he asked cautiously.

"She was the most sensitive."

Wallander quickly decided to take a chance.

"Did your Dad touch her?"

"What do you mean?"

"I think you know what I mean."

"Yes, I do. But he never touched her."

There it is, thought Wallander, and tried to avoid revealing his reaction. He may have abused his own daughter. Maybe the younger brother too. Maybe even Stefan. Wallander didn't want to go any further. The question of where the sister was and what may have been done to her was something he didn't want to deal with alone. The thought of abuse upset him.

"Did your Dad have any good friends?" he asked.

"He hung around with a lot of people. But whether any of them were real friends, I don't know."

"Who do you think that I should talk to?"

The boy smiled involuntarily but then regained his composure at once.

"Peter Hjelm," he replied.

Wallander wrote down the name.

"Why did you smile?"

"I don't know."

"Do you know Peter Hjelm?"

"I've met him."

"Where can I find him?"

"He's in the phone book under 'Handyman'. He lives on Kungsgatan."

"How did they know each other?"

"They used to drink together. I know that. What else they did, I can't say."

Wallander looked around the room. "Did your Dad have any of his things here in the flat?"

"No."

"Nothing at all?"

"Not a thing."

Wallander stuffed the paper into his trouser pocket. He had no more questions.

"What's it like to be a policeman?" the boy asked.

Wallander could tell that he was really interested. His eyes gleamed.

"It's a little of this, a little of that," said Wallander, unsure of what he thought about his profession at that moment.

"What's it like to catch a murderer?"

"Cold and grey and miserable," he replied, thinking with distaste of all the TV shows the boy must have seen.

"What are you going to do when you catch the person who killed my Dad?"

"I don't know," said Wallander. "That depends."

"He must be dangerous. Since he's already killed several other people."

Wallander found the boy's curiosity annoying.

"We'll catch him," he said firmly, to put an end to the conversation. "Sooner or later we'll catch him."

He got up from the chair and asked where the bathroom was. The boy pointed to a door in the hall leading to the bedroom. Wallander closed the door behind him. He looked at his face in the mirror. What he needed most was some sunshine. After he'd had a pee he opened the medicine cabinet. There were a few bottles of pills in it. One of them had Louise Fredman's name on it. He saw that she was born on November 9th. He memorised the name of the medicine and the doctor who had prescribed it. *Saroten.* He had never heard of this drug before. He would have to look it up when he got back to Ystad.

In the living-room the boy was sitting in the same position. Wallander wondered whether he was normal after all. His preco-ciousness and self-control made a strange impression. But then Stefan turned towards him and smiled, and for a moment the wariness in his eyes seemed to vanish. Wallander pushed away the thought, and picked up his jacket.

"I'll be calling you again," he said. "Don't forget to tell your mother that I was here. It would be good if you told her what we talked about."

"Can I come and visit you some time?" asked the boy.

Wallander was surprised by the question. It was like having a ball tossed at you and not being able to catch it.

"You mean you want to come to the station in Ystad?"

"Yes."

"Of course," said Wallander. "But call ahead of time. I'm often out. And sometimes it's not convenient."

Wallander went out to the landing and pressed the lift button. They nodded to each other. The boy closed the door. Wallander rode down and walked out into the sunshine.

It had turned into the hottest day yet. He stood for a moment, enjoying the heat, deciding what to do next, then drove down to the Malmö police station. Forsfält was in. Wallander told him about his talk with the boy. He gave Forsfält the name of the doctor, Gunnar Bergdahl, and asked him to get hold of him as soon as possible. Then he told him about his suspicions that Fredman might have abused his daughter and possibly the two boys as well. Forsfält couldn't recall that allegations of that nature had ever been directed at Fredman, but he promised to look into the matter.

Wallander moved on to Peter Hjelm. Forsfält told him that he was a man who resembled Björn Fredman in many ways. He'd been in and out of prison. Once he was arrested with Fredman for taking part in a joint fencing operation. Forsfält was of the opinion that Hjelm was the one who supplied the stolen goods, and Fredman then resold them. Wallander wondered whether Forsfält would mind if he talked to Hjelm alone.

"I'm happy to get out of it," said Forsfält.

Wallander looked up Hjelm's address in Forsfält's phone book. He also gave Forsfält his mobile number. They decided to have lunch together. Forsfält hoped that by then he would have copied all the material the Malmö police had on Björn Fredman.

Wallander left his car outside the station and walked towards Kungsgatan. He went into a clothing shop and bought a shirt, which he put on. Reluctantly he threw away the ruined one Baiba had given him. He went back out into the sunshine. For a few minutes he sat on a bench. Then he walked over to the building where Hjelm lived. The door had an entry code, but Wallander was lucky. After a few minutes an elderly man came out with his dog. Wallander gave him a friendly nod and stepped in the main door. He saw that Hjelm lived on the fourth floor. Just as he was about to open the lift door, his phone rang. It was Forsfält.

"Where are you?" he asked.

"I'm standing outside the lift in Hjelm's building."

"I was hoping you hadn't got there yet."

"Has something happened?"

"I got hold of the doctor. We know each other. I'd totally forgotten about it."

"What'd he say?"

"Something he probably shouldn't have. I promised I wouldn't mention his name. So you can't either."

"I promise."

"He thought that the person we're talking about – I won't mention the name since we're on mobile phones – was admitted to a psychiatric clinic."

Wallander held his breath.

"That explains why she left," he said.

"No, it doesn't," said Forsfält. "She's been there for three years."

Wallander stood there in silence. Someone pressed the button for the lift and it rumbled upwards.

"We'll talk later," Forsfält said. "Good luck with Hjelm."

He hung up. Wallander thought for a long time about what he had just heard. Then he started up the stairs to the fourth floor.

CHAPTER 25

Wallander knew that he'd heard the music coming from Hjelm's flat before. He listened with one ear pressed against the door, and remembered that Linda had played it, and that the band was called the Grateful Dead. He rang the doorbell and took a step back. The music was very loud. He rang again, and then banged hard on the door. Finally the music was turned down. He heard footsteps and then the door was opened wide, and Wallander took a step back so as not to be hit in the face. The man who opened it was completely naked. Wallander also saw that he was under the influence of something. His large body was swaying imperceptibly. Wallander introduced himself and showed his badge. The man didn't bother looking at it. He kept staring at Wallander.

"I've seen you," he said. "On the telly. And in the papers. I never actually read the papers, so I must have seen you on the front page. The policeman they were looking for. The one who shoots people without asking permission. What did you say your name was? Wahlgren?"

"Wallander. Are you Peter Hjelm?"

"Yeah."

"I want to talk to you."

The naked man made a suggestive gesture inside the flat. Wallander assumed this meant he had female company.

"It can't be helped," said Wallander. "It probably won't take very long anyway."

Hjelm reluctantly let him into the hall.

"Put some clothes on," Wallander said firmly.

Hjelm shrugged, pulled an overcoat from a hanger, and put it on. As if at Wallander's request, he also jammed an old hat down over his ears. Wallander followed him down a long hall. Hjelm lived in an old-fashioned, spacious flat. Wallander sometimes dreamed of finding one like it in Ystad. Once he inquired about the flats above the bookshop in the red building on the square, but was shocked at how high the rent was.

When they reached the living-room, Wallander was astonished to discover another man wrapping a sheet around himself. Wallander wasn't prepared for this. A naked man who gestured suggestively had a woman with him, not a man. To conceal his embarrassment, Wallander assumed a formal tone. He sat down in a chair and waved Hjelm to a seat facing him.

"Who are you?" he asked the other man, who was much younger than Hjelm.

"Geert doesn't understand Swedish," said Hjelm. "He's from Amsterdam. He's just visiting."

"Tell him I want to see some identification," said Wallander. "Now."

Hjelm spoke very poor English, worse than Wallander's. The man in the sheet disappeared and came back with a Dutch driver's licence. As usual, Wallander had nothing to write with. He memorised the man's last name, Van Loenen, and handed back the driver's licence. Then he asked a few brief questions in English. Van Loenen said that he was a waiter in a café in Amsterdam and that he had met Hjelm there. This was the third time he'd been to Malmö. He was going back to Amsterdam on the train in a couple of days. When he'd finished, Wallander asked him to leave the room. Hjelm was sitting on the floor, dressed in his overcoat with the hat pulled low over his forehead. Wallander felt himself getting angry.

"Take off that damned hat!" he shouted. "And sit in a chair. Otherwise I'll call a squad car and have you taken in."

Hjelm did as he was told. He tossed the hat in a wide arc so that it landed between two flowerpots on one of the windowsills. Wallander's anger made him start to sweat.

"Björn Fredman is dead," he said brutally. "But I suppose you already know that."

Hjelm's smile disappeared. He didn't know, Wallander realised.

"He was murdered," Wallander continued. "Someone poured acid in his eyes. And cut off part of his scalp. This happened three days ago. Now we're looking for the person who did it. The killer has already murdered two other people. A former politician by the name of Gustaf Wetterstedt and an art dealer named Arne Carlman. But maybe you knew this."

Hjelm nodded slowly. Wallander tried without success to interpret his reactions.

"Now I understand why Björn didn't answer his phone," he said after a while. "I tried to call him all day yesterday. And this morning I tried again."

"What did you want from him?"

"I was thinking of inviting him over for dinner."

Wallander saw at once that this was a lie. Since he was still furious at Hjelm's arrogant attitude, it was easy for him to tighten his grip. In all his years as a police officer Wallander had only lost control twice and struck individuals he was interrogating. He could usually control his rage.

"Don't lie to me," he said. "The only way you're going to see me walk out that door is if you give me clear, truthful answers to my questions. If you don't, all hell will break loose. We're dealing with a serial killer. Which means the police have special powers."

The last part wasn't true, of course. But it made an impression on Hjelm.

"I was calling him about a gig we had together."

"What sort of gig?"

"A little import and export. He owed me money."

"How much?"

"A little. A hundred thousand, maybe. No more than that."

This "little" sum of money was equivalent to many months' wages for Wallander. This made him even angrier.

"We can get back to your business with Fredman later," he said. "That's something the Malmö police will deal with. What I want to know is whether you can tell me who killed him."

"Not me, that's for sure."

"I wasn't suggesting you did. Anyone else?"

Wallander saw that Hjelm was trying to concentrate.

"I don't know," he said finally.

"You seem hesitant."

"Björn was into a lot of things I didn't know about."

"Such as?"

"I don't know."

"Give me a straight answer!"

"Well, shit! I just don't know. We did some deals. What Fredman did with the rest of his time I can't tell you. In this business you're not supposed to know too much. You can't know too little either. But that's something else again."

"What do you think Fredman might have been into?"

"I think he was doing collections quite a bit."

"He was an enforcer, you mean?"

"Something like that."

"Who was his boss?"

"Dunno."

"Don't lie to me."

"I'm not lying. I just don't know."

Wallander almost believed him.

"What else?"

"He was a pretty secretive type. He travelled a lot. And when he came back he was always sunburnt. And he brought back souvenirs."

"Where from?"

"He never said. But after his trips he usually had plenty of money."

Björn Fredman's passport, Wallander thought. We haven't found it.

"Who else knew Fredman besides you?"

"Lots of people."

"Who knew him as well as you do?"

"Nobody."

"Did he have a woman?"

"What a question! Of course he had women!"

"Was there anyone special?"

"He switched around a lot."

"Why did he switch?"

"Why does anyone switch? Why do I switch? Because I meet somebody from Amsterdam one day and somebody from Bjärred the next."

"Bjärred?"

"It's just an example, damn it! Halmstad, if that's any better!"

Wallander stopped asking questions. He frowned at Hjelm. He felt an instinctive animosity towards him. Towards a thief who regarded a hundred thousand kronor as "a little money".

"Gustaf Wetterstedt," he said finally. "And Arne Carlman. You knew they had been killed."

"I watch TV."

"Did Fredman ever mention their names?"

"No."

"Do you think you may have forgotten? Is it possible he did know them?"

Hjelm sat in silence for more than a minute. Wallander waited.

"I'm positive," he said finally. "But he might not have told me about it."

"This man who's on the loose is dangerous," said Wallander. "He's ice-cold and calculating. And crazy. He poured acid in Fredman's eyes. It must have been incredibly painful. Do you get my point?"

"Yes, I do."

"I want you to do some work for me. Spread it around that the police are looking for a connection between these three men. I assume you agree that we have to get this lunatic off the streets. A man who pours acid in somebody's eyes."

Hjelm grimaced.

"OK."

Wallander got up.

"Call Detective Forsfält," he said. "Or give me a call. In Ystad. Anything you can come up with might be important."

"Björn had a girlfriend named Marianne," said Hjelm. "She lives over by the Triangle."

"What's her last name?"

"Eriksson, I think."

"What kind of work does she do?"

"I don't know."

"Have you got her phone number?"

"I can look it up."

"Do it."

Wallander waited while Hjelm left the room. He could hear whispering voices, at least one of which sounded annoyed. Hjelm came back and handed Wallander a piece of paper. Then he followed him out to the hall.

Hjelm had sobered up, but he still seemed completely unfazed by what had happened to his friend. Wallander felt a great uneasiness at the coldness Hjelm exhibited. It was incomprehensible to him.

"That crazy man . . ." Hjelm began, without finishing his sentence. Wallander understood his unasked question.

"He's after specific individuals. If you can't see yourself in any connection with Wetterstedt, Carlman, and Fredman, you have nothing to worry about."

"Why haven't you caught him?"

Wallander stared at Hjelm, his anger returning.

"One reason is that people like you find it so hard to answer simple questions," he said.

When he got down to the street he stood there facing the sun and closed his eyes. He thought over the conversation with Hjelm, and the anxiety that the investigation was on the wrong track returned. He opened his eyes and walked over to the side of the building, into the shade. He couldn't shake off the feeling that he was steering the whole investigation into a blind alley. He remembered the half-formed idea that he'd had, that something he'd heard was significant. There's something missing, he thought. There's a link between Wetterstedt and Carlman and Fredman that I'm tripping over. The man they were searching for could strike again, and Wallander knew one thing about the case for certain. They had no idea who he was. And they didn't even know where to look. He left the shadow of the wall and hailed a cab.

It was past midday when he got out in front of the Malmö station. When he reached Forsfält's office he got a message to call Ystad. Again he had the terrible feeling that something serious had happened. Ebba answered. She reassured him and then switched him over to Nyberg. They had found a fingerprint on Fredman's left eyelid. It was smudged, but it was still good enough for them to confirm a match with the prints they had found. There was no longer any doubt they were after a single killer. The forensic examination confirmed that Fredman was murdered less than twelve hours before the body was discovered, and that acid had been poured into his eyes while he was alive.

Next Ebba put him through to Martinsson, who had received a positive confirmation from Interpol that Dolores María Santana's father recognised the medallion. It had belonged to her. Martinsson also mentioned that the Swedish embassy in the Dominican Republic was extremely unwilling to pay to transport the girl's remains back to Santiago.

Wallander was listening with half an ear. When Martinsson finished complaining about the embassy, Wallander asked him what Svedberg and Höglund were working on. Martinsson said that neither of them had come up with much. Wallander told him he'd be back in Ystad that afternoon and hung up. Forsfält stood out in the hall sneezing.

"Allergies," he said, blowing his nose. "Summer is the worst."

They walked in the dazzling sunshine to a restaurant where Forsfält liked to eat spaghetti. After Wallander told him about his meeting with Hjelm, Forsfält started talking about his summer house, up near Älmhult. Wallander guessed that he didn't want to spoil their lunch by talking about the investigation. Normally this would have made Wallander impatient, but he listened with growing fascination as the old detective described how he was restoring an old smithy. Only when they were having coffee did they return to the investigation. Forsfält would try to interview Marianne Eriksson that same day. But most important was the revelation that Louise Fredman had been a patient in a psychiatric hospital for the past three years.

"I'm not sure," said Forsfält. "But I'd guess that she's in Lund. At St Lars Hospital. That's where the more serious cases finish up, I think."

"It's hard to bypass all the obstacles when you want to get patient records," said Wallander. "And that's a good thing, of course. But I think we must know everything about Louise Fredman. Especially since the family haven't told the truth."

"Mental illness isn't something people want to talk about," Forsfält reminded him. "I had an aunt who was in and out of institutions her whole life. We almost never talked about her to strangers. It was a disgrace."

"I'll ask one of the prosecutors in Ystad to get in touch with Malmö," said Wallander.

"What reason are you going to give?" asked Forsfält.

Wallander thought for a moment.

"I don't know," he said. "I have a suspicion that Fredman may have abused her."

"That's not good enough," said Forsfält firmly.

"I know," said Wallander. "Somehow I have to show that it's crucial to the whole murder investigation to obtain information on Louise Fredman. About her and from her."

"What do you think she could help you with?"

Wallander threw out his hands.

"I don't know," he said. "Maybe nothing will be cleared up by finding out what it is that's keeping her locked up. Maybe she's incapable of holding a conversation with anyone."

Forsfält nodded, deep in thought. Wallander knew that Forsfält's objections were well-founded, but he couldn't ignore his hunch that Louise Fredman was important. Wallander paid for lunch. When they got back to the station Forsfält went to the reception desk and got a black plastic bag.

"Here are a few kilos of papers on Björn Fredman's troubled life," he said, smiling. But then he turned serious, as if his smile had been inappropriate.

"That poor devil," he said. "The pain must have been incredible. What could he possibly have done to deserve it?"

"That's just it," said Wallander. "What did he do? What did Wetterstedt do? Or Carlman? And to whom?"

"Scalping and acid in the eyes. Where the hell are we headed?"

"According to the national police board, towards a society where a police district like Ystad doesn't need to be manned at all on weekends," said Wallander.

Forsfält stood silent for a moment before he replied. "I hardly think that's the answer," he said.

"Tell the national commissioner."

"What can he do?" Forsfält asked. "He's got a board of directors on his back. And above them are the politicians."

"He could always refuse," said Wallander. "Or he could resign if things get too far out of hand."

"Perhaps," said Forsfält absently.

"Thanks for all your help," said Wallander. "And especially for the story about the smithy."

"You'll have to come up and visit sometime," said Forsfält. "I don't know whether Sweden is as fantastic as all the magazines say it is. But it's a great country all the same. Beautiful. And surprisingly unspoiled. If you take the trouble to look."

"You won't forget Marianne Eriksson?"

"I'm going to see if I can find her right now," replied Forsfält. "I'll call you later."

Wallander unlocked his car and tossed in the plastic bag. Then he drove out of town and onto the E65. He rolled down the window and let the summer wind blow across his face. When he arrived in Ystad he stopped at the supermarket and bought groceries. He was already at the checkout when he discovered he had to go back for washing powder. He drove home and carried the bags up to his flat, but found that he had lost his keys.

He went back downstairs and searched the car without finding them. He called Forsfält and was told that he had gone out. One of his colleagues went into his office and looked to see whether they were on his desk. They weren't there. He called Peter Hjelm, who picked up the phone almost at once. He came back minutes later and said he couldn't find them.

Wallander fished out the piece of paper with the Fredmans' number in Rosengård. The son answered. Wallander waited while he looked for the keys, but he couldn't find them. Wallander wondered whether to tell him that he now knew his sister Louise had been in a hospital for several years, but decided not to.

He thought for a while. He might have dropped his keys at the place where he ate lunch with Forsfält, or in the shop where he had bought the new shirt. Annoyed, he went back to his car and drove to the station. Ebba kept a spare set of keys for him. He told her the name of the clothing shop and the restaurant in Malmö. She said she would check whether they had found them. Wallander left the station and went home without talking to any of his colleagues. He needed to think over all that had happened that day. In particular, he wanted to plan his conversation with Åkeson. He carried in the groceries and put them away. He had missed the laundry time he had signed up for. He took the box of washing powder and gathered up the huge pile of laundry. When he got downstairs, the room was still empty. He sorted the pile, guessing which types of clothes required the same water temperature. With some fumbling he managed to get two machines started. Satisfied, he went back up to his flat.

He had just closed the door when the phone rang. It was Forsfält, who told him that Marianne Eriksson was in Spain. He was going to keep trying to reach her at the hotel where the travel agent said she was staying. Wallander unpacked the contents of the black plastic bag. The files covered his whole kitchen table. He took a beer out of the refrigerator and sat down in the living-room. He listened to Jussi Björling on the stereo. After a while he stretched out on the sofa with the can of beer beside him on the floor. Soon he was asleep.

He woke with a start when the music ended. Lying on the sofa, he finished the can of beer. The phone rang. It was Linda. Could she stay at his place for a few days? Her friend's parents were coming home. Wallander suddenly felt energetic. He gathered up all the papers spread out on the kitchen table and carried them to his bedroom. Then he made up the bed in the room where Linda slept. He opened all the windows and let the warm evening breeze blow through the flat. He went downstairs and got his laundry out of the machines. To his surprise none of the colours had run. He hung the laundry in the drying room. Linda had told him that she wouldn't want any food, so he boiled some potatoes and grilled a piece of meat for his supper. As he ate he wondered whether he should call Baiba. He also thought about his lost keys. About Louise Fredman. About Peter Hjelm. And about the stack of papers waiting for him in his bedroom. And he thought about the man who was out there somewhere in the summer night. The man they would have to catch soon. When he'd finished, he stood by the open window until he saw Linda coming down the street.

"I love you," he said aloud.

He dropped the keys from the window and she caught them with one hand.

CHAPTER 26

Wallander sat up half the night talking with Linda, but he still forced himself to get up at 6 a.m. He stood in the shower for a long time before managing to shake off his weariness. He moved quietly through the flat and thought that it was only when either Baiba or Linda was there that it really felt like home. When he was alone it felt like little more than a temporary roof over his head. He made coffee and went down to the drying room. One of his neighbours pointed out that he hadn't cleaned up after himself the day before. She was an old woman who lived alone, and he greeted her when they ran into each other, but didn't know her name. She showed him a spot on the floor where there was some spilled washing powder. Wallander apologised and promised to do better in the future. What a nag, he thought as he went upstairs. But he knew she was right, he had been too lazy to clean up.

He dumped his laundry on the bed and then carried the papers Forsfält had given him out to the kitchen. He felt guilty because he hadn't read them the night before. But the talk with Linda had been important. They had sat out on the balcony in the warm night. Listening to her, he felt for the first time that she was an adult. She told him that Mona was talking about remarrying. Wallander was depressed at this news. He knew that Linda had been asked to inform him. But for the first time he talked about why he thought the marriage had fallen apart. From her response he could tell that Mona saw it quite differently. Then she asked him about Baiba, and he tried to answer her as honestly as he could, though there was a lot that was still unresolved about their relationship. And when they finally turned in, he felt sure that she didn't blame him for what had happened, and that now she could view her parents' divorce as something that had been necessary.

He sat down at the kitchen table and looked at the extensive material describing Björn Fredman's life. It took him two hours just to skim through it all. Once in a while he would jot down notes. By the time he pushed aside the last folder and stretched, it was after 8 a.m. He poured another cup of coffee and stood by the open window. It was going to be a beautiful day. He couldn't remember the last time that it had rained.

He tried to think through what he had read. Björn Fredman had been a sorry character from the outset. He had had a difficult and troubled home life as a child, and his first brush with the police, over a stolen bicycle, occurred when he was seven. He had been in constant trouble ever since. Björn Fredman had struck back at a life that had never given him any pleasure. Wallander thought of how many times during his career he'd read these grey, colourless sagas in which it was clear from the first sentence that the story would end badly.

Sweden had pulled herself out of material poverty, largely under her own steam. When Wallander was a child there had still been desperately poor people, even though they were few in number by then. But the other kind of poverty, he thought, we've never dealt with that. And now that progress seemed to have stopped for the time being, and the welfare state was being eroded, the spiritual poverty that had been there all along was beginning to surface.

Fredman was not the only one. We haven't created a society where people like him could feel at home, Wallander thought. When we got rid of the old society, where families stuck together, we forgot to replace it with something else. The great loneliness that resulted was a price we didn't know we were going to have to pay. Or perhaps we chose to ignore it.

He put the folders back in the black plastic bag and then listened once again outside Linda's door. She was asleep. He couldn't resist the temptation to open the door a crack, and peek in at her. She was sleeping curled up, turned to the wall. He left a note on the kitchen table and wondered what to do about his keys. He called the station. Ebba was at home. He looked up her home number. Neither the restaurant nor the clothing shop had found his keys. He added to the note that Linda should put the house keys under the doormat. Then he drove to the station.

Hansson was sitting in his office, looking greyer than ever. Wallander felt sorry for him, and wondered how long he would last. They went to the canteen and had some coffee. There was little sign that the biggest manhunt in the history of the Ystad police force was under way. Wallander told Hansson that he realised now that they needed reinforcements. And that Hansson needed a break. They had enough manpower to send out in the field, but Hansson needed relief on the home front. He tried to protest, but Wallander refused to back down. Hansson's grey face and harried eyes were evidence enough. Finally Hansson gave in and promised to speak to the county chief of police on Monday. They would have to borrow a sergeant from another district.

The investigative team had a meeting set for 10 a.m. Wallander left Hansson, who already seemed relieved. He went to his office and called Forsfält, who couldn't be located. It took 15 minutes before Forsfält called back. Wallander asked about Björn Fredman's passport.

"It should be in his flat, of course," said Forsfält. "Funny we haven't found it."

"I don't know if this means anything," said Wallander. "But I want to find out more about those trips Peter Hjelm was talking about."

"E.U. countries hardly use entry and exit stamps any more," Forsfält pointed out.

"I think Hjelm was talking about trips further afield," replied Wallander. "But I could be wrong."

Forsfält said that they would start searching for Fredman's passport immediately.

"I spoke with Marianne Eriksson last night," he said. "I thought about calling you, but it was late."

"Where did you find her?"

"In Malaga. She didn't even know that Fredman was dead."

"What did she have to say?"

"Not much, I must say. Obviously she was upset. I couldn't spare her any details, unfortunately. They had met occasionally over the past six months. I got a feeling that she actually liked Fredman."

"In that case, she's the first," said Wallander. "If you don't count Hjelm."

"She thought he was a businessman," Forsfält continued. "She had no idea he had been involved in illegal activities. She also didn't know he was married and had three children. She was quite upset. I smashed the image she had of Fredman to smithereens with one phone call, I'm afraid."

"How could you tell she liked him?"

"She was hurt that he had lied to her."

"Did you learn anything else?"

"Not really. But she's on her way back to Sweden. She's coming home on Friday. I'll talk to her then."

"And then you're going on holiday?"

"I was planning to. Weren't you supposed to start yours soon too?"

"I don't even want to think about it."

"Once they start moving, things could happen quickly."

Wallander didn't respond to Forsfält's last remark. They said goodbye. Wallander dialled the switchboard, and asked the receptionist to track down Åkeson. After more than a minute she told him that Åkeson was at home. Wallander looked at the clock. Just after 9 a.m. He made a quick decision and left his office. He ran into Svedberg in the hall, still wearing his silly cap.

"How is the sunburn?" asked Wallander.

"Better. But I don't dare go out without the cap."

"Do you think locksmiths are open on Saturday?" asked Wallander.

"I doubt it. But there are locksmiths on call."

"I need to get a couple of keys copied."

"Did you lock yourself out?"

"I've lost my house keys."

"Were your name and address on them?"

"Of course not."

"Then at least you don't need to change your lock."

Wallander told Svedberg that he might be a little late for the meeting. He had to see Åkeson about something important. Åkeson lived in a residential neighbourhood near the hospital. Wallander had been to the house before and knew the way. When he arrived and got out of the car, he saw Åkeson mowing his lawn. He stopped when he saw Wallander.

"Has something happened?" he asked when they met at the gate.

"Yes and no," said Wallander. "Something is always happening. But nothing crucial. I need your help with part of the investigation."

They went into the garden. Wallander thought gloomily that it looked like every other garden he'd been in. He turned down an offer of coffee. They sat in the shade of a roofed patio.

"If my wife comes out I'd appreciate it if you didn't mention that I'm going to Africa this autumn. It's still quite a sensitive topic," said Åkeson.

Wallander said he wouldn't. He explained about Louise Fredman and his suspicion that she might have been abused by her father. He was honest and said that this could well be a false trail and might not add anything to the investigation. He outlined the new tack they were trying in the case, which was based around the knowledge that Fredman had been killed by the same person as Wetterstedt and Carlman. "Björn Fredman was the black sheep in the scalped 'family'," he said, realising immediately how inappropriate the description was.

How did he fit into the picture? How didn't he fit? Maybe they could find the connection by starting with Fredman at a place where a link was by no means obvious. Åkeson listened intently.

"I talked to Ekholm," he said when Wallander had finished. "A good man, I thought. Competent. Realistic. The impression I got from him was that the man we're looking for may strike again."

"I'm always thinking about that."

"What about getting reinforcements?" Åkeson asked.

Wallander told him about his conversation with Hansson earlier that morning.

"I think you're mistaken," Åkeson said. "It's not enough for Hansson to have support. I think you have a tendency to overestimate the work that you and your colleagues can handle. This case is big, in fact it's too big. I want to see more people working on it. More manpower means more things can be done at the same time. We're dealing with a man who could kill again. That means we have no time to lose."

"I know," said Wallander. "I keep worrying that we're already too late."

"Reinforcements," Åkeson repeated. "What do you think?"

"For the time being no, that's not the problem."

Tension rose between them.

"Let's say that I, as the leader of the investigation, can't accept that," said Åkeson. "But you don't want more manpower. Where does that leave us?"

"In a difficult situation."

"Very difficult. And unpleasant. If I request more manpower against the wishes of the police, my argument has to be that the present investigative team isn't up to the task. I'd have to declare your team incompetent, even though I'd phrase it in more kindly terms. And I don't want to do that."

"I assume you'll do it if you have to," said Wallander. "And that's when I'll resign from the force."

"God damn it, Kurt!"

"You were the one who started this discussion, not me."

"You've got your regulations. I've got mine. So I regard it as a dereliction of my duty if I don't request that you have more personnel put at your disposal."

"And dogs," said Wallander sarcastically. "I want police dogs. And helicopters."

The discussion was at an end. Wallander regretted flying off the handle. He wasn't sure why he was so opposed to getting reinforcements. He knew that problems in cooperation could damage and delay an investigation. But he couldn't argue with Åkeson's point that more things could be investigated simultaneously with more people.

"Talk to Hansson," Wallander said. "He's the one who makes the decision."

"Hansson doesn't do anything without asking you. And then he does whatever you say."

"I'll refuse to give him my opinion. I'll give you that much help."

Åkeson stood up and turned off a dripping tap with a green hose attached to it. Then he sat down again.

"Let's wait until Monday," he said.

"Let's do that," said Wallander. Then he returned to Louise Fredman. He reiterated that there was no proof that Fredman had abused his daughter. But it might be true; he couldn't rule out anything, and that was why he needed Åkeson's help.

"It's possible I'm making a big mistake," Wallander concluded. "And it wouldn't be the first time. But I can't afford to ignore any leads. I want to know why Louise Fredman is in a psychiatric hospital. And when I find out, we'll decide whether there's any reason to take the next step."

"Which would be?"

"Talking to her."

Åkeson nodded. Wallander was sure he could count on his cooperation. They knew each other well. Åkeson respected Wallander's instincts, even when they lacked solid evidence.

"It can be complicated," said Åkeson. "But I'll try to do something over the weekend."

"I'd appreciate it," said Wallander. "You can call me at the station or at home whenever you like."

Åkeson went inside to make sure he had all of Wallander's phone numbers. The tension between them had evaporated. Åkeson followed him to the gate.

"Summer is off to a good start," he said. "But I'm afraid you haven't had much time to think about that."

Wallander sensed that Åkeson was feeling sympathetic.

"Not much," he replied. "But Ann-Britt's grandmother predicted that the good weather is going to last for a long time."

"Can't she predict where we should be looking for the killer instead?" said Åkeson.

Wallander shook his head in resignation.

"We're getting lots of tip-offs all the time. The usual prophets and psychics have been calling in. There are trainees sorting through the information. Then Höglund and Svedberg go through it, but so far nothing useful has come in. No-one saw a thing, either outside Wetterstedt's house or at Carlman's farm. There aren't many leads about the pit outside the railway station or the van at the airport either."

"The man you're hunting for is careful," said Åkeson.

"Careful, cunning, and totally devoid of human emotions," said Wallander. "I can't imagine how his mind works. Even Ekholm seems dumbstruck. For the first time in my life I've got the feeling that a monster is on the loose."

For a moment Åkeson seemed to be pondering what Wallander had said.

"Ekholm told me he's putting all the data into the computer. He's using the F.B.I. programme. It might produce something."

"Let's hope so," said Wallander.

Wallander said no more. But Åkeson understood what was implied. Before he strikes again.

Wallander drove back to the station. He arrived in the conference room a few minutes late. To cheer up his hard-working detectives, Hansson had driven down to Fridolf's bakery and bought pastries. Wallander sat down in his usual spot and looked around. Martinsson was wearing shorts for the first time that season. Höglund had the first hint of a tan. He wondered enviously how she had had time to sunbathe. The only one dressed appropriately was Ekholm, who had established his base at the far end of the table.

"One of our evening papers had the good taste to provide its readers with historical background on the art of scalping," Svedberg said gloomily. "We can only hope that it won't be the next craze, given all the lunatics we've got running around."

Wallander tapped the table with a pencil.

"Let's get started," he said. "We're searching for the most vicious killer we've ever had to deal with. He has committed all three murders.

But that's all we know. Except for the fact that there's a real risk that he'll strike again."

A hush fell around the table. Wallander hadn't intended to create an oppressive atmosphere. He knew from experience that it was easier if the tone was light, even when the crimes being investigated were brutal. Everyone in the room was just as despondent as he was. The feeling that they were hunting a monster, whose emotional degeneracy was unimaginable, haunted each of them.

It was one of the most demoralising meetings Wallander had ever attended. Outside, the summer was almost unnaturally beautiful, Hansson's pastries were melting and sticky in the heat, and his own revulsion made him feel sick. Although he paid attention to everything said, he was also wondering how he could bear to remain a policeman. Hadn't he reached a point where he ought to realise he had done his share? There had to be more to life. But he also knew that what made him down-hearted was the fact that they couldn't see a single prospect of a break, a chink in the wall that they could squeeze through. They still had a great many leads to pursue, but they lacked a specific direction. In most cases there was an invisible navigation point against which they could correct their course. This time there was no fixed point. They were even starting to doubt that a connection between the murdered men existed.

Three hours later, when the meeting was over, they knew that the only thing to do was keep going. Wallander looked at the exhausted faces around him and told them to try and get some rest. He cancelled all meetings for Sunday. They would meet again on Monday morning. He didn't have to mention the one exception: unless something serious happened. Unless the man who was out there somewhere in the summertime decided to strike again.

Wallander got home in the afternoon and found a note from Linda saying that she would be out that evening. He was tired, and slept for a few hours. When he awoke, he called Baiba twice without success. He talked to Gertrud, who told him everything was fine with his father. He was talking a lot about the trip to Italy. Wallander hoovered the flat and mended a broken window latch. The whole time the thought of the unknown killer occupied his thoughts. At 7 p.m. he made himself a supper of cod fillet and boiled potatoes. Then he sat on the balcony with a cup of coffee and absentmindedly leafed through an old issue of *Ystad Recorder*. When Linda got home they drank tea in the kitchen. The next day Wallander would be allowed to see a rehearsal of the revue she was working on with Kajsa, but Linda was very secretive and didn't want to tell him what it was about. At 11.30 p.m. they both went to bed.

Wallander fell asleep almost at once. Linda lay awake in her room listening to the night birds. Then she fell asleep too, leaving the door to her room ajar.

Neither of them stirred when the front door was opened very slowly at 2 a.m. Hoover was barefoot. He stood motionless in the hall, listening. He could hear a man snoring in a room to the left of the living-room. He stepped into the flat. The door to another room stood ajar. A girl who might have been his sister's age was in there sleeping. He couldn't resist the temptation to go in and stand right next to her. His power over the sleeper was absolute. He went on towards the room where the snoring was coming from. The policeman named Wallander lay on his back and had kicked off all but a small part of the sheet. He was sleeping heavily. His chest heaved with his deep breathing.

Hoover stood utterly still and watched him. He thought about his sister, who would soon be freed from all this evil. Who would soon return to life. He looked at the sleeping man and thought about the girl in the next room, who must be his daughter. He made his decision. In a few days he would return.

He left the flat as soundlessly as he had come, locking the door with the keys he had taken from the policeman's jacket. A few moments later the silence was broken by a moped starting up. Then all was quiet again, except for the night birds singing.

CHAPTER 27

When Wallander awoke on Sunday morning he felt that he had slept enough for the first time in a long while. It was past 8 a.m. Through a gap in the curtains he could see a patch of blue. He stayed in bed and listened for Linda. Then he got up, put on his newly washed dressing gown, and peeked into her room. She was still asleep. He felt transported back to her childhood. He smiled at the memory and went to the kitchen to make coffee. The thermometer outside the kitchen window showed 19°C. When the coffee was ready he laid a breakfast tray for Linda. He remembered what she liked. One three-minute egg, toast, a few slices of cheese, and a sliced-up tomato. Only water to drink.

He drank his coffee and waited a while longer. She was startled out of her sleep when he called her name. When she saw the tray she burst out laughing. He sat at the foot of the bed while she ate. He hadn't thought of the investigation except briefly when he'd woken.

Linda set the tray aside, leaned back in bed, and stretched.

"What were you doing up last night?" she asked. "Did you have trouble sleeping?"

"I slept like a rock," said Wallander. "I didn't even get up to go to the bathroom."

"Then I must have been dreaming," she said, yawning. "I thought you opened my door and came into my room."

"You must have been," he said. "For once I slept the whole night through."

They agreed that they would meet at Österport Square at 7 p.m. Linda asked him if he knew that Sweden would be playing Saudi Arabia in the quarter-finals at that time. Wallander said he didn't give a damn, although he had bet that Sweden would win it 3–1 and advanced Martinsson another hundred kronor. The girls had managed to borrow an empty shop for their rehearsals.

After she left, Wallander took out his ironing board and started ironing his clean shirts. After doing a passable job on two of them, he got bored and called Baiba. She was glad to hear from him, he could tell. He told her that Linda was visiting and that he felt rested for the first time in weeks. Baiba was busy finishing her work at the university before the summer break. She talked about the trip to Skagen with childlike anticipation. After they hung up, Wallander went into the living-room and put on *Aïda*, the volume turned up high.

He felt happy and full of energy. He sat out on the balcony and read through the newspapers from the past few days, skipping reports on the murders. He had granted himself half a day off, total escape until midday. Then he was going to get cracking again. But Åkeson called him at 11.15 a.m. He had been in touch with the chief prosecutor in Malmö and they had discussed Wallander's request. Åkeson thought it would be possible for Wallander to get answers to some of his questions about Louise Fredman within the next few days. But he had one reservation.

"Wouldn't it be simpler to get the girl's mother to give you the answers you need?" he asked.

"I'm not sure I'd get the truth from her," Wallander answered.

"Which is what?"

"The mother is protecting her daughter," said Wallander. "It's only natural. I would do the same. No matter what she told me, it would be coloured by the fact that she's protecting her. Medical records and doctors' reports speak another language."

"You know best," said Åkeson, promising that he'd be in touch again as soon as he had something concrete to tell him.

The talk with Åkeson set Wallander thinking about the case again. He decided to take a notebook and sit on the balcony to go over the plan of the investigation for the coming week. He was getting hungry, though, and thought he'd allow himself to eat out. Just before noon he left the flat, dressed all in white like a tennis player, wearing sandals. He drove east out of town along Österleden, thinking that he could drop in on his father later on. If he hadn't had the investigation hanging over his head, he could have taken Gertrud and his father to lunch somewhere. But right now he needed time to himself. Over the past few weeks he had been constantly surrounded by people, involved in team meetings, and in discussions with others. Now he wanted to be alone.

Hardly aware of where he was going, he drove all the way to Simrishamn. He parked by the marina and took a walk. He found a corner table to himself at the Harbour Inn, and sat watching the holiday makers all around him. One of these people could be the man I'm looking for, he thought. If Ekholm's theories are right – that the killer lives a completely normal life, with no outward signs that he subjects his victims to the worst violence imaginable – then he could be sitting right here eating lunch. And at that instant the summer day slipped out of his hands. He went over everything one more time. He didn't know why, but he began with the girl who died in the rape field. She had nothing to do with the other events; it had been a suicide, prompted by some as yet unknown cause. Still, that's where Wallander began each time he started one of his reviews of the case.

But on this particular Sunday, in the Harbour Inn in Simrishamn, something started churning in his subconscious. It came to him that someone had said something in connection with the girl's death. He sat there with his fork in his hand and tried to coax the thought to the surface. Who had said it? What had been said? Why was it important? After a while he gave up. Sooner or later he'd remember what it was. His subconscious always demanded patience. As if to prove that he actually possessed that patience, he ordered dessert. With satisfaction he noted that the shorts he'd put on for the first time that summer weren't quite as tight as they had been the year before. He ate his apple pie and ordered coffee.

He tried to follow his thoughts the way a discerning actor reads through his part for the first time. Where were the gaps? Where were the faults? Where did he combine fact and circumstance too sloppily and draw a wrong conclusion? He went through Wetterstedt's house again, through the garden, out onto the beach; he imagined Wetterstedt in front of him, and Wallander became the killer stalking Wetterstedt like a silent shadow. He climbed onto the garage roof and read a torn comic book while he waited for Wetterstedt to settle at his desk and maybe leaf through his collection of pornographic photographs.

Then he did the same thing with Carlman; he put a motorcycle behind the road workers' hut and followed the tractor path up to the hill where he had a view over Carlman's farm. Now and then he made a note on his pad. *The garage roof. What did he hope to see? Carlman's hill. Binoculars?* He went over everything that had happened, deaf to the noise around him. He paid another visit to Hugo Sandin, he talked once more with Sara Björklund, and he made a note that he ought to get in touch with her again. Maybe the same questions would provoke different, fuller answers. What would the difference be? He thought for a long time about Carlman's daughter. He thought about Louise Fredman, and her polite brother. He was rested, his fatigue was gone, and his thoughts rose easily and soared on the updraughts inside him.

He glanced at what he had scribbled on his pad, as if it were magic, automatic writing, and left the Harbour Inn. He sat on one of the benches in the park outside the Hotel Svea and looked out over the sea. There was a warm, gentle breeze blowing. The crew of a yacht with a Danish flag was struggling with an unruly spinnaker. Wallander read his notes again.

The connection was always shifting, from parents to children. He thought about Carlman's daughter and Louise Fredman. Was it just a coincidence that one of them had tried to commit suicide after her father died and the other had been in a psychiatric clinic for a long time?

Wetterstedt was the exception. He had two adult children. Wallander recalled something Rydberg had once said. *What happens first is not necessarily the beginning.* Could that be true in this case? He tried to imagine that the killer they were looking for was a woman. But it was impossible. He thought of the physical strength needed for the scalpings, the axe blows, and the acid in Fredman's eyes. It had to be a man. A man who kills men. While women commit suicide or suffer mental illness.

He got up and moved to another bench, as if to register the fact that there were other conceivable explanations. Gustaf Wetterstedt was involved in shady deals. There was a vague but still unexplained connection between him and Carlman. It had to do with art, art theft, maybe forgery. It all had to do with money. It wasn't inconceivable that Björn Fredman could also be involved in the same area. He hadn't found anything useful in the dossier on his life, but he couldn't write it off yet. Nothing could be written off yet; that presented both a problem and an opportunity.

Wallander watched the Danish yacht. The crew had begun folding up the spinnaker. He took out his pad and looked at the last word he had written. *Mystery*. There was a hint of ritual to the murders. He had thought so himself, and Ekholm had pointed it out at the last meeting. The scalps were a ritual, as trophy collecting always was. The significance was the same as that of a moose's head mounted on a hunter's wall. It was the proof. The proof of what? For whom? For the killer alone, or for someone else as well? For a god or a demon conjured up in a sick mind? For someone else, whose demeanour was just as inconspicuous as the killer's?

Wallander thought about what Ekholm had said about invocations and initiation rites. A sacrifice was made so that another could obtain grace. Become rich, make a fortune, get well? There were many possibilities. There were motorcycle gangs with rules about how new members proved themselves worthy. In the United States it wasn't unusual to have to kill someone, whether picked at random or specially chosen, to be deemed worthy of membership. This macabre rite had spread, even to Sweden. Wallander thought of the motorcycle gangs in Skåne, and he remembered the road workers' hut at the bottom of Carlman's hill. The thought was dizzying – that the tracks might lead them to motorcycle gangs. Wallander put aside this idea for the moment, although he knew that nothing could be ruled out.

He walked back to the other bench where he had sat before. He was back at the starting point. He realised that he couldn't go any further without discussing it with someone. He thought of Ann-Britt Höglund. Could he bother her on a Sunday? He got up and went over to his car to call her. She was at home. He was welcome to drop by. Guiltily, he postponed his visit to his father. He had to have someone else confront his ideas, and if he waited, there was a good chance he would get lost among multiple trains of thought. He drove back towards Ystad, keeping just above the speed limit. He hadn't heard about any speed traps planned for this Sunday.

It was 3 p.m. when he pulled up in front of Höglund's house. She was in a light summer dress. Her two children were playing in a neighbour's garden. She offered Wallander the porch swing while she sat in a wicker chair.

"I really didn't want to bother you," he said. "You could have said no."

"Yesterday I was tired," she replied. "As we all were. *Are*, I mean. But today I feel better."

"Last night was definitely the night of the sleeping policemen," said Wallander. "It reaches a point where you can't push yourself any further. All you get is empty, grey fatigue. We'd reached that point."

He told her about his trip to Simrishamn, about how he went back and forth between the benches in the park down by the harbour.

"I went over everything again," he said. "Sometimes it's possible to make unexpected discoveries. But you know that already."

"I'm hoping something will come of Ekholm's work," she said. "Computers that are correctly programmed can cross-reference investigative material and come up with links that you wouldn't have dreamed were there. They don't *think*. But sometimes they *combine* better than we can."

"My distrust of computers is partly because I'm getting old," said Wallander. "But it doesn't mean I don't want Ekholm to succeed with his behavioural method. For me, of course, it's of no importance who sets the snare that catches the killer just as long as it happens. And soon."

She gave him a sombre look.

"Do you think that he will strike again?"

"I do. Without being able to get a handle on why, I think there's something *unfinished* about this murder scenario. If you'll pardon the expression. There's something missing. It scares me. And yes, it makes me think he'll strike again."

"How are we going to find where Fredman was killed?" she asked.

"Unless we're lucky, we won't," said Wallander. "Or unless somebody heard something."

"I've been checking up on whether there have been any calls coming in from people who heard screams," she said. "But I have found nothing."

The unheard scream hung over them. Wallander rocked slowly back and forth on the swing.

"It's rare that a solution comes clean out of the blue," he said when the silence had lasted too long. "I was walking back and forth between the benches in the park, and I wondered whether I had already had the idea that would give me the solution. I might have got something right without being aware of it."

She was thinking about what he had said. Now and then she glanced over at the neighbour's garden.

"We didn't learn anything at the police academy about a man who takes scalps and pours acid into the eyes of his victims," she said. "Life really turns out to be as unpredictable as I imagined."

Wallander nodded without replying. Then he started, unsure whether he could pull it off, and went over what he had been thinking about by the sea. He knew that telling someone else would shed a different light on it. But even though Ann-Britt listened intently, almost like a student at her master's feet, she didn't stop him to say that he had made a mistake or drawn a wrong conclusion. All she said when he had finished was that she was bowled over by his ability to dissect and then summarise the whole investigation, which seemed so overwhelming. But she had nothing to add. Even if Wallander's equations were correct, they lacked the crucial components. Höglund couldn't help him, no-one could.

She went inside and brought out some cups and a thermos of coffee. Her youngest girl came and crept onto the porch swing next to Wallander. She didn't resemble her mother, so he assumed she took after her father, who was in Saudi Arabia. Wallander realised he still hadn't met him.

"Your husband is a puzzle," he said. "I'm starting to wonder if he really exists. Or if he's just someone you dreamed up."

"I sometimes ask myself the same question," she answered, laughing.

The girl went inside.

"What about Carlman's daughter?" asked Wallander, watching the girl. "How is she?"

"Svedberg called the hospital yesterday," she said. "The crisis isn't over. But I had the feeling that the doctors were more hopeful."

"She didn't leave a note?"

"Nothing."

"It matters most that she's a well human being," said Wallander. "But I can't help thinking of her as a witness."

"To what?"

"To something that might have a bearing on her father's death. I don't believe that the timing of the suicide attempt was coincidental."

"What makes me think that you're not convinced of what you're saying?"

"I'm not," said Wallander. "I'm groping and fumbling my way along. There's only one incontrovertible fact in this investigation, and that is that we have no concrete evidence to go on."

"So we have no way of knowing if we're on the right track?"

"Or if we're going in circles."

She hesitated before she asked the next question.

"Do you think that maybe there aren't enough of us?"

"Until now I've dug my heels in on that issue," said Wallander.

"But I'm beginning to have my doubts. The question will come up tomorrow."

"With Per Åkeson?"

Wallander nodded.

"What have we got to lose?"

"Small units move more easily than large ones, but you could also argue that more heads do better thinking. Åkeson's argument is that we can work on a broader front. The infantry is spread out and covers more ground."

"As if we were all sweeping the area."

Wallander nodded. Her image was telling. What was missing was that the sweep they were doing was happening in a terrain where they were only barely able to take their bearings. And they had no idea of whom they were looking for.

"There's something we're all missing," said Wallander. "I'm still searching for something someone said right after Wetterstedt was murdered. I can't remember who said it. I only know that it was important, but it was too soon for me to recognise the significance."

"You like to say that police work is most often a question of patience."

"And it is. But patience has its limits. Someone else could get killed. We can never escape the fact that our investigation is not just a matter of solving crimes that have already been committed. Right now it feels as though our job is to prevent more murders."

"We can't do any more than we're doing already."

"How do we know that?" asked Wallander. "How do we know we're using our resources to their best effect?"

She had no answer.

He sat there for a while longer. At 4.30 p.m. he turned down an invitation to stay and have dinner with them.

"Thanks for coming," she said as she followed him to the gate. "Are you going to watch the game?"

"No. I have to meet my daughter. But I think we're going to win, 3–1."

She gave him a quizzical look.

"That's what I bet, too."

"Then we'll both win or we'll both lose," said Wallander.

"Thanks for coming," she said again.

"Thanks for what?" he asked in surprise. "For disturbing your Sunday?"

"For thinking I might have something worthwhile to say."

"I've said it before and I'll say it again, I think you're a talented policewoman. You believe in the ability of computers not only to make our work easier, but to improve it. I don't, and maybe you can change my mind."

Wallander drove towards town. He stopped at a shop that was open on Sundays and bought groceries. Then he lay back in the deckchair on his balcony. His need for sleep was enormous, and he dozed off. But just before 7 p.m. he was standing on the square at Österport. Linda came to get him and took him to the empty shop nearby. They had rigged up some lights and put out a chair for him. At once he felt self-conscious. He might not understand or might laugh in the wrong place. The girls vanished into an adjoining room. Wallander waited. More than 15 minutes passed. When they finally returned they had changed clothes and now looked exactly alike. After arranging the lights and the simple set, they got started. The hour-long performance was about a pair of twins. Wallander was nervous at being the only audience. Most of all he was fearful that Linda might not be very good. But it wasn't long before he realised that the two girls had written a witty script that presented a critical view of Sweden with dark humour. Sometimes they lost the thread, sometimes he thought that their acting wasn't convincing. But they believed in what they were doing, and that gave him pleasure. When it was over and they asked him what he thought, he told them that he was surprised, that it was funny, that it was thought-provoking. He could see that Linda was watching to see whether he was telling the truth. When she realised he was, she was very happy. She escorted him out.

"I didn't know you could do this sort of thing," he said. "I thought you wanted to be a furniture upholsterer."

"It's never too late," she said. "Let me give it a try."

"Of course you have to," he said. "When you're young you have plenty of time. Not like when you're an old policeman like me."

They were going to rehearse for a few more hours. He would wait for her at home. The summer evening was beautiful. He was walking slowly towards Mariagatan, thinking about the performance, when it dawned on him that cars were driving by, horns honking, people cheering. Sweden must have won. He asked a man he met on the footpath what the score was. 3–1 to Sweden. He burst out laughing. Then his thoughts returned to his daughter, and how little he really knew about her. He still hadn't asked her if she had a boyfriend.

He had just closed the door to his flat when the phone rang. At once he felt a twinge of fear. When he heard Gertrud's voice, he was instantly relieved. But Gertrud was upset. At first he couldn't understand what she was saying. He asked her to slow down.

"You must come over," she said. "Right away."

"What happened?"

"Your father has started burning his paintings. He's burning everything in his studio. And he's locked the door. You've got to come now."

Wallander wrote a quick note to Linda, put it under the doormat, and moments later was on his way to Löderup.

CHAPTER 28

Gertrud met him in the courtyard of the farmhouse. He could see that she'd been crying, but she answered his questions calmly. His father's breakdown, if that was what it was, had come on unexpectedly. They had had their dinner as normal. They hadn't had anything to drink. After the meal his father had gone out to the barn to continue painting, as usual. Suddenly she'd heard a great racket. When she went out on the front steps she'd seen the old man tossing empty paint cans into the yard. At first she thought he was cleaning out his chaotic studio. But when he started throwing out new frames she went and asked what he was doing. He didn't reply. He gave the impression of not being there at all, not hearing her. When she took hold of his arm he pulled himself free and locked himself inside the barn. Through the window, she watched him start a fire in the stove, and when he started tearing up his canvases and stuffing them into the flames she called Kurt.

They crossed the courtyard as she talked. Wallander saw smoke billowing from the chimney. He went up to the window and peered inside. His father looked wild and demented. His hair was on end, he was without his glasses, and the studio was a wreck. He was squishing around barefoot amongst spilled pots of paint, and trampled canvases were strewn everywhere. He was ripping up a canvas and stuffing the pieces into the fire. Wallander thought he saw a shoe burning in the stove. He knocked on the window, but there was no response. He tried the door. Locked. He banged on it and yelled that he had come to visit. There was no answer, but the racket inside continued. Wallander looked around for something to break down the door. But his father kept all his tools in the studio.

Wallander studied the door, which he had helped build. He took off his jacket and handed it to Gertrud. Then he slammed his shoulder against it as hard as he could. The whole doorjamb came away, and Wallander tumbled into the room, banging his head on a wheelbarrow. His father glanced at him vacantly and went on tearing up canvases.

Gertrud wanted to come in, but Wallander warned her away. He had seen his father like this once before, a strange combination of detachment and manic confusion. On that occasion he had found him walking in his pyjamas through a muddy field with a suitcase in his hand. Now he went up to him, took him by the shoulders, and began talking soothingly to him. He asked if there was something wrong. He said the paintings were fine, they were the best he'd ever done, the grouse were beautifully painted. Everything was all right. Anyone could have a bad day once in a while. But he had to stop burning things for no reason. Why should they have a fire in the middle of summer, anyway? They could get cleaned up and talk about the trip to Italy. Wallander kept talking, with a strong grip on his father's shoulders, as the old man squinted myopically at him. While Wallander kept up his reassuring chatter he discovered his glasses trampled to bits on the floor. He asked Gertrud, who was hovering by the door, whether there was a spare pair. She ran to the house to get them and handed them to Wallander, who wiped them on his sleeve and then set them on his father's nose. He continued to speak in a soothing voice, repeating his words as if he were reading the verses of a prayer. His father looked at him in bewilderment at first, then astonishment, and finally it seemed as though he had come to his senses again. Wallander released his grip. His father looked cautiously about him at the destruction.

"What happened here?" he asked. Wallander could see that he had forgotten everything. Gertrud began to weep. Wallander told her firmly to go and make some coffee. They'd be there in a minute. At last the old man seemed to grasp that he had been involved in the havoc.

"Did I do all this?" he asked, looking at Wallander with restless eyes, as if he feared the answer.

"Who doesn't get sick and tired of things?" Wallander said. "But it's all over now. We'll soon get this mess cleaned up."

His father looked at the smashed door.

"Who needs doors in the middle of summer?" said Wallander. "There aren't any closed doors in Rome in the summer. You'll have to get used to that."

His father walked slowly through the debris from the frenzy that neither he nor anyone else could explain. Wallander felt a lump in his throat. There was something helpless about his father, and he didn't know how to deal with it. He lifted the broken door and leaned it against the wall. He began tidying up the room, discovering that many of the canvases had survived. His father sat on a stool at his workbench and watched. Gertrud came in and told them that coffee was ready. Wallander gestured to her to take his father inside. Then he cleaned up the worst of the mess.

Before he went into the kitchen he called home. Linda was there. She wanted to know what had happened; she could barely decipher his quickly scribbled note. Wallander didn't want to worry her, so he said that her grandfather had just been feeling bad, but was fine now. To be on the safe side he'd decided to stay overnight in Löderup. He went in the kitchen. His father was feeling tired and had gone to lie down. Wallander stayed with Gertrud for a couple of hours, sitting at the kitchen table. There was no way to explain what had happened except that it was a symptom of the illness. But when Gertrud said this attack ruled out the trip to Italy in the autumn, Wallander protested. He wasn't afraid of taking responsibility. He would manage. It was going to happen, so long as his father wanted to go and was able to stand on his own two feet.

That night he slept on a fold-out bed in the living-room. He lay staring out into the light summer night for a long time before he fell asleep.

In the morning, over coffee, his father seemed to have forgotten the whole episode. He couldn't understand what had happened to the studio door. Wallander told him the truth, that he was the one who had broken it down. The studio needed a new door, and anyway, he would make it himself.

"When are you going to be able to do that?" asked his father. "You don't even have time to call ahead of time and tell me you're coming to visit."

Wallander knew then that everything was back to normal. He left Löderup just after 7 a.m. It wasn't the last time something like this might happen, he knew, and with a shiver imagined what might have occurred if Gertrud hadn't been there.

Wallander went straight to the station. Everyone was talking about the match. He was surrounded by people in summer clothes. Only the ones who had to wear uniforms looked remotely like police officers. Wallander thought that in his white clothes he could have stepped out of one of the Danish productions of Italian opera he'd been to. As he passed the reception desk Ebba waved to him that he had a call. It was Forsfält. They had found Fredman's passport, well hidden in his flat, along with large sums of foreign currencies. Wallander asked about the stamps in the passport.

"I have to disappoint you," Forsfält told him. "He had the passport for four years, and it has stamps from Turkey, Morocco and Brazil. That's all."

Wallander was indeed disappointed, although he wasn't sure what he had expected. Forsfält promised to fax over the details on the passport. Then he said he had something else to tell him that had no direct bearing on the investigation.

"We found some keys to the attic when we were looking for the passport. Among all the junk up there we found a box containing some antique icons. We were able to determine pretty quickly that they were stolen. Guess where from."

Wallander thought for a moment but couldn't come up with anything. "I give up."

"About a year ago there was a burglary at a house near Ystad. The house was under the administration of an executor, because it was part of the estate of a deceased lawyer named Gustaf Torstensson."

Wallander remembered him. One of two lawyers murdered the year before. Wallander had seen the collection of icons in the basement that belonged to the older of the two lawyers. He even had one of them hanging on the wall of his bedroom, a present he'd received from the dead lawyer's secretary. Now he also recalled the break-in; it was Svedberg's case.

"So now we know," said Wallander.

"You'll be getting the follow-up report," Forsfält told him.

"Not me," said Wallander. "Svedberg."

Forsfält asked how it was going with Louise Fredman.

"With a little luck we'll know something later today," said Wallander, and told him about his last conversation with Åkeson.

"Keep me informed."

After they hung up he checked his list of unanswered questions. He could cross out some of them, while others he would have to bring up at the team meeting. But first he had to see the two trainees who were keeping track of the tip-offs coming in from the public. Had anything come in that might indicate exactly where Fredman was murdered? Wallander knew this could be highly significant for the investigation.

One of the trainees had close-cropped hair and was named Tyrén. He had intelligent eyes and was thought of as competent. Wallander quickly explained what he was looking for.

"Someone who heard screams?" asked Tyrén. "And saw a Ford van? On the night of Tuesday, 28 June?"

"That's right."

Tyrén shook his head.

"I would have remembered that," he said. "A woman screamed in a flat in Rydsgård. But that was on Wednesday. And she was drunk."

"Let me know immediately if anything comes in," said Wallander.

He left Tyrén and went down to the meeting room. Hansson was talking to a reporter in reception. Wallander remembered seeing him before. He was a stringer for one or other of the big national evening papers. They waited a few minutes until Hansson got rid of the reporter, and then closed the door. Hansson sat down and gave Wallander the floor at once. Just as he was about to start, Åkeson came in and sat at the far end of the table, next to Ekholm. Wallander raised his eyebrows and gave him an inquiring look. Åkeson nodded. Wallander knew that meant there was news about Louise Fredman. With difficulty, he contained his curiosity, and called on Höglund. She reported the news from the hospital. Carlman's daughter was in a stable condition. It would be possible to talk to her within 24 hours. No-one could see an objection to Höglund and Wallander visiting the hospital.

Wallander went quickly down the list of unanswered questions. Nyberg was well prepared, as usual, able to fill in many of the gaps with laboratory results. But nothing was significant enough to provoke long discussion. Mostly they had confirmation of conclusions they had already drawn. The only new information was that there were faint traces of kelp on Fredman's clothes. This could be an indication that Fredman had been near the sea on the last day of his life. Wallander thought for a moment.

"Where are the traces of kelp?" he asked.

Nyberg checked his notes.

"On the back of his jacket."

"He could have been killed near the sea," said Wallander. "As far as I can recall, there was a slight breeze that night. If the surf was loud enough, it might explain why no-one heard screams."

"If it happened on the beach we would have found traces of sand," said Nyberg.

"Maybe it was on a boat," Svedberg suggested.

"Or a dock," said Höglund.

The question hung in the air. It would be impossible to check the thousands of pleasure boats and docks. Wallander noted that they should watch out for tip-offs from people who lived near the sea. Then he gave the floor to Åkeson.

"I succeeded in gathering some information about Louise Fredman," he said. "I remind you that this is highly confidential and cannot be mentioned to anyone outside the investigative team."

"We understand this," Wallander said.

"Louise Fredman is at St Lars Hospital in Lund," Åkeson continued. "She has been there for more than three years. The diagnosis is severe psychosis. She has stopped talking, sometimes has to be force-fed, and there is no sign of improvement. She's 17 years old. Judging from a photograph I saw she's quite pretty."

The group was silent.

"Psychosis is usually caused by something," said Ekholm.

"She was admitted on 9 January 1991," said Åkeson, after looking through his papers. "Her illness seems to have struck like a bolt from the blue. She had been missing from home for a week. She was having serious problems at school and was often truant. There were signs of drug abuse. Not heavy narcotics, mostly amphetamines and possibly cocaine. She was found in Pildamm Park, completely irrational."

"Were there signs of external injuries?" asked Wallander, who was listening intently.

"Not according to the material I've received."

Wallander thought about this.

"Well, we can't talk to her," he said finally. "But I want to know whether she had any injuries. And I want to talk to the person who found her."

"It was three years ago," said Åkeson. "But the people involved could probably be traced."

"I'll talk to Forsfält in Malmö," said Wallander. "Uniformed officers most probably found her. There will be a report on it."

"Why do you wonder if she had any injuries?" Hansson asked.

"I just want to fill in the picture as completely as possible," Wallander replied.

They left Louise Fredman and went on to other topics. Since Ekholm was still waiting for the F.B.I. programme to finish cross-referencing all the investigative material, Wallander turned the discussion to the question of reinforcements. Hansson had already received a positive response from the county chief of police as to the possibility of a sergeant from Malmö. He would be in Ystad by lunchtime.

"Who is it?" asked Martinsson, who had so far been silent.

"His name is Sture Holmström," said Hansson.

"Do we know anything about him?" Martinsson asked.

No-one knew him. Wallander promised to call Forsfält to check on him.

Then Wallander turned to Åkeson.

"The question now is whether we should ask for additional reinforcements," Wallander began. "What's the general view? I want everyone's opinion. I also undertake to bow to the will of the majority. Even though I'm not convinced that extra personnel will improve the quality of our work. I'm afraid we might lose the pace of our investigation. At least in the short run. But I want to hear your views."

Martinsson and Svedberg were in favour of requesting extra personnel. Höglund sided with Wallander, and Hansson and Ekholm didn't offer an opinion. Wallander saw that another burdensome mantle of responsibility had been draped around his shoulders. Åkeson proposed that they postpone the decision for a few more days.

"If there's another murder, it'll be unavoidable," he said. "But for the time being let's keep going the way we have been."

The meeting finished just before 10 a.m. Wallander went to his room. It had been a good meeting, much better than the last, even though they hadn't made any progress. They had shown one another that their energy and will were still strong.

Wallander was about to call Forsfält when Martinsson appeared in his doorway.

"There's one more thing that's occurred to me," he said, leaning against the doorframe. "Louise Fredman was found wandering around on a path in the park. There's a similarity to the girl running in the rape field."

Martinsson was right. There was a similarity, albeit a remote one.

"I agree," he said. "It's a shame that there's no connection."

"Still, it's weird," said Martinsson.

He remained in the doorway.

"You bet right this time."

Wallander nodded.

"I know," he said. "So did Ann-Britt."

"You'll have to split a thousand."

"When's the next match?"

"I'll let you know," said Martinsson and left.

Wallander called Malmö. While he waited, he looked out of the open window. Another beautiful day. Then Forsfält came on the line, and he pushed all thoughts of summer aside.

He took a long time selecting the right axe from the ones lying polished on the black silk cloth. Finally he chose the smallest one, the one he hadn't used yet. He stuck it in his wide leather belt and pulled the helmet over his head.

As before, he was barefoot when he locked the door behind him. The evening was warm. He rode along side roads that he had selected on the map. It would take him almost two hours. He would get there a little before 11 p.m.

He'd had to change his plans. The man who had gone abroad suddenly had returned. He decided not to risk his taking off again. He had listened to Geronimo's heart. The rhythmic thumping of the drums inside his chest had delivered their message to him. He must not wait. He would seize the opportunity.

The summer landscape seen from inside his helmet took on a bluish tinge. He could see the sea to his left, the blinking lights of ships, and the coast of Denmark. He felt elated and happy. It wouldn't be long now before he could bring his sister the last sacrifice that would liberate her from the fog that surrounded her. She would return to life in the loveliest part of the summer.

He got to the city just after 11 p.m., and 15 minutes later stopped on a street next to the large villa, hidden away in a garden full of tall, sheltering trees. He chained his moped to a lamppost and locked it. On the opposite footpath an old couple were walking their dog. He waited until they disappeared before he pulled off his helmet and stuffed it into his backpack. In the shadows he ran to the back of the property, which looked out over a football pitch. He hid his backpack in the long grass and crept through the hedge, at a point where he had long ago prepared an opening. The hedge scratched his bare arms and feet. But he steeled himself against all pain. Geronimo would not stand for weakness. He had a sacred mission, as written in the book he had received from his sister. The mission required all his strength, which he was prepared to sacrifice with devotion.

He was inside the garden now, closer to the beast than he had ever been. The entire ground floor was in darkness, but there was a light on upstairs. He remembered with anger how his sister had been here before him. She had described the house, and one day he would burn it to the ground. But not yet. Cautiously he ran up to the wall of the house and prised open the basement window from which he had earlier removed the latch. It was easy to crawl inside. He knew that he was in an apple cellar, surrounded by the faint aroma of sour apples. He listened. All quiet. He crept up the cellar stairs, into the big kitchen. Still quiet. The only thing he heard was the faint sound of water pipes. He turned on the oven and opened the door. Then he made his way upstairs. He had taken the axe out of his belt. He was completely calm.

The door to the bathroom was ajar. In the darkness of the hall he caught a glimpse of the man he was going to kill. He was standing in front of the bathroom mirror rubbing cream onto his face. Hoover slipped in behind the bathroom door, waiting. When the man turned off the light in the bathroom he raised the axe. He struck only once. The man fell to the floor without a sound. With the axe he sliced off a piece of the man's hair from the top of his head. He stuffed the scalp into his pocket. Then he dragged the man down the stairs. He was in pyjamas. The bottoms slipped off the body and were dragged along by one foot. He avoided looking at him.

He pulled the man into the kitchen and leaned the body against the oven door. Then he shoved the man's head inside. Almost at once he smelled the face cream starting to melt. He left the house the way he had come in.

He buried the scalp beneath his sister's window in the dawn light. Now all that was left was the extra sacrifice he would offer her. He would bury one last scalp. Then it would be over.

He thought about the man he had watched sleeping. The man who had sat across from him on the sofa, understanding nothing of the sacred mission he had to perform. He still hadn't decided whether he should also take the girl sleeping in the next room. He would make his final decision the next day, but now he had to rest.

Skåne

5–8 July 1994

CHAPTER 29

Waldemar Sjösten was a criminal detective in Helsingborg who devoted all his free time during the summer to a 1930s mahogany boat he had found by accident. And this was just what he planned to do on Tuesday morning, 5 July, when he let the shade on his bedroom window roll up with a snap just before 6 a.m. He lived in a newly renovated block of flats at the centre of town. One street, the railway line and the docks were all that separated him from the Sound. The weather was as beautiful as the weather reports had promised. His holiday didn't start until the end of July, but whenever he could he spent a few early mornings on his boat, docked at the marina a short bike ride away. Sjösten was going to celebrate his 50th birthday this autumn. He had been married three times, had six children and was planning his fourth marriage. The woman shared his love of the boat, *Sea King II*. He had taken the name from the beautiful boat that he'd spent his childhood summers on board with his parents, *Sea King I*. His father had sold it to a man from Norway when he was ten, and he had never forgotten it. He often wondered whether the boat still existed, or whether it had sunk or rotted away.

He had finished a cup of coffee and was getting ready to leave when the telephone rang. He was surprised to hear it at such an early hour. He picked up the receiver.

"Waldemar?" It was Detective Sergeant Birgersson.

"Yes."

"I hope I didn't wake you."

"I was just on my way out."

"Lucky I caught you then. You'd better get down here right away." Birgersson wouldn't have called unless it was something serious.

"I'll be right there," he said. "What is it?"

"There was smoke coming out of one of those old villas up in Tågaborg. When the fire brigade got there they found a man in the kitchen."

"Dead?"

"Murdered. You'll understand why I called you when you see him."

Sjösten could see his morning disappearing, but he was a dutiful policeman, so he had no trouble changing his plans. Instead of the key to his bicycle lock he grabbed his car keys and left at once. It took him only a few minutes to drive to the station. Birgersson was on the steps waiting. He got in the car and gave him directions.

"Who's dead?" Sjösten asked.

"Åke Liljegren."

Sjösten whistled. Åke Liljegren was well known, not just in the city but all over Sweden. He called himself "the Auditor" and had gained his notoriety as the *éminence grise* behind some extensive shell company dealing done during the 1980s. Apart from one six-month suspended sentence, the police had had no success in prosecuting the illegal operation he ran. Liljegren had become a by-word for the worst type of financial scams, and the fact that he got off scot-free demonstrated how ill-equipped the justice system was to handle criminals like him. He was from Båstad, but in recent years had lived in Helsingborg when he was in Sweden. Sjösten recalled a newspaper article that had set out to uncover how many houses Liljegren owned across the world.

"Can you give me a time frame?" asked Sjösten.

"A jogger out early this morning saw smoke coming out of the house. He raised the alarm. The fire department got there at 5.15 a.m."

"Where was the fire?"

"There was no fire."

Sjösten gave Birgersson a puzzled look.

"Liljegren was leaning into the oven," Birgersson explained. "His head was in the oven, which was on full blast. He was literally being roasted."

Sjösten grimaced. He was beginning to get an idea what he was going to have to look at.

"Did he commit suicide?"

"No. Someone stuck an axe in his head."

Sjösten stomped involuntarily on the brake. He looked at Birgersson, who nodded.

"His face and hair were almost completely burnt off. But the doctor thought he could tell that someone had sliced off part of his scalp."

Sjösten said nothing. He was thinking about what had happened in Ystad. That was this summer's big news. A serial killer who axed people to death and then took their scalps.

They arrived at Liljegren's villa on Aschebergsgatan. A fire engine was parked outside the gates along with a few police cars and an ambulance. The huge property was cordoned off. Sjösten got out of the car and waved off a reporter. He and Birgersson ducked under the cordon and walked up to the villa. When they entered the house Sjösten noticed a sickly smell, and realised that it was Liljegren's burnt corpse. He borrowed a handkerchief from Birgersson and held it to his nose and mouth. Birgersson nodded towards the kitchen. A very pale uniformed officer stood guard at the door. Sjösten peered inside. The sight that greeted him was grotesque. The half-naked man was on his knees. His body was bent over the oven door. His head and neck were out of sight inside the oven. With disgust Sjösten recalled the fairy tale of Hänsel and Gretel and the witch. A doctor was kneeling down beside the body, shining a torch into the oven. Sjösten tried to breathe through his mouth. The doctor nodded at him. Sjösten leaned forward and looked into the oven. He was reminded of a charred steak.

"Jesus," he said.

"He took a blow to the back of the head," said the doctor.

"Here in the kitchen?"

"No, upstairs," said Birgersson, standing behind him.

Sjösten straightened up.

"Take him out of the oven," he said. "Has the photographer finished?"

Birgersson nodded. Sjösten followed him upstairs, avoiding the traces of blood. Birgersson stopped outside the bathroom door.

"As you saw, he was wearing pyjamas," said Birgersson. "Here's how it probably happened: Liljegren was in the bathroom. The killer was waiting for him. He struck Liljegren with an axe in the back of the head and then dragged the body to the kitchen. That could explain why the pyjama bottoms were hanging from one leg. Then he put the body in front of the oven, turned it on, and left. We don't know yet how he got into the house and out again. I thought you might be able to take care of that."

Sjösten said nothing. He was thinking. He went back down to the kitchen. The body was on a plastic sheet on the floor.

"Is it him?" asked Sjösten.

"It's Liljegren," said the doctor. "Even though he doesn't have much face left."

"That's not what I meant. Is it the man who takes scalps?"

The doctor pulled back the plastic sheet covering the blackened face.

"I'm convinced that he cut or tore off the hair at the front of his head," said the doctor.

Sjösten nodded. Then he turned to Birgersson.

"I want you to call the Ystad police. Get hold of Kurt Wallander. I want to talk to him. Now."

For once Wallander had fixed a proper breakfast. He had fried some eggs and was just sitting down at the table with his newspaper when the telephone rang. The caller introduced himself as Detective Sergeant Sture Birgersson of the Helsingborg police. What he had feared had finally happened. The killer had struck again. He swore under his breath, an oath that contained equal parts rage and horror. Waldemar Sjösten came to the phone. In the early 1980s they had collaborated on the investigation of a drugs ring extending all over Skåne. Although they were very different people, they had had an easy time working together and had formed the beginnings of a friendship.

"Kurt?"

"Yes, it's me."

"It's been a long time."

"So what's happened? Is what I hear true?"

"Unfortunately it is. Your killer has turned up here in Helsingborg."

"Is it confirmed?"

"There's nothing to indicate otherwise. An axe blow to the head. Then he cut off the victim's scalp."

"Who was it?"

"Åke Liljegren. Does that name ring a bell?"

Wallander thought for a moment. "The one they call 'the Auditor'?"

"Precisely. A former minister of justice, an art dealer and now a white-collar criminal."

"And a fence too," said Wallander. "Don't forget him."

"You should come up here. Our superiors can sort out the red tape so that we can cross into each other's jurisdictions."

"I'll come right away," said Wallander. "It might be a good idea if I bring Sven Nyberg, our head forensic technician."

"Bring whoever you want. I won't stand in your way. I just don't like it that the killer has shown up here."

"I'll be in Helsingborg in two hours," said Wallander. "If you can tell me whether there's some connection between Liljegren and the others who were killed, we'll be ahead of the game. Did the killer leave any clues?"

"Not directly, although we can see how it happened. This time he didn't pour acid into his victim's eyes. He roasted him. His head and half his neck, at least."

"Roasted?"

"In an oven. Be glad you won't have to look at it."

"What else?"

"I just got here, so nothing really."

After Wallander hung up he looked at his watch. It was very early. He called Nyberg, who answered at once. Wallander told him what had happened, and Nyberg promised to be outside Wallander's building in 15 minutes. Then Wallander dialled Hansson's number, but changed his mind and called Martinsson instead. As always, Martinsson's wife answered. It took a couple of minutes before her husband came to the phone.

"He's killed again," said Wallander. "This time in Helsingborg. A crook named Åke Liljegren. They call him 'the Auditor.'"

"The corporate raider?" asked Martinsson.

"That's him."

"The murderer has taste."

"Bullshit," Wallander said. "I'm driving up there with Nyberg. They've asked us to come. I want you to tell Hansson. I'll give you a call as soon as I know more."

"This means that the National Criminal Bureau will be called in," Martinsson said. "Maybe it's the best thing."

"The best thing would be if we caught this killer," Wallander replied. "I'll call you later."

He was outside when Nyberg drove up in his old Amazon. It was a beautiful morning. Nyberg drove fast. At Sturup they turned off towards Lund and reached the motorway to Helsingborg. Wallander told him what he knew. After they had passed Lund, Hansson called. He was out of breath. He's been even more afraid of this than I have, Wallander thought.

"It's terrible," said Hansson. "This changes everything."

"For the time being it doesn't change a thing," Wallander replied. "It depends entirely on what actually happened."

"It's time for the National Criminal Bureau to take over," said Hansson. Wallander could tell from Hansson's voice that to be relieved of his responsibility was what he wanted most of all. Wallander was annoyed. He couldn't ignore the hint of disparagement of the work of the investigative team.

"That's your responsibility – yours and Åkeson's," Wallander said tersely. "What occurred in Helsingborg is their problem. But they've asked me to go up there. We'll talk about what we're going to do later."

Wallander hung up. Nyberg didn't say a word. But Wallander knew he had been listening carefully.

They were met by a squad car at the exit to Helsingborg. Wallander realised that it must have been somewhere nearby that Sven Andersson had stopped to give Dolores María Santana a lift on her last journey. They followed the car up to Tågaborg and stopped outside Liljegren's villa. Wallander and Nyberg passed through the police cordon and were met by Sjösten at the bottom of the steps to the villa, which Wallander guessed had been built around the turn of the century. They said hello and exchanged a few words. Sjösten introduced Nyberg to the forensic technician from Helsingborg. The two of them went inside.

Sjösten put out his cigarette and buried the butt in the gravel with his heel.

"It's your man who did this," he said.

"What do you know about the victim?"

"Åke Liljegren was famous."

"Infamous, you mean."

Sjösten nodded. "There are probably plenty of people who have dreamt of killing him," he said. "With a criminal justice system that worked better, with fewer loopholes in the laws on financial fraud, he would have been locked up."

Sjösten took Wallander into the house. The air was thick with the stench of burnt flesh. Sjösten gave Wallander a mask, which he put on reluctantly. They went into the kitchen where the body still lay under the plastic sheet. Wallander nodded to Sjösten to let him see, thinking that he might as well get it over with. He didn't know what he had expected, but he flinched involuntarily. Liljegren's face was gone. The skin was burnt away and large sections of the skull were clearly visible. There were just two holes where the eyes had been. The hair and ears were also burnt off. Wallander nodded to Sjösten to put back the sheet. Sjösten quickly described how Liljegren had been found leaning into the oven. Wallander got some Polaroids from the photographer. It was almost worse to see the pictures. Wallander shook his head with a grimace and handed them back. Sjösten took him upstairs, pointing out the blood, and describing the apparent sequence of events. Wallander occasionally asked a question about a detail, but Sjösten's scenario seemed convincing.

"Were there any witnesses?" asked Wallander. "Clues left by the murderer? How did he get into the house?"

"Through a basement window."

They returned to the kitchen and went down to the basement that extended under the whole house. A little window stood ajar in a room where Wallander smelt the faint aroma of apples stored for the winter.

"We think he got in this way," said Sjösten. "And left that way too. Even though he could have walked straight out the front door. Liljegren lived alone."

"Did he leave anything behind?" Wallander wondered. "So far he has been careful to leave no clues. On the other hand, he hasn't been excessively meticulous. We have a whole set of fingerprints. According to Nyberg, we're missing only the left little finger."

"Fingerprints he knows the police don't have on file," said Sjösten.

Wallander nodded. Sjösten was right.

"We found a footprint in the kitchen next to the stove," said Sjösten.

"So he was barefoot again," said Wallander.

"Barefoot?"

Wallander told him about the footprint they had found in the blood in Fredman's van. He would have to provide Sjösten and his colleagues with all the material they had on the first three murders.

Wallander inspected the basement window. He thought he could see faint scrape marks near one of the latches, which had been broken off. When he bent down he found it, although it was hard to see against the dark floor. He didn't touch it.

"It looks as though it might have been loosened in advance," he said.

"You think he prepared for his visit?"

"It's conceivable. It fits with his pattern. He puts his victims under surveillance. He stakes them out. Why, and for how long, we have no idea. Our psychologist from Stockholm, Mats Ekholm, claims this is characteristic of serial killers."

They went into the next room. The windows were the same. The latches were intact.

"We should probably search for footprints in the grass outside that window," Wallander said. He regretted his words immediately. He had no right to tell an experienced investigator like Sjösten what to do. They returned to the kitchen. Liljegren's body was being removed.

"What I've been looking for the whole time is the connection," said Wallander. "First I looked for one between Gustaf Wetterstedt and Arne Carlman. I finally found it. Then I looked for one between Björn Fredman and the two others. We haven't been able to find a link yet, but I'm convinced there is one. Perhaps this is one of the first things we should do here. Is it possible to find some connection between Åke Liljegren and the other three? Preferably to all of them, but at least to any one of them."

"In a way we already have a very clear connection," said Sjösten quietly.

Wallander gave him a questioning glance.

"What I mean is, the killer is an identifiable link," Sjösten went on. "Even if we don't know who he is."

Sjösten nodded towards the door to the garden. Wallander realised that Sjösten wanted to speak privately. Outside in the garden, they both squinted in the bright light. It was going to be another hot day. Sjösten lit a cigarette and led Wallander over to a table and chairs a little way from the house. They moved the chairs into the shade.

"There are plenty of rumours about Åke Liljegren," Sjösten began. "His shell companies are only a part of his operations. Here in Helsingborg we've heard about a lot of other things. Low-flying Cessnas making drops of cocaine, heroin and marijuana. Pretty hard to prove, and I have difficulty associating this type of activity with Liljegren. It may just be my limited imagination, of course. I go on thinking that it's possible to sort crimes into categories. Criminals are supposed to stay within those boundaries and not encroach on other people's territory, which messes up our classifications."

"I've sometimes thought along those same lines," Wallander admitted. "But those days are gone. The world we live in is becoming more comprehensible and more chaotic at the same time."

Sjösten waved his cigarette at the huge villa.

"There have been other rumours too," he said. "These ones more concrete. About wild parties in this house. Women, prostitution."

"Wild?" asked Wallander. "Have you ever had to get involved?"

"Never," said Sjösten. "Actually I don't know why I called the parties wild. But people used to come here a lot. And disappear just as quickly as they came."

Wallander didn't answer. A dizzying image flitted through his mind. He saw Dolores María Santana standing at the southern motorway entrance from Helsingborg. Could there be a connection? Prostitution? But he pushed the thought away. There was no evidence for this, he was confusing two different investigations.

"We're going to have to work together," Sjösten said. "You and your colleagues have several weeks on us. Now that we add Liljegren to the picture, how does it look? What's changed? What seems clearer?"

"The National Criminal Bureau will certainly get involved now," Wallander answered. "That's good, of course. But I'm afraid that we'll have problems working together, that information won't get to the right person."

"I have the same concern," Sjösten agreed. "That's why I want to suggest something. That you and I become an informal team, so we can step aside for discussion when we need to."

"That's fine by me," Wallander said.

"We both remember the days of the old national homicide commission," Sjösten said. "Something that worked very efficiently was dismantled. And things have never really been the same since."

"Times were different. Violence had a different face, and there were fewer murders. Criminals operated in patterns that were recognisable in a way that they aren't today. I'm not sure that the commission would have been as effective now."

Sjösten stood up. "But we're in agreement?"

"Of course," Wallander replied. "Whenever we think it's necessary, we'll talk."

"You can stay with me," Sjösten said, "if you have to be here overnight. It's no pleasure to have to stay at a hotel."

"I'd like that," Wallander thanked him. But he didn't mind staying at a hotel when he was away. He needed to have at least a few hours to himself every day.

They walked back to the house. To the left was a large garage with two doors. While Sjösten went inside, Wallander decided to take a look in the garage. With difficulty he lifted one of the doors. Inside was a black Mercedes. The windows were tinted. He stood there thinking.

Then he went into the house, called Ystad, and asked to speak with Höglund. He told her briefly what had happened.

"I want you to contact Sara Björklund," he said. "Do you remember her?"

"Wetterstedt's housekeeper?"

"Right. I want you to bring her here to Helsingborg. As soon as you can."

"Why?"

"I want her to take a look at a car. And I'll be standing next to her hoping that she recognises it."

Höglund asked no more questions.

CHAPTER 30

Sara Björklund stood for a long time looking at the black car. Wallander stayed in the background. He wanted his presence to give her confidence, but didn't want to stand so close to her that he would be a disturbing factor. He could tell that she was doing her best to be absolutely certain. Was this the car she had seen on the Friday morning that she'd come to Wetterstedt's house, thinking it was a Thursday? Had it looked like this one, could it even be the very same car she had seen drive away from the house where the old minister of justice lived?

Sjösten agreed with Wallander when he explained his idea. Even if the "charwoman" held in such contempt by Wetterstedt said that it could have been a car of the same make, that wouldn't prove a thing. All they would get was an indication, a possibility. But it was important even so; they both realised that.

Sara Björklund hesitated. Since there were keys in the ignition, Wallander asked Sjösten to drive it once round the block. If she closed her eyes and listened, did she recognise the sound of the engine? Cars had different sounds. She listened.

"Maybe," she said afterwards. "It looks like the car I saw that morning. But whether it was the same one I can't say. I didn't see the number plate."

Wallander nodded.

"I didn't expect you to," he said. "I'm sorry I had to ask you to come all the way here."

Höglund had brought Norén with her, who would now drive Sara Björklund back to Ystad. Höglund wanted to stay. It was barely midday, yet the whole country seemed to know already what had happened. Sjösten held an impromptu press conference out on the street, while Wallander and Höglund drove down to the ferry terminal and had lunch. He told her all that he had learned.

"Åke Liljegren appeared in our investigative material on Alfred Harderberg," she said when he'd finished. "Do you remember?"

Wallander let his mind travel back to the year before. He remembered the businessman and art patron who lived behind the walls of Farnholm Castle with distaste. The man they had eventually prevented from leaving the country in a dramatic scene at Sturup Airport. Liljegren's name had indeed come up in the investigation, but he had been on the periphery. They had never considered questioning him.

Wallander sat with his third cup of coffee and gazed out over the Sound, filled with yachts and ferries.

"We didn't want this, but we've got it," he said. "Another dead, scalped man. According to Ekholm our chances of identifying the killer will now increase dramatically. That's according to the F.B.I. models. Now the similarities and differences should be much clearer."

"I think somehow the level of violence has increased," she said hesitantly. "If you can grade axe murders and scalpings."

Wallander waited with interest for her to continue. Her hesitation often meant that she was on the trail of something important.

"Wetterstedt was lying underneath a rowing boat," she went on. "He had been hit once from behind. His scalp was sliced off, as if the killer had taken the time to do it carefully. Or maybe there was some uncertainty. The first scalp. Carlman was killed from the front. He must have seen his killer. His hair was torn off, not sliced. That seems to indicate more frenzy, or maybe rage, almost uncontrolled. Then Fredman. He apparently lay on his back. Probably tied up, or he'd have resisted. He had acid poured in his eyes. The killer forced open his eyelids. The blow to the head was tremendous. And now Liljegren, with his head stuck in an oven. Something is getting worse. Is it hatred? Or a sick person's thrill at demonstrating his power?"

"Outline this to Ekholm," Wallander suggested. "Let him put it into his computer. I agree with you. Certain changes in his behaviour are evident. Something is shifting. But what does it tell us? Sometimes it seems as though we're trying to interpret footprints that are millions of years old. What I worry about most is the chronology, which is based on the fact that we found the victims in a certain order, since they were killed in a certain order. So for us a natural chronology is created. But the question is whether there's some other order among them that we can't see. Are some of the murders more important than others?"

She thought for a moment. "Was one of them closer to the killer than the others?"

"Yes, that's it," said Wallander. "Was Liljegren closer to the heart of it than Carlman, for example? And which of them is furthest away? Or do they all have the same relationship to him?"

"A relationship which may only exist in his mind?"

Wallander pushed aside his empty cup. "At least we can be certain that these men were not chosen at random," he said.

"Fredman is different," she said as they got up.

"Yes, he is," said Wallander. "But you can also turn it around and say that it's the other three who are different."

They returned to Tågaborg, where they were given the message that Hansson was on his way to meet with the chief of police in Helsingborg.

"Tomorrow the National Criminal Bureau will be here," said Sjösten.

"Has anyone talked to Ekholm?" asked Wallander. "He should come up here as soon as possible."

Höglund went to see to this, and Wallander made an examination of the house again with Sjösten. Nyberg was on his knees in the kitchen with the other technicians. When they were heading up the stairs to the top floor, Höglund caught up with them, saying that Ekholm was on his way with Hansson. They continued their inspection. None of them spoke. They were each following their own train of thought.

Wallander was trying to feel the killer's presence, as he had done at Wetterstedt's house, and in Carlman's garden. Not twelve hours ago the man had climbed these same stairs. Wallander moved more slowly than the others. He stopped often, sometimes sitting down to stare at a wall or a rug or a door, as if he were in a museum, deeply engrossed in the objects on display. Occasionally he would retrace his steps.

Watching him, Höglund had the sense that Wallander was acting as though he were walking on ice. And in a sense, he was. Each step involved a risk, a new way of seeing things, a re-examination of a thought he'd just had. He moved as much in his mind as through the rooms. Wallander had never sensed the presence of the man he was hunting in Wetterstedt's house. It had convinced him that the killer had never been inside. He had not been closer than the garage roof where he had waited, reading *The Phantom* and then ripping it to pieces. But here, in Liljegren's house, it was different.

Wallander went back to the stairs and looked down the hall towards the bathroom. From here he could see the man he was about to kill. If the bathroom door was open, that is. And why would it have been closed if Liljegren was alone in the house? He walked towards the bathroom door and stood against the wall. Then he went into the bathroom and assumed the role of Liljegren. He walked out of the door, imagining the axe blow strike him with full force from behind, at an angle. He saw himself fall to the floor. Then he switched to the other role, the man holding an axe in his right hand. Not in his left; they had determined in examining Wetterstedt's body that the man was right-handed. Wallander walked slowly down the stairs, dragging the invisible corpse behind him. Into the kitchen, to the stove. He continued down to the basement and stopped at the window, which was too narrow for him to squeeze through. Only a slight man could use that window as a way of getting into Liljegren's house. The killer must be thin.

He went back to the kitchen and out into the garden. Near the basement window at the back of the house the technicians were looking for footprints. Wallander could have told them in advance that they wouldn't find anything. The man had been barefoot, as before. He looked towards the hedge, the shortest distance between the basement window and the street, pondering why the killer had been barefoot.

He'd asked Ekholm about it several times, but still didn't have a satisfactory answer. Going barefoot meant taking a risk of injury. Of slipping, puncturing his foot, getting cut. And yet he still did it. Why did he go barefoot? Why choose to remove his shoes? This was another of the inexplicable details he had to keep in mind. He took scalps. He used an axe. He was barefoot. Wallander stopped in his tracks. It came to him in a flash. His subconscious had drawn a conclusion and relayed the message.

An American Indian, he said to himself. A warrior. He knew he was right. The man they were looking for was a lone warrior moving along an invisible path. He was an impersonator. Used an axe to kill, cut off scalps, went barefoot. But why would an American Indian go around in the Swedish summertime killing people? Who was really committing these murders? An Indian or someone playing the role?

Wallander held on tight to the thought so he wouldn't lose it before he had followed it through. He travelled over great distances, he thought. He must have a horse. A motorcycle. Which had leant against the road workers' hut. You drive in a car, but you *ride* a motorcycle.

He walked back to the house. For the first time he'd caught a glimpse of the man he sought. The excitement of the discovery was immediate. His alertness sharpened. For the time being, however, he would keep his idea to himself.

A window on the top floor opened. Sjösten leaned out.

"Come up here," he shouted.

Wallander went in, wondering what they had found. Sjösten and Höglund were standing in front of a bookcase in a room that must have been Liljegren's office. Sjösten had a plastic bag in his hand.

"I'm guessing cocaine," he said. "Could be heroin."

"Where was it?" Wallander asked.

Sjösten pointed to an open drawer.

"There may be more," Wallander said.

"I'll see about getting a dog in here," said Sjösten.

"I wonder whether you shouldn't send out a few people to talk to the neighbours," said Wallander. "Ask if they noticed a man on a motorcycle. Not just last night, but earlier too. Over the last few weeks."

"Did he come on a motorcycle?"

"I think so. It seems to be his means of getting around. You'll find it in the investigative material."

Sjösten left the room.

"There's nothing about a motorcycle in the investigative material," said Höglund, surprised.

"There should be," said Wallander, sounding distracted. "Didn't we confirm that it was a motorcycle that stood behind the road workers' hut?"

Wallander looked out the window. Ekholm and Hansson were on their way up the path, with another man whom Wallander assumed was the Helsingborg chief of police. Birgersson met them halfway.

"We'd better go down," he said. "Did you find anything?"

"The house reminds me of Wetterstedt's," she replied. "The same gloomy bourgeois respectability. But at least here there are some family photos. Whether they make it more cheerful I don't know. Liljegren seems to have had cavalry officers in his family, Scanian Dragoons if you can believe it."

"I haven't looked at them," Wallander apologised. "But I believe you. His scams undoubtedly had much in common with primitive warfare."

"There's a photo of an old couple outside a cottage," she said. "If I understood what was written on the back, the picture was of his maternal grandparents on the island of Öland."

They went down. Parts of the stairs were cordoned off to protect the blood traces.

"Old bachelors," said Wallander. "Their houses resemble each other's because they were alike. How old was Åke Liljegren, anyway? Was he over 70?"

Höglund didn't know.

A conference room was set up in the dining room. Ekholm, who didn't have to attend, was assigned an officer to fill him in. When they had all introduced themselves and sat down, Hansson surprised Wallander by being quite clear-cut about what should happen. During the trip up from Ystad he had spoken with both Åkeson and the National Criminal Bureau in Stockholm.

"It would be a mistake to state that our situation has changed significantly because of this murder," Hansson began. "The situation has been dramatic enough ever since we realised that we were dealing with a serial killer. Now we might say that we have crossed a sort of boundary. There's nothing to indicate that we will actually crack these murders. But we have to hope. As far as the Bureau is concerned, they are prepared to give us whatever help we request. The formalities involved shouldn't present any serious difficulties either. I assume no-one has anything against Kurt being assigned leader of the new cross-boundary investigative team?"

No-one had any objections. Sjösten nodded approval from his side of the table.

"Kurt has a certain notoriety," Hansson said, without a trace of irony. "The chief of the National Criminal Bureau regarded it as obvious that he should continue to lead the investigation."

"I agree," said the chief of the Helsingborg police. That was the only thing he said during the meeting.

"Guidelines have been drawn on how a collaboration such as this can be implemented as quickly as possible," Hansson continued. "The prosecutors have their own procedures to follow. The key thing is to agree what type of assistance from Stockholm we actually require."

Wallander had been listening to what Hansson was saying with a mixture of pride and anxiety. At the same time he was self-assured enough to realise that no-one else was more suitable to lead the investigation.

"Has anything resembling this series of murders ever occurred in Sweden?" asked Sjösten.

"Not according to Ekholm," said Wallander.

"It's just that it would be good to have some colleagues who have experience with this type of crime," said Sjösten.

"We'd have to get them from the continent, or the United States," said Wallander. "And I don't think that's such a good idea. Not yet, at any rate. What we need, obviously, is experienced homicide investigators, who can add to our overall expertise."

It took them less than 20 minutes to make the necessary decisions. When they'd finished, Wallander hastily left the room in search of Ekholm. He found him upstairs and took him into a guest room that smelt musty. Wallander opened the window to air the stuffy room. He sat on the edge of the bed and told Ekholm what had occurred to him that morning.

"You could be right," Ekholm said. "A person with serious psychosis who has taken on the role of a lone warrior. There are many examples of that, though not in Sweden. Such a person generally metamorphoses into another before they go out to exact a revenge. The disguise frees them from guilt. The actor doesn't feel the pangs of conscience for actions performed by his character. But don't forget that there's a type of psychopath who kills with no motive other than for his own intense enjoyment."

"That's doesn't seem to fit this case," said Wallander.

"The difficulty lies in the fact that the role the killer has adopted doesn't tell us anything about the motive for the murder. If we assume that you're right – a barefoot warrior who has chosen his disguise for reasons unknown to us – then he could just as easily have chosen to turn himself into a Japanese samurai or a *tonton macoute* from Haiti. There's only one person who knows the reasons for the choice. The killer himself."

Wallander recalled one of the earliest conversations he had had with Ekholm.

"That would mean that the scalps are a red herring," he said. "That he's taking them as a ritual act in the performance of the role he's selected for himself. Not that he's collecting trophies to reach some objective that serves as the basis for all the murders he has committed."

"That's possible."

"Which means that we're back to square one."

"The combinations have to be tested over and over," said Ekholm. "We never return to the starting point once we have left it. We have to move the same way the killer does. He doesn't stand still. What happened last night confirms what I'm saying."

"Have you formed any opinion?"

"The oven is interesting."

Wallander flinched at Ekholm's choice of words.

"In what way?"

"The difference between the acid and the oven is striking. In one case he uses a chemical agent to torture a man who's still alive. It's an element of the killing itself. In the second case it serves more as a greeting to us."

Wallander looked at Ekholm intently. He tried to interpret what he'd just heard.

"A greeting to the police?"

"It doesn't really surprise me. The murderer is not unaffected by his actions. His self-image is growing. It may reach a point where he has to start looking for contact. He's terribly pleased with himself. He has to seek confirmation of how clever he is from the outside world. The victim can't applaud him. Sometimes he turns to the very ones who are hunting him. This can take various forms. Anonymous telephone calls or letters. Or why not a dead man arranged in a grotesque position?"

"He's taunting us?"

"I don't think he sees it that way. He sees himself as invulnerable. If it's true that he selected the role of a barefoot warrior, the invulnerability might be one of the reasons. Warrior peoples traditionally smear themselves with salves to make themselves immune from swords and arrows. In our day and age the police might symbolise those swords."

Wallander sat silently for a while.

"What's our next move?" he asked. "He's challenging us by stuffing Liljegren's head in the oven. What about next time? If there is one."

"There are many possibilities. Psychopathic killers sometimes seek contact with individuals within the police force."

"Why is that?"

Ekholm hesitated. "Policemen have been killed, you know."

"You mean this madman has his eye on us?"

"It's possible. Without our knowing it, he might be amusing himself by getting very close to us. And then vanishing again. One day this may not be enough of a thrill."

Wallander remembered the sensation that he'd had outside the cordon at Carlman's farm, when he thought he'd recognised one of the faces among the onlookers. Someone who had also been on the beach beyond the cordon when they'd turned over the boat and revealed Wetterstedt.

Ekholm looked at him gravely.

"You most of all should be aware of this," he said. "I was thinking of talking to you about it anyway."

"Why me?"

"You're the most visible one of us. The search for the man who committed these four murders involves a lot of people. But the name and face that are most regularly seen are yours."

Wallander grimaced. "You can't expect me to take this seriously?"

"That's for you to decide."

When Ekholm had left, Wallander stayed behind, trying to gauge his true reaction to Ekholm's warning. It was like a cold wind blowing through the room, he thought. But nothing more.

That afternoon Wallander drove back to Ystad with the others. It was decided that the investigation would continue to be directed from Ystad. Wallander sat in silence for the whole trip, giving only terse replies when Hansson asked him something. When they arrived they held a short briefing with Svedberg, Martinsson and Åkeson. Svedberg told them that it was now possible to speak with Carlman's daughter. They decided that Wallander and Höglund would pay a visit to the hospital the next morning. When the meeting was over, Wallander called his father. Gertrud answered. All was back to normal. His father had no recollection of what had happened.

Wallander also called home. No answer. Linda wasn't there. On his way out of the station he asked Ebba whether there was any word on his keys. Nothing. He drove down to the harbour and walked along the pier, then sat down in the harbour café and had a beer. He sat and watched the people passing by. Depressed, he got up and went back out on the pier, and sat on a bench next to the sea rescue hut.

It was a warm, windless evening. Someone was playing a concertina on a boat. One of the ferries from Poland was coming in. Without actually being conscious of it, he started to make a connection in his mind. He sat perfectly still and let his thoughts work. He was beginning to discern the contours of the drama. There were a lot of gaps still, but he could see where they should concentrate their investigation.

He didn't think that the way they had been working so far was to blame. The problem was with the conclusions he had made. He drove home and wrote down a summary at his kitchen table. Linda arrived back just before midnight. She had seen the papers.

"Who is doing this? What is someone like this made of?" she asked.

Wallander thought for a while before he replied.

"He's like you and me," he said at last. "By and large, just like you and me."

CHAPTER 31

Wallander woke with a start.

His eyes flew open and he lay completely still. The light of the summer night was grey. Someone was moving around in the flat. He glanced quickly at the clock on the bedside table. It was 2.15 a.m. His terror was instantaneous. He knew it wasn't Linda. Once she fell asleep, she didn't get up again until morning. He held his breath and listened. The sound was very faint.

The person moving around was barefoot.

Wallander got out of bed noiselessly. He looked for something to defend himself with. He had locked his service revolver in his desk at the station. The only thing in the bedroom he could use was the broken arm of a chair. He picked it up and listened again. The sound seemed to be coming from the kitchen. He came out of the bedroom and looked towards the living-room. He passed the door to Linda's room. It was closed. She was asleep. Now he was very scared. The sounds *were* coming from the kitchen. He stood in the doorway of the living-room and listened. Ekholm was right after all. He prepared himself to meet someone who was very strong. The chair arm wouldn't be much help. He remembered that he had a replica of a pair of old-fashioned brass knuckles in one of the drawers in the bookshelf. They had been the prize in a police lottery. He decided that his fists were better protection than the chair arm. He could still hear sounds in the kitchen. He moved cautiously across the parquet floor and opened the drawer. The brass knuckles were underneath a copy of his tax return. He put them on his right hand. At the same instant he realised that the sounds in the kitchen had stopped. He spun round and raised his arms.

Linda was in the doorway looking at him with a mixture of amazement and fear. He stared back at her.

"What are you doing?" she said. "What's that on your hand?"

"I thought it was somebody breaking in," he said, taking off the brass knuckles.

She could see that he was shaken.

"It was me. I couldn't sleep."

"The door to your room was closed."

"I must have shut it behind me. I needed a drink of water."

"But you never wake up in the night."

"Those days are long gone. Sometimes I don't sleep well. When I've got a lot on my mind."

Wallander knew he ought to feel foolish. But his relief was too great. His reaction had confirmed something. He had taken Ekholm much more seriously than he thought. He sat down. Linda was still standing there staring at him.

"I've often wondered how you can sleep as well as you do," she said. "When I think of the things you have to look at, the things you're forced to do."

"You get used to it," said Wallander, knowing that wasn't true at all.

She sat down next to him.

"I was looking through an evening paper while Kajsa was buying cigarettes," she went on. "There was quite a bit about what happened in Helsingborg. I don't know how you stand it."

"The papers exaggerate."

"How do you exaggerate somebody getting their head stuffed into an oven?"

Wallander tried to avoid her questions. He didn't know whether it was for his sake or for hers.

"That's a matter for the doctor," he said. "I examine the scene and try to work out what happened."

She shook her head, resigned.

"You never could lie to me. To Mama, maybe, but never to me."

"I never lied to Mona, did I?"

"You never told her how much you loved her. What you don't say can be a false affirmation."

He looked at her in surprise. Her choice of words astonished him.

"When I was little I used to sneak looks at all the papers you brought home at night. I invited my friends too, sometimes, when you were working on something we thought was exciting. We would sit in my room and read transcripts of witness testimonies."

"I had no idea."

"You weren't supposed to. So who did you think was in the flat?"

He decided to tell her at least part of the truth. He explained that sometimes, but very rarely, policemen in his position who had their pictures in the paper a lot or were on TV, might catch the attention of criminals who then became fixated on them. Perhaps "fascinated" was a better term. Normally there was nothing to worry about. But it was a good idea to acknowledge the phenomenon and to stay alert.

She didn't believe him for a second.

"That wasn't somebody standing there with brass knuckles on, showing how aware he was," she said at last. "What I saw was my Dad who's a policeman. And he was scared."

"Maybe I had a nightmare," he said unconvincingly. "Tell me why you can't sleep."

"I'm worried about what to do with my life," she said.

"You and Kajsa were very good in the revue."

"Not as good as we ought to be."

"You've got time to feel your way."

"But what if I want to do something else entirely?"

"Like what?"

"That's what I think about when I wake up in the middle of the night. I open my eyes and think that I still don't know."

"You can always wake me up," he said. "As a policeman at least I've learned how to listen, even if you can get better answers from someone else."

She leaned her head on his shoulder.

"You're a good listener. A lot better than Mama. But I have to find the answers for myself."

They talked for a long time. Not until it was light outside did they go back to bed. Something Linda said made Wallander feel good: he listened better than Mona did. In some future life he wouldn't mind doing everything better than Mona. But not now, when there was Baiba.

Wallander got up a little before 7 a.m. Linda was still asleep. He had a quick cup of coffee and left. The weather was beautiful, but the wind had started to blow. When he got to the station he ran into an agitated Martinsson, who told him that the whole holiday schedule had been thrown into chaos. Most holidays had been postponed indefinitely.

"Now I probably won't be able to get time off until September," he said angrily. "Who the hell wants a holiday at that time of year?"

"Me," said Wallander. "I can go to Italy with my father."

It was already Wednesday, 6 July. He was supposed to meet Baiba at Kastrup Airport in three days. For the first time he faced up to the fact that their holiday would have to be cancelled, or at least postponed. He had avoided thinking about it during the last hectic weeks, but he couldn't continue to do so. He would have to cancel flights and the hotel reservations. He dreaded Baiba's reaction. He sat at his desk feeling his stomach begin to ache with the stress. There must be some alternative, he thought. Baiba can come here. Maybe we could still catch this damned killer soon. This man who kills people and then scalps them.

He was terrified of her disappointment. Even though she had been married to a policeman, she probably imagined that everything was different in Sweden. But he couldn't wait any longer to tell her that they wouldn't be going to Skagen. He should pick up the phone and call Riga straight away. But he put off the unpleasant conversation. He wasn't ready yet. He took his notebook and listed all the calls he'd have to make.

Then he turned into a policeman again. He put the summary he had written the day before on the desk in front of him and read it through.

The notes made sense. He picked up the phone and asked Ebba to get hold of Sjösten in Helsingborg. A few minutes later she called back.

"He seems to spend his mornings scraping barnacles off a boat," she said. "But he was on his way in. He'll call you in the next ten minutes."

When Sjösten called back, he told Wallander that they'd located some witnesses, a couple, who claimed to have seen a motorcycle on Aschebergsgatan on the evening Liljegren was murdered.

"Check carefully," said Wallander. "It could be very important."

"I thought I'd do it myself."

Wallander leaned forward over his desk, as if he had to brace himself before tackling the next question.

"I'd like to ask you to do one more thing," he said. "Something that should take the highest priority. I want you to find some of the women who worked at the parties that were held at Liljegren's villa."

"Why?"

"I think it's important. We have to find out who was at those parties. You'll understand when you go through the investigative material."

Wallander knew very well that his question wouldn't be answered in the material they had assembled for the other three murders. But he needed to hunt alone for a while longer.

"So you want me to pick out a whore," said Sjösten.

"I do. If there were any at those parties."

"It was rumoured that there were."

"I want you to get back in touch with me as soon as possible. Then I'll come up to Helsingborg."

"If I find one, should I bring her in?"

"I just want to talk to her, that's all. Make it clear she has nothing to worry about. Someone who's afraid and says what she thinks I want to hear won't help at all."

"I'll try," said Sjösten. "Interesting assignment in the middle of summer."

They hung up. Wallander concentrated on his notes from the night before until Höglund called. They met in reception and walked down to the hospital so they could plan what they would say to Carlman's daughter. Wallander didn't even know the name of this young woman who had slapped his face.

"Erika," said Höglund. "Which doesn't suit her."

"Why not?" asked Wallander, surprised.

"I get the impression of a robust sort when I hear that name," she said. "The manager of a hotel smörgåsbord or a crane operator."

"Is it OK that my name is Kurt?" he asked.

She nodded cheerfully.

"It's nonsense that you can match a personality to a name of course," she said. "But it amuses me. And you could hardly imagine a cat called Fido. Or a dog called Kitty."

"There probably are some," said Wallander. "So what do we know about Erika Carlman?"

They had the wind at their backs as they walked towards the hospital. Höglund told him that Erika Carlman was 27 years old. That for a while she had been a stewardess for a small British charter airline. That she had dabbled in many different things without ever sticking to them for long. She had travelled all over the world, no doubt supported by her father. A marriage with a Peruvian football player had been quickly dissolved.

"A normal rich girl," said Wallander. "One who had everything on a silver platter from the start."

"Her mother says she was hysterical as a teenager. That's the word she used, hysterical. It would probably be more accurate to describe it as a neurotic predisposition."

"Has she attempted suicide before?"

"Not that anyone knows of, and I didn't think the mother was lying."

"She really wanted to die," Wallander said.

"That's my impression too."

Wallander knew that he had to tell Ann-Britt that Erika had slapped him. It was very possible that she might mention the incident. And there wouldn't be any explanation for his not having done so, other than masculine vanity, perhaps. As they reached the hospital,

Wallander stopped and told her. He could see that she was surprised.

"I don't think it was more than a manifestation of the hysteria her mother spoke of," he said.

"This might cause a problem," Ann-Britt said. "She may be in bad shape. She must know that she nearly died. We don't even know if she regrets the fact that she didn't manage to kill herself. If you walk into the room, her fragile ego might collapse. Or it might make her aggressive, scared, unreceptive."

Wallander knew she was right. "You should speak to her alone. I'll wait in the cafeteria."

"First we'll have to go over what we actually want to learn from her."

Wallander pointed to a bench by the taxi rank. They sat down.

"We always hope that the answers will be more interesting than the questions," he said. "What did her suicide attempt have to do with her father's death? How you get to that question is up to you. You'll have to draw your own map. Her answers will prompt more questions."

"Let's assume that she says she was so crushed by grief that she didn't want to go on living."

"Then we'll know that much."

"But what else do we actually know?"

"That's where you have to ask other questions, which we can't predict. Was it a normal loving relationship between father and daughter? Or was it something else?"

"And if she denies it was something else?"

"Then you have to start by not believing her. Without telling her so."

"In other words," said Höglund slowly, "a denial would mean that I should be interested in the reasons she might have for not telling the truth?"

"More or less." Wallander answered. "But there's a third possibility, of course. That she tried to commit suicide because she knew something about her father's death that she couldn't deal with in any other way except by taking the information with her to the grave."

"Could she have seen the killer?"

"It's possible."

"And doesn't want him to be caught?"

"Also conceivable."

"Why not?"

"Once again, there are at least two possibilities. She wants to protect him. Or she wants to protect her father's memory."

Höglund sighed hopelessly. "I don't know if I can handle this."

"Of course you can. I'll be in the cafeteria. Or out here. Take as long as you need."

Wallander accompanied her to the front desk. A few weeks earlier he had been here and found out that Salomonsson had died. How could he have imagined then what havoc was in store for him? Höglund disappeared down the hall. Wallander went towards the cafeteria, but changed his mind and went back outside to the bench. Once again he went over his thoughts from the night before. He was interrupted by his mobile phone ringing in his jacket pocket. It was Hansson, and he sounded harried.

"Two investigators from the National Criminal Bureau are arriving at Sturup this afternoon. Ludwigsson and Hamrén. Do you know them?"

"Only by name. They're supposed to be good. Hamrén was involved in solving that case with the laser man, wasn't he?"

"Could you possibly pick them up?"

"I don't think that I can," said Wallander. "I have to go back to Helsingborg."

"Birgersson didn't mention that. I spoke to him a little while ago."

"They probably have the same communication problems that we do," Wallander said patiently. "I think it would be a nice gesture if you went to pick them up yourself."

"What do you mean by gesture?"

"Of respect. When I went to Riga I was picked up in a limousine. An old Russian one, but even so. It's important for people to feel that they're being welcomed and taken care of."

"All right," said Hansson. "I'll do it. Where are you now?"

"At the hospital."

"Are you sick?"

"Carlman's daughter. Did you forget about her?"

"To tell you the truth, I did."

"We should be glad we don't all forget the same things," Wallander said. He didn't know whether Hansson had recognised that he was being ironic. He put the phone down on the bench and watched a sparrow perched on the edge of a rubbish bin. Ann-Britt had been gone for almost half an hour. He closed his eyes and raised his face to the sun, rehearsing what he would say to Baiba. A man with his leg in a cast sat down with a thud next to him. After five minutes a taxi arrived. The man with the cast left. Wallander paced back and forth in front of the hospital entrance. Then he sat down again.

After more than an hour Ann-Britt came out and sat down next to him. He couldn't tell from the expression on her face how it had gone.

"I think we missed one reason why a person would want to commit suicide," she said. "Being tired of life."

"Was that her answer?"

"I didn't even have to ask. She was sitting in a white room, in a hospital gown, her hair uncombed, pale, out of it. Still immersed in a mixture of her own crisis and heavy medication. 'Why go on living?' That was her greeting. To be honest, I think she'll try to kill herself again. Out of sheer loathing."

Wallander had overlooked the most common motive for committing suicide. Simply not wanting to go on living.

"But did you talk about her father?"

"She despised him, but I'm quite sure that she wasn't abused by him."

"Did she say so?"

"Some things don't have to be actually said."

"What about the murder?"

"She was strangely uninterested in it. She wondered why I had come. I told her the truth. We're searching for the killer. She said there were probably plenty of people who wanted her father dead. Because of his ruthlessness in business. Because of the way he was."

"She didn't say anything about him having another woman?"

"No."

Wallander watched the sparrow despondently.

"Well, at least we know that much," he said. "We know that we don't know anything else."

When they were halfway back to the station, Wallander's phone rang. He turned away from the wind to answer it. It was Svedberg.

"We think we found the place where Fredman was killed," he said. "At a dock just west of town."

Wallander felt his spirits rise.

"Great news," he said.

"A tip-off," Svedberg continued. "The person who called mentioned blood stains. It could have been somebody cleaning fish, of course. But I don't think so. The caller was a laboratory technician. He's worked with blood samples for 35 years. And he said that there were tyre tracks nearby. A vehicle had been parked there. Why not a Ford van?"

"We can drive over there and work it out very shortly," said Wallander.

They continued up the hill, much more quickly now. Wallander told Höglund the news. Neither of them was thinking about Erika Carlman any more.

Hoover got off the train in Ystad just after 11 a.m. He had decided to leave his moped at home today. When he came out of the railway station and saw that the cordon around the pit where he had dumped his father was gone, he felt a twinge of disappointment and anger. The policemen who were hunting him were much too weak. They would never have passed the easiest entrance exam to the F.B.I.'s academy. He felt Geronimo's heart start to drum inside him. He understood the message, simple and clear. He was going to fulfil the mission he had been chosen for. He would bring his sister two final sacrifices before she returned to life. Two scalps beneath her window. And the girl's heart. As a gift. Then he would walk into the hospital to get her and they would leave together. Life would be very different. One day they might even read her diary together, remembering the events that had led her back, out of the darkness.

He walked into Ystad. He was wearing shoes so as not to attract attention, but his feet didn't like it. He turned right at the square and went to the house where the policeman lived with the girl who must be his daughter. He had come to take a closer look. The action itself he was planning for the next evening. Or at the latest, one day later. Not more. His sister shouldn't have to stay in that hospital any longer. He sat down on the steps of one of the neighbouring buildings. He practised forgetting time. Just sitting, empty of thought, until he again took hold of his mission. He still had a lot to learn before he mastered the art to perfection, but he had no doubt that one day he would succeed.

His wait lasted for two hours. Then she came out of the front door, obviously in a hurry, and set off towards the town centre. He followed her and never let her out of his sight.

CHAPTER 32

When they got to the dock, ten kilometres west of Ystad, Wallander was immediately sure that it was the right place. It was just as he had imagined it. They had driven along the coast road and stopped where a man in shorts and a T-shirt advertising the golf course in Malmberget waved them down and directed them to a barely visible dirt road. They stopped just short of the dock, so they wouldn't disturb the tyre marks.

The laboratory technician, Erik Wiberg, told them that in the summer he lived in a cabin on the north side of the coast road. He often came down to this dock to read his morning paper, as he had on 29 June. He'd noticed the tyre tracks and the dark spots on the brown wood, but thought nothing of it. He left that same day for Germany with his family, and it wasn't until he saw in the paper on his return that the police were looking for a murder site, probably near the sea, that he remembered those dark spots. Since he worked in a laboratory, he knew that what was on the dock at least looked like blood. Nyberg, who had arrived just after Wallander and the others, was on his knees by the tyre tracks. He had toothache and was more irritable than ever. Wallander was the only one he could bear to talk to.

"It could be Fredman's van," he said, "but we'll have to do a proper examination."

They walked out on the dock together. Wallander knew they had been lucky. The dry summer helped. If it had rained there wouldn't have been tracks. He looked for confirmation from Martinsson, who had the best memory for the weather.

"Has it rained since 28 June?" he asked.

"It drizzled on the morning of Midsummer Eve," he said. "Ever since then it's been fine."

"Arrange to cordon off the whole place," said Wallander, nodding to Höglund. "And be careful where you put your feet."

He stood near the land end of the dock and looked at the patches of blood. They were concentrated in the middle of the dock, which was four metres long. He turned around and looked up towards the road. He could hear the noise, but he couldn't see the cars, just the roof of a tall lorry flashing by. He had an idea. Höglund was on the phone to Ystad.

"And tell them to bring me a map," he said. "One that includes Ystad, Malmö, and Helsingborg." Then he walked to the end of the dock and looked into the water. The bottom was rocky. Wiberg was standing on the beach.

"Where's the nearest house?" asked Wallander.

"A couple of hundred metres from here," replied Wiberg. "Across the road."

Nyberg had come out onto the dock.

"Should we call in divers?" he asked.

"Yes," said Wallander. "Start with a radius of 25 metres around the dock."

Then he pointed at the rings set into the wood.

"Prints," he said. "If Fredman was killed here he must have been tied down. Our killer goes barefoot and doesn't wear gloves."

"What are the divers looking for?"

Wallander thought.

"I don't know," he said. "Let's see if they come up with anything. But I think you're going to find traces of kelp on the slope, from the place where the tyre tracks stop all the way down to the dock."

"The van didn't turn around," said Nyberg. "He backed it all the way up to the road. He couldn't have seen whether any cars were coming. So there are only two possibilities. Unless he's totally crazy."

Wallander raised his eyebrows.

"He *is* crazy," he said.

"Not in that way," said Nyberg.

Wallander understood what he meant. He wouldn't have been able to back up onto the road unless he had an accomplice who signalled when the road was clear. Or else it happened at night. When he'd see headlights and know when it was safe to back out onto the road.

"He doesn't have an accomplice," said Wallander. "And we know that it must have happened at night. The only question is why did he drive Fredman's body to the pit outside the railway station in Ystad?"

"He's crazy," said Nyberg. "You said so yourself."

When a car arrived with the map, Wallander asked Martinsson for a pen and then sat on a rock next to the dock. He drew circles around Ystad, Bjäresjö and Helsingborg. Then he marked the dock. He wrote numbers next to his marks. He waved over Höglund, Martinsson and Svedberg, who had arrived last, wearing a dirty sun hat instead of his cap for a change. He pointed at the map on his knee.

"Here we have his movements," he said. "And the murder sites. Like everything else they form a pattern."

"A road," Svedberg said. "With Ystad and Helsingborg as the end points. The scalp murderer on the southern plain."

"That isn't funny," Martinsson snapped.

"I'm not trying to be funny," Svedberg protested. "It's how it is."

"Looking at the big picture, you're probably right," said Wallander. "The area is limited. One murder takes place in Ystad. One murder occurs here, perhaps, we aren't sure yet, and the body is taken to Ystad. One murder happens just outside Ystad, in Bjäresjö, where the body is also discovered. And then we have Helsingborg."

"Most of them are concentrated around Ystad," said Höglund. "Does that mean that the man we're looking for lives here?"

"With the exception of Fredman the victims were found close to or inside their homes," said Wallander. "This is the map of the victims, not the murderer."

"Then Malmö should be marked too," said Svedberg. "That's where Fredman lived."

Wallander circled Malmö. The breeze tugged at the map.

"Now the picture is different," said Höglund. "We get an angle, not a straight line. Malmö is in the middle."

"It's always Fredman who's different," said Wallander.

"Maybe we should draw another circle," said Martinsson. "Around the airport. What do we get then?"

"An area of movement," said Wallander. "Revolving around Fredman's murder."

He knew that they were on their way towards a crucial conclusion.

"Correct me if I'm wrong," he said. "Fredman lives in Malmö. Together with the man who kills him, either held captive or not, he is driven east in the van. They come here, where Fredman dies. The journey continues to Ystad. The body is dumped in a hole under a tarpaulin in Ystad. Later the van returns west. It's parked at the airport, about halfway between Malmö and Ystad. There the tracks vanish."

"There are plenty of ways to get away from Sturup," said Svedberg. "Taxis, airport buses, rental cars. Another vehicle parked there earlier."

"So the murderer probably doesn't live in Ystad," Wallander said. "Malmö's a good possibility. But it could just as well be Lund. Or Helsingborg. Or why not Copenhagen?"

"Unless he's leading us on a wild-goose chase," Höglund said. "And he really does live in Ystad."

"That's possible, of course," said Wallander, "but I don't buy it."

"Which means that we ought to concentrate on Sturup more than we have so far," Martinsson said.

Wallander nodded. "I believe that the man we're looking for uses a motorcycle," he said. "We talked about this before. Witnesses may have seen one outside the house in Helsingborg. Sjösten is working on that right now. Since we're getting reinforcements this afternoon, we can afford to do a careful examination of the transport options from Sturup. We're looking for a man who parked the van there on the night of 28 June. And somehow left. Unless he works at the airport."

"There's one question we can't yet answer," said Svedberg. "And that is: what does this monster look like?"

"We know nothing about his face," Wallander said. "But we know he's strong, and a basement window in Helsingborg tells us that he's thin. We're dealing with someone in good shape, who goes barefoot."

"You mentioned Copenhagen just now," Martinsson said. "Do you think he's a foreigner?"

"I doubt it," Wallander replied. "I think we're dealing with a 100 per cent Swedish serial killer."

"That's not much to go on," said Svedberg. "Haven't we found a single hair? Does he have light or dark hair?"

"We don't know. According to Ekholm he probably tries not to attract attention. And we can't say anything about the way he's dressed when he commits the murders."

"What about his age?" asked Höglund.

"His victims have been men in their 70s, except for Fredman. But he's in good shape, goes barefoot, and may ride a motorcycle, and these facts don't imply an older man. We just can't guess."

"Over 18," said Svedberg. "If he rides a motorcycle."

"Can't we start with Fredman?" asked Höglund. "He differs from the other men, who are considerably older. Maybe we can assume that Fredman and the man who killed him are the same age. Then we're talking about a man who's under 50. And there are quite a few of them who are in good shape."

Wallander gave his colleagues a gloomy look. They were all under 50; Martinsson, the youngest, was barely 30. None of them was in particularly good shape.

"Ekholm is working on the psychological profile," said Wallander, getting to his feet. "It's important that we all read through it every day. It might give us some ideas."

Norén came towards Wallander with a telephone in his hand. Wallander squatted down out of the wind. It was Sjösten.

"I think I've got someone for you," he said. "A woman who was at parties at Liljegren's villa."

"Well done," Wallander said. "When can I meet her?"

"Any time."

Wallander looked at his watch. "I'll be there no later than 3 p.m.," he said. "By the way, we think we've found the place where Fredman died."

"I heard about it," Sjösten said. "I also heard that Ludwigsson and Hamrén are on their way from Stockholm. They're good men, both of them."

"How's it going with the witnesses who saw a man on a motorcycle?"

"They didn't see a man," Sjösten answered. "But they did see a motorcycle. We're trying to establish what kind it was. But it's not easy. Both the witnesses are old. They're also passionate health nuts who despise all petrol-powered vehicles. In the end it may turn out to be a lawnmower they saw."

A scratchy noise came from the phone. The conversation sputtered out in the wind. Nyberg was looking at the dock, rubbing his swollen cheek.

"How's it going?" Wallander asked him cheerily.

"I'm waiting for the divers."

"Are you in a lot of pain?"

"It's a wisdom tooth."

"Get it removed."

"I will. But first I want those divers here."

"Is it blood on the dock?"

"Almost certainly. Tonight you'll know whether it ever ran around inside Fredman's body."

On his way to the car Wallander remembered something. He went back.

"Louise Fredman," he said to Svedberg. "Did Åkeson come up with anything else on her?"

Svedberg didn't know, but said he'd talk to Åkeson.

Wallander turned off at Charlottenlund, thinking that if they'd found the place where Fredman was murdered, it was chosen with great care. The closest house was too far away for screams to be heard. He drove to the E65 and headed towards Malmö. The wind was buffeting the car, but the sky was still totally clear. He thought about the map. There were a lot of reasons to think the killer lived in Malmö. He didn't live in Ystad, that seemed certain. But why did he go to the trouble of dumping Fredman's body in a pit at the railway station? Was Ekholm right, that he was taunting the police? Wallander took the road to Sturup and briefly considered stopping at the airport. But what good would that do? The interview in Helsingborg was more important.

Her name was Elisabeth Carlén. They were in the Helsingborg police station in Sjösten's office. As Wallander shook hands with her he thought of the female vicar he had met the week before. Maybe it was because she was dressed in black and wore heavy make-up. She was about 30. Sjösten's description of her was quite apt. Sjösten had said that she was attractive because she looked at the world with a cold, disparaging expression. To Wallander it seemed as if she had decided to challenge any man who came near her. He'd never seen eyes like hers before. They blazed contempt and interest at the same time. He went over Sjösten's account of her as she lit a cigarette.

"Elisabeth Carlén is a whore," he had said. "I doubt she's been anything else since she was 20. She left middle school and then worked as a waitress on one of the ferries crossing the Sound. Got tired of that and opened a boutique with a girlfriend. That was a flop. Her parents had guaranteed a loan she took out for the business. After the money was gone, she did nothing but fight with them, and she drifted around a lot. Copenhagen for a while, then Amsterdam. When she was 17 she went there as a courier with a haul of amphetamines. Probably she was a user herself, but she seemed to be able to control it. That was the first time I met her. Then she was away for a few years, a black hole I don't know anything about, before she popped up in Malmö, working in a chain of brothels."

Wallander had to interrupt. "Are there still brothels?" he asked in surprise.

"Whorehouses, then," said Sjösten. "Call them what you like. But yes, there are still plenty of them. Don't you have them in Ystad? Just wait."

Wallander didn't interrupt again.

"She never walked the streets, of course. She built up an exclusive clientele. She had something that was attractive and raised her market value to the skies. She didn't even need to put those classified ads in the porn magazines. You can ask her what it is that makes her so special. It might be interesting to find out. During the last few years she's turned up in certain circles that are connected to Liljegren. She's been seen at restaurants with a number of his directors. Stockholm has a record of quite a few occasions when the police were interested in the man who happened to be escorting her. That's Elisabeth Carlén in a nutshell. Quite a successful Swedish prostitute."

"Why did you choose her?"

"She's fun. I've spoken with her many times. She isn't timid. If I tell her she isn't suspected of anything, she believes me. Also I imagine that she has a whore's sense of self-preservation. She notices things. She doesn't like the police. A good way to keep us out of the way is to stay on good terms with us."

Wallander hung up his jacket and shifted a heap of papers on the table. Elisabeth Carlén followed all his movements with her eyes. Wallander was reminded of a wary bird.

"You know that you aren't suspected of anything," he began.

"Åke Liljegren was roasted in his kitchen," she said. "I've seen his oven. Quite fancy. But I wasn't the one who turned it on."

"Nor do we think you were," said Wallander. "What I'm looking for is information. I'm trying to build a picture. I've got an empty frame. I'd like to put a photo in it. Taken at a party at Liljegren's. I want you to point out his guests."

"No," she said, "that's not what you want. You want me to tell you who killed him. And I can't."

"What did you think when you heard Liljegren was dead?"

"I didn't think anything. I burst out laughing."

"Why? No-one's death should be funny."

"He had plans other than winding up the way he did. The mausoleum in the cemetery outside Madrid? That's where he was going to be buried. A virtual fortress built according to his own sketches. Out of Italian marble. But he fetched up dying in his own oven. I think he would have laughed himself."

"His parties," said Wallander. "Let's get back to them. I've heard they were wild."

"They sure were."

"In what way?"

"In every way."

"Can you be a little more specific?"

She took a couple of deep drags on her cigarette while she thought about this, all the time looking Wallander in the eye.

"Liljegren liked to bring people together who lived life to the fullest," she said. "Let's say they were insatiable. Insatiable with regard to power, wealth and sex. And Liljegren had a reputation for being discreet. He created a safety zone around his guests. No hidden cameras, no spies. Nothing ever leaked out about his parties. He also knew which women he could invite."

"Women like you?"

"Yes, women like me."

"And who else?"

She didn't seem to understand his question at first.

"What other women were there?"

"That depended on their desires."

"Whose desires?"

"The desires of the guests. The men."

"And what might they be?"

"Some wanted *me* to be there."

"I understood that. Who else?"

"You won't get any names."

"Who were they?"

"Young girls, some very young, blonde, brown, black. Older ones sometimes, some of them hefty. It varied."

"You knew them?"

"Not always. Not often."

"How did he get hold of them?"

332

She put out her cigarette and lit a new one before she answered. She didn't release his gaze even when she was stubbing it out.

"How does a person like Liljegren get what he wants? He had unlimited money. He had helpers. He had contacts. He could fly in a girl from Florida to attend a party. She probably had no idea she was going all the way to Sweden. Not to mention Helsingborg."

"You say he had helpers. Who were they?"

"His chauffeurs. His assistant. He often had a butler with him. English, of course."

"What was his name?"

"No names."

"We'll find out about them anyway."

"You probably will. But that doesn't mean the names are going to come from me."

"What would happen if you gave me some names?"

She seemed utterly unmoved when she replied.

"Then I might be killed. Maybe not with my head in an oven, but in an equally unpleasant manner, I'm sure."

"Were many of his guests public figures?"

"Many."

"Politicians?"

"Yes."

"Gustaf Wetterstedt?"

"I said no names."

Suddenly he realised that she was sending him a message. Her answers had a subtext. She knew who Wetterstedt was, but he had not been at the parties.

"Businessmen?"

"Yes."

"Arne Carlman, the art dealer?"

"Did he have almost the same name as me?"

"Yes."

"I'll say it one last time. Don't push me for names, or I'll get up and go."

Not him either, thought Wallander. Her signals were very clear.

"Artists? Celebrities?"

"Once in a while. But seldom. I don't think Åke trusted them. Probably with good reason."

"You talked about young girls. Brown girls. Did you mean brunettes, or girls with brown skin?"

"Brown skin."

"Do you remember ever meeting a girl named Dolores María?"

"No."

"A girl from the Dominican Republic?"

"I don't even know where that is."

"Do you remember a girl named Louise Fredman? A teenager. A blonde."

"No."

Wallander turned the conversation in another direction. She still seemed willing to continue.

"You say that the parties were wild."

"Yes, they were."

"Tell me about wild."

"Do you want details?"

"Please."

"Descriptions of naked bodies?"

"Not necessarily."

"They were orgies. You can imagine the rest."

"Can I?" said Wallander. "I'm not so sure."

"If I undressed and lay down on your desk it would be completely unexpected," she said. "Something like that."

"Unexpected events?"

"That's what happens when insatiable people get together, isn't it?"

"Insatiable men?"

"Exactly."

Wallander made a hasty outline in his head. He was still scratching the surface.

"I've got a proposal," he said. "And another question."

"I'm still here."

"My proposal is that you give me the opportunity to meet you one more time. Soon, within a few days."

She nodded her assent. Wallander got an unpleasant feeling that he was entering into some sort of agreement.

"My question is simple," he said. "You were speaking of Liljegren's chauffeurs. And his butlers. But you said that he had an assistant. Not plural. Is that correct?"

He saw a faint change in her expression. She knew she had said too much even without providing names.

"This conversation is strictly for my memoirs," said Wallander. "Did I hear correctly or not?"

"You heard wrong," she said. "Of course he had more than one assistant."

So, I was right, thought Wallander. "That'll be all this time, then," he said, getting up.

"I'll leave when I finish my cigarette," she said. For the first time in the conversation she released him from her gaze.

Wallander opened the door. Sjösten was sitting outside reading a sailing magazine. Wallander nodded. She put out her cigarette, stood up, and shook his hand. When Sjösten had shown her out and returned, Wallander was by the window, watching her get into her car.

"Did it go well?" Sjösten asked.

"Maybe," said Wallander. "She agreed to meet me again."

"What did she say?"

"Nothing, actually."

"And you think that was good?"

"It was what she didn't know that interested me," Wallander said. "I want 24-hour surveillance of Liljegren's house, and I want you to put a tail on Carlén. Sooner or later somebody will show up who we'll want to talk to."

"That sounds like an inadequate reason for surveillance," said Sjösten.

"I'll take responsibility for that decision," said Wallander kindly, "as the chosen leader of this investigation."

"I'm glad it wasn't me," replied Sjösten. "Are you staying overnight?"

"No, I'll drive home."

They went down the steps to the ground floor.

"Did you read about a girl who burned herself to death in a field near here?" Wallander asked just before they said goodbye.

"Yes. Terrible story."

"She had hitchhiked from Helsingborg," Wallander went on. "And she was scared. I'm just wondering whether she might have had something to do with Liljegren's fun and games. Although it's a long shot."

"There were rumours about Liljegren trading in girls," said Sjösten. "Among a thousand other rumours."

Wallander looked at him intently. "Trading girls?"

"There were rumours that Sweden was being used as a transit country for poor girls from South America, on their way to brothels in southern Europe and the former Eastern bloc countries. We've found a couple of girls who have managed to escape but we've never caught the ones running the business. And we haven't been able to build a proper case."

Wallander stared at Sjösten.

"And you waited until now to tell me this?"

Sjösten shook his head, surprised.

"You never asked me about this before now."

Wallander stood stock still. The girl had started running through his head again.

"I've changed my mind," he said. "I'll stay the night."

They took the lift back up to Sjösten's office.

CHAPTER 33

On that lovely summer evening Wallander and Sjösten took the ferry to Helsingør on the Danish side and had dinner at a restaurant Sjösten liked. He entertained Wallander while they ate with stories about the boat he was restoring, his numerous marriages and his yet more numerous children. They didn't begin talking about the investigation until they were having coffee. Wallander listened gratefully to Sjösten, who was a charming storyteller. He was very tired. After the excellent dinner he was feeling drowsy, but his mind was rested. Sjösten had drunk a few shots of aquavit with beer, while Wallander stuck to mineral water.

When the coffee came they exchanged roles. Sjösten listened while Wallander talked. He went over everything that had happened. He talked to Sjösten in a way that forced him to clarify things for himself as well. For the first time he let the girl who had burned herself to death serve as the prelude to the murders. It had seemed improbable to him before that her death might be connected to them. Now he admitted that it had been careless to draw this conclusion. Sjösten was an attentive listener who pounced on him whenever he was vague.

Wallander would think of that evening in Helsingør later as the point when the investigation sloughed off its skin. The pattern he thought he had discovered as he'd sat on the bench on the pier was confirmed. Gaps were filled, holes sealed; questions found their answers, or at least were formulated more clearly and arranged in order. He marched back and forth through the landscape of the case and for the first time felt that he had an overview. But he also had a nagging, guilty feeling that he should have seen it all sooner, that he had been sidetracked, instead of realising that he must go in an entirely different direction. Although he avoided mentioning it to Sjösten, there was one question always on his mind. Could any of the murders have been prevented? Or at least the last one – if it was the last one – Liljegren's? He couldn't help but ask. And he knew that it would haunt him for a very long time; maybe he'd never get an answer that he could live with.

The problem was that they didn't have a suspect, not even a group of people among whom they could cast their net. Nor were there any solid clues that led in a specific direction.

Earlier in the day, when Sjösten had mentioned in passing that it was suspected that Sweden, and especially Helsingborg, served as a transit point for girls destined for brothels, Wallander's reaction had been immediate. Sjösten was amazed at Wallander's sudden burst of energy. Without thinking, Wallander had sat down behind the desk, so Sjösten had to take the visitor's chair in his own office. Wallander told him all he knew about Dolores María Santana, that she seemed to be running away when she hitchhiked from Helsingborg.

"A black car came once a week to Gustaf Wetterstedt's house," Wallander said. "By chance the housekeeper noticed it. She thought she might recognise the car in Liljegren's garage. What conclusion can you draw from that?"

"None," said Sjösten. "There are plenty of black Mercedes with tinted windows."

"Put it together with the rumours about Liljegren. The rumours of the trade in girls. Is there anything that would prevent him from having parties somewhere else besides his house? Why couldn't he also run a home delivery service?"

"No reason at all," said Sjösten. "But there doesn't seem to be any basis for believing it."

"I want to know whether that car left Liljegren's house on Thursdays," said Wallander. "And came back on Fridays."

"How can we find that out?"

"There are neighbours. Who drove the car? There seems to be such a vacuum around Liljegren. He had personal employees. He had an assistant. Where are all these people?"

"We're working on that," said Sjösten.

"Let's set our priorities," said Wallander. "The motorcycle is important. Liljegren's assistant is too. And the car on Thursdays. Start there. Assign all your available people to look into these areas."

Sjösten went to set this in train. He told Wallander when he came back that the surveillance of Elisabeth Carlén had begun.

"What's she doing?"

"She's in her flat," Sjösten said. "Alone."

Wallander called Ystad and talked to Åkeson.

"I must talk with Louise Fredman now," he said.

"You'll have to come up with a strong case for doing so," Åkeson said, "or I can't help you."

"It might be crucial."

"It has to be something concrete, Kurt."

"There's always a way round this bureaucratic crap."

"What do you think she can tell you?"

"Whether she ever had the soles of her feet cut with a knife, for instance."

"Good Lord. Why would that have happened to her?"

Wallander didn't feel like telling him.

"Can't her mother give me permission?" he said. "Fredman's widow?"

"That's what I was wondering," said Åkeson. "That's the way we'll have to proceed."

"I'll drive to Malmö tomorrow," Wallander said. "Do I need any kind of papers from you?"

"Not if she gives you her permission," said Åkeson. "But you mustn't put pressure on her."

"Do I do that?" Wallander asked, surprised. "I didn't realise."

"I'm just telling you the rules. That's all."

Sjösten had suggested they take a ferry across to Denmark and have dinner, so they could talk, and Wallander had agreed. It was still too early to call Baiba. Maybe not too early for her, but certainly too early for him. It occurred to him that Sjösten, with all his marriages behind him, might be able to give him some advice on how to present his dilemma to Baiba. They took the ferry across the Sound, with Wallander wishing the journey was longer. They had dinner, which Sjösten insisted on paying for. Then they strolled back through Helsingør towards the terminal. Sjösten stopped at a doorway.

"In here lives a man who appreciates Swedes," he said, smiling.

Wallander read on a brass plate that a doctor had his practice here.

"He writes prescriptions for diet drugs that are banned in Sweden," said Sjösten. "Every day there's a long line of overweight Swedes outside."

They were on their way up the stairs to the terminal when Sjösten's mobile phone rang. He kept walking as he listened.

"That was Larsson, one of my colleagues. He's found what may be a real gold mine," Sjösten said, putting away his phone. "A neighbour of Liljegren's who saw a number of things."

"What did he see?"

"Black cars, motorcycles. We'll talk to him tomorrow."

"We'll talk to him tonight," Wallander said. "It'll only be 10 p.m. by the time we get back to Helsingborg."

Sjösten nodded without replying. Then he called the station and asked Larsson to meet them at the terminal. The young police officer waiting for them reminded Wallander of Martinsson. They got into his car and drove to Tågaborg. Wallander noticed a banner from the local football team hanging from his rear-view mirror. Larsson filled them in.

"His name is Lennart Heineman, and he's a retired diplomat," he said, in a Skåne accent so broad that Wallander had to strain to understand him. "He's almost 80, but quite sharp. His wife seems to be away. Heineman's garden is just across from the main entrance to Liljegren's grounds. He's observed a number of things."

"Does he know we're coming?" asked Sjösten.

"I called," said Larsson. "He said it was fine. He says he rarely goes to bed before 3 a.m. He told me he was writing a critical study of the Swedish foreign office's administration."

Wallander remembered with distaste an officious woman from the foreign office who had visited them in Ystad some years earlier, in connection with the investigation that led him to Latvia to meet Baiba. He tried to think of her name. Something to do with roses. He pushed the thought aside as they pulled up outside Heineman's house. A police car was parked outside Liljegren's villa across the street. A tall man with short white hair came walking towards them. He had a firm handshake, and Wallander trusted him instantly. The handsome villa he ushered them into was from the same period as Liljegren's, but this house had an air of vitality about it, a reflection of the energetic old man who lived there. He asked them to have a seat and offered them a drink. They all declined. Wallander sensed that he was used to receiving people he hadn't met before.

"Terrible things going on," said Heineman.

Sjösten gave Wallander an almost imperceptible nod to lead the interview.

"That's why we couldn't postpone this conversation until tomorrow," Wallander replied.

"Why postpone it?" said Heineman. "I've never understood why Swedes go to bed so early. The continental habit of taking a siesta is much healthier. If I'd gone to bed early I'd have been dead long ago."

Wallander pondered Heineman's strong criticism of Swedish bed-time hours for a moment.

"We're interested in any observations you may have made of the traffic in and out of Liljegren's villa," he said. "But there are some things that are of particular interest to us. Let's begin by asking about Liljegren's black Mercedes."

"He must have had at least two," said Heineman.

Wallander was surprised at the answer. He hadn't imagined more than one car, even though Liljegren's big garage could have held two or three.

"What makes you think he had more than one?"

"I don't just think so," said Heineman, "I know. Sometimes two cars left the house at the same time. Or returned at the same time.

When Liljegren was away the cars remained here. From my upper floor I can see part of his grounds. There were two cars over there."

One is missing, Wallander thought. Where is it now?

Sjösten took out a notebook.

"Can you recall whether one or perhaps both cars regularly left Liljegren's villa late in the afternoon or evening on Thursdays?" Wallander said. "And returned during the night or in the next morning?"

"I'm not much for remembering dates," said Heineman. "But it's true that one of the cars used to leave the villa in the evening. And return the next morning."

"It's crucial that we ascertain that it was on Thursdays," Wallander said.

"My wife and I have never observed the idiotic Swedish tradition of eating pea soup on Thursdays," Heineman said. Wallander waited while Heineman tried to remember. Larsson sat looking at the ceiling, and Sjösten tapped his notebook lightly on one knee.

"It's possible," said Heineman all of a sudden. "Perhaps I can piece together an answer. I recall definitely that my wife's sister was here on one occasion last year when the car left on one of its regular trips. Why I'm so certain of this I don't know. But I'm positive. She lives in Bonn and doesn't visit very often."

"Why do you think it was a Thursday?" asked Wallander. "Did you write it down on the calendar?"

"I've never had much use for calendars," Heineman said with distaste. "In all my years at the foreign office I never wrote down a single meeting. But during 40 years of service I never missed one either, unlike people who did nothing but write notes on their calendars."

"Why Thursday?" Wallander repeated.

"I don't know whether it was a Thursday," said Heineman. "But it was my wife's sister's name day. I know that for sure. Her name is Frida."

"What month?" asked Wallander.

"February or March."

Wallander patted his jacket pocket. His pocket calendar didn't have the previous year in it. Sjösten shook his head. Larsson couldn't help.

"Might there be an old calendar somewhere in the house?" asked Wallander.

"It's possible that one of the grandchildren's Christmas calendars is still in the attic," Heineman said. "My wife has the bad habit of saving a lot of old junk. I'm the opposite. Also a trait I picked up at the ministry. On the first day of each month I threw out everything that didn't need to be saved from the previous one. My rule was, better to throw out too much than too little. I never missed a thing I had discarded."

Wallander turned to Larsson. "Call and find out what day is the name day for Frida," he said. "And what day of the week it was in 1993."

"Who would know that?" Larsson asked.

"Damn it," said Sjösten. "Call the station. You have five minutes to get the answer."

"There's a telephone in the hall," said Heineman.

Larsson left the room.

"I must say that I appreciate it when clear orders are given," Heineman said contentedly. "That ability seems to have been lost."

To fill in time, Sjösten asked where Heineman had been stationed abroad. It turned out that he had been posted to many places.

"It got better towards the end," he said. "But when I started my career, the people who were sent overseas to represent this country were often of a deplorably low calibre."

When Larsson reappeared, almost ten minutes had passed. He was holding a piece of paper.

"Frida has her name day on February 17th," he said. "In 1993 it fell on a Thursday."

Police work was just a matter of refusing to give up until a crucial detail was confirmed in writing, Wallander thought.

He decided to ask Heineman the other questions he had for him later, but for appearances' sake he raised a few more queries: whether Heineman had observed that anything could have indicated a "possible traffic in girls" as Wallander chose to describe it.

"There were parties," Heineman said stiffly. "From our top floor, seeing into some of the rooms was unavoidable. Of course there were women involved."

"Did you ever meet Åke Liljegren?"

"Yes," replied Heineman, "I met him once in Madrid. It was during one of my last years as an active member of the foreign office. He had requested introductions to some large Spanish construction companies. We knew quite well who Liljegren was, of course. His shell company scam was in full swing. We treated him as politely as we could, but he was not a pleasant man to deal with."

"Why not?"

Heineman paused for a moment. "To put it bluntly, he was disagreeable. He treated everyone around him with undisguised contempt."

Wallander brought the interview to an end.

"My colleagues will be contacting you again," he said, getting to his feet.

Heineman followed them to the gate. The police car opposite was still there. The house was dark. After saying goodbye to Heineman, Wallander went across the street. One of the officers in the car got out and saluted. Wallander raised his hand in response to the exaggerated deference.

"Anything going on?" he asked.

"All's calm here. A few curiosity-seekers is about it."

Larsson dropped them off at the station. Wallander started by calling Hansson, who told him that Ludwigsson and Hamrén from the National Criminal Bureau had arrived. He had put them up at the Hotel Sekelgården.

"They seem to be good men," said Hansson. "Not at all as arrogant as I feared."

"Why would they have been arrogant?"

"Stockholmers," said Hansson. "You know how they are. Don't you remember that prosecutor who filled in for Per? What was her name? Bodin?"

"Brolin," said Wallander. "But I don't remember her."

In fact Wallander remembered quite well. Embarrassment crept over him when he recalled totally losing control when drunk and making a pass at her. It was one of the things he was most ashamed of. And it didn't help that she had later spent the night with him in Copenhagen.

"They're going to start working the airport tomorrow," said Hansson.

Wallander told him what had happened at Heineman's house.

"So we've got a break," said Hansson. "So you think that Liljegren sent a prostitute to Wetterstedt in Ystad once a week?"

"I do."

"Could it have been going on with Carlman too?"

"Maybe not in the same way. But I should think that Carlman's and Liljegren's circles have overlapped. We still don't know where."

"And Fredman?"

"He's the exception. He doesn't fit in anywhere. Least of all in Liljegren's circles. Unless he was one of his enforcers. I'm going to go back to Malmö tomorrow to talk to his family. I especially want to meet his daughter."

"Åkeson told me about your conversation. You'll have to tread carefully. We don't want it to end as badly as your meeting with Erika Carlman, do we?"

"Of course not."

"I'll get hold of Höglund and Svedberg tonight," Hansson said. "You've finally found a real lead."

"Don't forget Ludwigsson and Hamrén," Wallander said. "They're also part of the team now."

Wallander hung up. Sjösten had gone to get coffee. Wallander dialled his own number in Ystad. Linda answered at once.

"I just got home," she said. "Where are you?"

"In Helsingborg. I'm staying here overnight."

"Has something happened?"

"We went over to Helsingør and had dinner."

"That's not what I meant."

"We're working."

"We are too," Linda said. "We rehearsed the whole thing again tonight. We had an audience too."

"Who?"

"A boy who asked if he could watch. He was standing outside on the street and said he'd heard we were working on a play. I think the people at the hot dog stand must have told him about it."

"So it wasn't anyone you know?"

"He was just a tourist here in town. He walked home with me afterwards."

Wallander felt a pang of jealousy.

"Is he in the flat now?"

"He walked me home to Mariagatan. Then he went home."

"I was only wondering."

"He had a funny name. He said it was Hoover. But he was very nice. I think he liked what we were doing. He said he'd come back tomorrow if he had time."

"I'm sure he will," Wallander said.

Sjösten came in with two cups of coffee. Wallander asked him for his home number, which he gave to Linda.

"My daughter," he said, after he hung up. "The only child I have. She's going to Visby shortly to take a theatre course."

"One's children give life a glimmer of meaning," Sjösten said, handing the coffee cup to Wallander.

They went over the conversation with Heineman. Wallander could tell that Sjösten was not convinced that Wetterstedt's connection to Liljegren meant they were closer to finding the killer.

"Tomorrow I want you to find all the material about the traffic in girls that mentions Helsingborg. Why here, anyway? How did they get here? There must be an explanation. Besides, this vacuum surrounding Liljegren is unbelievable. I don't get it."

"That stuff about the girls is mostly speculation," said Sjösten. "We've never done an investigation of it. We simply haven't had any reason to. One time Birgersson brought it up with one of the prosecutors, but he said we had more important things to do. He was right too."

"I still want you to check it out," Wallander said. "Do a summary for me tomorrow. Fax it to me in Ystad as soon as you can."

It was late by the time they drove to Sjösten's flat. Wallander knew he had to call Baiba. There was no escaping it. She would be packing. He couldn't postpone telling her the news any longer.

"I have to make a phone call to Latvia," he said. "Just a couple of minutes."

Sjösten showed him where the phone was. Wallander waited until Sjösten had gone into the bathroom before he dialled the number. When it rang the first time he hung up. He had no idea what to say. He didn't dare tell her. He would wait until tomorrow night and then make up a story: that the whole thing had come up suddenly and now he wanted her to come to Ystad instead. He couldn't think of a better solution. At least for himself.

They talked for another half hour over a glass of whisky. Sjösten made a call to check that Elisabeth Carlén was still under surveillance.

"She's asleep," he said. "Maybe we ought to go to bed too."

Sjösten gave him sheets and Wallander made up a bed for himself in a room with children's drawings on the walls. He turned off the light and was asleep immediately.

He woke drenched in sweat. He must have had a nightmare, although he remembered nothing. He had only slept for a couple of hours. He wondered why he'd woken, and turned over to go back to sleep. But he was wide awake. Where the feeling came from he had no idea. He was gripped with panic.

He had left Linda alone in Ystad. She shouldn't be there by herself. He had to go home. Without another thought he got up, dressed, and quickly scribbled a note to Sjösten. He drove out of town. Perhaps he should call her. But what would he say? She'd just be frightened. He drove as fast as he could through the light summer night. He didn't understand where the panic had come from. But it was definitely there, and it wouldn't let go.

It was light when he parked on Mariagatan. He unlocked the door carefully. The terror had not abated. Not until he pushed open Linda's door gently, saw her head on the pillow and heard her breathing, did he calm down.

He sat on the sofa. Now fear had been replaced by embarrassment. He wrote a note to her, which he left on the coffee table in case she got up, saying that his plans had changed and that he'd come home. He set the alarm clock for 5 a.m, knowing that Sjösten got up early to work on his boat. He had no idea how he was going to explain his departure in the middle of the night. He lay in bed and wondered what lay behind his panic, but he couldn't find an answer. It took a long time before he fell asleep.

CHAPTER 34

When the doorbell rang he knew at once that it had to be Baiba. Oddly, he wasn't nervous at all, even though it wasn't going to be much fun explaining to her why he hadn't told her that their holiday had to be postponed. Then he started and sat up in bed. Of course she wasn't there. It was only the alarm clock ringing, the hands positioned like a gaping mouth at 5.03 a.m. The confusion passed, he put his hand over the alarm button and then sat motionless. Reality slowly dawned. The town was quiet. Few sounds other than birdsong penetrated his room. He couldn't remember whether he'd dreamed about Baiba or not. The flight from the child's room in Sjösten's flat now seemed wildly irrational. Not like him at all.

With a yawn he got up and went into the kitchen. On the table he found a note from Linda. I communicate with my daughter through a series of notes, he thought. When she makes one of her occasional stops in Ystad. He read over what she had written and realised that the dream about Baiba, waking up and believing that she was standing outside his door, had contained a warning. Linda's note said that Baiba had called and would he call right away. Baiba's irritation was recognisable from the note.

He couldn't call her, not now. He'd call her tonight, or maybe tomorrow. Or should he have Martinsson do it? He could give her the unfortunate news that the man she was intending to go to Skagen with, the man she assumed would be standing at Kastrup Airport to meet her, was up to his neck in a hunt for a maniac who smashed axes into the heads of his fellow human beings and then cut off their scalps. What he might tell Martinsson to say was true, and yet not true. It could never explain or excuse the fact that he was too weak to do the decent thing and call Baiba himself.

He picked up the phone, not to call Baiba, but Sjösten in Helsingborg, to explain why he had left during the night. What could he possibly say? The truth was one option: sudden concern for his daughter, a concern all parents feel without being able to explain. But when Sjösten answered he said something quite different, that he'd forgotten about a meeting he had arranged with his father for early that morning. It was something that couldn't be revealed by accident, since Sjösten and his father would never cross paths. They agreed to talk later, after Wallander had been to Malmö.

Then everything seemed much easier. It wasn't the first time in his life he had started his day with a bunch of white lies, evasions and self-deceptions. He took a shower, had some coffee, wrote a new note to Linda, and left the flat just after 6.30 a.m. Everything was quiet at the station. It was this early, lonely hour, when the weary graveyard shift was on its way home and it was still too early for the daytime staff, that Wallander took pleasure in. Life took on a special meaning in this solitude. He never understood why this was so, but he could remember the feeling from deep in his past, maybe as far back as 20 years.

Rydberg, his old friend and mentor, had been the same way. *Everyone has small but extremely personal sacred moments*, Rydberg had told him on one of the few occasions when they had sat in either his or Wallander's office and split a small bottle of whisky behind a locked door. No alcohol was permitted in the station. But sometimes they had something to celebrate. Or to grieve over, for that matter. Wallander sorely missed those brief and strangely philosophical times. They had been moments of friendship, of irreplaceable intimacy.

Wallander read quickly through a stack of messages. In a memo he saw that Dolores María Santana's body had been released for burial and now rested in a grave in the same cemetery as Rydberg. This brought him back to the investigation; he rolled up his sleeves as though going out into the world to do battle, and skimmed as fast as he could through the copies of investigative material his colleagues had prepared. There were papers from Nyberg, laboratory reports on which Nyberg had scrawled question marks and comments, and charts of the tip-offs that had come in from the public. Tyrén must be an extraordinarily zealous young man, Wallander thought, without being able to decide whether that meant he would be a good policeman in the field in the future, or whether he was already showing signs that he belonged somewhere in the hunting grounds of the bureaucracy. Wallander read quickly, but nothing of value escaped him. The most important thing seemed to be that they had established that Fredman had indeed been murdered on the dock below the side road to Charlottenlund.

He pushed the stacks of papers aside and leaned back pensively in his chair. What *do* these men have in common? Fredman doesn't fit the picture, but he belongs just the same. A former minister of justice, an art dealer, a criminal fraudster and a petty thief. They're all murdered by the same killer, who takes their scalps. Wetterstedt, the first, is barely hidden, just shoved out of sight. Carlman, the second, is killed in the middle of a summer party in his own arbour. Fredman is kidnapped, taken to an out-of-the-way dock and then dumped in the middle of Ystad, as if being put on display. He lies in a pit with a tarpaulin over his head, like a statue waiting to be unveiled. Finally, the killer moves to Helsingborg and murders Liljegren. Almost immediately we pin down a connection between Wetterstedt and Liljegren. Now we need the links between the others. After we know what connected them, we have to discover who might have had reason to kill them. And why the scalps? Who is the lone warrior?

Wallander sat for a long time thinking about Fredman and Liljegren. There was a similarity there. The kidnapping and the acid in the eyes on the one hand, and the head in the oven on the other. It hadn't been enough to kill these two. Why? He took another step. The water got deeper around him. The bottom was slippery. Easy to lose his footing. There was a difference between Fredman and Liljegren, a very clear one. Fredman had hydrochloric acid poured into his eyes while he was alive. Liljegren was dead before he was stuck in the oven. Wallander tried to conjure up the killer again. Thin, in good condition, barefoot, insane. If he hunts evil men, Fredman must have been the worst. Then Liljegren. Carlman and Wetterstedt in about the same category.

Wallander got up and went to the window. There was something about the sequence that bothered him. Fredman was the third. Why not the first? Or the last – at least so far? The root of evil, the first or the last to be punished, by a killer who was insane but canny and well-organised. The dock must have been chosen because it was handy. *How many docks did he look at before he chose that one?* Is this a man who is always near the sea? A well-behaved man; a fisherman, or someone in the coast guard? Or why not a member of the sea rescue service, which has the best bench for meditating on in Ystad? Someone who also managed to drive Fredman away, in his own van. Why did he go to all that trouble? Because it was his only way to get to him? They met somewhere. They knew each other. Peter Hjelm had been quite clear. Fredman travelled a lot and always had plenty of money afterwards. It was rumoured that he was an enforcer. But Wallander only knew of parts of Fredman's life. They must try to bring the unknown past to light.

Wallander sat down again. The sequence didn't make sense. What could the explanation be? He went to get some coffee. Svedberg and Höglund had arrived. Svedberg had a new cap on. His cheeks were a blotchy red. Höglund was more tanned, and Wallander was paler. Hansson arrived with Mats Ekholm in tow. Even Ekholm had managed to get a tan. Hansson's eyes were bloodshot with fatigue. He looked at Wallander with astonishment, and at the same time he seemed to be searching for some misunderstanding. Hadn't Wallander said he'd be in Helsingborg? It wasn't even 7.30 a.m. yet. Had something happened? Wallander shook his head almost imperceptibly. No-one had misunderstood anything. They hadn't planned to have a meeting of the investigative team. Ludwigsson and Hamrén had already driven out to Sturup, Höglund was going to join them, while Svedberg and Hansson were busy with follow-up work on Wetterstedt and Carlman. Someone stuck in his head and said that Wallander had a phone call from Helsingborg. Wallander took the call on the phone next to the coffee machine. It was Sjösten, who told him that Elisabeth Carlén was still sleeping. No-one had visited her, and no-one except some curiosity-seekers had been seen near Liljegren's villa.

"Did Liljegren have no family?" Martinsson asked angrily, as if he'd behaved inappropriately by not marrying.

"He left behind only a few grieving, plundered companies," Svedberg said.

"They're working on Liljegren in Helsingborg," Wallander said. "We'll get the information in time."

Wallander knew that Hansson had been meticulous about passing on the latest developments. They agreed that it was likely that Liljegren had been supplying women to Wetterstedt on a regular basis.

"He's living up to the old rumour about him," said Svedberg.

"We have to find a similar link to Carlman," Wallander went on. "It's there, I know it is. Forget about Wetterstedt for the time being. Let's concentrate on Carlman."

Everyone was in a hurry. The link that had been established was like a shot in the arm for the team. Wallander took Ekholm to his office. He told him what he had been thinking earlier that morning. Ekholm was an attentive listener, as always.

"The acid and the oven," Wallander said. "I'm trying to interpret the killer's language. He talks to himself and he talks to his victims. What is he actually saying?"

"Your idea about the sequence is interesting," said Ekholm. "Psychopathic killers often have an element of pedantry in their bloody handiwork. Something may have happened to upset his plans."

"Like what?"

"He's the only one who can answer that."

"Still, we have to try."

Ekholm didn't answer. Wallander got the feeling that he didn't have a lot to say at the moment.

"Let's number them," Wallander said. "Wetterstedt is number one.

What do we see if we rearrange them?"

"Fredman first or last," Ekholm said. "Liljegren just before or after, depending on which variant is correct. Wetterstedt and Carlman in positions which tie them to the others."

"Can we assume that he's finished?" asked Wallander.

"I have no idea," Ekholm answered.

"What does your programme say? What combinations has it managed to come up with?"

"Not a thing, actually." Ekholm seemed surprised by his own answer.

"How do you interpret that?" Wallander said.

"We're dealing with a serial killer who differs from his predecessors in crucial ways."

"And what does that tell us?"

"That he'll provide us with totally new data. If we catch him."

"We must," said Wallander, knowing how feeble he sounded.

He got up and they both left the room.

"Criminal psychologists at both the F.B.I. and Scotland Yard have been in touch," said Ekholm. "They're following our work with great interest."

"Have they got any suggestions? We need all the help we can get."

"I'm supposed to let them know if anything comes in."

They parted at the reception desk. Wallander took a moment to exchange a few words with Ebba. Then he drove straight to Sturup. He found Ludwigsson and Hamrén in the office of the airport police. Wallander was disconcerted to meet a young policeman who had fainted the year before when they were arresting a man trying to flee the country. But he shook his hand and tried to pretend that he was sorry about what had happened.

Wallander realised he had met Ludwigsson before, during a visit to Stockholm. He was a large, powerful man with high colour from blood pressure, not the sun. Hamrén was his diametrical opposite: small and wiry, with thick glasses. Wallander greeted them a little offhandedly and asked how it was going.

"There seems to be a lot of rivalry between the different taxi companies out here," Ludwigsson began. "Just like at Arlanda. So far we haven't managed to pin down all the ways he could have left the airport during the hours in question. And nobody noticed a motorcycle. But we've only just begun."

Wallander had a cup of coffee and answered a number of questions the two men had. Then he left them and drove on to Malmö. He parked outside the building in Rosengård. It was very hot. He took the lift up to the fifth floor and rang the doorbell. This time it wasn't the son but Björn Fredman's widow who opened the door. She smelled of wine. At her feet cowering close by was a little boy. He seemed extremely shy. Or afraid, rather. When Wallander bent down to greet him he seemed terrified. A fleeting memory entered Wallander's mind. He couldn't catch it, but filed the thought away. It was something that had happened before, or something someone had said, that had been imprinted on his subconscious.

She asked him to come in. The boy clung to her legs. Her hair wasn't combed and she wore no make-up. The blanket on the sofa told him she had spent the night there. They sat down, Wallander in the same chair for the third time. Stefan, the older son, came in. His eyes were as wary as the last time Wallander had visited. He came forward and shook hands, again with adult manners. He sat down next to his mother on the sofa. Everything was as before. The only difference was the presence of the younger brother, curled up on his mother's lap. Something didn't seem quite right about him. His eyes never left Wallander.

"I came about Louise," Wallander said. "I know it's hard to talk about a family member who's in a psychiatric hospital. But it's necessary."

"Why can't she be left in peace?" the woman said. Her voice sounded tormented and unsure, as if she doubted her ability to defend her daughter.

Wallander would have liked to avoid this conversation more than anything. He was unsure of how to handle it.

"Of course she'll be left in peace," he said. "But unfortunately it's part of the duty of the police to gather all the information we can to help solve a brutal crime."

"She hadn't seen her father in many years," the woman said. "She can't tell you anything important."

"Does Louise know that her father is dead?"

"Why should she?"

"It's not unreasonable, is it?"

Wallander saw that she was about to break down. His distaste at what he was doing increased with each question and answer. Without wanting to, he had put her under a pressure she could hardly endure. Stefan said nothing.

"First of all, you have to understand that Louise no longer has any relationship to reality," the woman said in a voice that was so faint that Wallander had to lean forward to hear her. "She has left everything behind. She's living in her own world. She doesn't speak, she doesn't listen. She's pretending that she doesn't exist."

Wallander thought carefully before he continued.

"Even so, it could be important for the police to know why she became ill. I actually came here to ask for your permission to meet her. Speak to her. I realise now that it may not be appropriate. But then you'll have to answer my questions instead."

"I don't know what to tell you," she said. "She got sick. It came out of nowhere."

"She was found in Pildamm Park," Wallander prompted her.

Both the son and the mother stiffened. Even the little boy on her lap seemed to react, affected by the others.

"How do you know that?" she asked.

"There's a report on how and when she was taken to the hospital," said Wallander. "But that's all I know. Everything to do with her illness is confidential. I understand that she was having some difficulty in school before she got sick."

"She never had any trouble, but she was always very sensitive."

"I'm sure she was. Still, usually specific events trigger acute cases of mental illness."

"How do you know that? Are you a doctor?"

"No, I'm a police officer. But I know what I'm talking about."

"Nothing happened."

"But you must have wondered about it. Night and day."

"I've hardly thought about anything else."

Wallander felt the atmosphere becoming so intolerable that he wished he could break off the conversation and leave. The answers he was getting were leading him nowhere, though he believed they were mostly truthful, or at least partly so.

"Do you have a photograph of her I could look at?"

"Is it necessary?"

"Please."

The boy sitting next to her began to speak, but checked himself instantly. Wallander wondered why. Didn't the boy want him to see his sister? Why not?

The mother got up with the little boy hanging on to her. She opened a drawer and handed him some photographs. Louise was blonde, smiling, and resembled Stefan, but there was nothing of that wariness he sensed now in the room, or that he'd seen in the family photograph in Fredman's flat. She smiled openly and trustingly at the camera. She was pretty.

"A nice-looking girl," he said. "Let's hope she gets better some day."

"I've stopped hoping," the mother said. "Why should I hope any more?"

"Doctors can work wonders these days," Wallander said.

"One day Louise is going to leave that hospital," the boy said suddenly. He smiled at Wallander.

"And it's vital that when she does she has a family to support her," Wallander replied, annoyed that he expressed himself so stiffly.

"We support her in every way," the boy went on. "The police have to search for the person who killed our Dad. Not go bothering her."

"If I visit her at the hospital it's not to bother her," Wallander said. "It's as part of the investigation."

"We'd prefer it if you left her in peace."

Wallander nodded. The boy was quite determined.

"If the prosecutor, the leader of the preliminary investigation, makes the decision, then I'll have to visit her," said Wallander. "And I presume that will happen. Very soon. Either today or tomorrow. But I give you my word that I won't tell her that her father is dead."

"Then why are you going there at all?"

"To see her," said Wallander. "A photograph is still just a photograph. Although I'll have to take this with me."

"Why?" The response was immediate. Wallander was surprised by the animosity in the boy's voice.

"I have to show it to some people," he said. "To see whether they recognise her. That's all."

"You're going to give it to the newspapers," said the boy. "Her face will be plastered all over the country."

"Why would I do that?" asked Wallander.

The boy jumped up from the sofa, leaned over the table, and grabbed the photographs. It happened so fast that Wallander didn't have time to react. He regained his composure, but he was angry.

"I'm going to be forced to come back here with a warrant to make you hand over those pictures," he said, although this wasn't true. "There's a risk that some reporters will hear about it and follow me here. I can't stop them. If I can borrow a picture now, this won't have to happen."

The boy stared at Wallander. His previous wariness had now evolved into something else. Without a word he handed back one of the photos.

"I have only one more question," said Wallander. "Do you know if Louise ever met a man named Gustaf Wetterstedt?"

The mother looked perplexed. The boy got up and stood looking out of the open balcony door with his back to them.

"No," she said.

"Does the name Arne Carlman mean anything to you?"

She shook her head.

"Åke Liljegren?"

"No."

She doesn't read the papers, Wallander thought. Under that blanket there's probably a bottle of wine. And in that bottle is her life. He got up from his chair. The boy by the balcony door turned round.

"Are you going to visit Louise?" he asked again.

"It's a possibility."

Wallander said goodbye and left. When he got to the street he felt relieved. The boy was standing in the fifth-floor window looking down at him. As he got into his car, he decided he would put off visiting Louise Fredman for the time being, but he'd check straight away whether Elisabeth Carlén recognised her. He rolled down his window and called Sjösten. The boy was gone from the window. As the phone rang, he searched for an explanation for the uneasiness he had felt at the sight of the frightened little boy. But he couldn't identify it. Wallander told Sjösten he was on his way to Helsingborg with something that he wanted Elisabeth Carlén to see.

"According to the latest report she's lying on her balcony sun-bathing," Sjösten said.

"How's it going with Liljegren's employees?"

"We're working on locating the one who was supposed to be his right-hand man. Name is Hans Logård."

"Did Liljegren have any family?"

"Apparently not. We spoke with his lawyer. Strangely enough, he left no will, and there's no indication of direct heirs. Liljegren seems to have lived in his own universe."

"That's good," Wallander said. "I'll be in Helsingborg within the hour."

"Should I bring Elisabeth Carlén in?"

"Do that, but be nice to her. I've got a feeling we're going to be needing her for a while. She might stop cooperating if it doesn't suit her any more."

"I'll pick her up myself," said Sjösten. "How's your father?"

"My father?"

"You were going to meet him this morning."

"Oh, he's fine," Wallander said. "But it was very important that I saw him."

He hung up. He glanced up at the window on the fifth floor. No-one was there.

Hoover went into the basement just after 1 p.m. The coolness from the stone floor permeated his whole body. The sunlight shone weakly through some cracks in the paint he had put on the window. He sat down and looked at his face in the mirrors.

He couldn't allow the policeman to visit his sister. They were so close to their goal now, the sacred moment, when the evil spirits in her head would be driven out for good. He couldn't let anyone get near her.

The policeman's visit had been a sign that now was the time to act. He thought about the girl it had been so easy for him to meet. She had reminded him of his sister somehow. That was a good sign, too. Louise would need all the strength he could give her.

He took off his jacket and looked around the room. Everything he needed was there. The axes and knives gleamed, laid out on the black silk cloth. Then he took one of the wide brushes and drew a single line across his forehead.

Time was running out.

CHAPTER 35

Wallander put the photograph of Louise Fredman face down on the desk in front of him. Elisabeth Carlén followed his movements with her eyes. She was dressed in a white summer dress, which Wallander guessed was very expensive. They were in Sjösten's office, Sjösten in the background, leaning against the doorframe, Elisabeth Carlén in the visitor's chair. The summer heat swept in through the open window. Wallander felt himself sweating.

"I'm going to show you a photograph," he said. "And I simply want you to tell me whether you recognise the person in it."

"Why do policemen have to be so dramatic?" she asked.

Her haughty, imperturbable manner irritated Wallander, but he controlled himself.

"We're trying to catch a man who has killed four people," he said. "And he scalps them too. Pours acid into their eyes. And stuffs their heads into ovens."

"Well obviously you can't let a maniac like that run around loose, can you?" she replied calmly. "Shall we look at that photograph?"

Wallander slid it over and watched Elisabeth Carlén's face. She picked it up and seemed to be thinking. Almost half a minute passed, then she shook her head.

"No," she said. "I've never seen her before. At least not that I can remember."

"It's very important," said Wallander.

"I have a good memory for faces," she said. "I'm sure I've never met her. Who is she?"

"That doesn't matter for the time being," Wallander said. "Think carefully."

"Where do you want me to have seen her? At Åke Liljegren's?"

"Yes."

"She may have been there sometime when I wasn't."

"Did that happen a lot?"

"Not recently."

"How many years are we talking about?"

"Maybe four."

"But she could have been there?"

"Young girls are popular with some men. The real creeps."

"What creeps?"

"The ones with a single fantasy. To go to bed with their own daughters."

What she said was true, of course, but her indifference angered him. She was part of this market that sucked in innocent children and wrecked their lives.

"If you can't tell me whether she was ever at any of Liljegren's parties, who could?"

"Somebody else."

"Give me a straight answer. Who? I want a name and address."

"It was always completely anonymous," said Elisabeth Carlén patiently. "That was one of the rules for these parties. You recognised a face now and then. But nobody exchanged cards."

"Where did the girls come from?"

"All over. Denmark, Stockholm, Belgium, Russia."

"They came and then they disappeared?"

"That's about it."

"But you live here in Helsingborg?"

"I was the only one who did."

Wallander looked at Sjösten, as if wanting confirmation that the conversation hadn't completely got off the track before continuing.

"The picture is of a girl called Louise Fredman," he said. "Does the name mean anything to you?"

She gave him a puzzled look.

"Wasn't that *his* name? The one who was murdered? Fredman?"

Wallander nodded. She looked at the photograph again. For a moment she seemed moved by the connection.

"Is this his daughter?"

"Yes."

She shook her head again.

"I've never seen her before."

Wallander knew she was telling the truth, if only because she had nothing to gain by lying. He retrieved the photograph and turned it over again, as if to spare Louise Fredman from further participation.

"Were you ever at the house of a man named Gustaf Wetterstedt?" he asked. "In Ystad?"

"What would I be doing there?"

"The same thing you normally do to make your living. Was he your client?"

"No."

"Are you sure?"

"Yes."

"Completely sure?"

"Yes."

"Were you ever at the house of an art dealer named Arne Carlman?"

"No."

Wallander had an idea. Maybe names weren't used in those cases either.

"I'm going to show you some other photographs," he said, getting to his feet. He took Sjösten outside.

"What do you think?" Wallander asked.

Sjösten shrugged. "She's not lying."

"We need photos of Wetterstedt and Carlman," Wallander said. "Fredman too. They're in the investigative material."

"Birgersson has the folders," said Sjösten. "I'll get them."

Wallander went back into the room and asked whether she'd like coffee.

"I'd rather have a gin and tonic," she said.

"The bar isn't open yet," Wallander answered.

She laughed. His reply appealed to her. Wallander went out into the hall. Elisabeth Carlén was very beautiful. Her body was clearly visible through her dress. Sjösten came of out Birgersson's office with a plastic folder. They went back into the room. Elisabeth Carlén was sitting there smoking. Wallander put a picture of Wetterstedt in front of her.

"I recognise him," she said. "From TV. Wasn't he the one who ran around with whores in Stockholm?"

"He may have still been at it later on."

"Not with me," she replied calmly.

"And you've never been to his house?"

"Never."

"Do you know anyone else who's been there?"

"No."

Wallander replaced the picture with one of Carlman. He was standing next to an abstract painting, smiling broadly at the camera.

"This one I've seen," she said firmly.

"At Liljegren's?"

"Yes."

"When was that?"

Elisabeth Carlén thought for a moment. Wallander surreptitiously studied her body. Sjösten took a notebook out of his pocket.

"About a year ago," she said.

"Are you sure about that?"

"Yes."

Wallander nodded. Another connection, he thought. Now all we have to do is find the right box to put Fredman in.

He showed her Björn Fredman. Fredman was playing guitar. It was a prison photograph, and must have been old. Fredman had long hair and was wearing bell-bottoms; the colours were faded.

She shook her head again. She had never seen him.

Wallander let his hands drop with a smack on the desk.

"That's all I wanted to know for now," he said. "I'll swap places with Sjösten."

Wallander took up the position by the door. He also took over Sjösten's notebook.

"How the hell can you live a life like yours?" Sjösten began, surprisingly. He asked the question with a big smile. He sounded quite friendly, but Elisabeth Carlén didn't let down her façade for a moment.

"What business is that of yours?"

"None. Just curious, that's all. How can you stand to look at yourself in the mirror every morning?"

"What do you think when *you* look in the mirror?"

"That at least I'm not making a living by lying on my back for anyone who happens to have enough cash. Do you take credit cards?"

"Go to hell."

She made a move to get up and leave. Wallander was annoyed at the way he was needling her. She might still be useful.

"Please forgive me," Sjösten said, still just as friendly. "Let's forget about your private life. Hans Logård? Is that name familiar?"

She looked at him without replying. Then she turned and looked at Wallander.

"I asked you a question," Sjösten said.

Wallander understood her glance. She wanted to give only him the answer. He signalled to Sjösten to follow him into the hall. There he explained that Sjösten had destroyed Elisabeth Carlén's trust.

"Then we'll arrest her," said Sjösten. "I'll be damned if I'll let a whore give me trouble."

"Arrest her for what?" asked Wallander. "Wait here, I'll go in and get the answer. Calm down, damn it!"

Sjösten shrugged. Wallander went back in and sat down behind the desk.

"Logård used to hang out with Liljegren," she said.

"Do you know where he lives?"

"In the country somewhere."

"Do you know where?"

"Only that he doesn't live in town."

"What does he do?"

"I don't know that either."

"But he was at the parties?"

"Yes."

"As guest or host?"

"As the host. And as a guest."

"Do you know how I can get hold of him?"

"No."

Wallander still believed she was telling the truth. Probably they wouldn't be able to track down Logård through her.

"How did they get along?"

"Logård always had plenty of money. Whatever he did for Liljegren, he was well paid."

She stubbed out her cigarette. Wallander felt as if he had been granted a private audience with her.

"I'm going," she said, getting to her feet.

"Let me see you out," said Wallander.

Sjösten came sauntering down the hall. She looked straight through him as they passed. Wallander waited on the steps until he saw someone follow her, then went back up to the office.

"Why were you needling her?" he asked.

"She stands for something I despise," Sjösten said.

"We need her. We can despise her later."

They got coffee and sat down to go over what they knew. Sjösten brought in Birgersson to help out.

"The problem is Fredman," said Wallander. "He doesn't fit. Otherwise we now have a number of links that seem to hang together, fragile points of contact."

"Or maybe it just looks that way," Sjösten said thoughtfully.

Wallander could tell that Sjösten was worried about something. He waited for him to continue, but he didn't.

"What are you thinking?" he asked.

Sjösten kept staring out of the window.

"Why couldn't this be possible?" he said. "That he was killed by the same man, but for a completely different reason."

"That doesn't make sense," said Birgersson.

"Nothing makes sense in this case."

"So you mean that we should be looking for two different motives," said Wallander.

"That's about it. But I could be wrong. It was just an idea, that's all."

Wallander nodded. "We shouldn't disregard that possibility"

"It's a sidetrack," said Birgersson. "A blind alley, a dead end. It doesn't seem likely at all."

"We can't rule it out," Wallander said. "We can't rule out anything. But right now we have to find Logård. That's the priority."

"Liljegren's villa is a very strange place," said Sjösten. "There wasn't one piece of paper there. No address book. Nothing. And no-one has had the opportunity to go in and clean up."

"Which means we haven't searched hard enough," Wallander replied. "Without Logård we're not going to get anywhere."

Sjösten and Wallander had a quick lunch at a restaurant next to the station, and drove to Liljegren's villa. The cordons were still up. An officer opened the gates and let them in. Sunlight filtered through the trees. Suddenly the case seemed surreal. Monsters belonged in the cold and dark. Not in a summer like this one. He recalled Rydberg's joke. *It's best to be hunting insane killers in the autumn. In the summer give me a good old-fashioned bomber.* He laughed at the thought. Sjösten gave him a funny look, but he didn't explain.

Inside the huge villa the forensic technicians had finished their work. Wallander took a look in the kitchen. The oven door was closed. He thought of Sjösten's idea about Björn Fredman. A killer with two motives? Did such birds exist? He called Ystad, and Ebba got hold of Ekholm for him. It was almost five minutes before he came to the phone. Wallander watched Sjösten wandering through the rooms on the ground floor, drawing back the curtains from the windows. The sunlight was very bright.

Wallander asked Ekholm his question. It was actually intended for Ekholm's programme. Had there been serial killers who combined very different motives? Did criminal psychology have a collective view on this? As always, Ekholm found Wallander's question interesting. Wallander wondered whether Ekholm really was so charmed by everything he told him. It was beginning to remind him of the satirical songs about the absurd incompetence of the Swedish security police. Recently they relied more and more on various specialists. And no-one could really explain why.

Wallander didn't want to be unfair to Ekholm. During his time in Ystad he had proved to be a good listener. In that sense he had learned something basic about police work. The police had to be able to listen, as well as question. They had to listen for hidden meanings and motives, for the invisible impressions left by offenders. Just like in this house. Something is always left behind after a crime is committed. An experienced detective should be able to listen his way to what it was. Wallander hung up and went to join Sjösten, who was sitting at a desk. Wallander didn't say a thing. Neither did Sjösten. The villa invited silence. Liljegren's spirit, if he had one, hovered restlessly around them.

Wallander went upstairs and wandered through room after room. There were no papers anywhere. Liljegren had lived in a house in which emptiness was the most noticeable characteristic. Wallander thought back to what Liljegren had been famous or infamous for. The shell company scams, the looting of company finances. He had made his way in the world by hiding his money. Did he do the same thing in his private life? He had houses all over the world. The villa was one of his many hide-outs. Wallander stopped by a door up to the attic. When he was a child he had built a hide-out for himself in the attic. He opened the door. The stairs were narrow and steep. He turned the light switch. The main room with its exposed beams was almost empty. There were just some skis and a few pieces of furniture. Wallander smelled the same odour as in the rest of the house. The forensic technicians had been here too. He looked around. No secret doors. It was hot underneath the roof.

He went back down and started a more systematic search. He pulled back the clothes in Liljegren's large wardrobes. Nothing. Wallander sat on the edge of the bed and tried to think. Liljegren couldn't have kept everything in his head. There had to be an address book somewhere. Something else was missing too. At first he couldn't figure out what it was. Who was Åke Liljegren, "the Auditor"? Liljegren was a travelling man, but there were no suitcases in the house. Not even a briefcase. Wallander went downstairs to see Sjösten.

"Liljegren must have had another house," he said. "Or at least an office."

"He has houses all over the world," Sjösten said distractedly.

"I mean here in Helsingborg. This place is too empty"

"We would have known about it."

Wallander nodded without saying any more. He was still sure his hunch was right. He continued his search. But now he was more persistent. He went down to the basement. In one room there was an exercise machine and some barbells. There was a wardrobe down there, too, which contained some exercise clothes and rain gear. Wallander thoughtfully regarded the clothes. Then he went back upstairs to Sjösten.

"Did Liljegren have a boat?"

"I'm sure he did. But not here. I would have known about it."

Wallander nodded mutely. He was just about to leave Sjösten when an idea struck him.

"Maybe it was registered under another name. Why not in Hans Logård's name?"

"Why do you think Liljegren had a boat?"

"There are clothes in the basement that look like they're for sailing."

Sjösten followed Wallander to the basement. They stood in front of the open wardrobe.

"You may be right." Sjösten said.

"It's worth looking into," said Wallander. "This house is too empty to be normal."

They left the basement. Wallander opened the balcony doors and stepped into the sunshine. He thought of Baiba again and felt a knot in his stomach. Why didn't he call her? Did he still think it would be possible for him to meet her? He wasn't happy about asking

Martinsson to lie for him, but now it was his only way out. He went back inside, into the shadows, with a feeling of utter self-loathing. Sjösten was on the phone. Wallander wondered when the killer would strike next. Sjösten hung up and dialled another number. Wallander went into the kitchen and drank some water, trying to avoid looking at the stove. As he came back, Sjösten slammed the phone down.

"You were right," he said. "There's a boat in Logård's name down at the yacht club. The same one I belong to."

"Let's go," said Wallander, feeling the tension rise.

A dock watchman showed them where Logård's boat was berthed. Wallander could see that it was a beautiful, well-maintained boat. The hull was fibreglass, but it had a teak deck.

"A Komfortina," said Sjösten. "Very nice. They handle well, too."

He hopped on board like a sailor. The entrance to the cabin was locked.

"Do you know Hans Logård?" Wallander asked the watchman. He had a weatherbeaten face and wore a T-shirt advertising canned Norwegian fish-balls.

"He's not talkative, but we say hello to each other when he comes down here."

"When was he here last?"

"Last week, I think. But it's high summer, you know, our busiest time, so I might be mistaken."

Sjösten had managed to pick the cabin lock. From inside he opened the two half-doors. Wallander clambered clumsily aboard, as though walking on newly polished ice. He crept down into the cockpit and then into the cabin. Sjösten had had the foresight to bring along a torch. They searched the cabin without finding anything.

"I don't get it," Wallander said when they were back on the dock. "Liljegren must have been running his affairs from somewhere."

"We're checking his mobile phones," said Sjösten. "Maybe that will produce something."

They headed back. The man with the T-shirt followed them.

"I expect that you'll want to take a look at his other boat too," he said as they stepped off the long dock. Wallander and Sjösten reacted as one.

"Logård has another boat?" Wallander asked.

The man pointed towards the furthest pier.

"The white one, all the way at the end. A Storö class. It's called the *Rosmarin.*"

"Of course we want to look at it," Wallander said.

They ended up in front of a long, powerful, sleek launch.

"These cost money," said Sjösten. "Lots and lots of money."

They went aboard. The cabin door was locked. The man on the dock was watching them.

"He knows I'm a policeman," Sjösten said.

"We don't have time to wait," said Wallander. "Break the lock. But do it the cheapest way."

Sjösten managed it without breaking off more than a piece of the doorframe. They entered the cabin. Wallander saw at once that they had hit the jackpot. Along one wall was a whole shelf of folders and plastic binders.

"Find an address for Hans Logård," said Wallander. "We can go through the rest later."

In a few minutes they had found a membership card to a golf club outside Ängelholm with Logård's name and address on it.

"Bjuv," Sjösten said. "That's not far from here."

As they were leaving the boat, Wallander opened a cupboard. To his surprise there was women's clothing inside.

"Maybe they had parties on board, too," Sjösten said.

"I'm not so sure." Wallander said pensively.

They left the boat and went back to the dock.

"I want you to call me if Logård shows up," Sjösten told the dock watchman.

He gave him a card with his phone number on it.

"But I shouldn't let on that you're looking for him, right?" the man asked, excitedly.

Sjösten smiled.

"Right in one," he replied. "Pretend that everything's normal. And then call me. No matter what time."

"There's nobody here at night," said the man.

"Then we'll have to hope he comes in the day."

"May I ask what he did?"

"You can," said Sjösten, "but you won't get an answer."

"Should we take more men along?" Sjösten asked.

"Not yet," Wallander replied. "First we have to find his house and see if he's home."

They drove towards Bjuv. They were in a part of Skåne that Wallander didn't know. The weather had turned muggy. There would be a thunderstorm that evening.

"When's the last time it rained?" he asked.

"Around Midsummer," Sjösten said, after thinking for a bit. "And it didn't rain much."

They had just reached the turn-off to Bjuv when Sjösten's mobile phone rang. He slowed down and answered it.

"It's for you," he said, handing it to Wallander.

It was Ann-Britt Höglund. She got straight to the point. "Louise Fredman has escaped from the hospital."

It took a moment before Wallander grasped what she said.

"Could you repeat that?"

"Louise Fredman has escaped from the hospital."

"When?"

"About an hour ago."

"How did you find out?"

"The hospital contacted Åkeson. He called me."

Wallander thought for a moment.

"How did it happen?"

"Someone came and got her."

"Who?"

"No-one saw it happen. Suddenly she was gone."

"God damn it to hell!"

Sjösten hit the brakes.

"I'll call you back in a while," Wallander said. "In the meantime, find out absolutely everything you can. Above all, who it was that picked her up."

"Louise Fredman has escaped from hospital," he told Sjösten.

"How?"

Wallander gave it some thought before he replied.

"I don't know," he said. "But this has something to do with our killer. I'm sure of it."

"Should I go back?"

"No. Let's keep going. Now it's more important than ever to get hold of Logård."

They drove into the village and stopped. Sjösten rolled down the window and asked the way to the street. They asked three people and got the same answer. Not one of them knew the address they were looking for.

CHAPTER 36

They were just on the point of giving up when they finally picked up the trail to Hans Logård and his address. Some scattered showers had started over Bjuv by that time. But the main thunderstorm passed by to the west.

The address they had been looking for was "Hördestigen". It had a Bjuv postal code, but they couldn't find it. Wallander went into the post office himself to check it. Logård didn't have a post office box either, at least not in Bjuv. Finally there was nothing to do but think Logård's address was false. At that point, Wallander walked into the bakery and struck up a conversation with the two ladies behind the counter while he bought a bag of cinnamon rolls. One of them knew the answer. Hördestigen wasn't a road. It was the name of a farm north of the village, a place that was hard to find if you didn't know the way.

"There's a man living there named Hans Logård," Wallander told them. "Do you know him?"

The two women looked at each other as if searching a shared memory, then shook their heads in unison.

"I had a distant cousin who lived at Hördestigen when I was a girl," said one of the women. "When he died it was sold to a stranger. But Hördestigen is the name of the farm, I know that. It must have a different postal address, though."

Wallander asked her to draw him a map. She tore up a bread bag and drew the route on it for him. It was almost 6 p.m. They drove out of town, following the road to Höganäs. Wallander navigated with the bread bag. They reached an area where the farms thinned out. That's where they took the first wrong turn. They ended up in an enchantingly beautiful beech forest, but they were in the wrong place.

Wallander told Sjösten to turn around, and when they got back to the main road they started again. They took the next side road to the left, then to the right, and then left. The road ended in a field. Wallander swore to himself, got out of the car, and looked around for a church spire the ladies had told him about. Out there in the field he felt like someone floating out to sea, searching for a lighthouse to navigate by. He found the church spire and then understood, after a conference with the bread bag, why they had got lost. Sjösten was directed back; they started again, and this time they found it.

Hördestigen was an old farm, not unlike Arne Carlman's, and it was in an isolated spot with no neighbours, surrounded by beech woods on two sides and gently sloping fields on the others. The road ended at the farmhouse. There was no letter box. His post must go elsewhere.

"What can we expect?" asked Wallander.

"You mean is he dangerous?"

"He might be the one who killed Liljegren. Or all of them. We don't know a thing about him."

Sjösten's reply surprised Wallander.

"There's a shotgun in the boot. And ammunition. You take that. I've got my service revolver."

Sjösten reached under the seat.

"Against regulations," he said, smiling. "But if you had to follow all the regulations that exist, police work would have been forbidden long ago by the health and safety watchdogs."

"Forget the shotgun," Wallander said. "Have you got a licence for the revolver?"

"Of course I have a licence," Sjösten said. "What do you think?"

They got out of the car. Sjösten stuffed his revolver in his jacket pocket. They stood and listened. There was thunder in the distance. Around them it was quiet and extremely humid. No sign of a car or a living soul. The farm seemed abandoned. They walked up to the house, shaped like an L.

"The third wing must have burned down," Sjösten said. "Or else it was torn down. But it's a nice house. Well preserved. Just like the boat."

Wallander went and knocked on the door. No answer. Then he banged on it hard. Nothing. He peered in through a window. Sjösten stood in the background with one hand in his jacket pocket. Wallander didn't like being so close to a gun. They walked around the house. Still no sign of life. Wallander stopped, lost in thought.

"There are stickers all over saying that the windows and doors are alarmed," Sjösten said. "But it would take a hell of a long time for anyone to get here if it was set off. We'll have time to go inside and get out of here before then."

"Something doesn't fit here," said Wallander, as if he hadn't heard Sjösten.

"What's that?"

"I don't know."

They went over towards the wing that served as a tool shed. The door was locked with a big padlock. Through the windows they could see all kinds of equipment and rubbish inside.

"There's nobody here," said Sjösten flatly. "We'll have to put the farm under surveillance."

Wallander looked around. Something was wrong, he was sure of it. He walked round the house again and looked in at several of the windows, listening. Sjösten followed. When they had gone round the house for a second time, Wallander stopped by some black rubbish bags next to the house. They were sloppily tied with string. Flies buzzed around them. He opened one of the sacks. Food remains, paper plates. He picked up a plastic bag from the Scan Deli between his thumb and forefinger. Sjösten stood next to him, watching. He looked at the various expiry dates. He could smell the meat. They hadn't been here many hours. Not in this heat. He opened the other sack. It too was filled with frozen food containers. It was a lot of food to eat in a few days.

Sjösten stood next to Wallander looking at the sacks.

"He must have had a party."

Wallander tried to think. The muggy heat was making the pressure build in his head. Soon he would have a headache, he could feel it.

"We're going in," he said. "I want to look around inside the house. Isn't there any way to get around the alarm?"

"Maybe down the chimney."

"Then I guess we'll have to take our chances."

"I've got a crowbar in the car," Sjösten said.

Wallander examined the front door of the house. He thought about the door he had broken down at his father's studio in Löderup. He went to the back of the house with Sjösten carrying the crowbar. The door there seemed less solid. Wallander decided to prise it open. He jammed the crowbar between the hinges. He looked at Sjösten, who glanced at his watch.

"Go," he said.

Wallander braced himself and pushed on the crowbar with all his strength. The hinges broke off, along with some chunks of wall plaster and tile. He jumped to one side so the door wouldn't fall on him.

The house looked even more like Carlman's on the inside, if that were possible. Walls had been torn down, the space opened up. Modern furniture, newly laid hardwood floor. They listened again. Everything was quiet. Too quiet, Wallander thought. As if the house were holding its breath. Sjösten pointed to a telephone and fax machine on a table. The light on the answer machine was blinking. Wallander nodded. Sjösten pushed the play button. It crackled and clicked. Then there was a voice. Wallander saw Sjösten jump. A man's voice asked Hans to call him as soon as possible. Then it was silent again. The tape stopped.

"That was Liljegren," Sjösten said, obviously shaken. "God damn."

"Then we know that message has been here for quite a while," Wallander said.

"So Logård hasn't been here since then."

"Not necessarily," Wallander said. "He might have listened to the message but not erased it. If the power goes off later, the light will start blinking again. They may have had a thunderstorm here. We don't know."

They went through the house. A narrow hall led to the part of the house at the angle of the L. The door there was closed. Wallander suddenly raised his hand. Sjösten stopped short behind him. Wallander heard a sound. At first he couldn't tell what it was. It sounded like a growling animal, then like a muttering. He looked at Sjösten, who'd heard it too. Then he tried the door. It was locked. The muttering had stopped.

"What the hell is going on?" he whispered.

"I don't know," said Wallander. "I can't break this door open with the crowbar."

"We're going to have the security company here in about 15 minutes."

Wallander thought hard. He didn't know what was on the other side, except that it was at least one person, maybe more. He was feeling sick. He knew that he had to get the door open.

"Give me your revolver," he said.

Sjösten took it out of his pocket.

"Get back from the door," Wallander shouted as loud as he could. "I'm going to shoot it open."

He looked at the lock, took a step back, cocked the gun, and fired. The blast was deafening. He shot again, then once more. The ricochets hit the far wall in the hall. He handed the revolver back to Sjösten and kicked open the door, his ears ringing.

The room was large. It had no windows. There were a number of beds and a partition enclosing a toilet. A refrigerator, glasses, cups, some thermoses. Huddled together in a corner of the room, obviously terrified, were four young girls clutching one another. Two of them reminded Wallander of the girl he had seen from 20 metres away in Salomonsson's rape field. For a brief moment, with his ears ringing, Wallander thought he could see it all before him, one event after another, how it all fitted together and how everything suddenly made sense. But in reality he saw nothing at all. There was just a feeling rushing straight through him, like a train going through a tunnel at high speed, leaving behind only a light shaking of the ground.

"What the hell is going on?" Sjösten asked.

"We have to get some back-up from Helsingborg," Wallander said. "As fast as we can."

He knelt down, and Sjösten did the same. Wallander tried to talk to the frightened girls in English. But they didn't seem to understand the language, or at least not the way he spoke it. Some of them couldn't be much older than Dolores María Santana.

"Do you know any Spanish?" he asked Sjösten. "I don't know a word."

"What do you want me to say?"

"Do you know Spanish or not?"

"I can't speak Spanish! Shit! I know a few words. What do you want me to say?"

"Anything! Just tell them to be calm."

"Should I say I'm a policeman?"

"No! Whatever you do, don't say that!"

"*Buenas dias*," Sjösten said hesitantly.

"Smile," Wallander said. "Can't you see how scared they are?"

"I'm doing the best I can," complained Sjösten.

"Say it again," said Wallander. "Friendly this time."

"*Buenas dias*," Sjösten repeated.

One of the girls answered. Her voice was unsteady. Wallander felt as if he was now getting the answer he'd been looking for, ever since that day when the girl stood in the field and stared at him with her terrified eyes.

At the same moment they heard a sound behind them in the house, perhaps a door opening. The girls heard it too, and huddled together again.

"It must be the security guards," Sjösten said. "We'd better go and meet them. Otherwise they'll wonder what's going on here and start making a fuss."

Wallander gestured to the girls to stay put. Then the two of them went back down the narrow hall, this time with Sjösten in the lead.

It almost cost him his life. When they stepped into the open room, several shots rang out. They came in such rapid succession that they must have been fired from a semi-automatic weapon. The first bullet slammed into Sjösten's left shoulder, smashing his collarbone. He was thrown backwards by the impact and rammed into Wallander. The second, third and maybe fourth shots landed somewhere above their heads.

"Don't shoot! Police!" Wallander shouted.

Whoever was shooting fired off another burst. Sjösten was hit again, this time in the right ear. Wallander threw himself behind one of the walls. He pulled Sjösten with him, who screamed and passed out. Wallander found Sjösten's revolver and fired it into the room. He knew there must only be two or three shots left.

There was no answer. He waited with his heart pounding, revolver raised and ready to shoot. Then he heard the sound of a car starting. He let Sjösten go and crouching low, ran over to a window. He saw the back end of a black Mercedes disappearing down the farm road, vanishing into the beech woods. He went back to Sjösten, who was bleeding and unconscious. He found a pulse. It was fast. This was good. Better than too slow. Still holding the revolver in his hand, he picked up the phone and dialled 90–000.

"Officer down," he shouted when they answered. Then he managed to calm down, tell them who he was, what had happened, and where they were. He went back to Sjösten, who had regained consciousness.

"It'll be all right," Wallander said, over and over again. "Help is on the way."

"What happened?" Sjösten asked.

"Don't talk," Wallander said. "Everything will be fine."

He searched feverishly for wounds. He'd thought Sjösten had been hit by at least three bullets, finally realised that it was only two. He made two simple pressure bandages, wondering what had happened to the security company and why it was taking so long for help to arrive. He also thought about the Mercedes and knew he wouldn't rest until he caught the man who had shot Sjösten.

Eventually he heard the sirens. He got up and went outside to meet the cars from Helsingborg. First came the ambulance, then Birgersson and two other squad cars and last the fire department. All of them were shocked when they saw Wallander. He hadn't noticed how covered in blood he was. And he still had Sjösten's revolver in his hand.

"How is he?" Birgersson asked.

"He's inside. I think he'll be OK."

"What the hell happened?"

"There are four girls locked up here," said Wallander. "They're probably some of the ones being taken through Helsingborg to brothels in southern Europe."

"Who shot at you?"

"I never saw him. But I assume it was Logård. This house belongs to him."

"A Mercedes crashed into a car from the security company down by the main road," Birgersson said. "No injuries, but the driver of the Mercedes stole the security guards' car."

"Then they saw him," said Wallander. "It must be him. The guards were on their way here. The alarm went off when we broke in."

"You broke in?"

"Never mind that now. Put out the word on that security company car. And get the technicians out here right away. I want them to check for prints. They'll have to be compared to the ones we found at the other murder scenes. Wetterstedt, Carlman, all of them."

Birgersson turned pale. The connection seemed to dawn on him for the first time.

"You mean it was him?"

"It could have been, but we don't know that. Now get going. And don't forget the girls. Take them all in. Treat them nicely. And find some Spanish interpreters."

"It's amazing how much you know already," Birgersson said.

Wallander stared at him. "I don't know a thing," he said. "Now get moving."

Sjösten was carried out. Wallander went into town with him in the ambulance. One of the ambulance drivers gave him a towel. He wiped himself clean with it as best he could. Then he checked in with Ystad.

It was just after 7 p.m. He got hold of Svedberg and explained what had happened.

"Who is this Logård?" Svedberg asked.

"That's what we have to find out. Is Louise Fredman still missing?"

"Yes."

Wallander felt the need to think. What had seemed so clear in his mind a while before was no longer making sense.

"I'll be in touch later," he said. "But you'll have to pass all of this on to the investigative team."

"Ludwigsson and Hamrén have found an interesting witness at Sturup," Svedberg said. "A night watchman. He saw a man on a moped. The timetable fits."

"A moped?"

"Yep."

"You don't think our killer is riding around on a moped, do you? Those are for children, for God's sake."

Wallander felt himself starting to lose his cool. He didn't want to, least of all at Svedberg. He said goodbye quickly and hung up.

Sjösten looked up at him from the stretcher.

Wallander smiled. "It's going to be fine," he said.

"It was like getting kicked by a horse," moaned Sjösten. "Twice."

"Don't talk," said Wallander. "We'll be at the hospital soon."

The night of 7 July was one of the most chaotic Wallander had ever experienced. There was an air of unreality about everything that happened.

He would never forget it. Sjösten was admitted to hospital, and the doctors confirmed that his life was not in danger. Wallander was driven to the station in a squad car.

Sergeant Birgersson had proven to be a good organiser, and he'd understood everything Wallander had said at the farmhouse. He had the presence of mind to establish an area past which all the reporters who had started gathering weren't permitted. Inside, where the actual police were working, no reporters were allowed.

It was 10 p.m. when Wallander arrived from the hospital. Someone had lent him a clean shirt and pair of trousers. They were so tight around the waist that he couldn't zip them up. Birgersson, noticing the problem, called the owners of Helsingborg's most elegant tailor and put Wallander on the line. It was a strange experience to stand in the middle of the chaos and try to remember his waist size, but in an astonishingly swift time, several pairs of trousers were delivered to the station, and one of them fitted.

Höglund, Svedberg, Ludwigsson and Hamrén had already arrived and been briefed on the work that was under way. There was no sighting of the security company's car yet. Interviews were being conducted in different rooms. The Spanish-speaking girls had each been supplied with an interpreter. Höglund was talking to one of them, while three female officers from Helsingborg took care of the others. The guards whose car had collided with the Mercedes had also been interviewed, while forensic technicians were busy cross-checking fingerprints. Finally, several officers were leaning over a number of computers, entering all the information that they had on Hans Logård. The activity was intense. Birgersson concentrated on keeping order so that their work stayed on track.

When Wallander had been briefed, he took his colleagues from Ystad into a room and closed the door. He had obtained Birgersson's approval to do so. Birgersson was an exceptional policeman who performed his job impeccably, and didn't seem to suffer from the jealousy and rivalry that so often degraded the quality of police work. He was interested only in catching the man who had shot Sjösten, working out exactly what had happened and who the killer was.

Wallander told his version of events, but what he wanted to resolve was the reason for his unease. Too many things didn't add up. The man who had shot Sjösten, was he really the same man who had assumed the role of a lone warrior? It was difficult to believe. He would have to do his thinking out loud, with all of them together and just one thin door separating them from the frenzied investigative work. Wallander wanted his colleagues to step aside – and Sjösten would have been there too if he wasn't in hospital – so that they could serve as a kind of counterweight to the work being done. Wallander looked around and wondered why Ekholm wasn't there.

"He left for Stockholm this morning," Svedberg said.

"Just when we need him most," Wallander said, dismayed.

"He's supposed to be back tomorrow morning," Höglund said. "I think one of his children was hit by a car. Nothing serious. But even so ..."

Wallander nodded. The phone rang. It was Hansson for Wallander.

"Baiba Liepa has called several times from Riga," he said. "She wants you to call her right away."

"I can't right now," said Wallander. "Explain to her if she calls again."

"If I understood her correctly, you're supposed to meet her at Kastrup on Saturday. To go on a holiday together. How were you planning to pull that off?"

"Not now," Wallander said. "I'll call you later."

No-one except Höglund seemed to notice that the conversation with Hansson was over a personal matter. Wallander caught her eye. She smiled, but didn't say a word.

"Let's continue," he said. "We're searching for a man who shot at both Sjösten and me. We find some girls locked up inside a farmhouse in the countryside near Bjuv. We can assume that Dolores María Santana once came from such a group, passing through Sweden on the way to brothels and the devil knows what else in other parts of Europe. Girls lured here by people associated with Liljegren. In particular, a man named Hans Logård, if that's his real name. We think he was the one who shot at us, but we aren't sure. We don't have a picture of him. Maybe the guards can give us a usable description, but they're pretty shaken up. They may have seen nothing but his gun. Now we're hunting for him. But are we actually tracking our killer? The one who killed Wetterstedt, Carlman, Fredman and Liljegren? I'm doubtful. We must catch this man as soon as possible. In the meantime, I think we have to keep working as if this were simply one event on the periphery of the major investigation. I'm just as interested in what has happened to Louise Fredman. And what was discovered at Sturup. But first, of course, I'd like to hear if you have any reactions to my view of the case."

The room was silent, then Hamrén spoke up. "Looking from outside, and not needing to be afraid of causing offence, the whole thing seems like a problem in approach. The police have a tendency to focus on one thing at a time, while the offenders they're hunting are thinking about ten."

Wallander listened approvingly, though he wasn't sure Hamrén meant what he was saying.

"Louise Fredman disappeared without a trace," said Höglund. "She had a visitor. She followed the visitor out. The name written in the visitors' book was illegible. Because there were only summer temps working, the normal system had almost fallen apart."

"Someone must have seen the person who came to get her," Wallander said.

"Someone did," Höglund said. "An assistant nurse named Sara Pettersson."

"Did anyone talk to her?"

"She's left on holiday."

"Where to?"

"She's bought an Interrail card. She could be anywhere."

"Damn!"

"We can trace her through Interpol," Ludwigsson said. "That'll probably work."

"Yes," said Wallander. "I think we should do that. And this time we won't wait. I want someone to contact Åkeson about it tonight."

"This is Malmö's jurisdiction," Svedberg pointed out.

"I don't give a shit whose jurisdiction we're in," Wallander said. "Do it. It'll have to be Åkeson's headache."

Höglund said she would get hold of him. Wallander turned to Ludwigsson and Hamrén.

"I heard rumours about a moped," he said. "A witness who saw something at the airport."

"That's right," Ludwigsson said. "The timing fits. A moped drove off towards the E65 on the night in question."

"Why is that of interest?"

"Because the night watchman is sure that the moped was driven off just about the same time Björn Fredman's van arrived."

Wallander recognised the significance of this.

"We're talking about a time of night when the airport is closed," Ludwigsson went on. "Nothing's happening. No taxis, no traffic. Everything is quiet. A van comes up and stops in the car park. Then a moped drives off."

The room grew still. If there were magic moments in a complex criminal investigation, this was definitely one of them.

"A man on a moped," Svedberg said. "Can this be right?"

"Is there a description?" Höglund asked.

"According to the watchman, the man was wearing a helmet that covered his whole head. He's worked at Sturup for many years. That was the first time a moped left there at night."

"How can he be sure that he headed towards Malmö?"

"He wasn't. And I didn't say that either."

Wallander held his breath. The voices of the others were far away, like the distant, unintelligible noise of the universe. He knew that now they were very, very close.

CHAPTER 37

Somewhere in the distance Hoover could hear thunder. He counted the seconds between the lightning and the thunder. The storm was passing far away. It wouldn't come in over Malmö. He watched his sister sleeping on the mattress. He had wanted to offer her something better, but everything had happened so fast. The policeman whom he now hated, the cavalry colonel with the blue trousers, whom he'd christened "Perkins" and "the Man with the Great Curiosity" when he drummed his message to Geronimo, had demanded pictures of Louise. He had also threatened to visit her.

Hoover had realised that he had to change his plans right away. He would pick up Louise even before the row of scalps and the last gift, the girl's heart, were buried. That's why he had only managed to take a mattress and a blanket down to the basement. He had planned to do something quite different. There was a big empty house in Limhamn. The woman who lived there alone went to Canada every summer to see her family. She had been his teacher and he sometimes ran errands for her, so he knew she was away. He had copied a key to her front door long ago. They could have lived in her building while they planned their future. But now Perkins had got in the way. Until he was dead, and that would be soon, they would have to settle for the mattress in the basement.

She was asleep. He had taken medicine from a cabinet when he went to get her. He had gone there without painting his face, but he had an axe and some knives with him, in case anyone tried to stop him. It had been strangely quiet at the hospital, with almost no-one around. Everything went more smoothly than he could have imagined. Louise hadn't recognised him at first, but when she'd heard his voice she put up no resistance. He had brought some clothes for her. They walked across the hospital grounds and then took a taxi, without any problem. She didn't say a word, never questioning the bare mattress, and she fell asleep almost at once. He had lain down and slept a while beside her. They were closer to the future than ever before. The power from the scalps had already started working. She was on her way back to life again. Soon everything would be changed.

He looked at her. It was evening, past 10 p.m. He had made his decision. At dawn he would return to Ystad for the last time.

In Helsingborg a great crowd of reporters besieged Birgersson's outer perimeter. The chief of police was there. At Wallander's stubborn insistence, Interpol was trying to trace Sara Pettersson. They had contacted the girl's parents and tried to put together a possible itinerary. It was a hectic night at the station.

Back in Ystad, Hansson and Martinsson were handling the incoming calls. They sent over materials when Wallander needed them. Åkeson was at home but was willing to be reached at any time.

Although it was late, Wallander sent Höglund to Malmö to talk to the Fredman family. He wanted to make sure they weren't the ones who had taken Louise from the hospital. He would rather have gone there himself, but he couldn't be in two places at once. She had left at 10.30 p.m., after Wallander had phoned Fredman's widow. He estimated she'd be back by 1 a.m.

"Who's taking care of the children while you're away?" he'd asked.

"Do you remember my neighbour who has children of her own?" she asked. "Without her I couldn't do this job."

Wallander called home. Linda was there. He explained as best he could what had happened. He didn't know when he'd be home, maybe sometime that night, maybe not until dawn.

"Will you get here before I leave?" she asked.

"Leave?"

"Did you forget I'm going to Gotland? Kajsa and I. And you're going to Skagen."

"Of course I didn't forget," he said."

"Did you talk to Baiba?"

"Yes," Wallander said, hoping she couldn't hear that he was lying.

He gave her the number in Helsingborg. Then he wondered whether he ought to call his father, but it was late. They were probably already in bed. He went to the command centre where Birgersson was directing the manhunt. Five hours had passed, and no-one had seen the stolen car. Birgersson agreed with Wallander that it could only mean that Logård, if it was him, had taken the car off the road.

"He had two boats at his disposal," Wallander said. "And a house outside Bjuv that we could barely locate. I'm sure he has other hide-outs."

"We've got a man going over the boats," said Birgersson. "And Hördestigen. I told them to look for other possibilities."

"Who is this damned Logård, anyway?" Wallander said.

"They've started checking the prints," Birgersson said. "If he's ever had a run-in with the police, we'll know very soon."

Wallander went over to where the four girls were being interviewed. It was a laborious process, since everything had to go through interpreters. Besides, the girls were terrified. Wallander had told the officers to explain that they weren't accused of a crime. But he wondered how frightened they were. He thought about Dolores María Santana, about the worst fear he had ever seen. But now, at midnight, a picture had finally begun to take shape.

The girls were all from the Dominican Republic. They had each separately left their villages and gone to the cities to look for work as domestic helps or factory workers. They had been contacted by men, all very friendly, and offered work in Europe. They had been shown pictures of beautiful houses by the Mediterranean, and were promised wages ten times what they could hope to earn at home. They'd all said yes.

They were supplied with passports but were never allowed to keep them. First they were flown to Amsterdam – at least that was what they thought the city was called. Then they were driven to Denmark. A week ago they had been taken across to Sweden at night by boat. There were different men involved at each stage and their friendliness decreased as the girls travelled further from home. The fear had set in in earnest when they were locked up at the farm. They had been given food, and a man had explained in poor Spanish that they would soon be travelling the last stretch of the way. But by now they had begun to understand that nothing would happen as promised. The fear had turned to terror.

Wallander asked the officers to question the girls carefully about the men they had met during the days at the farm. Was there more than one? Could they give a description of the boat that took them to Sweden? What did the captain look like? Was there a crew? He told them to take one of the girls down to the yacht club to see whether she recognised Logård's launch. A lot of questions remained. Wallander needed an empty room where he could lock himself away and think.

He was impatient for Höglund to return. And he was waiting for information on Logård. He tried to connect a moped at Sturup Airport, a man who took scalps and killed with an axe, and another who shot at people with a semi-automatic weapon. The myriad of details swam back and forth in his head. The headache he had felt coming earlier had arrived, and he tried unsuccessfully to fight it off with painkillers. It was very humid. There were thunderstorms over Denmark. In less than 48 hours he was supposed to be at Kastrup Airport.

Wallander was standing by a window, looking out at the light summer night and thinking that the world had dissolved into chaos, when Birgersson came stamping down the hall, triumphantly wielding a piece of paper.

"Do you know who Erik Sturesson is?" he asked.

"No, who?"

"Then do you know who Sture Eriksson is?"

"No."

"They're one and the same. And later he changed his name again. This time he didn't settle for switching his first and last names. He took on a name with a more aristocratic ring to it. Hans Logård."

"Great," he said. "What have we got?"

"The prints we found at Hördestigen and in the boats are in our records, under Erik Sturesson and Sture Eriksson. But not Hans Logård. Erik Sturesson, if we start with him, since that was Hans Logård's real name, is 47. Born in Skövde, father a career soldier, mother a housewife. The father was also an alcoholic. Both died in the late 1960s. Erik wound up in bad company, was first arrested at 14, downhill from there. He's done time in Österåker, Kumla and Hall prisons. And a short stretch at Norrköping. He changed his name for the first time when he got out of Österåker."

"What type of crimes?"

"From simple jobs to specialisation, you might say. Burglaries and con games at first. Occasionally assault. Then more serious crimes. Narcotics. The hard stuff. He seems to have worked for Turkish and Pakistani gangs. This is an overview, mind. We'll have more information through in the night."

"We need a picture of him," Wallander said. "And the fingerprints have to be cross-checked against the ones we found at Wetterstedt's and Carlman's. And the ones on Fredman too. Don't forget the ones we got from the left eyelid."

"Nyberg is onto it," Birgersson said. "But he seems so pissed off all the time."

"That's just the way he is," Wallander replied. "But he's good at his job."

They sat down at a table overflowing with used plastic coffee cups. Telephones rang all around them. They erected an invisible wall around themselves, admitting only Svedberg.

"The interesting thing is that Logård suddenly stopped paying visits to our prisons," Birgersson said. "The last time he was inside was 1989. Since then he's been clean. As if he found salvation."

"That corresponds pretty well with when Liljegren got himself a house here in Helsingborg."

Birgersson nodded. "We're not too clear on that yet. But it seems that Logård bought Hördestigen in 1991. That's a gap of a couple of years. But there's nothing to prevent him from having lived some-where else in the meantime."

"We'll need an answer to that one right away," Wallander said, reaching for the phone. "What's Elisabeth Carlén's number? It's on Sjösten's desk. Have we still got her under surveillance, by the way?"

Birgersson nodded again. Wallander made a quick decision.

"Pull them off," he said.

Someone put a piece of paper in front of him. He dialled the number. She answered almost immediately.

"This is Inspector Wallander," he said.

"I won't come to the station at this time of night," she said.

"I don't want you to. I just have one question: was Hans Logård hanging out with Liljegren as early as 1989? Or 1990?"

He could hear her lighting a cigarette and blowing smoke straight into the receiver.

"Yes," she said, "I think he was there then. In 1990 anyway."

"Good," said Wallander.

"Why are you tailing me?" she asked.

"I was wondering myself," Wallander said. "We don't want anything to happen to you, of course. But we're lifting the surveillance now. Just don't leave town without telling us. I might get mad."

"Fair enough," she said, "I bet you can get mad."

She hung up.

"Logård was there," said Wallander. "It seems he appeared at Liljegren's in 1989 or 1990. Then he acquired Hördestigen. Liljegren seems to have taken care of his salvation."

Wallander tried to fit the different pieces together.

"And about then the rumours of the trade in girls surfaced. Isn't that right?"

Birgersson nodded.

"Does Logård have a violent history?" Wallander asked.

"A few charges of aggravated assault," Birgersson said. "But he's never shot anyone, that we know of."

"No axes?"

"No, nothing like that."

"In any case, we've got to find him," said Wallander, getting up.

"We'll find him," Birgersson said. "Sooner or later he'll crawl out of his hole."

"Why did he shoot at us?" Wallander asked.

"You'll have to ask him that yourself," Birgersson said, as he left the room.

Svedberg had taken off his cap. "Is this really the man we're looking for?" he asked.

"I don't know," said Wallander. "Frankly I doubt it, although I could be wrong. Let's hope I am."

Svedberg left the room. Wallander was alone again. More than ever he missed Rydberg. *There's always another question you can ask.* Rydberg's words, repeated often. So what was the question he hadn't asked yet? He searched and found nothing. All the questions had been asked. Only the answers were missing.

That was why it was a relief when Höglund stepped into the room. It was just before 1 a.m. They sat down together.

"Louise wasn't there," she said. "Her mother was drunk. But her concern about her daughter seemed genuine. She couldn't understand how it had happened. I think she was telling the truth. I felt really sorry for her."

"You mean she actually had no idea?"

"Not a clue. And she'd been worrying about it."

"Had it happened before?"

"Never."

"And her son?"

"The older or the younger one?"

"The older one. Stefan."

"He wasn't there."

"Was he out looking for his sister?"

"If I understood the mother correctly, he stays away occasionally. But there was one thing I did notice. I asked to have a look around. Just in case Louise was there. I went into Stefan's room. The mattress was gone from his bed. There was just a bedspread. No pillow or blanket either."

"Did you ask her where he was?"

"I don't think she would have been able to tell me."

"Did she say how long he'd been gone?"

She thought about it and looked at her notes.

"Since midday."

"Not long before Louise disappeared."

She looked at him in surprise.

"You think he was the one who went and got her? Then where are they now?"

"Two questions, two answers. I don't know. I don't know."

Wallander felt a deep unease creep over him. He couldn't tell what it meant.

"Did you happen to ask her whether Stefan has a moped?"

He saw that she immediately understood where he was heading.

"No."

Wallander gestured towards the phone.

"Call her," he said. "Ask her. She drinks at night. You won't wake her up."

It was a long time before she got an answer. The conversation was very brief. She hung up again.

"He doesn't have a moped," she said. "Besides, Stefan isn't 15 yet, is he?"

"It was just a thought," Wallander said. "We have to know. Anyway, I doubt that young people today pay much attention to what is permitted or not."

"The little boy woke up when I was about to leave," she said. "He was sleeping on the sofa next to his mother. That's what upset me the most."

"That he woke up?"

"I've never seen such frightened eyes in a child before."

Wallander slammed his fist on the table. She jumped.

"I've got it," he cried. "What it was I've been forgetting all this time. Damn it!"

"What?"

"Wait a minute. Wait a minute . . ."

Wallander rubbed his temples to squeeze out the image that had been bothering him for so long. Finally he captured it.

"Do you remember the doctor who did the autopsy of Dolores María Santana in Malmö?"

She tried to remember.

"Wasn't it a woman?"

"Yes, it was. A woman. What was her name? Malm something?"

"Svedberg's got a good memory," she said. "I'll get him."

"That's not necessary," said Wallander. "I remember now. Her name was Malmström. We've got to get hold of her. And we need to get hold of her right now. I'd like you to take care of it. As fast as you can!"

"What is it?"

"I'll explain later."

She got up and left the room. Could the Fredman boy really be mixed up in this? Wallander picked up the phone and called Åkeson. He answered at once.

"I need you to do me a favour," he said. "Now. In the middle of the night. Call the hospital where Louise was a patient. Tell them to copy the page of the visitors' book with the signature of the person who picked her up. And tell them to fax it here to Helsingborg."

"How the hell do you think they can do that?"

"I have no idea," Wallander said. "But it could be important. They can cross out all the other names on the page. I just want to see that one signature."

"Which was illegible?"

"Precisely. I want to see the illegible signature."

Wallander stressed his final words. Åkeson understood that he was after something that might be important.

"Give me the fax number," Åkeson said. "I'll try."

Wallander gave him the number and hung up. The clock on the wall said 2.05 a.m. He was sweating in his new shirt. He wondered vaguely whether the state had paid for the shirt and trousers. Höglund returned and said that Agneta Malmström was on a sailing holiday with her family somewhere between Landsort and Oxelösund.

"What's the name of the boat?"

"It's supposed to be some kind of Maxi class. The name is *Sanborombon*. It also has a number."

"Call Stockholm Radio," Wallander said. "They must have a two-way radio on board. Ask them to call the boat. Tell them it's a police emergency. Talk to Birgersson. I want to get in touch with her right away."

Wallander had his second wind. Höglund left to go and find Birgersson. Svedberg almost collided with her in the doorway as he came in with the security guards' account of the theft of their car.

"You're right," he said. "Basically all they saw was the gun. And it all happened very fast. But he had blond hair, blue eyes and was dressed in some kind of jogging suit. Normal height, spoke with a Stockholm accent. Gave the impression of being high on something."

"What did they mean by that?"

"His eyes."

"I assume the description is on its way out?"

"I'll check."

As Svedberg left, excited voices came from the hall. Wallander guessed that a reporter had tried to cross the boundary that Birgersson had drawn. He found a notebook and quickly wrote a few notes in the sequence he remembered them. He was sweating profusely now, checking the wall clock, and in his mind Baiba was sitting by the phone in her spartan flat in Riga waiting for the call he should have made long ago.

It was close to 3 a.m. The security company's car was still missing. Hans Logård was hiding. The Dominican girl who had been taken to the yacht club couldn't make a positive identification of the boat. Maybe it was the same one, maybe not. A man who had always kept in the shadows had been at the wheel. She couldn't remember any crew. Wallander told Birgersson that the girls had to get some sleep now.

Hotel rooms were arranged. One of the girls smiled shyly at Wallander when they met in the hall. Her smile made him feel good, for a brief moment almost exhilarated. At regular intervals Birgersson would find Wallander and provide information on Logård. At 3.15 a.m. Wallander learned that Logård had been married twice and had two children under 18. One of them, a girl, lived with her mother in Hagfors, the other in Stockholm, a boy of nine. Next Birgersson came back and reported that Logård might have had one other child, but that they hadn't managed to confirm it.

At 3.30 a.m. an exhausted officer came into the room where Wallander was sitting with a coffee cup in his hand and his feet on the desk and told him that Stockholm Radio had contacted the Malmströms' Maxi. Wallander jumped up and followed him to the command centre, where Birgersson stood yelling into a receiver. He handed it to Wallander.

"They're somewhere between two lightships named the *Hävringe* and the *Gustaf Dalén*," he said. "I've got Karl Malmström on the line."

Wallander quickly handed the phone back to Birgersson.

"I've got to talk to his wife. Only the wife."

"I hope you realise that there are hundreds of pleasure boats out there listening to the conversation going out over the coastal radio."

In his haste, Wallander had forgotten that.

"A mobile phone is better," he said. "Ask if they have one on board."

"I've already done that," Birgersson said. "These are people who think you should leave mobile phones at home when you're on holiday."

"Then they'll have to put into shore," Wallander said. "And call me from there."

"How long do you think that will take?" said Birgersson. "Do you have any idea where the *Hävringe* is? Plus, it's the middle of the night. Are they supposed to set sail now?"

"I don't give a shit where the *Hävringe* is," Wallander said. "Besides, they might be sailing at night and not lying at anchor. Maybe there's some other boat nearby with a mobile phone. Just tell them that I have to get in touch with her within an hour. With her. Not him."

Birgersson shook his head. Then he started yelling into the phone again. Half an hour later Agneta Malmström called from a mobile phone borrowed from a boat they'd met out in the channel. Wallander got straight to the point.

"Do you remember the girl who burned herself to death?" he asked. "In a rape field a few weeks ago?"

"Of course I remember."

"Do you also recall a phone conversation we had at that time? I asked you how a young person could do such a thing to herself. I don't remember my exact words."

"I have a vague memory of it," she replied.

"You answered by giving an example of something you had recently experienced. You told me about a boy, a little boy, who was so afraid of his father that he tried to put out his own eyes."

"Yes," she said. "I remember that. But it wasn't something I had experienced myself. One of my colleagues told me about it."

"Who was that?"

"My husband. He's a doctor too."

"Then I'll have to talk to him. Please get him for me."

"It'll take a while. I'll have to row over and get him in the dinghy. We put down a drift anchor some way from here."

Wallander apologised for bothering her.

"Unfortunately, it's necessary," he said.

"It'll take a while," she said.

"Where the hell is the *Hävringe*?" asked Wallander.

"Out in the Baltic," she said. "It's lovely where we are. But just now we're making a night sail to the south. Even though the wind is poor."

It took 20 minutes before the phone rang again. Karl Malmström was on the line. In the meantime Wallander had learnt that he was a paediatrician in Malmö. Wallander reverted to the conversation he had had with his wife.

"I remember the case," he said.

"Can you remember the name of the boy off the top of your head?"

"Yes, I can. But I can't stand here yelling it into a mobile phone."

Wallander understood his point. He thought feverishly.

"Let's do this, then," he said. "I'll ask you a question. You can answer yes or no. Without naming any names."

"We can try," said Malmström.

"Does it have anything to do with Bellman?" asked Wallander.

Malmström instantly understood the reference to *Fredman's Epistles* by the famous Swedish poet.

"Yes, it does."

"Then I thank you for your help," said Wallander. "I hope I won't have to bother you again. Have a good summer."

Karl Malmström didn't seem annoyed. "It's nice to know we have policemen who work hard at all hours," was all he said.

Wallander handed the phone to Birgersson.

"Let's have a meeting in a while," he said. "I need a few minutes to think."

"Take my office," Birgersson said.

Wallander suddenly felt very tired. His sense of revulsion was like a dull ache in his body. He still didn't want to believe that what he was thinking could be true. He had fought against this conclusion for a long time. But he couldn't do that any longer. The truth that confronted him was unbearable. The little boy's terror of his father. A big brother nearby. Who pours hydrochloric acid into his father's eyes as revenge. Who acts out an insane retribution for his sister, who had been abused in some way. It was all very clear. The whole thing made sense and the result was appalling. He also thought that his subconscious had seen it long ago, but he had pushed the realisation aside. Instead he had allowed himself to be sidetracked, distracted from his goal.

A police officer knocked on his door.

"We just got a fax from Lund," he said. "From a hospital."

Wallander took it. Åkeson had acted fast. It was a copy of a page from the visitors' book for the psychiatric ward. All the names but one were crossed out. The signature really was illegible. He took out a magnifying glass from Birgersson's desk drawer and tried to make it out. Illegible. He put the paper on the table. The officer was still standing in the doorway.

"Get Birgersson over here," Wallander said. "And my colleagues from Ystad. How's Sjösten, by the way?"

"He's sleeping. They've removed the bullet from his shoulder."

A few minutes later they were gathered in the room. It was almost 4.30 a.m. Everyone was exhausted. Still no sign of Logård. Still no trace of the security guards' car. Wallander nodded to them to sit down.

The moment of truth, he thought. This is it.

"We're searching for Hans Logård," he began. "We have to keep doing so of course. He shot Sjösten in the shoulder and he's mixed up in the traffic of young girls. But he isn't the one who committed four murders and scalped his victims. That was somebody else entirely."

He paused.

"Stefan Fredman is the person who did this," he said. "We're looking for a 14-year-old boy who killed his father, along with the others."

There was silence in the room. No-one moved. They were all staring at him. When Wallander had finished his explanation, there was no doubt in anyone's mind. The team decided to return to Ystad. The greatest secrecy would have to attach to what they had just discussed. Wallander couldn't tell which feeling was stronger among his colleagues, shock or relief.

Wallander called Åkeson and gave him a brisk précis of his conclusions. As he did so, Svedberg stood next to him, staring at the fax that had come from Lund.

"Strange," he said.

Wallander turned to him.

"What's strange?"

"This signature. It looks as if he's signed himself Geronimo."

Wallander grabbed the fax out of Svedberg's hand. He was right.

CHAPTER 38

They said goodbye in the dawn outside the station in Helsingborg. Everyone looked haggard, but more than anything they were shaken by what they now realised was the truth about the killer they had been hunting for so long. They agreed to meet at 8 a.m. at the Ystad police station. That meant they would have time to get home and shower, but not much else. They had to keep working. Wallander had been blunt in outlining his conclusions. He believed that the murders had happened because of the sick sister. But they couldn't be sure. It was possible that she herself was in danger. There was only one approach to take: to fear the worst.

Svedberg went in Wallander's car. It was going to be another beautiful day. They spoke very little during the trip. Svedberg discovered that he must have left his keys somewhere. It reminded Wallander that his own keys had never shown up. He told Svedberg to come home with him. They reached Mariagatan just before 7 a.m. Linda was asleep. After they had each taken a shower and Wallander had given Svedberg a clean shirt, they sat in the living-room and had coffee.

Neither of them noticed that the door to the cupboard next to Linda's room, which had been closed when they arrived, was ajar.

Hoover had arrived at the flat at 6.50 a.m. He was on his way into the policeman's bedroom with the axe in his hand when he heard a key turn in the lock. He hid in the cupboard. He heard two voices. When he could tell that they were in the living-room, he opened the door a crack. Hoover assumed that the other man was a policeman too. He gripped the axe the whole time, listening to them talking softly. At first Hoover didn't understand what they were talking about. The name

Hans Logård was mentioned repeatedly. The policeman whom he had come to kill was clearly trying to explain something to the other man. He listened carefully and finally understood that it was holy providence, the power of Geronimo, that had started working again. Hans Logård had been Åke Liljegren's right-hand man. He had smuggled girls in from the Dominican Republic, and maybe from other parts of the Caribbean too. He was also the one who probably brought girls to Wetterstedt and maybe even Carlman. He also heard the policeman predict that Logård was on the death list that must exist in Stefan Fredman's mind.

Then the conversation stopped. A few moments later Wallander and Svedberg left the flat. Hoover emerged from the cupboard and stood utterly still. Then he left, as soundlessly as he had come. He had gone to the empty shop where Linda and Kajsa had held their rehearsals. He knew they wouldn't be using it again, so he had left Louise there while he went to the flat on Mariagatan to kill Perkins and his daughter. But as he'd stood in the cupboard, the axe ready in his hand, and heard the conversation he started to have doubts. There was one more person he had to kill. A man he had overlooked. Hans Logård. When the policeman described him, Hoover understood that he must have been the one who had brutally raped and abused his sister. That was before she had been drugged and taken to both Gustaf Wetterstedt and Arne Carlman – events that had forced her into the darkness. All of it was written down in the book he had taken from her. The book that contained the words that controlled him. He had assumed that Hans Logård was someone who didn't live in Sweden. A foreign visitor, an evil man. Now he knew that he had made a mistake.

It was easy to get into the empty shop. Earlier he had seen Kajsa hide the key. Since he was moving around in broad daylight, he hadn't painted his face. He didn't want to frighten Louise, either. When he came back she was sitting on a chair, staring blankly into space. He had already decided to move her. And he knew where. Before he went to Mariagatan he went on the moped to see that the situation was as he'd thought. The house he'd selected was empty. But they weren't going to move there until evening. He sat down on the floor at her side and tried to work out how to find Logård before the police did. He turned inward and asked Geronimo for advice. But his heart was strangely still this morning. The drums were so faint that he couldn't hear their message.

At 8 a.m. they gathered in the conference room. Åkeson was here, as was a sergeant from Malmö. Birgersson was hooked up via speaker phone from Helsingborg. Wallander looked around the table and said they'd start by bringing everyone up to date. The sergeant from Malmö was looking for a hiding place they assumed Stefan Fredman had access to. They still hadn't found it. But one of the neighbours in the building told them that he had seen Stefan Fredman on a moped several times. The building where the family lived was under surveillance. Birgersson told them that Sjösten was doing well, although his ear would be permanently damaged.

"Plastic surgeons can work wonders," Wallander shouted encouragingly. "Say hello to him from all of us."

Birgersson went on to say that they weren't Logård's fingerprints on the comic book, the paper bag, Liljegren's stove or Fredman's left eyelid. This confirmation was crucial. The Malmö police were getting Stefan Fredman's prints from objects taken from his room in the Rosengård flat. Nobody doubted that they would match, now that Logård's didn't.

They talked about Logård. The hunt had to continue. They had to assume he was dangerous, since he had shot at Wallander and Sjösten.

"Stefan Fredman is only 14, but he is dangerous," Wallander said. "He may be crazy, but he's not stupid. He's very strong and he reacts fast. We have to be careful."

"This is all so damned disgusting!" Hansson exploded. "I still can't believe it's true."

"Nor can any of us," Åkeson said. "But what Kurt says is absolutely right. And we need to act accordingly."

"Fredman got his sister Louise out of the hospital," Wallander went on. "We're looking for the nurse who will be able to identify him. Let's assume it'll be a positive identification. We still don't know whether he intends to hurt Louise. It's crucial that we find them. He has a moped and must ride with her on the back. They can't get very far. Besides, the girl is sick."

"A nutcase on a moped with a mentally ill girl on the back," Svedberg said. "It's so macabre."

"He can also drive a car," Ludwigsson pointed out. "He used his father's van. So he may have stolen one by now."

Wallander turned to the detective from Malmö.

"Stolen cars," he said. "Within the past few days. Above all in Rosengård. And near the hospital."

The detective went to a phone.

"Stefan Fredman carries out his actions after careful planning," continued Wallander. "Naturally we have no way of knowing whether the abduction of his sister was also planned. Now we have to try and get into his mind to guess what he plans to do next. Where are they headed? It's a shame Ekholm isn't here when we need him most."

"He'll be here in about an hour," Hansson said, glancing at the clock. "Someone's picking him up at the airport."

"How is his daughter?" asked Höglund.

Wallander was ashamed that he'd forgotten the reason for Ekholm's absence.

"She's OK," said Svedberg. "A broken foot, that's all. She was very lucky."

"This autumn we're going to have a big traffic safety campaign in schools," said Hansson. "Too many children are being killed."

The detective returned to the table.

"I presume you've also looked for Stefan in his father's flat," Wallander said.

"We've already searched there and everywhere else his father usually hung out. And we've picked up Peter Hjelm and asked him to try and think of other hide-outs Fredman may have had access to that his son might know about. Forsfält is taking care of it."

The meeting dragged on, but Wallander knew that they were really just waiting for something to happen. Stefan Fredman was somewhere with his sister. Logård was out there too. A large contingent of police officers were looking for them. They went in and out of the conference room, getting coffee, sending out for sandwiches, dozing in their chairs, drinking more coffee. The German police found Sara Pettersson in Hamburg. She'd been able to identify Stefan Fredman at once. Ekholm arrived from the airport, still shaken and pale.

Around 11 a.m. they got the confirmation they were waiting for. Stefan Fredman's fingerprints had been identified on his father's eyelid, on the comic book, the bloody scrap of paper and Liljegren's stove. The only sound in the conference room was the faint hiss of the speaker phone linked to Birgersson. There was no turning back. All the false leads, especially those they had thought up themselves, had been erased. All that was left was the realisation of the appalling truth: they were searching for a 14-year-old boy who had committed four cold-blooded, premeditated and atrocious murders.

Finally Wallander broke the silence and turned to Ekholm.

"What's he doing? What's he thinking?"

"I know this is very risky," Ekholm said. "But I don't think he intends to hurt his sister. There's a pattern, call it logic if you will, to his behaviour. Revenge for his little brother and his sister is the goal. If he diverges from that goal, then everything he so laboriously built up will collapse."

"Why did he take her from the hospital?" Wallander asked.

"Maybe he was afraid that you would influence her somehow."

"How?" asked Wallander in surprise.

"Picture a confused boy who has taken on the role of a lone warrior. Suppose men have done his sister irreparable harm. That's what drives him. Assuming this theory is correct, that means he'll want to keep all men away from her. He's the only exception. And you can't rule out the fact that he may have suspected you were on his trail. Certainly he knows that you're in charge of the investigation."

Wallander remembered something.

"The pictures that Norén took," he said. "Of the spectators outside the cordons? Where are they?"

Nyberg, who most of the time had sat quiet and meditative at the meeting table, went to get them. Wallander spread them out on the table. Someone got a magnifying glass. They gathered around the pictures. It was Höglund who found him.

"There he is," she said, pointing.

He was almost hidden behind some other onlookers, but part of his moped was visible, along with his head.

"I'll be damned," Hamrén said.

"It should be possible to identify the moped," Nyberg said. "If we blow up the details."

"Do that," Wallander said.

It was obvious now that there had been a good reason for the feeling gnawing at Wallander's subconscious. Grimly he thought that at least he could close the case on his own anxiety.

Save for one thing. Baiba. It was midday. Svedberg was asleep in his chair, and Åkeson was on the phone to so many different people that no-one could keep track of them. Wallander gestured to Höglund to follow him out into the hall. They sat down in his office and closed the door. Without beating around the bush, he told her of the mess he'd made. In doing so he broke his cardinal rule: never to confide a personal problem to a colleague. He had stopped doing that when Rydberg died. Now he was doing it again. He was unsure whether he could develop the same trusting relationship with Ann-Britt Höglund that he had enjoyed with Rydberg, especially since she was a woman. She listened attentively.

"What the hell am I going to do?"

"Nothing," she said. "You're right. It's already too late. But I could talk to her if you like. I assume she speaks English. Give me her number."

Wallander wrote it down, but when she reached for his telephone he asked her to wait.

"A couple more hours," he said.

"Miracles don't happen very often," she said.

At that moment Hansson burst through the door.

"They found his hide-out. A basement in a condemned school building. It's right near the flats where he lives."

"Are they there?" Wallander asked, getting up from his chair.

"No. But they've been there."

They went back to the meeting room. Another speaker phone was hooked up. Wallander heard Forsfält's friendly voice. He described what they had found. Mirrors, brushes, make-up. A cassette player with a tape of drums on it. He played a few seconds of the tape. It echoed spookily in the meeting room. War paint, thought Wallander. How had he signed at the hospital? Geronimo. There were axes on a piece of cloth, and knives too. They could hear that Forsfält was upset.

"We didn't find scalps," he said. "We're still looking."

"Where the hell are they?" said Wallander.

"Either he has them with him, or else he's left them as a sacrifice somewhere," Ekholm said.

"Where? Does he have his own sacrificial grove?"

"Could be."

The waiting continued. Wallander lay down on the floor of his office and managed to sleep for half an hour. When he woke up he felt more tired than before. His body ached all over. Now and then Höglund gave him a questioning look, but he shook his head and felt his self-loathing grow.

At 6 p.m. that evening, there was still no trace of Logård, Fredman or his sister. They had discussed at length whether to put out a nation-wide alert for the Fredmans. Everyone was reluctant to do so. The risk that something would happen to Louise was too great. Åkeson agreed. They kept waiting.

Just after 6 p.m. Hoover took his sister to the house he had chosen. He parked the moped on the beach side. He quickly picked the lock on the gate to the garden. Wetterstedt's villa was deserted. They walked up the path to the main door. Suddenly he stopped and held Louise back.

There was a car in the garage. It hadn't been there this morning. He carefully pushed Louise down to sit on a rock behind the garage wall. He took out an axe and listened. He walked forward and looked at the car. It belonged to a security company. One of the front windows was open. He peered inside. There were some papers lying on the seat. He picked them up and saw that there was a receipt among them, made out to Hans Logård. He put it back and stood still, holding his breath. The drums started to pound. He remembered the conversation he had heard that morning. Hans Logård was on the run too.

So he'd had the same idea about the empty house. He was somewhere inside. Geronimo had not failed him. He had helped him track the monster to his lair. He didn't have to search any further. The cold darkness that had penetrated his sister's soul would soon be gone. He went back to her and told her to stay there for a while, and keep as quiet as she could. He would be back very soon.

He went into the garage. There were some cans of paint, and he opened two of them carefully. With his fingertip he drew two lines across his forehead. One red line, then a black one. He picked up his axe and took off his shoes. Just as he was about to leave he had an idea. He held his breath again, which he had learned from Geronimo. Compressed air in the lungs made thoughts clearer. He knew that his idea was a good one. It would make everything easier. Tonight he would bury the last of the scalps outside the hospital window alongside the others. There would be two of them. And he would bury a heart. Then it would be all over. In the last hole he would bury his weapons. He gripped the axe handle and started walking towards the house and the man he was to kill.

At 6.30 p.m. Wallander suggested to Hansson that they could start sending people home. Everyone was exhausted. They might as well be waiting, and resting, in their own homes. They would remain on call through the night.

"So who should stay here?" asked Hansson.

"Ekholm and Höglund," Wallander answered. "And one more.

Whoever's the least tired."

Ludwigsson and Hamrén both stayed.

They all moved down to one end of the table instead of spreading out as usual.

"The hide-out," Wallander said. "What would be a secret and impregnable fortress? What would an insane boy who transforms himself into a lone warrior seek?"

"I think his plans must have fallen apart," Ekholm said. "Otherwise they would have stayed in the basement room."

"Smart animals dig extra exits," Ludwigsson said thoughtfully.

"You mean that he might have a second hide-out in reserve?"

"Maybe. In all likelihood it's also in Malmö."

The discussion petered out. Hamrén yawned. A phone rang down the hall and someone appeared in the doorway, saying that there was a call for Wallander. He got up, much too tired to ask who it was. It didn't occur to him that it might be Baiba, not until he had picked up the phone in his own office. By then it was too late. But it wasn't Baiba. It was a man who spoke with a broad Skåne accent.

"Who is this?" Wallander asked.

"Hans Logård."

Wallander almost dropped the receiver. "I need to meet with you. Now."

Logård's voice was strained, as if he was having a lot of trouble forming his words. Wallander wondered whether he was on drugs.

"Where are you?"

"First I want a guarantee that you'll come. And that you'll come alone."

"You won't get it. You nearly killed me and Sjösten."

"God damn it! You have to come!"

The last words sounded almost like a shriek. Wallander grew cautious. "What do you want?"

"I can tell you where Stefan Fredman is. And his sister."

"How can I be sure of that?"

"You can't. But you should believe me."

"I'll come. You tell me what you know. And then we'll bring you in."

"All right."

"Where are you?"

"Are you coming?"

"Yes."

"Wetterstedt's villa."

A feeling that he should have thought of that possibility raced through Wallander's mind.

"Do you have a gun?" he asked.

"The car is in the garage. The revolver is in the glove compartment. I'll leave the door to the house open. You'll see me when you come in the door. I'll keep my hands in sight."

"All right, I'm coming."

"Alone?"

"Yes, alone."

Wallander hung up, thinking feverishly. He had no intention of going alone. But he didn't want Hansson to start organising a major strike force. Ann-Britt and Svedberg, he thought. But Svedberg was at home. He called him and told him to meet him outside the hospital in five minutes. With his service revolver. Did he have it? He did. Wallander told him briefly that they were going to arrest Logård. When Svedberg tried to ask questions, Wallander cut him off. Five minutes, he said, outside the hospital. Until then, don't use the phone.

He unlocked a desk drawer and took out his revolver. He detested even holding it. He loaded it and tucked it in his jacket pocket, then went to the conference room and waved Höglund outside. He took her into his office and explained. They would meet in the car park right away. Wallander told her to bring her service revolver. They would take Wallander's car. He told Hansson he was going home to shower. Hansson yawned and waved him goodbye. Svedberg was outside the hospital. He got into the back seat.

"What's going on?" he asked.

Wallander told them about the phone call. If the revolver wasn't in the car they'd call it off. Same thing if the door wasn't open. Or if Wallander suspected something was wrong. The two of them were supposed to stay out of sight but ready.

"He might have another gun," Svedberg said. "He might try to take you hostage. I don't like this. How could he know where Stefan Fredman is? What does he want?"

"Maybe he's stupid enough to try and make a deal with us. People think Sweden is just like the United States."

Wallander thought about Logård's voice. Something told him he really did know where the boy was.

They parked the car out of sight of the house. Svedberg was to watch the beach side. When he got there he was alone, except for a girl sitting on the boat under which they'd found Wetterstedt's dead body. She seemed to be completely entranced by the sea and the black rain cloud bearing down on the land. Höglund took up a position outside the garage. Wallander saw that the front door was open. He moved slowly. The car was in the garage. The revolver was in the glove compartment. He took out his own gun, put the safety catch off, and advanced cautiously to the door. Everything was still.

He stepped up to the door. Hans Logård stood in dark hall. He had his hands on his head. Wallander sensed danger. But he went inside. Logård looked at him. Then everything happened very fast. One of Logård's hands slipped down and Wallander saw a gaping wound in his head. Logård's body fell to the floor. Behind him stood Stefan Fredman. He had lines painted on his face. He threw himself furiously at Wallander, an axe lifted high. Wallander raised his revolver to shoot, but too late. Instinctively he ducked and a rug slipped under him. The axe grazed his shoulder. He fired a shot and an oil painting jumped on one of the walls. At the same instant Höglund, appeared in the doorway. She stood crouched and ready to fire. Fredman saw her just as he was raising the axe to slam it into Wallander's head. He leapt to the left. Wallander was in the line of fire.

Fredman vanished towards the open terrace door. Wallander thought of Svedberg. Slow Svedberg. He yelled to Höglund to shoot. But he was gone. Svedberg, who had heard the first shot, didn't know what to do.

He yelled at the girl sitting on the boat to take cover, but she didn't move. He ran towards the garden gate. It hit him in the head as it flew open. He saw a face he would never forget. He dropped his revolver. The man had an axe in his hand. Svedberg did the only thing he could do, he ran yelling for help. Fredman got his sister, motionless still on the boat, and dragged her to his moped. They rode off just as Wallander and Höglund came running out.

"Call for back-up!" Wallander shouted. "Where the hell is Svedberg? I'll try and follow them in the car."

Heavy rain begain to fall. Wallander ran to his car, trying to work out which way they would have gone. Visibility was poor even with the windscreen wipers on full. He thought he had lost them but suddenly caught sight of the moped again. They were going down the road towards the Saltsjöbad Hotel. Wallander kept a safe distance behind. He didn't want to frighten them. The moped was going very fast. Wallander frantically tried to think how to put an end to the chase. He was just about to call in his location when the moped wobbled. He braked. The moped was heading straight for a tree. The girl was thrown off, right into the tree. Stefan Fredman landed somewhere off to the side.

"Damn!" said Wallander. He stopped the car in the middle of the road and ran towards the moped.

Louise Fredman was dead, he could see that at once. Her white dress seemed strangely bright against the blood streaming from her face. Stefan appeared uninjured. Wallander watched the boy fall to his knees beside his sister. The rain poured down. The boy started to cry. It sounded as if he was howling. Wallander knelt next to him.

"She's dead," he said.

Stefan looked at him, his face distorted. Wallander quickly got up, afraid that the boy would jump on him. But he didn't. He kept howling.

Somewhere behind him in the rain he heard a siren. It wasn't until Hansson was standing next to him that he realised he was crying himself. Wallander left all the work to the others. He told Höglund briefly what had happened. When he saw Åkeson, he took him to his car. The rain was drumming on the roof.

"It's over," Wallander said.

"Yes," said Åkeson, "it's over."

"I'm going on holiday," said Wallander. "I realise there's a pile of reports that have to be written. But I thought I'd go anyway."

Åkeson's reply came without hesitation.

"Do that," he said. "Go."

Åkeson got out of the car. Wallander thought he should have asked him about his trip to the Sudan. Or was it Uganda?

He drove home. Linda wasn't there. He took a bath and was drying himself off when he heard her close the front door. That evening he told her what had really happened. And how he felt.

Then he called Baiba.

"I thought you were never going to call," she said, keeping her anger in check.

"Please forgive me," Wallander said. "I've had so much to do lately."

"I think that's a pretty poor excuse."

"It is, I know. But it's the only one I've got."

Neither of them said anything else. The silence travelled back and forth between Ystad and Riga.

"I'll see you tomorrow," Wallander finally said.

"All right," she said. "I guess so."

They hung up. Wallander felt a knot in his stomach. Maybe she wouldn't come. After supper he and Linda packed their bags. The rain stopped just after midnight. The air smelled fresh as they stood out on the balcony.

"The summer is so beautiful," she said.

"Yes," Wallander said. "It *is* beautiful."

The next day they took the train together to Malmö. Then Wallander took the hydrofoil to Copenhagen. He watched the water racing past the sides of the boat. Distracted, he ordered coffee and cognac. In two hours Baiba's plane would be landing. Something close to panic gripped him. He suddenly wished that the crossing to

Copenhagen would take much longer. But when she arrived at the airport he was waiting for her.

Not until then did the image of Louise Fredman, dead and broken, finally disappear from his mind.

Skåne

16–17 September 1994

EPILOGUE

On Friday, 16 September, autumn suddenly rolled in to Skåne. Kurt Wallander woke up early that morning. His eyes flew open in the dark, as if he had been cast violently out of a dream. He lay still and tried to remember. But there was only the echo of something that was gone and would never return. He turned his head and looked at the clock next to the bed. The fluorescent hands showed 4.45 a.m. He turned over on his side to go back to sleep. But the knowledge of what day it was kept him awake.

He got up and went to the kitchen. The streetlight hanging over the street swayed forlornly in the wind. He checked the thermometer and saw that the temperature had dropped. It was 7°C. He smiled at the thought that tomorrow night he would be in Rome where it was still warm. He sat at the kitchen table and had some coffee, going over the preparations for the trip in his mind. A few days earlier he had finally fixed his father's studio door. He had also taken a look at his father's new passport. He had exchanged some money for Italian lire at the bank and had bought traveller's cheques. He was going to leave work early to pick up the tickets.

Now he had to go to work for one last day before his holiday. He left the flat and went down to his car. He zipped up his jacket and shivered when he got into the driver's seat. On the way to the station he thought about this morning's meeting.

It was exactly 8 a.m. when he knocked on the door of Lisa Holgersson's office and opened the door. She nodded and asked him to have a seat. She had been serving as their new chief for only three weeks, but Wallander thought she had already set her stamp on the atmosphere of the department.

Many had been sceptical about a woman who came from a police district in Småland. And Wallander was surrounded by colleagues who still believed that women weren't even suited to be police officers. How could one be their chief? But Lisa Holgersson had soon demonstrated how capable she was. Wallander was impressed by her integrity, her fearlessness and the clear presentations she gave, no matter what the topic.

The day before she had arranged a meeting. Now Wallander sat in her visitor's chair wondering what she wanted.

"You're going on holiday," she said. "I heard you were going to Italy with your father."

"It's his dream," Wallander said. "It may be the last chance we get. He's 80."

"My father is 85," she said. "Sometimes his mind is crystal clear. Sometimes he doesn't recognise me. But I've come to terms with the fact that you never escape your parents. The roles are simply reversed. You become your parents' parent."

"Exactly," Wallander replied.

She moved some papers on her desk.

"I don't have a specific agenda for this meeting," she said. "But I realised that I've never had a proper chance to thank you for your work this summer. It was model detective work."

Wallander gave her a surprised look. Was she serious?

"That's putting it a little strongly," he said. "I made a lot of mistakes. I let the whole investigation be sidetracked. It could have failed miserably."

"The ability to lead an investigation often means knowing when to shift tactics," she said. "To look in a direction you may have just ruled out. The investigation was a model in many ways, especially because of your tenacity and your willingness to think along unconventional lines. I want you to know this. I've heard it said that the national police chief has expressed his satisfaction. I think you'll be receiving an invitation to hold seminars about the investigation at the police academy."

"I can't do that," he said. "Ask someone else. I can't speak to people I don't know."

"We'll take this up again after you get back," she said, smiling. "Right now the most important thing is that I had a chance to tell you what I thought."

She stood to indicate that the meeting was over.

Wallander walked down the hall thinking that she'd meant what she said. He tried to dismiss it, but the appreciation made him feel good. It would be easy to work with her in the future.

He got some coffee from the canteen and exchanged a few words with Martinsson about one of his daughters who had tonsillitis. When he got to his office he made an appointment for a haircut. He had made a list the day before, which was on his desk. He'd planned to leave the station as early as midday so that he could deal with all his errands. But it was 4.15 p.m. by the time he left to go to the travel agency. He also stopped at the state off licence and bought a bottle of whisky. When he got home he called Linda. He promised to send her a postcard from Rome. She was in a hurry, and he didn't ask why. The conversation was over much sooner than he would have liked.

At 6 p.m. he called Löderup and asked Gertrud if everything was in order. She told him that his father had such travel fever that he could hardly sit still. Wallander walked into the centre of town and ate dinner at one of the pizzerias. When he got back to Mariagatan he poured himself a glass of whisky and spread out a map of Rome. He had never been there and didn't know a word of Italian. But there are two of us, he thought. My father has never been there either, except in his dreams. And he doesn't speak Italian either. We're heading into this dream together and will have to guide each other.

On impulse he called the tower at Sturup and asked one of the air traffic controllers, who he knew from an old case, what the weather was like in Rome.

"It's warm. Right now it's 21°C, even though it's evening. Light winds from the southeast. Light fog too. The forecast for the next 24 hours is for more of the same."

Wallander thanked him.

"Are you going away?"

"I'm going on holiday with my father."

"That sounds like a good idea. Are you flying Alitalia?"

"Yes, the 10.45."

"I'll be thinking of you. Have a nice trip."

Wallander went over his packing one more time, checking his money and travel documents. He tried to call Baiba, then remembered that she was visiting relatives.

He sat down with a glass of whisky and listened to *La Traviata*. He thought about the trip he had taken with Baiba in the summer. Tired and dishevelled, he had waited for her in Copenhagen. He stood there at Kastrup Airport like an unshaven ghost. He knew she was disappointed, though she said nothing. Not until they had reached Skagen and he had caught up on his sleep did he tell her everything that had happened. After that their holiday had started in earnest.

On one of the last days he asked her if she would marry him. She had said no. Not yet, at any rate, not now. The past was still too close. Her husband, police captain Karlis, whom Wallander had worked with, was still alive in her memory. His violent death followed her like a shadow. Above all she doubted she could ever consider marrying another policeman. He understood. But he wanted some kind of assurance. How long would she need to think about it? She was fond of him, he knew. But was that enough? What about him? Did he really want to live with someone else? Through Baiba he had escaped the loneliness that haunted him after his divorce from Mona. It was a big step, a great relief. Maybe he should settle for that. At least for the time being.

It was late when he went to sleep, questions swirling in his head. Gertrud picked him up the next morning. It was still raining. His father was in the front, dressed in his best suit. Gertrud had given him a haircut.

"We're off to Rome," his father said happily. "To think we're actually going."

Gertrud dropped them in Malmö at the terminal. On the ferry his father insisted on tottering around the rainswept deck. He pointed to the Swedish mainland, to a spot south of Malmö.

"That's where you grew up. Do you remember?"

"How could I forget?"

"You had a very happy childhood."

"I know."

"You had everything."

"Everything."

Wallander thought about Stefan Fredman. About Louise. About the brother who had tried to put out his own eyes. About all they lacked or had been deprived of. But he pushed the thoughts away. They would still be there, lurking in the back of his mind; they would return. For now, he was on holiday with his father. That was the most important thing. Everything else would have to wait.

The plane took off as scheduled. His father had a window seat, and Wallander sat on the aisle. It was the first time his father had been in a plane. Wallander watched him press his face to the window as the plane gathered speed and slowly lifted off. Wallander could see him smiling, the smile of an old man, who had been granted, one last time in his life, the chance to feel the joy of a child.

Please visit the Harvill Press website at

www.harvill.com